MUTINEER

ALEXIS CAREW #2

J A SUTHERLAND

D1715495

MUTINEER
Alexis Carew #2

by J.A. Sutherland

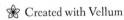 Created with Vellum

For Ash,

Love you Boo.

And to the memory of the crew of HMS Hermione (1782) and the events of September 1797.

ONE

H.M.S. Hermione's masthead shook and spun in dizzying circles as the forces of the *darkspace* winds struck her sails and hull. Alexis had her legs wrapped tightly around the yard, her muscles aching as she tried not to be shaken loose. Sweat rolled down her face in steady rivulets and her breath echoed inside her vacsuit's helmet. Her stomach rebelled at the violent motion, the sway and arc of each movement amplified by her height above the ship's hull — fully sixty meters, as Captain Neals had left the masts, all the way to the royals, extended, even while bringing in most of the sail to ride out the storm.

Just for me, so I'd get the full effect of his ... lesson.

The effect was to place Alexis so far from the hull and sails that the small amount of gallenium embedded in the thin royal mast and yard wasn't enough to offset the full effects of *darkspace*, especially with a storm raging over the ship. Tendrils of blackness flowed past her like mist, and she could feel her thoughts and movements become slowed and dull. Not as badly as she'd heard described by spacers who'd been fully outside of a ship's field, but quite disturbing none-theless.

It was enough to make her grateful that she'd had so little to eat the last day or more. Save for brief returns to the sail locker to charge her air and refill her water reservoir, sometimes wolf down a bit of ship's biscuit if it were available, she'd been at the masthead for nearly twenty hours by her estimate.

Her eyes burned with fatigue and her fingers cramped from gripping the safety lines on the yard. The storm had arrived some ten hours before, and she'd been sure that Captain Neals would send for her, but it didn't happen. Instead a spacer had climbed the mast at the change of each watch to tell her it was time for air and water, then, with no word of a reprieve, she returned to her place.

A swirl of *darkspace* energy struck the hull, knocking *Hermione* keelward, and Alexis yelped as the ship dropped away from her. Her grip held, but she felt her stomach flip-flop and her vision sparked as her helmet cracked into the yard. Far below she saw suited figures start up the mast, she assumed to take in another reef or two in the already well-furled topsail. The ship was carrying so little sail that the azure glow of their charged wire mesh barely cast any light at all.

One of them came higher, though, pulling his way up the topgallant mast and waving an arm to get Alexis' attention, as the vacsuits' radios, nor any electronics, wouldn't function in *darkspace*. She winced as she unclenched one of her hands, knuckles popping and painful as she released the line for the first time in hours. She raised her own hand in acknowledgment. The spacer stopped climbing toward her and signaled again, this time for her to come down.

Has it been a full watch again already?

In the starless black of *darkspace*, with the only light coming from the azure glow of the ship's sails, and that only from the bit of topsail currently let loose, she couldn't tell who the spacer was. She waved acknowledgment and flexed her fingers, trying to work some smoothness into their motion before she moved her safety lines from the masthead to the masts guidewires to make her way down. The figure below her signaled again, making the sign for *Lively Now* in an attempt to get her to move faster.

Aye, and I've some gestures for you, too, and I get my fingers uncramped!

It would have to be an officer or another midshipman, then, to dare make that gesture to her, or one of the senior warrants. No common spacer would act so peremptorily toward a midshipman, even one so clearly out of favor with the captain as she was.

With an effort and pain that brought tears to her eyes, Alexis managed to uncramp her hands and clip her lines to the mast's guidewires. She swung her legs off the yard and wrapped them around the mast, pulling herself down toward the hull hand over hand. She'd normally just let her legs dangle and trail behind her, relishing in the sensation of gliding along the mast in zero gravity, but not with the storm.

The ship jerked again, flinging her away from the mast to the limit of her arms and then back, knocking her breath from her. She clung to it tightly for a moment, gasping harshly, then started down again.

When she reached the suited figure, she recognized him as Ledyard, the junior midshipman aboard and just twelve-years old, but taking on the airs and actions that permeated the other officers-in-training. They touched helmets carefully, trying to keep them in contact on the jerking mast.

"Can't you move faster than that, Carew? Change of watch!" Ledyard shouted, his high-pitched voice echoing inside her helmet. "Lieutenant Dorsett says you're to come in!"

In and then back out? Or finally in?

Alexis didn't ask, she'd find out soon enough. Better, perhaps, not to know until she'd reached the airlock to the quarterdeck. Until then, she could at least imagine that this nightmare was over and she'd be allowed back inside the ship — a chance to eat, clean up, and even sleep. She wasn't entirely sure she could take another watch Outside at the masthead. This last one, she'd been afraid she'd fall asleep, unable to stay awake even with the storm, and wake to find herself flung off the mast and her safety line snapped, left to drift behind the ship as it carried on.

Sure and they'd never stop for me. Neals'd dance a jig while he watched me fall away.

Ledyard started to back down the mast, but Alexis reached out and grabbed his suit, stopping him and keeping his helmet in contact with hers. He tilted his head toward her and she could see his face, his eyes narrowed angrily, through their suit visors where they met.

"Ledyard," she said. "There's a question you should ask yourself when delivering these messages — which angers Captain Neals more, the officer you're speaking to or insubordination from a junior? Do you take my meaning?" Likely it would be the former, she knew, and Neals would take no note of whatever the other midshipmen did to her, but the possibility of the captain's displeasure was not something anyone aboard *Hermione* took lightly. It wouldn't help her in the gunroom when they were off-duty, but on-watch she was still senior and could demand at least some respect.

Alexis saw his throat work as he swallowed, but his glare didn't lessen. "Aye, sir."

She released him and he started down the mast. She followed, groaning with the pains that shot through her limbs with each movement. She made her own way down the mast to *Hermione's* cylindrical hull and clipped her safety line to one of the wires that ran back toward the stern. Unlike her first ship, the smaller, and much happier, sloop *Merlin*, *Hermione* was a full-size frigate. With three masts arrayed equidistant around her bow and a proper quarterdeck sitting atop the hull at the ship's stern.

She set her feet on the hull and felt the sharp *clicks* as the magnetic soles of her boots latched on to the gallenium embedded in the ship's thermoplastic hull. It was over thirty meters back along the hull to the quarterdeck's airlock, each of the long, sliding steps that kept one foot always firmly on the ship's hull sending daggers of pain through her cramped legs. She felt *Hermione* shudder beneath her as another wave of *darkspace* energy washed over her. She glanced up at the mast and saw the slight roll of the hull magnified in the swaying dip of the mast.

Please let it be over.

"WELCOME BACK, MISTER CAREW."

"Lieutenant Dorsett, sir," Alexis said, standing as straight as she could. Even the dry, stale air of the quarterdeck was a relief after the old-sweat scent permeating her vacsuit, though she could still sense the odor wafting out of her suit's neck. Ledyard passed her, carrying his own suit, which he'd removed in the quarterdeck lock. It irked Alexis that he, at twelve, was slightly taller than she. Unfortunately, she wasn't likely to grow much more than the bit over one and a half meters that she'd achieved.

"You may rejoin the regular watch schedule now," Dorsett said. "I trust your experience was educational."

"Yes, sir. Thank you, sir." She started for the hatch to the companionway down into the ship.

"Mister Carew."

Alexis stopped. "Sir?"

"Where do you think you're going?"

"I ... sir? To the gunroom, sir?"

"The watch schedule, I said, Mister Carew," Dorsett said.

Alexis furrowed her brow, confused, then the speakers on the quarterdeck began to sound with the soft *ding-ding* that marked the ship's time — four times the double tone sounded.

"Eight bells, Mister Carew. Start of the Middle Watch ... which is yours, if I'm not mistaken."

Alexis closed her eyes and her shoulders slumped at the prospect of a full watch, four hours, standing on the quarterdeck before she'd have the opportunity to eat, bathe, or sleep. And the threat of a much worse punishment if she fell asleep on watch. She opened her eyes and swallowed.

"Aye, sir."

"Very well, then." Dorsett nodded to her and stepped to the hatchway. "You'll be relieved at the start of the Morning Watch. The captain wishes to be informed of any sail changes, instanter."

"Aye, sir."

Dorsett left the quarterdeck and she took her place at the navigation plot. Inside the ship, under the influence of the inertial compensators and artificial gravity, the effects of the storm were barely noticeable. There was an occasional feeling that the ship had rolled or jerked to the side, but it was more a psychological effect of knowing the storm still blew around them and the images on the monitors than any real motion.

Alexis checked the helm to ensure they were on the expected course, but the helmsman, Batchelder, was a good lad and experienced. She noted that the log had not been thrown since seven bells, so that duty fell to her, and turned to the signals console.

"Please tell the sail watch that I'd admire that they threw the log, Hache," she said.

"Aye sir," the spacer said and began sliding his fingers over his console. Out on the hull, a display of fiber optic lights would relay the order to the men Outside. One of them would go to the keel and cast a heavy, weighted bag attached to a line away from the ship. Once away from the field generated by *Hermione's* gallenium-laced hull, the bag would stop moving. Never mind that they were in space, in vacuum, with no force to act on it — this was *darkspace*, and things behaved ... differently. Away from the ship's field, things just stopped. The bag would stick in the morass of *darkspace,* an effect of the dark matter that made up most of the universe, and be left behind, all the while trailing meter after meter of line as *Hermione* continued on her way.

The quarterdeck hatch slid open and a spacer, vacsuit helmet in hand, stepped through.

"Six knots, sir," he said. "Drift's four points t'leeward an' three down."

"Thank you, Cager," Alexis said. The force of the storm, the drift and how much *Hermione* was being driven from her preferred course, was not too great. She slid her fingers over the surface of the navigation plot to enter the information. The computer would calculate the ship's position, but Alexis began the task manually, as all of the officers did. There were even paper plots to the side of the quarterdeck, so that they would be able to navigate even if the computer and plot were damaged — or if they took an enemy ship as a prize and were unable to unlock its plot.

Six knots in the archaic usage of the Navy — 'traditional' as Lieutenant Caruthers, back on her first ship, *Merlin*, had been fond of calling it — gave her the ship's speed over the last half hour, or one bell as they measured the watches. Given that speed, their course, and the reported drift of four points to leeward, forty-five degrees directly away from the *darkspace* winds, and a touch over thirty-three degrees down ...

She entered her calculations for the ship's position and allowed the computer to update the plot with its own.

"Damn!" she said aloud as she saw the computer's calculated position diverge from her own. Flushing, she glanced around the quarterdeck, but the spacers kept their heads studiously trained on their consoles. She flushed more, but for a different reason. On *Merlin*, there'd have been some laughter at her outburst, perhaps even a good-natured quip or word of encouragement from the hands. Midshipman, and a very junior one at that, was not so exalted a rank ... at least, not on a happy ship. *Such is not the case on* Hermione, *though.*

No, on *Hermione* the hands would never joke or josh with an officer, not even a midshipman. Not even a midshipman who allowed it and treated them with courtesy, for if one of the *other* midshipmen heard it ... well, then that hand would likely find himself at the gratings next Captain's Mast, reported for insolence and his back laid bloody by the bosun's cat.

Alexis returned to studying the plot, seeing her error immediately. *Hermione* had passed close enough to a star system during the last watch to alter her speed. Or how far she traveled at a given speed. *Or something*, she thought.

None of the texts she'd read on *darkspace* adequately explained the effect — not because she couldn't understand it, but because no one did. The best scientists could only describe the effect, not the reason for it. But for those who sailed the Dark, it was the effect that mattered. An hour at six knots near a star system resulted in less normal-space distance traveled than an hour at six knots far from any system, resulting in the odd circumstance that it might take a day or more to sail between two planets in the same system, yet only a fort-night to reach a star system light years away.

She sighed and corrected her plot, but still noting her error in the log. She'd likely receive some sort of punishment from Captain Neals for her oversight, but less than if she tried to hide it. She was actually rather pleased to note that once she took the nearby system into account, her plot was not too far off that of the computer. Navigation was her weakest point, no doubt, but she thought she was improving somewhat — despite the sick feeling she got in her stomach every time she realized that ships flung themselves through *darkspace* by dead reckoning ... something little better than a guess, in her opinion.

Well, and Captain Neals would say that my weakest point is being a girl ... not something I can exactly improve upon.

What Neals' exact issues with women were, she didn't know, but he had certainly made it clear they had no place in his Navy. So very different from her first captain, Captain Grantham, who'd given her a place aboard his ship and a chance to leave her home planet of Dalthus. There were no regulations against women in the Navy, much to Neals' frequently voiced disgust — in fact, there were many female officers and crew, including some admirals. But Coreward, in the Core Worlds that made up the longest settled worlds of humanities expansion into the stars.

No, the official Naval regulations cared not one whit that she was a girl — ignored it all-entire, in fact, for those regulations said that she was to be referred to as "sir" and "Mister Carew" by the hands, like any other officer.

Out here on the Fringe, though, where so many worlds were just being colonized or had only been so for a few generations ... well, colonies tended to breed odd ideas. One of the most prevalent, for some reason, was that certain jobs were for men and others were for women.

Even if a colony didn't start out that way — and some did, for the colonies were generally free to set their own laws from the start — it wasn't uncommon for their customs to drift in that direction. And so the Navy's Fringe Fleet had drifted as well. It was no formal policy, but ships in the Fringe simply didn't enlist women.

Merchant ships did, both as crew and officers — in fact, shipping aboard a merchant vessel was one of the few, sure ways a woman could get herself off one of those planets. But merchantmen were free to pick and choose their ports of call, and merchant crews had the option of staying aboard in the more provincial systems. Navy ships didn't have that luxury. They went where they were ordered.

As *Hermione* had, traveling far from Alexis' home on Dalthus to the border between New London space and Hanover. Alexis wasn't even sure what the war between the two star kingdoms was about.

One would think, with so many habitable systems being discovered, that war would be rather pointless. Of course, what she thought of it mattered very little in the scheme of things — not when those on New London and Hanover had decided the two kingdoms would go to war. *How was it Captain Grantham announced it to us? "Gentlemen, some damn fool somewhere has gone and gotten us a war."*

The muted sound of a bell interrupted her reverie and made her realize just how long she'd been lost in her own thoughts.

"Another throw of the log, please," she ordered.

"Aye sir."

ALEXIS BIT her lip to keep from crying out in relief as the ship's bell began to strike its distinctive *ding-ding* pattern and marked the end of the watch. *Hermione's* second lieutenant, Williard, entered the quarterdeck and Alexis turned to face him, the time before the next bell seeming to stretch out unbearably. Finally the eighth bell rang out, eight bells of the Middle Watch, its end and four a.m., start of the Morning Watch.

"I have the deck, Mister Carew," Williard said, his look carrying more than a bit of sympathy it seemed to Alexis.

"Aye sir. The deck is yours." She slumped with relief and started for the hatchway, feet shuffling in fatigue. Just the thought of soon being able to fall into her cot and sleep was a comfort.

"The captain wishes to see you in his cabin, Mister Carew," Williard whispered.

Alexis clenched her eyes shut. *No, he wouldn't be done with me yet, now would he?*

"Aye sir." She slid the hatch open and made her way down the companionway to the captain's cabin.

The marine standing guard pounded on the hatch. "Midshipman Carew, *sir!*" he called out, nodding to her to enter at a call from within.

Alexis entered and made her way to stand before the captain's large dining table, which doubled as a desk. Captain Neals was well-awake and at his breakfast. He ignored Alexis, concentrating on his plate of eggs and bacon. Proper, real eggs, she saw, not from a powder rehydrated with ship's water and tasting of the recyclers. The captain and other officers all brought their own stores aboard. Anything to supplement the poor ship's rations of bread and beef. Beef grown in the purser's nutrient vats and resembling nothing so much as a gelatinous pudding. Even the midshipmen could, but Alexis had stopped doing so — and it had been quite a long time since she'd had food that wasn't the simple ship's rations fed to the crew.

Alexis felt her mouth fill as the scent hit her and she had to swallow. How long had it been since she'd had a real egg? How long since she'd tasted bacon, or any meat, for that matter, that hadn't been grown in the ship's vats? *Two, no, three port calls ago ... been that long since I was off this ship.*

Neals crumbled a bit of ship's biscuit, the dry, hard bread the purser stocked for when the ship's cook couldn't take the time to bake fresh, over his plate and spread it around to soak into the runny yolks. He looked up at her and his lip curled in distaste.

"Still in a vacsuit, Carew?"

"Yes, sir," Alexis said, fixing her eyes forward and not meeting his. Neals' eyes were pale and hooded. *Like a lizard*, she thought. *Cold and heartless as one, too.* The bags under them, and the fleshiness of his face, did nothing to make him look kinder.

"So unsure of your abilities that you're afraid you'll hole the ship while you're on watch?"

"I came on watch directly from the masthead, sir."

"Well you look disgusting, Carew. I expect you to be presentable when you're on my quarterdeck, do you understand?"

"Aye sir," she said. There was nothing else to say. How she'd manage that if she came to the watch directly from the masthead again, which she was sure Neals would arrange, she didn't know. *Which is much the point, I'm sure.*

Neals returned his attention to his breakfast, scooping up a forkful of eggs and biscuit. The archaic aiguillette, a loop of gilt, braided rope, he wore at his shoulder, instead of the more modern gilt epaulet, swayed back and forth. Alexis found herself swaying in time with it, catching herself, she hoped, before Neals noticed.

"Are you prepared to give me what I want, Carew?"

Alexis ground her teeth together. She felt her nostrils flare despite trying to keep her face impassive. She took a deep breath to calm herself.

"No, sir," she said. This was something she didn't have to acquiesce to, something he couldn't order her to do. She could tell him no and there was nothing he could do about it. *No, not nothing ... he can make my life a hell until I give in to him.*

"Come now," Neals said. He wiped his mouth with a napkin and smiled at her.

Short, gray hair barely visible under his beret with the gold band of ship's command. Neals was far older than she'd expect of a frigate captain — they were usually younger, more daring men. Frigates were the eyes and ears of the Fleet, sailing mostly independent commands, and the stepping stone to command of larger ships and eventual Flag rank. That Neals, at his age, was still in a Fifth Rate and not a ship of the line said something about his competence, she thought. But that he still held his command when frigates were so sought after for their independence and the opportunities for prize money spoke to some political connection.

"Such a small thing to end all this unpleasantness, don't you think?" Neals asked.

"I will not, sir."

Neals stood and came around the desk. He stood close to her, almost touching but not quite. So close that she couldn't see his face without looking up, which she wouldn't do. She kept her eyes forward, struggling to keep her face from betraying her disgust with the captain.

"But you will, you know," Neals said. "I'll have it from you eventually. You'll even thank me in the end."

That wasn't a question, so she wasn't required to answer.

Neals bent over and put his lips next to her ear.

"*Resign*, Carew," he whispered.

"No, sir."

Neals stepped back from her, his face flushed and angry.

"You have no place in my Navy, girl," he said. "*None!*" He turned from her and began pacing the cabin. "I cannot imagine what that fool Grantham was thinking to sign you aboard."

Alexis caught her breath and held it, willing herself not to speak out. Captain Grantham, who'd taken her aboard his ship as a midshipman when she'd determined to leave Dalthus and seek some option other than marriage to make her way in the world, was the

kindest, most honorable man she'd ever met. Certainly more so than
Neals. But to say so, to say anything in contradiction to what Neals
believed, would only garner more punishment.

"What did you give him, I wonder?" Neals asked, turning to look
at her. He ran his gaze up and down. "I can't imagine him to be so
desperate as to have a prurient motive, but one never knows."

Ah ... it's to be that one, then? Neals' rants had become, if not
predictable, at least identifiable. There was the women are too stupid
and weak to serve rant, the woman's place is on her back not in the
Navy rant, the women are bad for discipline rant ...

"Was he, Carew? Desperate, I mean? Forge too much of a reputa-
tion on the planet with your wantonness and seize upon a lonely
captain to make your way elsewhere, did you?"

"No, sir." And today would be the all women are slatterns rant, it
seemed. When she'd first come aboard *Hermione*, she'd thought that
Neals hated her specifically for some reason and wondered what she
could possibly do to gain his good opinion. As the days went by,
though, she'd come to realize that the man hated all women — why,
she didn't know, but he did. And most men, as well, if his treatment
of the crew was any gauge. Hated, at least, those men who were not
officers and willing to toady to him.

"I know your kind," Neals went on. "Spread your legs and lure
good, honest men to do your bidding — well I'll not have it aboard my
ship, do you hear me?"

"Aye sir."

"I find you've worked your disgusting ways with a decent officer
aboard my ship and I'll have you before a Court!"

"Yes, sir." *First have to find a decent officer aboard this ship. Like-
lier there'll be golden eggs on your plate come morning than that.*

"Oh, just resign, Carew," Neals said, sounding almost kindly
now. "I'll turn the ship around and make for the nearest port. You
could be back home and underneath some idiot village boy in two
months' time."

The truth was she almost would — resign, that was. Life aboard

Hermione was so much different than aboard *Merlin*. But if she did, if she resigned, she'd be giving in to Neals. She'd be letting him beat her, giving him what he wanted. She had to follow his orders in virtually everything, but not this, at least.

"No, sir."

Curiously, he could dismiss her without cause but didn't. As a midshipman, she held no commission from Admiralty, she served at the pleasure, laughable though the thought was, of her captain. They were locked into a struggle, Neals wanting to force her to resign and her refusing.

Neals stared at her for a time.

"You'll stand watch-and-watch until we make Penduli Station again, Carew," Neals said. "Perhaps that will change your mind."

TWO

Alexis staggered into her berth, sliding the hatch gently shut behind her. Her heavy boots clunked loudly on the deck as she braced herself with one hand on the top bunk. Thankfully she had the berth to herself. Timpson, the midshipman she shared it with, being up and about with the hands and she'd be able to get at least a little sleep. She stripped off her vacsuit and stored it neatly in her chest that sat under the lower bunk next to Timpson's. She considered taking the time to go to the head and shower, but her exhaustion was too great. Instead, she stuffed her soiled jumpsuit and underthings into a bag for later washing and pulled on a fresh set of the loose undershorts and baggy shirt, then crawled into the upper bunk.

She almost cried as the meager softness of the thin mattress cradled her body and she pulled the blanket over herself. She'd skip breakfast to have a few hours' sleep, at least. She rolled over and buried her face in her pillow. She did cry then.

Watch-and-watch until Penduli? Seven or more days, then, of having to be up and on duty every other watch. She'd have a bare three hours sleep now, until the end of the Morning Watch, then back on her feet to serve the Forenoon? Four more hours sleep through the Afternoon, and then up again for the shortened First Dog Watch and a choice between supper or sleep in the Second Dog? A week or more of it on top of the exhaustion she felt now.

She looked around the small space of the midshipman's berth for a moment. A bare two meters square, with two bunks on the wall opposite the hatchway. Two triangular desks in the corners, now folded up flush against the bulkheads. So much the same as the berth she'd shared with Philip Easely aboard her first ship, *H.M.S. Merlin*.

Not the same. She turned off the light and closed her eyes, feeling them burn with fatigue. At least that's what she told herself the burning was. *Nothing aboard this ship of the damned is the same.*

ALEXIS SPEARED another piece of the ship's beef, grown in the purser's vats from nutrient solution, and crammed it into her mouth, chewing rapidly to get it down with as little time tasting it as she could manage. She grasped her glass of wine to wash some of the taste away, though the wine was not much better than the beef, being the sweet and sharply alcoholic ship's wine the spacers referred to as Miss Taylor. Though still preferable to the thick, syrupy port they called blackstrap. She'd prefer to have a more palatable wine, of course, along with a meal made of something other than ship's stores, but she'd found that was simply not possible for her aboard *Hermione*.

Bushby, the senior midshipman, filled his glass from one of the bottles on the table. Bottles that they'd bought in, not from the ship's stores.

"More wine, gentlemen?" he asked, refilling everyone's glasses at their nods. Everyone's but hers, she noted. Also at the gunroom's table were two of *Hermione's* other midshipmen, Timpson, her berthmate, and Canion. The sixth, Brattle, had the watch and would eat at the start of the Second Dog Watch. The midshipmen were alone, the junior warrant officers and others who shared the gunroom, such as the captain's clerk, marine sergeants, and surgeon's mates being busy with other duties and would join Brattle for dinner in the Second Dog.

Bushby sat back in his chair, and brushed dark, unruly hair from his forehead. He shared a smirk with the other three at the table, before returning his gaze to Alexis. She followed his darting looks to the others, the little Ledyard, whose innocent face, she knew, hid a disturbing cruelty with the hands, Timpson, a fat, unpleasant boy of sixteen, and Canion, the oldest of the midshipmen at nineteen, but not the senior. That honor went to the absent Brattle. Alexis met Bushby's eyes.

"No bottle to share with us, Carew?" he asked.

"None," she answered.

Alexis missed the comforting surroundings of her previous ship, *Merlin*. On the much smaller sloop, there had been no separate wardroom for the lieutenants and senior warrant officers as there was here on *Hermione*. Here, alone with the other midshipmen, she felt things sometimes got out of hand and the presence of senior officers would cut some of the barbs and slights. The marines' presence, at least, would have put a bit of a damper on them, for Alexis had continued her habit of working out with the marines in an effort to improve her combat skills. Despite the traditional rivalry between the spacers and the marine complement, she felt oddly quite at home with them.

Bushby cleared his throat and waited for silence. "Is no one curious?" he asked.

"Is it good news, then?" Timpson asked.

Bushby's face broke into a wide grin. "Passed!" he announced to cheers and congratulations. Bushby had stood for lieutenant when last they'd stopped at Penduli Station, and news of the results must have reached him via the last packet ship they'd encountered.

Alexis raised her glass in turn when toasts were called for, not because she felt glad for the young man, but because not doing so would leave her singled out again. In truth, she was a little glad for him, but only because his passing the lieutenant's examination might see him promoted off of *Hermione* and some new midshipman brought aboard.

Bushby waived their cheers down with what Alexis knew was false modesty. "Now, gentlemen, I'm only passed, not promoted. Have to find ourselves in-system with some ship needing a newly-made lieutenant before I can hope for that." Until then, Bushby would remain a midshipman. But should *Hermione* encounter another ship that was short a lieutenant and had no midshipman aboard that her captain felt could act in the role, Bushby would likely be sent aboard. Or if one of *Hermione's* lieutenants were killed in action, Bushby would find himself promoted without the need for Captain Neals to name him 'acting'.

"To a bloody war or a sickly season!" Ledyard called out cheer-fully in the traditional gunroom toast naming the two things that most led to promotion.

"We've the one, at least," Canion said.

Alexis closed her eyes and sighed. They were such ... children. Parroting the toasts of the lieutenants without understanding their import. None of the midshipmen around the table had faced a real action, even with the war and *Hermione's* role as a free-sailing frigate, tasked with seeking out the Hanoverese warships and merchants. Thus far, they'd engaged no warships and the only merchants they'd closed with had been much smaller, striking their colors and surren-dering as soon as *Hermione* came into range.

They'd, none of them save Alexis, stood on the gundeck while incoming fire struck the man next to them, burning straight through vacsuit and man to exit the other side. *And won't care one bit for the men when they do — only so long as they themselves aren't harmed.*

"Yes," Bushby said. "It won't be long before I'm promoted to commander, and a ship of my own. Then a short hop to be made Post and my name on the Captains List."

"Then you've only to live long enough and you'll be Admiral Bushby," Canion said. He grinned and took a slow sip of his wine. "Of the Yellow, most like."

Bushby snorted and the other midshipmen shared a laugh at his expense. Alexis looked down at her plate, not wanting him to think she was joining in the laughter. When a captain reached the top of the Captains List and was promoted to admiral, it was to the Fleet's Blue Squadron, then to the White and Red Squadrons in time. To be 'yellowed', or promoted without distinction of squadron, was effectively to be retired — placed in a squadron that did not exist, with no ships, and left on half-pay.

"Bugger," Bushby muttered, but he shared a grin with the others.

"Did you see we've gotten the latest Gazette from that last packet, gentlemen?" Canion asked.

"Yes," Bushby answered. "And loads of mail, as well."

"Did you get news from home, Carew?" Timpson asked. "Know you've been waiting for it."

"No," Alexis admitted. She regretted having asked, after some weeks aboard with no messages, if any of them knew how long it would take for hers to catch up. Now, with so much more time passed and still nothing, she'd only given them something more to use against her.

"That's too bad," Bushby said, a look of what she knew to be false sympathy on his face.

"Do you think they've forgot about you?" Ledyard asked.

"Mister Ledyard!" Timpson barked in mock outrage. "Your manners, sir."

Ledyard raised his glass to take a sip of wine, eyebrows raised in innocence. "Only meant, well, out of sight and out of mind, don't you know?"

Alexis clenched her jaw tight and returned to her meal. She was well aware that anything she said would only prolong their game and entertain them more. As it was, they'd be about it for a quarter hour or more — all of them cackling at each other's latest riposte.

"Well, she is quite forgettable," Timpson said. "You may have a point after all."

"Perhaps the Navy's come around and realized their mistake,

Carew," Bushby said, "and your family's expecting you home any day?"

"Yes, Carew," Canion said. "Are you sure you didn't miss orders to return to your proper place? Some kitchen, perhaps?"

"A proper husband's bed?" Ledyard asked.

"Mister Ledyard!" Bushby said. "Now you do forget yourself!" Ledyard hung his head, but Alexis knew this outrage was false as well, which was proven as Bushby continued, "Apologize at once!"

Ledyard leapt to his feet and doffed his beret, face composed in contrition. He faced an empty chair that Alexis supposed was to represent her figurative husband.

"I do apologize, sir," he said, eyes wide and downcast. "And I implore you to forgive my wishing such a fate upon you."

"Fair enough," Bushby said.

Alexis took another, large gulp of the Miss Taylor, wrinkling her nose at the taste. Oh, they were on a tear now and she could tell it would get much worse before the meal was over. If she'd realize none of the warrants would be dining with them, she'd have skipped supper altogether and stayed in her bunk, or gone Outside to watch the *darkspace* clouds that so fascinated her. Anything to avoid having to sit here helpless and take their abuse.

She'd tried everything she knew early on, but nothing worked with this group. There were too many of them and all cut from the same vulgar, bullying cloth. Anger made them laugh, sly ripostes were shouted down, and the few times she'd resorted to striking them ... well, no matter how much time she spent training with the marines, outnumbered four or five to one and all of them but Ledyard bigger and stronger? No, that only got her beaten bloody and bruised, with the captain taking note of any marks she left on *them* and sending her to the masthead, or worse, for fighting.

"Hell!" Canion said with an exaggerated shudder. "Married to this tit? Can you imagine?"

"Tits're the one thing you *wouldn't* have to worry about! She's certainly a dearth of *that!*"

"Now there's a thought!" Bushby exclaimed as the laughter died.

He leaned forward and Alexis had no choice but to look up and meet his eyes, else they'd accuse her of being sullen and disrespectful to him as the senior. Mentioned in the captain's hearing would give him yet another excuse to punish her, not that he seemed to lack them.

Bushby's mouth curled up. "Not to play matchmaker, Carew, but I've an uncle might take a shine to you ... of course he's a Windward Passage sort of fellow and likes them smooth-chested." He looked around at the others as they roared laughter. "What? Be all the same to him from behind, wouldn't it? And no fear of hair sprouting out all over to ruin it some day!"

He turned back to Alexis, grinning, but his grin faltered as he met her eyes. Never in life had she so regretted the Navy's prohibition against dueling. She'd always been a fair hand with a pistol, and her work with the marines had made her more than proficient with the Navy's heavy bladed cutlass. She'd even turned her hand to the longer swords reserved for duels. The image of Bushby lying bleeding on a field some morning made her smile.

Bushby's grin faltered at the look on her face, he looked away from her, then back, his grin falling even more. He lowered his gaze, cleared his throat, and raised his glass to drink.

The others' laughter finally died away and their talk turned to news from the Naval Gazette and speculation about when the Prize Court might release the funds from their latest captures, small though they were. Alexis applied herself to her plate, allowing herself the hope that they might be done with her.

"Would you like the last of the chicken, Mister Bushby?"

"Why, yes, I would, Mister Ledyard, thank you for the offer."

Alexis watched as Ledyard handed the platter of roast chicken across the table to Bushby. *No, not done.* She knew what was coming next, from their tone and the elaborate formality of the charade they'd just started.

"I'd offer this last bit to you, Carew," Bushby said, scooping the chicken thigh onto his plate and pouring the last of the sauce from the platter over it. "But I note you've once again contributed no stores to our meal."

Alexis kept her head lowered, eyes on her plate as she cut yet another bite from the hunk of ship's beef. She raised it to her mouth, grimacing at the soft, mushy texture, and chewed. She'd lost weight, she knew, her already slight form becoming even more so in the time she'd been aboard *Hermione,* but she could only stomach so much of the ship's provisions.

"I've none to contribute, Mister Bushby," she said. "As you're aware."

"A shame," Bushby said. "I'd have thought you'd bring more aboard last we were in port."

And if you'd told me aboard Merlin that I'd one day wish for Stanford Roland's company at dinner ...

"I didn't see the point, Mister Bushby, as it would simply be pilfered again, as all my other stores have been."

"Pilfered, Carew?" he straightened in his chair. "That's a most dire accusation. Point the culprit out to us, if you please, and we'll see him done for you!"

Alexis sighed. This was quite the same conversation he'd been attempting to engage her in for weeks, ever since she'd first noticed that her personal stores were disappearing at an alarming rate. At first, she'd thought it was the gunroom steward, Boxer, but the amount of goods missing had quickly grown past anything a member of the crew would dare.

"I've no one to point to," she said. *And no one who'd listen if I did.*

She had, in fact, spoken to the second lieutenant about the matter, as the midshipmen were his responsibility. Williard had sighed and shaken his head.

"A bit of food and wine, Mister Carew?" he'd asked. "Is this not something you lot should settle amongst yourselves?"

"It's more than a bit, sir," she'd told him. "Nigh a full pound's value, all I brought aboard last port. And the port before that, as well. I've no objection to sharing, sir, but ..."

Williard had closed his eyes and hung his head. He'd seemed tired and resigned.

"Do you know who's done it?" He'd held up a hand to stop her speaking. "Know, mind you, not suspect. And can prove it, as well."

"No, sir."

"If I pursue the matter, Mister Carew, it will become known to Captain Neals."

And that had been the end of the matter for Alexis, for she'd learned already that there was nothing she desired aboard this ship so strongly as to be unnoticed by *Hermione's* captain.

"Then you should refrain from making idle accusations, I think," Bushby said with a wide grin. "Theft is quite a serious matter aboard ship, you know."

Alexis couldn't help it, she burst out laughing as the day's fatigue and the absurdity of Bushby's words washed over her. *Oh, yes, a serious matter.* Among the crew it was quite serious, she knew, and might result in the offender mysteriously disappearing one watch Outside. If the matter were brought before the captain on any ship, it would likely result in the offender facing a gauntlet of his mates, forced to walk slowly between two rows of them, as they kicked and pummeled him for his offense.

Among the officers, it was unheard of. Even the most destitute of midshipmen would have more honor than to steal from his mess-mates, and the consequences for one who did would be dire. In the unlikely event that he weren't disrated or dismissed from the service, no fellow officer would ever trust him again.

Unless you're so confident the captain himself wouldn't believe it, nor care if it could be proven to him.

"You laugh, Carew?"

"I do, Mister Bushby, I do, indeed." She looked up and met his eyes, knowing it was a mistake to engage him, but not caring. After a day and night atop the mast, she wanted the satisfaction of lashing out at someone herself.

"You should not make light about so serious a charge, Carew," Canion said.

"Oh, I do not make light of it, Mister Canion. Not light at all. It would be a serious charge indeed to make and I would not do so frivolously. To make such a charge would be to say that the man had no honor at all." She met each of their eyes in turn. "That he was a weak, useless excuse for an officer, indeed, and unfit for the company of respectable men. That he was a disgrace and embarrassment to the Queen's Service and should be ashamed to walk the deck of a Queen's Ship. No, sirs, I would not make light of such a charge. Were I to make it." She raised her glass, suppressing a grimace at the taste. "Which I do not, of course." She smiled and rose. "Good night, gentlemen."

ALEXIS ARLEEN CAREW, you are a fool. Sure as certain, they'll find a way to make you pay for that.

But it was worth it. To watch their eyes as she spoke, seeing that they knew she was speaking to them, about them — but they couldn't object, couldn't call her out for what she said — not without admitting that she was speaking about them, what they'd done, and that every word she'd said was nothing but the truth.

She lay back on her bunk and pulled out her tablet. The news that there'd been mail and the Gazette was welcome, but her anticipation quickly waned when she saw that no mail for her had arrived. Nothing from any of her former shipmates, nor even from her grandfather, back at home on Dalthus. *I'd have thought at least Philip would write to me — and certainly grandfather's written something in all this time. It's been months, I do wonder if the Navy's forgotten where I am.*

It wasn't at all unusual for mail to take weeks or even months to travel the vast distances between stars. Longer if the message's destination was a ship that was constantly in motion itself. But it had been so long and Alexis was certain that *something* should have arrived at Penduli and been waiting for *Hermione's* last port-call.

With no mail, she turned instead to the Naval Gazette. A quick search turned up news of her old ship and shipmates, the first of which made her exclaim with delight. There on the Captain's List, only fourth from the bottom, but still on it, was the entry: Captain William S. Grantham, made Post the seventeenth of October, into *H.M.S. Camilla* (20).

Only twenty guns and a sixth-rate, but still a frigate and he's made Post!

Formerly holding the rank of commander, though called "captain" by virtue of commanding *Merlin* — a bit of naval semantics that still made her head hurt a little bit — Grantham was now a full Post Captain, his name on the Captains List that dictated seniority and promotion. He'd now move steadily up it as those above him were promoted or died.

She moved on to the next result from her searches and found another name she recognized on the list of those promoted to lieutenant. *Good for you, Roland, it's about time.*

Certain that there must have been an action to result in the two promotions, she searched for the ship's name and found it. *Merlin* and another sloop, *H.M.S. Vulture,* had worked in concert to take a Hanoverese frigate. She read the account of the action eagerly for any news of her former shipmates, but for one name in particular.

UPON MAKING FAST to the enemy ship's port side, Midshipmen Stanford Roland and Philip Easely led the boarding parties. While Midshipman Roland's party forced the quarterdeck and with few injuries or deaths demanded the colors be struck, Midshipman Easely and his party so occupied the enemy that they were unable to fight their guns to either side, allowing the men of Vulture *to board from starboard.*

ALEXIS SCANNED the rest of the article and hurried on to the list of those injured or killed in the action, though the Gazette named only officers and gave but a count for the regular crew. *Three dead and eleven injured of the crew — and how I wish they'd care enough to give the names. Now I'll be forever worrying about the lads until there's some news. But Philip and Roland are both all right, and must be so proud to be mentioned in dispatches.*

She satisfied herself that the Gazette contained no more about her friends and sighed. She opened the latest letter she'd started writing to her grandfather and read.

GRANDFATHER,

I KNOW I should see things through and persevere, but I cannot. Life aboard Hermione *is too hard. It is a living hell that you could not comprehend and I cannot bring myself to describe to you.*

I've decided that I must leave — for my sanity and safety, for I fear what will happen if I remain.

When next we make port, I will resign my position and take passage upon some merchant vessel back to Dalthus.

The prize money I was awarded aboard Merlin *will certainly cover the cost of my passage home and allow me, even should I never hold our lands, some modest life. It will surely be enough and must be better than this.*

THERE WAS a soft knock at the hatchway. Alexis set the tablet aside and sat up, swinging her legs over the side of the bunk.

"Yes?"

The hatch slid open and Boxer, the gunroom steward, entered. He glanced once at Alexis, then down at the deck.

"Beggin' yer pardon, sir." He held out a cloth-covered plate to her. "But I've brought you some'at." Alexis hopped down from the bunk. "It's not much, sir, but ..."

"Boxer," she whispered, reaching out to raise the cloth. Underneath was a bit of chicken and a ship's biscuit covered in gravy.

"It's my bit, Mister Carew," he said quickly. "No more'n would be my due, you understand."

Alexis stared at him. There was an unwritten rule that the men who did extra work as servants for the gunroom, wardroom, and captain would pilfer a small amount of each meal, as a bit more compensation than the few extra coins they earned for the service.

"Not right what they doin' to you, sir."

She laid a hand on his forearm. "Nothing aboard this ship is right." She gently pushed the plate toward him. "But you can't do this, Boxer."

"My bit, sir," he insisted, his face set and stubborn. "Can do what I like with it, I 'spect."

"No. I'm grateful, Boxer, I truly, truly am, but if they find out ..."

"Checked, sir. They's all left the gunroom and —"

"They'll find out, Boxer. If I accept this once, you'll do it again, and one time they'll find out and they'll see it goes hard on you. I won't have you lose your place over me ... or worse." She nodded toward the hatchway. "Off with you now. Enjoy your bit yourself ... and thank you."

Alexis waited until he'd left, then slid the hatch closed and climbed to her bunk again. She took up her tablet and reread the words she'd written, then erased them as she'd written and erased similar words so many times over, and started again.

GRANDFATHER,

I WISH you to know I am well and hope you and all those I love at home are as well.

I have not received any messages from you since boarding Hermione, *but we have been traveling and patrolling so widely that I suspect they have simply not caught up to us yet. My own to you, I am certain, have a much surer route to travel, as Dalthus does not move about nearly so much as a warship.*

Hermione *is not so happy a ship as* Merlin, *and Captain Neals is certainly not so kind as Captain Grantham was, but I am determined to persevere. As with my time on* Merlin, *my time aboard* Hermione *will pass, as well. I am given to understand that she is due to pay off in some six months or a year, at which time her officers and crew will be disbursed to other ships while she is refitted. This is no more than twice or thrice the time I have already been aboard, so it can be no greater hardship to wait out my time on this ship.*

The men have a saying they use when facing even the most trying of times:

'You shouldn't have joined if you can't take a joke,' they say.

I often feel that, for all their roughness and the violence of their trade, the crews of these ships must certainly be the most tolerant ... and kindest ... of men. I truly hope that I will one day be worthy of leading their like.

Despite the war, please do not concern yourself as to my safety. Hermione *has seen little in the way of action, and that still only with lightly-armed merchantmen, all much smaller. Captain Neals is quite clever in that regard.*

ALL MY LOVE,
Alexis

SHE SENT the message off and lay back to try and sleep. She should, she sometimes thought, be grateful to Captain Neals for the time he gave her on the mast. At least when she'd slept earlier, there had been no dreams. Ever since she'd come aboard *Hermione*, she'd been haunted by dreams of the pirate leader Horsfall. *Merlin* had taken his ship and Alexis had been sent aboard to head the prize crew, but a storm had come up and the pirates had retaken it.

Alexis and the remainder of the prize crew had managed to surprise the pirates and take the ship back, but not without great cost, as all but Alexis and a single spacer had been killed or severely injured in the fighting. Horsfall had demanded she negotiate with him, as there was only himself and one other pirate who could pilot the ship. But Alexis, furious at the deaths of her men and knowing Horsfall would never negotiate in good faith, had shot him.

Defenseless and in cold blood, she admitted to herself. She would, she thought, always remember the feel of the trigger and the way his head had jerked backward. The fine mist of blood that had covered the bulkhead and the other pirates behind him. Oddly, she could not remember the sound of the shot — in her memory, the entire thing played out in absolute silence.

At the time and immediately after, she'd had no regrets, and no one had even suggested that she'd not done the right thing. She'd gotten the rest of her crew home. But the cost came later, and she'd come to question whether she wouldn't have been able to do it some other way.

Please not tonight.

THREE

"Sail, sir."

"Where away, Youngs?" Alexis turned from her place at the navigation plot, a large, round table at the center of the quarterdeck, and stepped over to the tactical console. The spacer there pointed to a bright spot on his monitor. The spot, blurry and indistinct after being brought inboard through a series of optics, the path protected by a series of fine gallenium mesh to protect the interior of the ship from *darkspace*, was small and clearly far away.

"Fine on the port quarter, sir, down fifteen," he said.

Alexis nodded and patted his shoulder. "Good work, Youngs."

She returned to the navigation plot and sighed. It was two bells into her watch, the Middle Watch again, and she'd just been starting to relax. She knew that Captain Neals considered it a punishment, but she rather enjoyed the quiet hours late in the ship's night, followed by the bustle of the crew waking, cleaning the ship for the day, then going to their breakfast at the start of the Morning Watch. Neals himself rarely left his cabin before well into the Forenoon Watch, and Alexis was quite willing to give up a few hours' sleep for the pleasure of some hours without the other officers about. She could almost, for a time, pretend it was the quarterdeck of some other ship entirely.

But not with a sail sighted.

"Wake Captain Neals," she said, not taking her eyes from the plot, "the lieutenants, and the sailing master."

"Aye, sir."

Alexis brought the image of the other ship up on the navigation plot and expanded it, studying the fuzzy blob of light in the distance. *Behind us and below.* She switched back to the plot that showed their course. *Hermione* was close-hauled, running as close to the wind as she could, with her keelboard fully extended. The other ship seemed to be on a similar course.

Could be three masts, she thought, studying the image of the other ship. *A large merchantman or another frigate.* She'd spent a good deal of time studying images of other ships at varying distances and angles, working to improve her ability to identify them and to pick out their signals. She narrowed her eyes at the plot, thinking of the size of the other ship's sails and its course, so close to the wind. *Another frigate, I think.*

With *Hermione* to windward of the other ship, she had the option of continuing on as she was or dropping back to close. The strange sail, on the other hand, would find it near impossible to close with her upwind — even another frigate would be unable to sail closer to the wind or faster. She heard the quarterdeck hatch slide open and footsteps as Neals entered, followed closely by Lieutenant Dorsett — the others would not be far behind. She half-smiled at the image of the other ship before closing it and leaving the navigation plot for the captain. *And so we'll never know for sure what you are, will we? For we're about to run.*

"Sail, sir," she said, turning to face Neals. "Youngs spotted it — fine on the port quarter and down fifteen."

Neals grunted acknowledgment and crossed to the tactical

console without looking at her. A moment later the two other lieutenants, Williard and Roope, along with the sailing master entered the quarterdeck.

"Thank you for finally joining us, gentlemen," Neals said. He stepped to the navigation plot.

The others joined him there and Alexis stepped back, hoping to go unnoticed.

"Mister Carew," Neals said, giving her a narrow look. "You've had the most time to study this Sail, what do you make of it?"

Alexis felt her stomach sink. She looked from the plot to the captain. *What I think or what he wants to hear?* She bit her lip — there'd been so many compromises to make aboard *Hermione* that she constantly questioned what was right.

She squared her shoulders. "A frigate, sir."

Neals looked back at the image. "Lieutenant Dorsett?"

Dorsett leaned over the plot, staring intently. "I am ... unsure, sir."

Neals straightened. "Yes, it is a difficult identification — and one should not speak until one is sure. A lesson Mister Carew would do well to take to heart." He tapped the image. "This is a merchant vessel."

"Yes, sir," Dorsett said. "I see it now."

"Do you other gentlemen concur?"

Alexis shared a glance with Youngs, the spacer at the tactical console, then he looked down, face blank and impassive.

The two other lieutenants and the sailing master all nodded. "Yes, sir."

"Do you see it now, Mister Carew?"

"I ... defer to your experience, captain. Thank you for correcting me."

"Man the signals console, Mister Carew. I will remain on the quarterdeck and we shall maintain our course. This merchantman is too far behind to pursue — she would take us on a long stern chase into Hanoverese territory and to little benefit."

"Yes, sir," Dorsett said.

Alexis took the place of the spacer at the signals console. The other ship was too far away for signals, but she brought up its image anyway.

"Pass the word for the bosun, Lieutenant Dorsett, let us have the royals bent on," Neals said.

"Aye, sir."

ALEXIS WATCHED the sequence of images again, wanting to be absolutely certain of what she'd seen. There'd been no call from the spacer on the tactical console. She looked over at him and saw that his shoulders were hunched and tense. Captain Neals was engaged in conversation with Lieutenant Dorsett, neither of them watching the navigation plot or its inset image of the other ship.

She ran the sequence again, looking carefully. It was there, a thin, brief line of light flashing away from the other ship on the far side, the leeward side. It could be nothing but the firing of a single gun — the distinctive, bolt of a laser, behaving so different in *darkspace* than it should. She turned toward the plot and started to speak, but Lieutenant Williard caught her eye and gave his head the smallest of shakes. Not entirely sure she'd understood his meaning, she opened her mouth, and he, quite clearly, mouthed the words "do not".

Confused, she turned back to her console. Could she truly be the only one on the quarterdeck who'd seen the ship fire a gun, and a single gun to leeward, at that? It was a sure sign that the ship was both a warship, not a merchant, and of the enemy. It was a challenge to come out and engage that even she recognized.

"This merchant's lookouts must be blind to have not seen us and turned away," Neals said loudly.

"Yes, sir," Dorsett agreed.

Alexis turned and stared at the officers in shock and sudden realization. She'd noticed early in her time aboard Hermione that

Captain Neals preferred to engage the Hanoverese merchant shipping, rather than their warships. In fact, Hermione had not fired her guns in anger, save a warning shot or two across a ship's bow, in all the time she'd been aboard.

Thinking back, though, she realized that even those merchant vessels had all been much smaller than Hermione. Sloops, pinnaces, cutters – never a ship of similar size, and no warships whatsoever. There was always a reason, of course, supplies low, poor conditions for a chase, and more.

Alexis had thought Neals simply greedy and lazy, preferring the easy prize money of a merchant and her cargo to the effort of engaging another ship of war. Now, though, with another warship not only pursuing them, but throwing a challenge in his face, he maintained some fiction that he hadn't seen.

He's a coward.

THE OTHER SHIP had been losing ground for some time and was barely visible. Whether *Hermione* was more lightly-laden or had more sail area or for some other reason, Alexis didn't know, but it was clear now that *Hermione* would soon be out of sight of the other ship.

Alexis watched as the image of the other ship changed as it turned aside and then away, taking the wind on her stern and sailing almost directly away from *Hermione's* course. There was a larger flash and lines of light streamed away from the other ship's sides, shot after shot in quick succession.

Both broadsides – emptied her guns.

It was a clear gesture of contempt, a message that Hermione wasn't worth even the precaution of keeping the guns loaded and ready.

Surely he can't ignore that?

"Put us on the port tack, Lieutenant Dorssett, and make for Penduli Station, I should like to resupply."

"Aye, sir."

"And I'll have the royals brought down at five bells." Neals paused and Alexis could sense the tension on the quarterdeck as the crew anticipated his next words. "I am displeased with the men's speed in raising them – see that they're brought in more quickly and twelve lashes for the last man down from the yards."

FOUR

T HE STREAMS of people parted and passed Alexis on both sides. The corridors of Penduli Station were filled, with seven Navy ships in-system and enumerable merchantmen delivering stores to the station. Stores that would be taken on by the warships and, thence, back to the border systems and the war.

She noted that the marine sentry posted outside the hatch to the Port Admiral's offices was staring at her. She couldn't blame him, she supposed, with that she'd been standing in the corridor for some time. Her realization of Neals' cowardice and the subsequent flogging of Brownlee, a skilled topman, but the last man down from the yards after Neals' order, had resolved her to do something, and speaking to the Port Admiral was the only thing she could think of to do.

I can barely count the number of men he's flogged just since I've come aboard. Surely they'll not want a man of his cruelty and cowardice in command of a Queen's Ship?

She straightened and stepped forward, just as a hand grasped her elbow and spun her to face down the corridor.

"Ah, there you are, Mister Carew," Lieutenant Williard said, keeping a tight grip on her arm and fairly dragging her away. He leaned close and whispered, "Not a word and come with me, Carew."

Without another word, he was off, dragging her alongside. She was too shocked by his sudden appearance and actions to protest, and could do nothing in any case. Though she was certain she could break his grip on her arm, he was still her superior officer, both in rank and in *Hermione's* chain of command.

Williard led her through the crowd and up several levels until he finally guided her into a small pub. Or, at least, she thought it was a pub until they entered and found a liveried servant waiting to greet them behind a podium of dark wood. The man raised an eyebrow at Alexis, then looked enquiringly at Williard.

Williard tapped his tablet to the podium and the man glanced down.

"Ah, Lord Atworth, a table for you and your guest?"

"Perhaps," Williard said. "But first someplace for a private conversation. The library?"

"Of course, sir." He stepped away from the podium and motioned them to follow him. "This way."

They followed him, Williard still not releasing his grip on her arm and she staring around in wonder. The narrow corridor they were walking through was lined in paneling with the distinctive purple swirl of *varrenwood* from her own home on Dalthus, and it appeared to be real. The cost of so much *varrenwood*, even were it a veneer, would be quite high.

They left the corridor and entered a large room, large for the limited space of a station, in any case, with low lighting and groups of heavy, leather-covered chairs. The walls were lined with glass-fronted shelves and behind the glass were books. *They look real – must be a fortune in antiques there.*

The man leading them stopped at a pair of chairs in the room's corner and raised an eyebrow to Williard. "Refreshment, sir?"

"No, thank you ... yes, in fact, now I think on it." Williard glanced at Alexis. "Scotch, two. Something decent."

"Of course, sir."

When he'd left, Williard shoved Alexis toward one of the chairs and sat himself in the other. The library was empty, save for them. Alexis looked around, fascinated.

"Are you a fool, Carew?"

She returned her gaze to Williard and found him staring at her.

"I do not believe so, sir, no."

"Standing around the Port Admiral's office as though you had some business there? You don't find this quite a foolish thing?"

"I ..."

"No, don't tell me what you intended. I can quite imagine, but I don't want to hear it. Were I to hear it, I might have to act."

Seems you've acted already, dragging me in here.

"What is this place?"

"Dorchester's, it's a gentleman's club. No," he said as her eyes widened, "not the sort the midshipmen speak of. It's a club for actual gentlemen."

"And you are a gentleman?" Alexis asked, rubbing her arm where he'd gripped it.

Williard had the good grace to look uncomfortable at that. "Lord Atworth, Baron, at present, through an accident of birth and the untimely death of my brother — Earl of Iota Talis, should I outlast my father." He paused as a servant arrived with two glasses. "Thank you." When they were alone again, Williard raised his glass and took a sip. "I will suggest to you a ... hypothetical situation, Mister Carew. An entire phantasm of events, you understand?"

"Yes, sir."

"Very well, then. Suppose an officer, a very junior officer — a sniveling snotty of a midshipman, perhaps — aboard a ship were to approach a far more senior member of Her Majesty's Navy, a Port Admiral, for the sake of argument, about some ... things which concerned him aboard ship. What do you suppose might happen, Mister Carew?"

"I ..."

"She'd be bounced out on her arse and her impertinence reported to her captain, you naive, bloody fool!"

Alexis stared at him in shock. "Sir, I ..."

"Do you not know how the Navy works, Carew? Well, I shall tell you. A captain is the representative of Her Majesty's Government in space. Do you understand what that means? It means his actions are those of Her Majesty. There is a *reason* a ship's captain is referred to as the 'sole master after God' — and God, Carew, seldom bothers Himself with frigates."

"But ..."

"Drink your drink, Carew, and listen closely, without interrupting me."

Well, and I wouldn't, if you'd stop asking questions. She raised her glass and took a small sip for courtesy's sake, then widened her eyes and took another. She'd never really enjoyed liquors, but this was quite good. It set her tongue tingling and drew a line of warmth down to her belly.

"The Navy will only acknowledge a captain's misdeeds in the most grievous and public circumstances ... or if they have need of a scapegoat, of course," Williard went on. "And anything that can be covered up, will be. To do otherwise would destroy the discipline required to man our ships months from home. And they do not take a kind view of those who try to force their hand. So, to return to our little hypothetical, the junior officer who reports a senior is likely to find herself in a much worse position than she was before."

"But he's a coward, sir," she said in a rush, "surely they must care about that."

Williard took a deep breath. "Prove it."

"The ship's logs ..."

"Yes, the logs. Again, our hypothetical captain and aboard our purely speculative ship, of course. What would the logs show, if such a man were careful? A series of entirely justified decisions, perhaps? Ships misidentified, but the identification concurred to by his senior officers? Pursuits not quite on the best point of sail, so that a Chase gets away? And, yet still, a not embarrassing string of Prizes – small, I grant you, but still ships taken from the enemy."

Alexis stared at him. That would, indeed, be what *Hermione's* logs would show, now that he pointed it out to her. She raised her glass again, surprised to find it empty, but before she'd even set it back on the table the servant had appeared again with fresh glasses for her and Williard, whisking the empties away and withdrawing. Alexis raised this new glass and drank. The warmth filled her and loosened some of the tension.

"The men, then, sir?" she asked. "There's not a Captain's Mast goes by that some man isn't flogged. The flimsiest of reasons and the number of lashes." She closed her eyes. "Sir, the regulations allow for no more than two dozen to be ordered by a captain, and yet Captain —"

"Carew ..." Williard said warningly.

Alexis bit her lip. "And yet ... I have heard of some captains ordering as many as four dozen. And that men have died of it aboard ... some ships."

Williard nodded. "Admiralty cares that a captain is successful, Carew, not a bit about his methods. Punishments go into the log, but when that log is reviewed at the end of a cruise ... assuming it actually is, of course ... well, one does not argue methods with God when He's successful, does one?"

"The Devil, rather."

Williard shrugged. "Aboard some ships, they're one and the same."

Alexis drained her glass, grateful for the sting and burn of the drink.

Williard smiled. "I should warn you, Mister Carew, that's an expensive taste to cultivate."

"I'm sorry, sir," Alexis said, setting the glass down.

"I wasn't complaining about the reckoning. Only that I'd not start a fellow officer down the dark path of fine Scotch whiskey without fair warning."

Alexis picked up the glass again and smiled as she took a sip. "I'll consider myself warned, sir." She studied the glass for a moment, the dim light sparkling amber through the liquid and the crystal of the glass. "So there's nothing to be done, then?"

"Come," Williard said, standing. As soon as he stood, the servant appeared. "We'll go in to dinner now, if you please."

"Of course, sir. Follow me?"

They followed the servant down another hallway and into a large dining room, again appointed in rich woods and leathers, the tables set far apart for privacy. Only a few of the tables were occupied, and those by older men, most in uniform and most of those had sleeves bearing the four narrow gold bands of a Post Captain. She was, Alexis noted, not merely the only woman in the room, but by far the most junior officer. A second servant appeared and held a chair for her at a table in a secluded corner.

"Should I really be here, Lieutenant Williard?" Alexis asked, sitting.

"I feel there may be unplumbed depths to that question."

Alexis smiled. "Nothing too philosophical, sir, only that I'm neither a gentleman nor of high rank."

"Dorchester's was founded on New London. You'll find them less than provincial, no matter where they've opened a branch — and they care far more about my peerage than naval rank."

"Well, neither am I a peer, for a certain."

Williard laughed and raised his glass. "That they care about. You'd not see the inside of the place without a title — or a very great deal of money, they do like that as well — and that would truly be a shame, for they've the best chops you'll find."

THE MEAL, when it came, was everything Williard had led her to believe it would be. Starting with a rich, creamy soup made with some sort of shellfish Alexis hadn't encountered before. Her grandfather's farm on Dalthus had been nowhere near the sea, and Denholm Carew avoided his coastal holdings for some reason that had never been explained to Alexis.

"This is quite good, sir, thank you," she said as the bowls were being removed and they waited for the next course.

Following naval custom, they'd not discussed "shop" once the meal started. Nothing about the war or *Hermione*. Instead, talk had turned to their pasts and families.

Alexis learned that Williard was a second son, bound for the Navy from birth as his older brother would inherit. When his brother died in an aircar crash, Williard had become the heir, but had decided to remain in the Navy, much to his father's displeasure.

"I'd much prefer to make my way in the Navy and my younger brother would do much better at managing the estate, but father is a bit of a traditionalist," Williard told her with a small smile. "But what of yourself? From Dalthus, was it? What brought you to the Navy?"

"Yes, Dalthus." Alexis hesitated. Once she'd seen what life aboard *Hermione* was like, she'd remained silent about her life before coming aboard. The other midshipmen would use anything they could against her and as for the lieutenants, well, personal conversations were few and far between. "One could say Dalthus is a planet of traditionalists, sir."

Williard frowned. "Not political or religious is it? I hadn't heard it mentioned as one of those."

Alexis shook her head. With habitable planets so common, any group with enough funds to form a colonization company could buy a star system. That was how her grandfather had come to Dalthus, as one of the three thousand or so original settlers who'd bought shares in the company. Those settlers had all been of mostly independent mindsets, not like some colonies that were founded by groups with strong opinions that were then codified into the system's laws.

"No," she said, "not one of those. Just ... well, they turned their tradition into law and decided that a woman can't hold lands there at all. And as I'm my grandfather's only heir ... potential heir, I suppose ..."

Williard frowned. "Yes, I'd noticed that about the Fringe. You're the first woman I've seen in uniform since I was transferred from the Core. The colonies do sprout odd ideas, I suppose." He grunted. "Not that the Core Worlds have room to judge, what with how some of them were founded."

Alexis smiled. "There's a New London founder or two who've some things to answer for in the afterlife, if my grandfather's oaths over the household accounts carry any weight. He's certain their decision to bring back the shilling proves they were all quite mad."

"Yes, well one would almost have to be a bit mad to be a first settler," Williard said. "Without offense to your grandfather, the thought of being dropped on a bare planet with nothing but the goods I could ship there is more than a bit unsettling."

"It was very difficult, I'm told," Alexis agreed.

The rest of the meal passed in idle talk as course after course was brought, and more than one bottle of wine.

"You did not exaggerate, sir. Not at all." Alexis sat back from the table as the last of the dishes was cleared. The meal had been truly spectacular. A thick, juicy slab of real beef, charred black on the outside and rare in the middle. So far removed from the provisions aboard *Hermione* that she could not credit them being called the same. The side dishes had been equally well prepared, and Alexis had allowed her enjoyment of the food to lull her into also enjoying far more wine than she should have — and this on top of her newfound love for the Scotch whiskey. The servants quickly scraped the tablecloth clean and set two glasses and a decanter of port between them.

"I never exaggerate about fine food and drink, Mister Carew," Williard said. "It is far too important." He poured them each a glass of the port.

Alexis took a sip and bit her lip. The conversation over dinner had remained innocuous, not touching on *Hermione* or Captain Neals, but both were still much on her mind.

"About our ... phantasm, lieutenant? You truly believe there's nothing to be done?"

"I truly believe it should not even be spoken of, Mister Carew. But as you seem determined." He sighed and drained his glass. "There are, in truth, two Navies. The first, which if I am to believe all I've heard of him, you encountered aboard *Merlin* with Captain Grantham. It is a Navy of honor and duty, where your worth is measured by merit and your deeds." He twirled his empty glass between his fingertips, watching the light through the remaining drops of port. "The other Navy is quite different, I'm afraid. It has gained much sway over the whole during the last few years of peace, and it measures worth in quite a different way. It is one of patronage and power, and it cares not for the rest. Our hypothetical captain would belong to the latter Navy, and he would certainly have many friends. Friends who, in addition to the Navy's own desire to avoid scandal, would go to great lengths to protect him personally."

He refilled his glass.

"Even when the nation is at peace, Mister Carew, our two Navies are at war, the one against the other. And as with any war, those of us in less exalted positions —" He smiled. "— and I assure you that lieutenant, no matter how far removed from your own position it may seem, is far from exalted. We must ... survive. For we can do our side of the battle little good when we wield little power. No, Mister Carew, I will survive. I will do my time with ... with any phantasm I am assigned to serve, and I will move on. When I am a Post Captain, myself, then I will have some influence over events, I think. This is what I recommend for you, as well."

ALEXIS STAGGERED a bit as she wandered the station's corridors. Dinner with Lieutenant Williard had gone long, and it was later than she'd thought. She considered, briefly, returning to the ship, but Captain Neals had granted all the officers liberty not only for the evening, but "all night in", with no one required to be back aboard *Hermione* until the forenoon watch. For the officers, at least — the hands were not so lucky, being confined to the ship, and the ship not even Out of Discipline for them to have some release from the pressures of constant sailing.

Her head was spinning more than a bit from the drink. Though dinner had been long, it hadn't been enough for the effects to wear off, and she staggered as someone bumped her in the still busy corridor. She needed to find a room for the night and relax away from the ship. Someplace fine, not one of the many pod-complexes where one could rent a coffin-like, enclosed space to sleep for a few hours. No, it had been entirely too long since she'd slept in a proper bed and she wanted something larger than her shipboard bunk, someplace where she could stretch and roll about. Perhaps even a proper bath all to herself.

There was a sharp tug at her sleeve and she looked down to find a young boy at her side.

"You looking?" he asked.

"Looking for what?" She paused and bit the inside of her cheek then blinked rapidly to try and clear her head a bit.

He smiled widely. "You tell me, I help you find it!"

Alexis smiled back. "How old are you? Should you be out so late?"

"Station runs all the time. I'll sleep later. Now, what you looking for?"

Alexis looked around, she didn't see any place that looked likely to rent a room for the night, and she could see the boy, like those in any village back on Dalthus, was anxious to earn a coin or two.

"A place to spend the night," she said. "Someplace nice."

"Yes, nice," the boy said, tugging her arm to get her moving. "Not here though — nothing nice on the Navy side. We go to the civvy-side. Nice places there for the nice lady, yes?"

"All right, yes."

The boy led her down the corridor and up several levels to leave the pubs and shops that catered to Navy crews. She saw more and more women in civilian ships' uniforms as they went, crew and officers on the merchant vessels in-system. Alexis nodded and smiled at those that met her eye and they nodded back, though some looked askance at her naval uniform.

They turned into a small side corridor with hatchways that looked more residential than commercial and the boy stopped before one and held out his hand, palm up.

"Nice place for the night. Very nice."

Alexis swayed a bit and eyed the hatchway. There was no signage to indicate it was a business or had rooms to let.

"Are you certain?"

"Very nice. Customers always pleased. Come back many, many times."

Alexis laughed. "All right, then." She took a few coins and placed them in the boy's outstretched hand. Apparently it was enough, because he clenched his fist tightly and smiled. "Nice lady have nice night," he called and dashed away grinning.

She watched him go, then looked at the hatchway again. If she had not had quite so much to drink she might go in search of another place. She pressed the call button beside the hatchway, expecting to find that it was, indeed, someone's home and the boy had taken her coins for naught. Though why he might do so, instead of leading her to an inn of some kind, she couldn't fathom. She smiled again. *Well, and if he has, then I'll look up the nearest inn with my tablet and be done with it.*

The hatch slid open and a well-dressed woman of middle-age peered out. "Yes, dear?"

Alexis tried to look apologetic for bothering her. "Pardon me, ma'am, but I was told you might have a room for the night?"

The woman smiled and slid the hatch fully open. "Of course, dear, come in." Alexis entered into a nicely appointed sitting room and the woman slid the hatch shut behind her. "What did you have in mind?"

Alexis felt herself sway, possibly the last glass of port catching up with her, and she closed her eyes to a wave of dizziness. "Just something nice for the night, before I have to go back aboard ship."

"Something nice?" the woman asked and Alexis opened her eyes to find her smiling curiously. "Nothing more specific for me to work with, dear?"

"Well, no, I suppose. It's just for one night, after all."

The woman reached out and took one of Alexis' hands in hers. "Is this your first time, dear?"

Alexis blinked. "I suppose it is, yes. I went straight from home to aboard one ship or another, and haven't spent much time in port, you see. Is that somehow important?"

The woman's face softened. "Oh, dear, yes, I think it is." She smiled. "But you just trust old Chelsea here, I'll see you right." She turned to a screen hanging on the bulkhead which showed rows of red and green circles. "Yes, that'll do nicely," she said, tapping one and changing it from green to red. "The whole night, you said?"

"Yes, I've to be back aboard for the Forenoon Watch."

"All right, then. One pound seven and we'll see you on your way in time to meet your ship."

Alexis stared at her in shock. A full pound and seven shillings for a night's stay in a room? *Well, I did ask for something nice, I suppose.* She'd never before even priced a room, so had no idea what it should cost. And she was definitely feeling the effects of the drink, her head felt stuffed with cotton and she wanted nothing more than to lay her head on pillow and sleep the night away.

And it's not as though I've aught else to spend my pay on otherwise. Without taking new stores aboard ship with her, and there was only so much she could eat and drink in port on those rare occasions she was allowed off *Hermione*, her accounts had accumulated a tidy sum on top of her earlier prize money. She'd also saved what she would have spent that night, what with Williard treating her to a fine dinner and finer drink. Nodding, she pulled out her tablet and made the payment.

"Compartment seven, dear, just at the top of the stairs there."

"Thank you."

Alexis climbed the stairs and slid the hatchway open on room seven. Though space was at a premium on board stations, it wasn't so bad as aboard ships, and the compartment she entered was, perhaps, four meters square — a large compartment aboard station. Softly lit, with chairs and an inviting divan. The bed itself was larger than the entire midshipman's berth she shared with Timpson. *And all to myself.* There was another hatch on the opposite bulkhead, which she assumed led to a private head. She smiled widely and slid the hatch shut behind her, then tossed her beret onto a chair and shrugged out of her uniform jacket and tunic. *A real bed again,* she thought, tossing her trousers after her jacket and climbing onto the bed in her underthings. *And a proper bath in the morning.* She spread her arms and legs to the corners, reveling in the space and the softness of the mattress.

"So y'ave me fer the night entire, eh, lass?"

Alexis sprang up. There was man standing in the now open hatchway to the head. The light silhouetted him from behind. He wore a towel wrapped around his waist and nothing else. *A short towel.* His long, curly, dark hair was tied back and his teeth shone brightly against his tanned skin. Muscles rippled under his skin as he stepped toward the bed and raised one leg to kneel on it. *A very short towel ...*

"Oh ... dear."

FIVE

Alexis came awake slowly and reluctantly. Her eyes felt filled with grit and her head pounded. She moved her mouth slowly, grimacing at the feel of her coated tongue. She clenched her eyes shut and burrowed her face into the smooth, warm body next to her.

Her eyes flew open, blinking.

Her cheek was pressed against someone's chest and she was looking down an expanse of brown, muscle-rippled skin to where her arm was draped over a blanket-covered waist. Her own legs were pressed against bare skin, one of them thrown over the man next to her.

Alexis froze, trying to make sense of the previous night. She remembered most of the dinner clearly, but things became quite ... blurry thereafter. She remembered looking for a room and following a boy who'd promised her something nice. *And wasn't that a brilliant thing to do.* A vague recollection of falling into a soft, warm bed. And, curiously, a towel, which made little sense. She blinked again and the clearer view of the swathe of skin she rested against brought a much more vivid image of the towel, as well as a flush of heat to her face.

She pondered, for a moment, how she might gather her clothes, she still seemed to be wearing her underthings, at least, and escape without waking ...

Oh ... my ... did I ever learn his name, at least?

"Awake, lass?"

Alexis clenched her jaw and swallowed as the blood drained from her face. *So much for that, then.* Now all she had to do was decide if she'd be less likely to die of embarrassment by sitting up and looking him in the eye, or staying where she was. The man shifted position and the blanket started to slide down his waist. Alexis bolted upright, spinning her legs around to face the wall behind the bed's headboard. Her eyes widened and her mouth dropped open at the sight of the man's face.

Black, curly hair framed a rugged face with a strong chin. For a moment, she focused on his eyes, a deep, brilliant blue that drew her in, until he smiled and her gaze dropped to his mouth and his even, white teeth surrounded by full lips.

He raised an eyebrow. "Something, lass?"

Alexis felt herself blushing again. "Um, yes, last night ..."

"A bit muddle-headed aboot things, are ye?"

Alexis nodded.

The man smiled again. "It were a bit awkward at the first, I'll admit, but after the cryin' and the carryin' on were over, it's settle in to a fine evening, we did, lass."

Alexis felt herself blanch, the blood draining from her face. *And if it would only pick a place and stay there, instead of ever moving about, I might find a way through this.*

"I ... that is to say, we ... and, by that, I mean you ..."

The man threw his head back and laughed. "We talked, lass. After you explained yer ... misunderstandin'."

Alexis swallowed again. For as dry as her mouth was, she seemed to be doing a lot of that. "Talked?"

"Well and it's you who did the talkin', fer the most part, and me the listenin'. We're right good at that bit, we are."

"We?"

"Us who work the houses."

Alexis flushed again. *Oh, sweet heavens, he said it. I spent the night in a house, there's no denying now. But talking?*

"What ... did I ..." She couldn't imagine what she might have said, about Captain Neals or *Hermione,* perhaps, and what might happen if anyone found out.

"A bit o' this and a bit o' that. It's nae a happy ship yer aboard, an' that's the truth." He brought his arms up and laced his fingers behind his head and Alexis found her eyes drawn from his face to the very interesting things this did to his chest muscles. "Lass?"

Alexis shook her head, tearing her eyes away. She bit her lip. "I ... should not have spoken so, I think."

He reached out and wrapped his hand around one of hers. "Nae fear, lass. Were us in the houses to speak aught o' what were cried into our bosoms, the Navy'd come a'screechin' to a halt, an' that's no lie." He smiled as her eyes widened. "What? And it's thinkin' yer the first midshipman to find a bit o' comfort an naught else? Nor lieutenant nor captain, neither, come to that."

Alexis glanced sideways at the bosom in question. *And was that a fancy or is there aught I'll wish I could remember clearer?*

"So ..." Alexis cleared her throat and glanced away. "So, we didn't ..."

"Nae, lass, yer Philip-lad's nae to worry aboot."

Alexis froze, eyes wide again. *What on earth else did I say last night?* Philip Easley from *Merlin* was a friend and nothing more. Yes, there'd been a moment or two and a bit of thought, but they'd never so much as spoken about anything more. He was far away, on another ship — and if they ever did again serve on the same ship, well, nothing could come of any feelings that might exist, for such things were forbidden between officers serving together.

A chime started sounding, gradually increasing in volume.

"That's my tablet." Alexis slid off the bed and dug through her uniform for the tablet. "It's time I went back to the ship." She started dressing quickly, blushing as she saw the man watching her. "Must you?"

The man laughed and slid off the opposite side of the bed. He was, Alexis was relieved to note, wearing a bit more than the towel she remembered from the night before, then her gaze rose to his back and she gasped. The expanse of brown skin was marred with a criss-cross mass of scars. He turned and saw her shocked look.

"Oh, aye, spent a bit of time afore the mast, I did." His face split in a wide smile. "Then found I were far too pretty to spend my days in a vacsuit." He pulled a loose, white shirt from a drawer and slid it over his head. "I'll say this aboot our talk, lass. Your lieutenant's a worse man than that Captain Neals you told me of."

Alexis froze in buttoning her uniform jacket. Had he really just suggested that Lieutenant Williard was worse than Captain Neals?

"That captain? He don't know what's wrong, or flat don't care. The lieutenant, though? He sees the wrong and does nae a thing? How much worse is that?"

Alexis frowned. "No lieutenant can stop a captain doing as he likes on his own ship."

"Nae what I'm saying, lass. Nae at all." He pursed his lips in thought. "A man meets yer captain," he said finally, "and he's the worse fer it. Same man meets yer lieutenant, is he the better?" He frowned. "His way seems t'be just givin' up. I dinnae ken givin' up in the face o' that. Fightin' what y'can, e'en a wee bit, that I ken."

Alexis considered this. She wasn't entirely sure that she remembered Lieutenant Williard's words at dinner all that clearly, but she did recall being uncomfortable with them at the time. So much of what Williard had suggested to her seemed to be about protecting himself until he was in some better position to do something, with little thought to helping others, such as the crew, who had no such option. Still, she wasn't at all certain what she could do.

"I'll think on that, thank you." She smoothed her jacket and set her beret atop her head. "And thank you, as well, for ... listening."

He came around the bed and slid the hatch to the hall open. He met her eye and grinned. "You paid for the time, lass. How we spend it's up to you." He raised his eyebrows. "Though, perhaps, next time ..."

Alexis flushed and hurried through the hatch and down the stairs. In the main room, she saw the woman she recognized from the night before speaking to another woman, younger and looking uncertain, dressed in the jumpsuit of a merchant shipping line. Alexis caught the younger woman's gaze and they each looked away quickly as she hurried to the hatch back to the corridor.

"Lass!"

She turned at the hatchway to find the man from upstairs — now wearing a long robe, but having left it untied — on the stairs.

"Cort," he said, grinning broadly at her look of confusion. "Cort Blackmon. Case you were wonderin' ... or fer next time yer in port, if you come askin'."

———

THE CHANDLER EYED the list of stores she'd transferred to his tablet and nodded.

"Aye and I've most of this lot I can have aboard afore your ship sails, but not the last bit. Not if it's the actuals you're after," he said.

"The actuals?" With still several hours before she was due back aboard *Hermione*, Alexis had stopped into one of the many chandleries to have personal stores sent aboard. If they were to be pilfered by the others in the midshipman's berth, then they'd be pilfered, but she'd no longer allow them to make her change her ways over it — or, at least, not in the way they might want or suspect. *Fight what I can and not give up, aye.*

"Is it the actual Scotch whiskey you're after? I've bourbons aplenty, rye if you want it, and Irish — well, anywheres there're two brogues and a copper pot there'll be the Irish made. But the Scotch now that's different — there's but three places it's made, do you see? The home province back on Earth, a few areas of New London, and

New Glasgow, a'course." He ran his fingers over his tablet. "Now there's Hendly & Sons, planet-side, they import a bit of it, but I'm not sure I could have it brought up a'fore your ship sails." He paused and looked Alexis over. "Meanin' no offense, sir, but it'd be right dear. An hundred or more pounds the bottle for the least ..."

Alexis raised her eyebrows, eyes wide. *An hundred pounds for a single bottle?* That was outrageous. A bottle of perfectly fine claret cost less than a pound, though she knew there were many vintages that would cost more. Still she'd never heard of anything that cost so much as that.

It wasn't entirely beyond her means. She still had over a thousand pounds on account from her time aboard *H.M.S. Merlin* and the Prize Court's odd accounting of the captured pirate ship *Grapple*. Though *Merlin* had taken the prize, Alexis had been in command of the small prize crew that was sailing her back to port. The pirates left aboard to sail the ship had managed to retake her during a *darkspace* storm, making Alexis and the three surviving *Merlins* captive. One of them, Robert Alan, had pretended to go over to the pirates, and only through his actions were Alexis and the others able to retake *Grapple* a second time and sail her into port.

The Prize Court, in reading about the taking, retaking, and then reretaking of the ship, had so bollixed up the events that they'd thought Alexis had been in command of a ship named *Grapple* that had taken a second ship, also named *Grapple*. They'd then awarded all of the prize money for the capture to Alexis and the three others, though Robert Alan's award had been to his estate, as he'd been killed in fighting.

Mister Gorbett, *Merlin's* elderly sailing master, the surviving spacer, Peters, and Alan's estate had each received over four hundred pounds in the award, while Alexis, having been placed in command, had received over two thousand — the three eighths of the award normally given to the commander of a ship under Admiralty Orders and not part of a fleet, as well as the two eighths that would have gone to any midshipmen or junior warrant officers aboard. Those two eighths she'd gotten the crew of *Merlin* to accept as their due, since they were the ones who'd originally taken *Grappel*, but the three-eighths remaining had still amounted to over twelve hundred pounds.

Even after making sizable donations to the families of two marines who'd been killed aboard *Grappel* before she was retaken, and thus received no award from the Prize Court, Alexis had been left with a considerable sum. Added to that was her share, quite a lot smaller, of the other ships *Merlin* had taken while she was aboard.

And the ships Hermione's *taken add up to a tidy sum, as well.* Though the Prize Courts, after a shocking display of alacrity just as the war with the Republic of Hanover had begun, had reverted to their more normal course of spending months in deliberation before rendering a judgment on each prize. Neither Alexis nor any of the other crew of *Hermione* had seen aught but promises and dreams from the frigate's captures. *Naught but a stack of drafts promising a share of some future decision, though that doesn't stop the crew from selling theirs at pennies on the pound to any prize agent they come across.* Perhaps the one bright point to Captain Neals' habit of confining his crew to the ship was that they weren't to be so easily cheated out of their future awards by the temptations of a moment's pleasure.

"Sir?" the chandler prompted.

Ah, yes, temptations. And a 'dark path', indeed, Lieutenant Willard. She considered the number of glasses that had been poured in Dorchester's the night before. *Baron must pay quite a bit better than lieutenant.*

"Could you, perhaps, recommend something?" she asked. "That would be a bit dear, but I was only introduced to this last evening — I fear I have no experience at all with whiskeys."

"Aye, now there's a fine bourbon from right here on Penduli that I could recommend. Three shillings the bottle — not the least cost, but a decent drink and not the dearest, neither."

"I'll be guided by you then. A bottle of that and I'll return for more if it's to my liking." The chandler's eyes lit up at the prospect of repeat business, but dimmed at her next words. "Please send it along with the other items to *Hermione*, will you? To the bosun's attention, as he'll be seeing to my packages for me." Alexis had learned early in her life aboard ship to not trust pursers or chandlers, and the threat of the bosun, who wasn't bound by the niceties of an officer, finding things amiss always kept them closer to honest.

"Of course, sir."

"And if I may, a bit of time alone with the things I've ordered before you send them off?" She shrugged. "I realize it's unusual —" She made as if to leave. "— if you cannot accommodate it, perhaps another —"

"No, sir, not necessary." He furrowed his brow at her request, but was clearly unwilling to lose a customer. "No trouble at all. I'll just put things together for you and leave you to it, yes?"

ALEXIS HURRIED BACK to the ship and found Boxer storing deliveries for the other officers in the pantry. She glanced quickly around to ensure they were alone in the gunroom and then slipped into the pantry with him. The empty shelves where her stores should have been made her clench her jaw. All the others had bottles of wine, canisters of tea or coffee, packages of biscuit, and a dozen more items, but hers were bare. And the gunroom's freezers would be the same. *Well, that'll be changed shortly.*

"Sir?"

"I've some stores being delivered, Boxer, and I wanted to speak to you before they arrived." She kept her voice low, so as not to be overheard if anyone entered the gunroom.

"That's good, sir, weren't right. I'll watch 'em close — mayhap I'll speak to the carpenter about a locking box fer 'em."

"No, Boxer, I want you to treat them no differently than before, do you understand? Save in one very important way." She caught his eye to be sure he was paying attention. "You're not to serve me, nor give to the cook for sharing, any of these stores save what I've given you directly. Do you understand?"

"Not rightly, no, sir."

Alexis laid a hand on his arm. "You don't need to understand the reason, just the order, yes? Nothing to me, the cook, nor even for your bit that you haven't had from my hand directly. Do you understand that?"

"So if there's a chicken needed?"

"I'll pull him out of the freezer myself and hand him to you. Can you do that?"

"Aye, sir. Seems a bit of trouble, though."

"There'll be more trouble if you forget, so follow me on this, will you?"

"Aye, sir."

"Good." She turned to go, then spun back. "Oh, but there'll be a bottle of something called bourbon in my things. That you can find a hiding place for, can't you?"

"One bottle? Of course, sir. Be nothin' ter hide that. Safe as houses."

"Thank you, Boxer."

She slipped out of the pantry and back to her berth. She quickly stripped out of the dress uniform she'd worn onto the station and donned the simpler ship's jumpsuit, glad that Timpson wasn't yet back aboard. He never said anything and he was subtle about it, but he watched her change with a look that made her uncomfortable.

She settled on to her bunk with her tablet. There were still no messages for her, which was a disappointment, but there were more articles from the Naval Gazette that told of several ships taken from the Hanoverese. Little about the cause of the war itself, though, which she was curious about. She'd studied little of the wider universe while at home on Dalthus, but felt she should gain some knowledge of more than the ships themselves now that she was in the Navy. Finished with the Gazette, she moved on to her studies.

There were always ever more complex navigation problems to go through, ship's systems to learn about, and tactical simulations to run through. *Not that the captain nor any of the others will ever ask me about them.* While Captain Neals grilled the other midshipmen more ruthlessly even than Captain Grantham had, he'd never once included Alexis. It wasn't that she wanted to face the brutal quizzing — having scenario after scenario thrown at her with demands for what orders she would give — but it was designed to prepare the midshipmen for their lieutenant's exam. An exam where three or more captains would demand answers to whatever they could dream up before finally passing the applicant to lieutenant or sending him back to the pool of midshipmen.

So Alexis was reduced to studying on her own and keeping her own answers to herself when Neals quizzed the others. That she felt she came to better decisions than the lot of them was small comfort when it couldn't be confirmed. Likely, though, if Neals ever did include her, he'd not accept anything she said, so perhaps his indifference was preferable.

She was almost done with yet another treatise on navigation when she heard the other midshipmen begin to arrive back aboard, talking in the gunroom outside her hatch. Timpson came in to change his own uniform, ostentatiously stripping out of his dress uniform and underthings before pulling fresh clothing from the drawer beneath his bunk. It was one of the reasons Alexis didn't mind, in fact preferred, having the upper bunk aboard *Hermione,* even though its height made it more difficult for her to get into. Taking the lower bunk would have put her right at eye level with things she honestly preferred not to think about.

"Saw you got some fresh stores, Carew," Timpson said, pulling on his boots. "About time, that."

"Yes, I received some good advice about giving up."

Timpson stood up and faced the bunks. "What's that mean?"

Alexis shrugged, never taking her eyes from her tablet. Timpson left and she returned to her studies.

There was a loud scream from the gunroom and she quickly

locked her tablet and slid off the bunk. She rushed through the hatch into the gunroom to find Timpson, Brattle, and Ledyard staring at Bushby in shock. The senior midshipman was staggering around outside his berth, eyes watering profusely and spitting on the deck. *Well, then, that didn't take long.*

"Bushby!" Brattle yelled. "What the devil—"

Bushby spat once more and looked up at them, his chin was covered in streaks of brown and bright red spittle that leaked from his mouth. Alexis covered her mouth and tried to look concerned. Bushby looked around wildly and his eyes widened as he spied the wine bottles the others had on the table. *Oh ... I'd not recommend that,* Alexis thought, doing her best to keep from laughing outright.

Bushby rushed to the table and grasped a bottle, throwing his head back and draining it. He lowered it finally, looking relieved, but then his eyes widened. He gasped and clutched at his throat, then his chest.

"*Surgeon,*" he croaked, rushing toward the companionway. "*Where's Rochford?*"

"Should we help him, do you think?" Timpson asked.

"He can find the orlop deck on his own, I suspect," Brattle said. He went instead to Bushby's berth. "What was the man doing?"

Alexis went to the pantry and examined her stores. She noted that a box of her chocolates was missing and took one of the others, carefully noting the discreet marks she'd made on the packaging. She returned to the gunroom as Brattle was coming out of Bushby's berth with a similar package, this one opened.

He held it at arm's length, his eyes squinted and watering, as he carried it to the table. He set it down and stepped back, as did all the others. One of the chocolates had been bitten in half and a viscous, bright red fluid seeped from it. It gave off fumes that didn't seem to have a scent, they simply stung the eyes and nose viciously.

"What is that?" Timpson asked.

Alexis stepped over to them, squinting and sniffing as she opened her own box of chocolates. "I believe it's a sauce of Shimea reaper

chilies. I've noted the men challenging each other to try the stuff —
quite soluble in alcohol, I'm given to understand." She looked at each
of the others, eyes wide. "I do hope my own chocolates don't have the
same issue." She took one from the box in her hand and popped it
into her mouth, feeling a bit of anxiety as she bit down that she might
have grabbed the wrong package. "No," she continued, chewing.
"These are quite fine." She held the box out to Timpson. "Would you
like one? I'm quite happy to share, of course."

SIX

THE SHADOWS WERE CLOSING *in on her from every side. Dark, flowing masses, reminiscent of the* darkspace *clouds all around her.*

Alexis knew what was next — dreaded it, but knew.

She turned and the shadows began to come together, solidifying into a figure. Head and face a mass of darkness, with barely the hint of features, but she could imagine them well enough. Dirty, pockmarked skin, long greasy hair, and a mouth filled with half-rotted teeth — the face of the pirate captain, Horsfall. Her last real sight of him vivid in her memory. His gloating, confident smile as he told her that she needed him to pilot the ship, Grappel, *with its sabotaged navigation plot.*

The pistol had bucked in her hand, not even leaving time for his confident grin to falter before the bullet she'd fired struck him, punching a neat, dark hole just to the left of his nose. The part of her horrified that she'd killed a man warred with the part that was disappointed she'd been off-center at less than five meters distance. Followed quickly by a roiling sickness in her belly that she could even notice her aim when a man was dead, and fear of what that meant about her.

The shadowy figure raised an arm, hand extended to point at her in accusation. Behind Horsfall, more figures formed. Only a few at first, but then dozens, hundreds more. One by one they raised a hand to point at her. Some she knew, though their faces too were lost in shadow. Hadd, a topman lost in the Dark when she'd failed to save him as she should. Corsey and Bays, two marines the pirates had killed when she'd failed to divine their intent to retake the ship. Robert Alan, who'd saved them all aboard that ship — and died for his trouble when she'd failed to see his intent. Even the pirate, young Brighty, whose last days had been filled with terror — terror of her and her threat that she'd put him over the ship's side to die alone in darkspace while she watched. Terror she'd put in him by telling him she'd do that very thing unless he obeyed her. Then, when he'd done what she demanded and piloted the ship for her, she'd let them hang him as a pirate without even trying to stop it. If she had thought to speak on his behalf, perhaps he could have been saved.

"I'm sorry," she whispered.

The figures she didn't know, though, were the worst. There were so very many of them, forming and crowding forward to accuse her. Who were they? Had she wronged so many? Failed so many? She didn't see how that could be ... there were hundreds of them now, and she was but sixteen-years old. Or did she not recognize them because she had yet to fail them?

That thought drew a moan from her as it always did.

The figures drew closer, merging into a single, rolling mass.

"I tried!" Alexis cried out.

The mass rolled over her, consuming her like the darkspace winds.

"I'm sorry!"

"OH, for all that's holy, Carew, will quit your moaning!"

Alexis' eyes flew open in the darkness of her berth as a pillow swung over the edge of her bunk and slapped her across the face.

"Could I get a fortnight without you carrying on at all hours some night?" Timpson asked from the lower bunk. "Is that so bloody much to ask?"

Alexis took a deep, shuddering breath. Her heart was racing and she was drenched in sweat — as she always was when that particular dream came. She slid her tablet from its pocket next to her bunk and checked the time. A bit past six bells of the First Watch, so she had the better part of an hour before midnight when she'd have to be on the quarterdeck to take the Middle Watch — but no sense in even trying for a few more minutes sleep, she knew. Not after the dream came.

"Or if you must go on with your noise," Timpson continued, "slide yourself in here with me and I'll give you something to moan about."

Alexis sat up and swung her legs over the side of the bunk. "Touch me again, Timpson, and your breakfast'll be nutmegs and sausage." She shuddered at the memory, from her first week aboard *Hermione,* when she'd woken to find Timpson standing beside her bunk, one hand slid under her blanket and what he must have felt was an inviting leer on his face. "One touch and I'll have them off you and into a pan to fry with bloody onions and garlic, you just see if I don't."

Timpson grunted, but she knew he was a bit afraid of her in that regard. The threat of punishment from Captain Neals made her take their bullying comments and even beatings on those rare occasions that she fought back and it turned physical, but she'd made it clear from that first incident that touching her in *that* way would mean someone would die and damn the consequences. They'd seen her at work with the marines, and knew she could take any one of them individually.

Acting solely by touch in the pitch black compartment, she slid off the bunk and opened the drawer below it to grab a clean jumpsuit, sliding it on quickly and taking up her boots and beret. She paused with her hand on the hatch.

"Turn aside, Timpson, I'm changing my underthings," she said, knowing that he wouldn't. In fact, he made a point of staring at her even when she was just changing her jumpsuit. She knew it was ingrained in the lecherous prat that he'd turn and look, even in the darkened berth. When she heard the rustle of his bedclothes, she flung the compartment's hatch open wide, letting in the bright light from the gunroom.

"*Argh!* You ruddy bitch!" Timpson cried, rolling to face the wall and cover his head with a pillow.

Alexis smiled to herself and made her way through the gunroom to the heads, leaving the compartment hatch open so Timpson would have to crawl out of bed and close it himself. It was a petty thing, but she was feeling petty this morning. Night, really, as it lacked but an hour until midnight and the start of her watch. The watch-and-watch schedule Neals had ordered ended when they'd reached Penduli, but he'd still scheduled her to take the Middle Watch, midnight to four, nearly every night.

She locked herself in the head and studied her image in the mirror. Despite the lack of a normal night's sleep taking the Middle Watch entailed, she rather enjoyed it usually. The ship was quiet, with most of the hands and officers asleep. If the *darkspace* winds were calm and steady, then there'd be no need to change the sails — meaning no need to wake Captain Neals and ask his permission, for his standing orders demanded that he approve any change to the sail plan. No, the Middle Watch was, perhaps, the only time of peace she'd found aboard *Hermione*.

When I've not been woken by that horrid dream and feel like I've not slept at all, that is.

She splashed some of her precious water allotment on her face, hoping it would both help her to wake up and reduce some of the swollenness under her eyes, then brushed her hair so that it could be pulled back into a tight ponytail instead of shooting off in all directions.

"I HAVE THE DECK, SIR," Alexis said as the eighth tone of the ship's bell sounded over the quarterdeck speakers.

"You have the deck, Mister Carew," Lieutenant Williard said, nodding. He started for the companionway, but paused and looked back at her. "Are you entirely well, Mister Carew? You appear a bit off."

"I didn't sleep well, sir," she said. "It's no real matter."

Williard came back to the navigation plot to stand beside her. His brow was furrowed and he was frowning. "Have you recovered from your ... distress aboard Penduli Station?" he asked quietly.

Alexis frowned. No matter how quietly they spoke, the closeness of the quarterdeck made it certain the men there would overhear. Williard's position as second lieutenant made him most responsible for the midshipman, so it wasn't unusual for him to ask after their welfare, but this seemed a public place to do so.

"I believe I have, sir, thank you for your concern." She grinned. "And for the introduction to Scotch. Too dear a 'dark path' for me just now, I fear, but I've made a fine foray into bourbons."

Williard chuckled. "That's better," he said. "All's not so dark."

Alexis nodded, though she didn't really agree with him. Williard must have seen the doubt on her face, for he frowned again.

"Have you noticed," he asked, "that you and Mister Bushby are the only midshipmen to stand a watch alone?"

Alexis nodded. "I have, sir."

"Does that suggest nothing to you, Mister Carew?" Williard asked, voice even quieter.

Putting her on watch-and-watch? Disrupting the established watch schedule to place her on the Middle Watch night after night? It suggested a great deal to her, none of which she could voice — certainly not on the quarterdeck to another officer. Criticism of the captain could be considered mutiny if Neals found out, and she'd not give him that opportunity.

"Much as a captain may dislike one of his officers," Williard went on, clearly choosing his own words with care, "he will always love his ship more. No captain would trust his ship to an officer he felt would endanger her." Alexis' eyes widened and Williard nodded. "Think on that a bit," he said, leaving the quarterdeck.

Alexis did. The *darkspace* winds outside the hull were light and steady, leaving her with little to do but call for the log to be thrown every half-hour and run her navigation plot, so she had plenty of time to do so.

Williard's observation was quite true, now it had been pointed out to her. Of the midshipman aboard, only she and Bushby stood a watch alone. The others always had a lieutenant or the sailing master on the quarterdeck with them. What did that say of Neals' true opinion of her skills?

Even with my navigational difficulties, she thought, adjusting her plot to match the computers after the last throw of the log. This one had not been *too* far off.

What did it mean that Neals constantly derided her abilities and wanted to drive her out of the Navy, yet still trusted her with *Hermione*? Could the man be so spiteful and derisive of women that he'd want her out of the Navy even knowing that she was more competent than some of the male midshipman?

"*Sail!*" the spacer on the tactical console called out, pulling Alexis from her thoughts.

"Where away, Askren?" she asked.

"Two points abaft the port beam … up a bit, though not much at all."

Alexis examined the navigation plot as he transferred the information to it. The strange sail was some distance away, barely visible even at the highest magnification, and just a bit behind *Hermione* on the port side. She studied the blurry image for a moment. There seemed to be three lobes to the blob of light, so it was likely a decently sized ship with three masts, but one of the lobes appeared less bright than the others. That could be the result of angle or even a strong bit of *darkspace* wind distorting the view, but it could also be from a worn or malfunctioning particle projector causing one of the sails to not fully charge.

That would make the ship a merchantman and not a warship, for a warship would have more stringent maintenance. It would also slow the other ship, making her easier prey for *Hermione*.

Alexis hesitated. She had a sudden urge to ignore the other ship and sail on. The standing orders said to alert Captain Neals to any strange sail, but she was reluctant to do so. Neals would see the ship as easy prey as well, and add her to the list of merchantman prizes awaiting adjudication with the Prize Court on Penduli. *Hermione* had taken so many merchantman, all much smaller and weaker than the frigate herself, that there was a great deal of prize money owing — or would be, once the Prize Court got around to it. The Court tended to hear the cases of captured warships first, leaving *Hermione's* prizes always at the bottom of the list, but they'd get around to them eventually.

Still she hesitated. Attacking the enemy's merchant trade was vital, she knew. It would cost the Hanoverese time and money, disrupt their trade, and force them to allocate warships to guard convoys in the areas hardest hit. Still, though, it irked her that this was *all Hermione* had done since she'd come aboard. The frigate had yet to meet a single Hanoverese warship in an action. Neals, instead, choosing to prey on smaller, weaker ships.

I started by fighting pirates aboard Merlin, *yet Hermione's no better than one herself.*

"Wake Captain Neals, Norville," she said at last, nodding to the spacer on the signals console. "And sound *All Hands*, as I'm sure he'll want to tack and close her."

Alexis sighed. The orders were clear, and even if she'd been willing to disobey them, the ship's log would already have recorded the sighting.

"GENTLEMEN," Ledyard said, raising his glass. "The Queen!"

"The Queen!" Alexis called along with the others. She raised her own glass and took a small sip. The wine at Captain Neals' table was quite good, much better than any shared in the gunroom, but she wanted to keep her wits well about her. It wasn't unusual for Neals to invite the lieutenants and one or two midshipmen to dine with him, but it was the first time that he'd invited Alexis to join them. And the first time that all of them, all of *Hermione's* lieutenants and midshipmen — all save Bushby, who was away as prize master of the captured merchantman — had been invited at once.

At least Ledyard's here, so I don't have to draw attention to myself by giving the Loyal Toast. As the most junior at the table, the toast to the Queen fell to Ledyard, and Alexis was quite glad for it. Something was afoot and she'd prefer not to be noticed by Neals.

After the toast, the officers remained silent. Neals was hunched forward, as though impatient to begin speaking, but he waited until his steward had removed the last of the dishes and refilled the glasses needing it. Alexis simply tried to enjoy the relative quiet. The meal, though the food was good, had been an interminable series of conversations she was pointedly excluded from. Why Neals had bothered to invite her, she didn't know, unless he had simply ordered that all of his officers were to attend and simply forgotten that she was one of them.

"Gentlemen," Neals said at last. "In some few hours I expect we shall arrive at Badra and have some hopes for a very rich find there." He smiled. "The master of that last merchant ship we took gave me some very interesting information, confirmed by his ship's logs, as he'd just come from Badra and there were no fewer than six fat merchantmen in port and not a single warship left behind to protect them. Apparently the Hanoverese fleet is busy elsewhere and needed all of their bottoms for it." He took a long drink of his wine. "I intend to drop in-system, dispatch all four of our boats, and have the lot of them in convoy as prizes before lunch tomorrow!"

The officers all cheered. Alexis along with them, for she didn't want to be singled out, but she wondered at the easy acceptance of the captive merchant's word. Like all the others, he'd struck his colors without firing a shot when it was clear *Hermione* would catch him up.

"The division shall be as follows," Neals continued. "Lieutenant Dorsett, you shall take the launch, along with Misters Timpson and Ledyard. Lieutenant Williard will take my barge, in company with Misters Canion and Brattle. Lieutenant Roope shall take one of the ship's cutters and a competent master's mate. Each of you select such men and marines as you feel prudent. I will designate your targets for you at such time as we have more information about the ships in-system, but, assuming our information is correct and there are six, I trust you shall each take one, leaving behind a prize crew in command, and then move on to a second.

"I will remain aboard *Hermione* and position her in such a way as to ensure none of our prizes shall escape." He grinned widely. "Now, we will transition at L2, just beyond their primary moon, and use the conventional drive and the moon's gravity to gain speed. Once we've swung around the moon and have a view of the planet, we'll see what ships are in orbit and choose our targets. We'll drop the boats and *Hermione* will swing into a high, fast orbit so that she may cut off any escape." He narrowed his eyes and looked toward Alexis.

"Carew, you and your division will take the other cutter as a sort of reserve. You're to maintain a high orbit as well and be prepared to drop down and assist any of the other boats that call for you, do you understand?"

"Yes, sir. Stay in a high orbit and drop down to assist if called."

"And mind that you do!" Neals narrowed his eyes and glared at her. "No holding back from the fight. I'll not stand for that!"

"No, sir, I understand."

"See that you do." His face cleared and he raised his glass. "To a profitable tomorrow, gentlemen!"

SEVEN

ALEXIS SCANNED the mostly dark consoles in front of her and glanced over at the boat's pilot, Hearst, to her right. Only those for the boat's internal systems were active, but as soon as *Hermione* transitioned to normal space, they'd begin receiving signals from the boat's sensors and could retract the gallenium laced panels that covered the forward viewports. The ship's cutter was cramped with all twenty-four men of her division aboard, but it would be a short time, no more than hours, before the action was completed and they were all back aboard *Hermione*.

She looked behind her through the open hatch into the boat's interior. Nabb was at the hatch, the rest of the division standing and crowded behind him.

"See that everyone's suited and has their helmet to hand, Nabb," she said. "And have those with flechettes well spread out amongst the others, I don't want them clumped together."

Since the action would be in normal-space, the men of the four boats were armed with laser and flechette weapons, as well as the projectile weapons they'd have been limited to in *darkspace*. On the other three boats, all of the men were so armed, but there weren't enough to arm all of *Hermione's* crew, so only one in three of Alexis' men had received a flechette gun and none were armed with lasers. Neals had explained that her division, being a reserve of sorts that would only come in after an engagement began, would likely encounter a more chaotic melee that would be better suited to stun rods and the edged weapons the men carried for use in *darkspace* where nothing electrical would function.

All things considered, she was just as glad to not have any lasers, as the size of the capacitor needed for each shot made them bulky and they had to be reloaded with a new capacitor after each shot, though chemical pistols would be welcome. She could only hope that the merchant crews would not be better armed.

"Aye, sir." Nabb slid the hatch shut.

Alexis caught her lower lip between her teeth. She'd never been part of a boarding action before, only fought from the gundeck. But the merchant ships they planned to take would not be heavily armed or manned. Likely they'd have fewer crew than the cutter carried, much less the larger boats with more men heavily reinforced with marines.

The consoles in front of her suddenly sprang to life and Hearst retracted the gallenium shutters that covered the viewports. *Hermione* had transitioned and directly in front of them was the planet's primary moon, already seeming to draw closer as the ship's conventional drive fired at full force.

Now came the waiting and Alexis settled back into her seat, forcing herself to remain calm. Hearst glanced at her once and seemed about to speak, but shrugged and settled back to waiting as well.

Hermione's speed increased, driven both by her drive and the pull of the moon's gravity, and the view forward changed as the ship turned to go around the moon. Just as they were about to round the moon and bring the planet itself into sight, the boat shuddered once.

"We're away, sir," Hearst said, settling his hands on the controls. He waited until *Hermione* had passed them, pulling off ahead, before he eased the boat into her path and fired their own drive. The ship still pulled away, having better acceleration, but the cutter was not far behind. The other boats would be launched shortly, once they were around the moon and could locate the merchant ships in orbit around the planet.

With a suddenness that surprised her, the planet came into view from behind the moon and Alexis scanned the console. The boat's optics and other sensors would begin picking out ships around the planet and plot their orbits for her. In addition, *Hermione's* superior sensors should be repeated to her so that she'd know where the potential targets were.

Minutes went by and they were past the moon. *Hermione* was still accelerating and had not yet released the other boats.

"I'm seeing nothing," Alexis said. "Can they all have sailed?"

"Behind the planet, sir?" Hearst suggested.

"Six of them?" Alexis shook her head. "No, I think they must have sailed. Most, in any case." She sighed. "Captain Neals will not be happy."

A new track appeared on the console, not near the planet but further around the moon and on a course to cut behind *Hermione*. Alexis studied the image and magnified it. The new ship was small, much smaller than *Hermione* or even *Merlin*. Not much bigger than the pilot boats that sailed only a little ways from a system's Lagrange points to escort arrivals. Like the pilot boats, it had a single mast mounted amidships, not on the bow as with larger ships.

"Fore and aft rigged," she murmured. "Some kind of customs cutter, do you suppose?"

Hearst glanced over. "Like as not, sir. No more than four guns and a dozen men, surely. Not a match for *Hermione* at all."

"I should think not," she agreed. "Well, it will be something for Neals to take or scuttle. At least he'll have something out of our visit." She watched the plots, *Hermione's* continuing on toward the planet, ignoring the other ship, and the new ship moving between the frigate and the moon. "Or he may see it as not worth his while. Best prepare to maneuver, Hearst. I'm not sure what they're up to, but if they come around this side they may fire on us in passing. They're likely hoping to circle the moon and get to L2 for an escape themselves."

"Aye, sir."

Her console *pinged* with an incoming message from *Hermione* and she accepted it, jerking with surprise to see Ledyard's face. He was supposed to be in one of the ship's boats, not manning the signals console.

"Best lay on, Carew," he said. "Captain's emptied the other boats and ordered you recalled."

Alexis quickly scanned the plot. *Hermione* was still accelerating toward the planet and her boat was falling further behind. "Where will you slow for us to catch up?"

"Didn't you hear me, Carew? *Lay on* as we're not slowing. Captain says it must be a trap and there're probably frigates or worse behind the planet with this little sot as a tripwire. We're transitioning at L1 instanter, and if you're not back aboard ..." He grinned. "Well good luck to you."

Alexis' mouth dropped open in shock and she found herself speechless for a moment. She looked over to Hearst, but he shook his head. He'd heard and could read the plot as well as she — there was no way they could catch *Hermione* before the ship reached the Lagrange point. Not unless the ship slowed.

"Ledyard, it's a bloody customs boat — one broadside from *Hermione* and it'll cease to exist!"

Ledyard glanced over his shoulder. "Aye, sir." He turned back. "Captain won't risk the ship for you, Carew. If you're at L1 before we transition, we'll take you aboard, else ..." He shrugged and ended the transmission.

They're going to abandon us.

Alexis stared at the blank screen in shock, then back to the plot where the enemy ship was rapidly coming into range. "Alter course, up ninety," she ordered. "Get us out of his path, at least."

"Aye, sir."

She ran her fingers over the plot, estimating distances and times. *Hermione* was closing on L1, the Lagrange point between the moon and planet. The ship would shortly transition and leave them behind with the enemy vessel. Her ship's boat lacked the ability to transition between normal-space and *darkspace,* and even if it could, they had no sails. If *Hermione* truly abandoned them, their only hope would be to take another ship.

"With luck," she said, "they'll continue on to L2 for safety and be behind the moon before *Hermione* transitions. Then we'll head for the planetary/solar L4 and hope to surprise some merchant transitioning in." She looked at Hearst and saw the skeptical look on his face. "It's what we have." She stood and slid the hatch to the main part of the boat open. "*Nabb!*"

When Nabb arrived she motioned him close and whispered. "Without frightening the men, go and check the stores locker. I want to know how much food, water, and air we have aboard." If the custom's boat did transition away, they might have a long wait at the Lagrange point before a merchantman arrived and they had a chance to take it. If it didn't, well, then they were so far outgunned that they didn't stand a chance.

"Aye, sir."

"Quietly, mind you."

Nabb nodded. Alexis slid the hatch closed and resumed her seat.

She watched the plot in silence. *Hermione* moving ever closer to the Lagrange point, the enemy ship circling the moon, and her boat moving perpendicular to both their courses.

Hermione reached the edge of the Lagrange point and slowed. *Too soon, damn them.* The Hanoverese ship could still see *Hermione* and would know that the ship's boat had been abandoned. *Hermione* transitioned, leaving them behind with the enemy.

Within moments, the enemy ship altered course, curving up in a clear attempt to intercept her boat. The signals console again *pinged* for attention and Alexis played the incoming message.

"New London boat, this is *Leutnant* Egenhauser of *Hannover*

System Patrouille. Shut down your drive and strike colors or you will be fired upon. Respond."

"Damn," she whispered. The other ship couldn't have more than a dozen men aboard while she had twice that, but it was faster and had larger guns with a longer range. She had only a single gun and a small case of grape shot, more than adequate against a merchant's thin hull and scared crew, but nothing against a warship. Even one so small as this. *They can lay off and pound us to dust and we'll have nothing to respond with.*

She had to somehow lure them into trying to board, but the only way they'd do that was if she struck her colors, taking down the New London colors that lit the boat and surrendering. *And once I do that I've surrendered and can't fight them.*

What could possibly make the Hanoverese lieutenant forget that the colors still flew and try to board anyway?

"Hearst?"

"Sir?"

"Do you suppose you could make this boat appear it's being conned by a terrified, sixteen-year old girl?"

"NEW LONDON BOAT, this is *Leutnant* Egenhauser of *Hannover System Patrouille*. Shut down your drive and strike colors or you will be fired upon. Respond."

Is he playing a bloody recording? That's all he's said the last ten minutes.

She spared a quick glance to the cockpit's hatchway. Nabb would have the lads well in hand, she knew. She'd briefed them on her plan, such as it was, and they knew they had only one chance to pull it off. She nodded to Hearst and the pilot grinned, gripping the boat's controls. He began flinging the controls back and forth, sending the boat jerking and twisting through space. He spun the boat to port and down, so that the planet slid past the viewport, then twisted it in space and swung back up, as though trying to steer for the planet but over-correcting each time. He slammed the throttle into reverse and Alexis was flung forward against her seat straps as the maneuver actually exceeded the inertial compensator's safety margins and allowed some of the inertia to bleed through. Then he slammed the throttle forward to full military power, pressing her into her seatback. Alexis looked at him with wide eyes, but he was paying her no attention, his gaze flicking from console to console and a manic grin on his face.

Well, I did ask for it.

"New London boat, this is *Leutnant* Egenhauser of *Hannover System Patrouille*. Shut down your drive — what are you doing? Stop that this instant! New London boat, strike colors and zero your drive or you will be fired upon!"

"Good luck hitting me, mate," Hearst muttered.

"Be quiet, Hearst, I'm about to begin my part," Alexis said. Hearst was right, the boat was too small and agile for the Hanoverese to target, but they couldn't evade her forever. Even if they could, eventually a larger ship would enter the system and they'd be unable to evade that.

Sixteen or twenty guns fired near us would get a hit eventually. Her plan relied upon the Hanoverese believing she was alone in the cockpit. *Alone and a scared little girl.* Her mouth twisted at the thought. *Bloody hell.*

She keyed the communications to the passenger compartment. "Get ready, lads," she said. "Nabb, have at the hatchway, please, and keep it up." The hatchway to the cockpit began shaking and rattling, as though someone were trying to get in. There was an occasional loud *thump* as something heavy was slammed against it.

Alexis hunched over her half of the console, adjusting the communications pickup so that it was closer to her and would show mostly her face. She didn't want the Hanoverese to be able to see that she wasn't, in fact, piloting the boat, nor catch a glimpse of Hearst beside her. She composed her face in what she hoped was an appropriately terrified expression and poised her finger over the transmit button and began speaking, turning the transmitter on and off randomly, as though she had no idea what she was doing and was randomly pressing things in the search for the right one.

"Hello? Hello? Hello? Are you there? Hello? Oh, which is the right button? Hello? Can you hear me? Please don't shoot! Hello?"

"New London boat, this is *Leutnant* Egenhauser of *Hannover System Patrouille*. Shut down your drive — what? Who is that? What are you doing? Stop that! *Verdammt!* Leave it alone! *Idiot!*"

Alexis stopped her pressing of the transmit button, ensuring that it was off, and turned to Hearst. Hearst put the boat into a looping spiral that spun the system's moon past the viewport every so often, forcing to Alexis to swallow heavily and look away before she became ill.

I wonder if it would help if this Egenhauser saw me be sick?

"New London boat, this is *Leutnant* Egenhauser of *Hannover System Patrouille*. You have stopped transmitting ... press the transmit button. Once! Press it once and leave it!"

Alexis leaned close the pickup again. "Hello? Hello?" She pressed transmit and left it set. "Hello? Hello? Hello?"

"Yes, yes," Egenhauser said. "Good, strike colors and zero your drive immediately!"

"Hello? Can you hear me? Hello?"

"Yes! I hear you! Stop speaking this instant!"

Well, that's rude. Alexis stopped speaking. She looked away from the pickup to the rest of the console and made sure to move her arms as though it was she who was piloting the boat.

"Take your hands off the controls immediately!"

Quite rude, him. She reached out to Hearst and touched his arm. Hearst stopped his wild maneuvers, but not before slamming the throttle fully forward. That would draw out the chase and give Alexis a bit more time.

"Who are you?" Egenhauser demanded.

Alexis looked into the pickup and let her lower lip tremble a bit.

"Midshipman Alexis Carew, captain," she said. "Please don't shoot! The men have gone mad! Mad, I tell you! They're terrified at being captured and I've had to lock myself in the cockpit! Please! Please don't shoot, captain!"

"I am not *kapitän*! I am *leutnant*! Strike your colors, girl!" He shook his head and muttered something guttural that Alexis didn't catch.

"Lootnut?" Alexis asked. "Is that at all like a lieutenant?"

Egenhauser's face grew red and Alexis thought she might have gone too far, but he took a deep breath and composed himself. "*Leutnant*," he said distinctly. "*Leutnant* Egenhauser. Yes, it is the same." He took another deep breath. "Tell me what is your situation."

Alexis caught her lower lip between her teeth. It was a bad habit she had and she knew it made her look even younger than she was, but it would serve her well now. "Sir," she said, "the men went mad when *Hermione* transitioned, sir! Said the captain abandoned us to rot in a Hanoverese prison!" She bit the inside of her cheek hard, wincing and blinking until her eyes watered. "The purser had casks of rum stored aboard, sir, and the men got into it! They're running wild back there, the pilot with them!" There was an especially loud *thump* from the cockpit hatchway that she was sure could be heard over the pickup. She swallowed hard. "The men are drunk, sir! Said they'd have a last bit of fun before they went to your prison, so I had to lock myself up here!" She squeezed her eyes tightly shut, quite proud of herself when she managed to get a single tear to run down her cheek. "Please, sir, I've only been aboard a few months! I don't know what to do!"

She almost felt guilty as Egenhauser's expression softened, but she forced that down. The lads were counting on her and this was their only chance, so far as she could see. *Oh, but there'll be a special place in hell for me after this, I suspect.*

"Calm yourself," Egenhauser said, voice calm and reassuring. "We will save you, but first you must strike your colors."

"I remember that!" Alexis said, careful of her wording. "I

remember reading about that!" She scanned the console and reached for a control. "That's this one, yes?"

Hearst fired the keel's bow thruster and the top stern thruster simultaneously, flipping the boat end for end over and over again. As the main engines were still firing, the boat was also looping in a tight spiral.

"Stop!" Egenhauser yelled. "Take your hands away!"

Alexis did, as did Hearst, and the boat straightened its course once more.

Egenhauser rubbed his face. He clasped his hands in front of him. "You do not know your console, *fräulein?*"

Alexis shook her head. "I've not been aboard long at all. I know some signals, sir ... I know *Heave-to*, and I know *Hermione's* number by heart, I do." She smiled in what she hoped was an appropriately vapid bit of pride.

"*Scheisse.*" Egenhauser hung his head. "Do you know where the throttle is, *fräulein?*"

Alexis bit her lip again and scanned the console.

"No," Egenhauser said. "No, touch nothing. Please — touch nothing. Leave all set as it is and we will match course and speed with you." He sighed. "Just say, *fräulein,* as you are in—" He shook his head as though he couldn't believe it. "— command of the boat, do you surrender?"

Alexis kept her face as bland and innocent as possible. She widened her eyes and said carefully, "I appear to have no other choice, Lieutenant Egenhauser."

EIGHT

ALEXIS CONTINUED to talk to Egenhauser as his ship closed with her boat. Occasionally, the cockpit hatch would rattle and thump, and Alexis would jump in her seat, staring fearfully behind her.

"Please, do hurry, lieutenant," she whispered. "I fear what the men will do, should they gain entry."

"Calm yourself, *fräulein*," Egenhauser said. "We will match speed with you in minutes and be aboard." He curled his lips in distaste. "Your New London crews lack discipline."

Alexis nodded, eyes wide. *My New London lads are about to beat your backside bloody,* leutnant. *And all for you're a gullible fool.*

She watched the plot as the Hanoverese ship matched the boat's speed and acceleration. It settled in on the boat's starboard side and began easing closer. Alexis edged a hand out of view of the pickup and flashed the passenger compartment lights twice. The ship was close enough now that it couldn't see the far side of the boat, and the crew would be opening the port lock and streaming out onto the boat's hull. Four remained inside the passenger compartment, flechette guns trained on the starboard lock, where the Hanoverese would enter.

The flechette guns would be no more than annoyance against a Navy crew, though. They were made for unsuited targets or the thinner vacsuits of merchant crews, not the heavier vacsuits navies used. They'd still penetrate, but the suits would seal around the thin flechettes and they hadn't enough force to do more than prick the man inside. They'd be enough to surprise and annoy the Hanoverese, though, until the crew could close enough to use their heavy cutlasses, as the stun rods they'd expected to use against a merchant crew were equally useless now.

She could only hope that the Hanoverese weren't better armed.

Alexis watched the ship drift closer, its boarding tube extended and just about to latch onto the boat's starboard lock.

"Lieutenant Eganhauser!" she said quickly when his gaze drifted from her to what his ship was doing. She hung her head. "Will being a prisoner be terribly difficult, sir?"

"Badra is a fine planet, *fräulein*," he said. He smiled for the first time and licked his fat lips. "Perhaps I shall call upon you, when I am in port."

Why, you lecherous cad!

The boat jostled slightly as the ship's boarding tube made fast. Hanoverese would be crowded into the tube, ready to blow the boat's lock and enter to subdue her crew. Her lads, though, were even now flinging themselves over the top and keel of the boat. The boat shuddered as the lock's hatch was blown and Eganhauser stumbled, looking away from the pickup in shock. Alexis smiled thinly. The jar to his ship was air streaming out of his boarding tube, through her boat and out the still open port lock. She heard shouts coming over the transmission and Eganhauser's face paled. He'd clearly not been expecting her boat to be in vacuum.

Alexis grabbed her vacsuit helmet from its place beside her seat and sealed it over her head. She flipped the faceplate closed and spun to the cockpit's hatch as she heard Eganhauser shout.

"*Mein Gott, du kleine miststück!*" He turned away from the pickup. "*Abfeuern! Abfeuern!*"

Alexis got to the hatchway just behind Hearst, who flung it open. They braced themselves against the brief rush of air from the cockpit into the vacuum of the passenger compartment.

Please let him have sent more men to the boarding tubes than stayed on the guns — and that he wants to take the boat undamaged, so ordered his men not to have firearms at the ready.

Eganhauser must have, for only a single shot from his guns was fired. It shot through the boat's hull, easily vaporizing a quarter-meter circle of the hull nearest the Hanoverese ship before doing the same on the boat's port side. Had the men been inside, the results would have been devastating. As it was, the shot passed through the empty passenger compartment without striking a single man.

At the far end of the compartment, near the starboard lock, a tangle of men in Hanoverese vacsuits were sorting themselves out from where they'd been sucked out of the boarding tube by the sudden decompression when they'd blown the lock. The four spacers Alexis had had stay inside the boat were tucked behind seats, flechette guns raised and peppering the men with the small darts.

Alexis triggered her suit radio and rushed past them, drawing her cutlass.

"At them, lads!" she yelled.

Hearst and the men drew their own blades and followed her. She reached the far end of the compartment and slashed her blade at the back of a Hanoverese just regaining his feet. She winced as the blade bit deep, blood and air jetting from the rent in his suit. She swallowed hard as her gorge rose and swung again. Beside her, Hearst blocked a blade swinging for her head and she shouldered forward, knocking the man she'd struck to the deck and swinging at the next.

The Hanoverese still in the boarding tube had turned and were rushing back to their own ship to rejoin the bulk of their crew. The rest of Alexis' crew would have gone over the top and keel of the boat to leap the gap and board the Hanoverese ship however they could. They'd be swinging themselves in through open gunports, blowing a lock or two, and even firing their flechettes into the boarding tube itself.

Alexis rushed through the tube onto the ship and into the backs of the Hanoverese, screaming what encouragement she could to her men. The Hanoverese were oblivious to her, concentrating on the bulk of the *Hermiones* who'd made it aboard through locks and gunports.

The *Hermiones* outnumbered them, but the Hanoverese knew their ship and were fighting for it. Her own crew's ship had abandoned them and Alexis wondered if they'd have the heart to take the fight to the end.

Virtually ignored at their rear, Alexis hopped up and down, trying to see over their heads to gauge the state of the action. Hearst and the others joined her and she grabbed Hearst's arm. "Up!" she yelled. He gave her an odd look. "Lift me, damn your eyes, I need to see!"

Nodding, Hearst grasped her waist and lifted her up so that she could see above the heads of the Hanoverese in front of her. The Hanoverese ship's deck was crowded with men, but she could see from their helmets' colors that the bulk of her crew were aboard.

"*Hermione!*" she yelled, giving the traditional battle cry of one's ship's name. "They're surrounded, lads!" She waved her cutlass above her head. "Don't let up!"

A cutlass waved from within the mass of New London helmets across the deck and she heard Nabb's voice. "Bugger *Hermione!* The cry's 'Carew', lads! And at 'em hard!"

Alexis' suit speakers crackled with two dozen voices screaming, "*Carew!*" and the mass of New London vacsuits surged into the Hanoverese. She pounded on Hearst's helmet to be let down and leapt forward as well. Her arm numbed as the rear of the Hanoverese turned and one blocked her first blow. She felt the impact and the vibration of the steel all the way to her shoulder, but she shoved her way forward, slashing again, feeling the bite of her blade against a vacsuit and the flesh beneath, then a rush of air and a burning in her side as someone stabbed past her guard. Her suit sealed itself, but she felt a rush of warm blood soaking her skin.

She heard her breath coming in harsh, quick gasps that echoed in her helmet. Her voice grew hoarse and her throat hurt from yelling encouragement. Her arm felt like a leaden weight from swinging the heavy cutlass, and the cut on her side stung. She could feel it opening and tearing with every movement.

Another lunge, a parry, the impact of steel on steel as she ground forward. Hearst dropped back with a startled cry, taking the blade from an enemy's hand where it lodged between his arm and side. Alexis swung viciously at the man's head, cracking his helmet visor and seeing the puff of air released, then swinging at the next. She realized at the last moment that the man had his arms raised, hands empty of a weapon, and she twisted her own hand barely in time, slapping him heavily with the side of the blade instead of the edge. She looked around and saw that other Hanoverese, too, had their hands raised or were kneeling on the deck. Her helmet speakers crackled with Lieutenant Egenhauser's voice.

"*Wir kapitulieren!* Quarter! We ask quarter!"

Alexis shuddered, stepping back from the fight. "We've won, lads! Quarter! Give quarter!"

Around her, men stepped back from each other, lowering their blades. The deck was strewn with bodies, some moving, some still. She knew that deaths would be rare — the vacsuits would seal over and reair themselves, constricting around tears to put pressure on wounds. The still men would be unconscious from a few moments vacuum or trying to remain still and out of the fight. She shook her head as sweat streamed into her eyes, stinging them.

"Make a lane!" she yelled, transmitting over all channels so that the Hanoverese would hear her, as well. They might not understand the words, but they'd know the meaning. "Make a lane and let me through, damn your eyes!"

She stepped forward, making for the ship's quarterdeck and Egenhauser. The mass of men parted before her, fighting done. She found Egenhauser on the ship's quarterdeck. The compartment's lock had been forced and the quarterdeck was in vacuum. Alexis brought four men with her and slapped a repair seal over the breach in the hatch, leaving orders with Nabb to seal and air the rest of the ship after securing the Hanoverese crew aboard their boat. Eganhauser stood stiffly while the quarterdeck was reaired. When the pressure settled, he took his helmet off and flung it to the deck. Alexis took hers off and regarded him calmly.

"You ..." Eganhauser began.

"Watch yerself, you," Matheny growled from beside her, raising his cutlass.

"Easy, Matheny," Alexis said. "Lieutenant Egenhauser is understandably distraught."

Eganhauser glared at her. "A dishonorable ruse," he said.

"You saw what you wished to see, lieutenant." Alexis crossed to the navigation plot and checked that the ship was unlocked and that she understood how to switch its controls to English instead of German. By asking for quarter, Eganhauser had surrendered and should turn the ship over to them, but if he felt she'd acted dishonorably he might have laid some sort of trap. Eganhauser looked away, jaw stiff. Alexi sighed. "Well, you'll be shut of me soon enough, lieutenant."

"You do not take us prisoner?"

"No," Alexis said. "I had quite enough of prisoners on a long voyage last time, thank you."

Nabb came through the quarterdeck lock.

"The ship's aired and sealed, sir, and the lot of 'em're in the boat."

"Thank you, Nabb." Alexis wanted to ask about the men, how many injured and how many dead, but they had to move fast. She wanted the Hanoverese off her new ship and to be underway as soon as possible. There was a chance, if they transitioned soon enough, that they might spot *Hermione* in *darkspace* and be able to catch her. "Be sure all the food and water is brought aboard this ship, please." Nabb nodded and left again. Alexis turned to Eganhauser. "If you'll go aboard the boat now, lieutenant? A patch or two and you should be able to reair her and make it to the planet's surface with little trouble."

"You are —"

"I am what I am, lieutenant. If being that gets my lads home safe, then I'll suffer your scorn." She nodded at his helmet. "You'll need that."

Eganhauser scooped up his helmet without another word. Alexis escorted him off the quarterdeck to the boarding tube. She met Nabb there leading a party of men back with boxes of supplies.

"The boat's console is locked, lieutenant," she said at the airlock. "I'll send you the codes before we transition." Eganhauser nodded, his lip curling. Alexis jerked her head at the lock, wanting to be shut of the man and his reproach. When the lock was closed and the boarding tube had begun to retract, she whispered to Nabb, "What was the butcher's bill?"

"Four of the Hanoverese dead," he said, "but not a one of ours."

"None?"

He grinned. "Took 'em with their skivvies down, you did, sir. That lieutenant told 'em to expect a bunch o' drunken sots, not fighting men. Oh, there's a lad or two of ours hurt. Hearst has a hunk o' skin carved off his ribs and there's four with blood in their eyes from cracked helmets. That's the worst, though, and they'll all heal."

Alexis grasped the bulkhead to steady herself. She'd been dreading the cost of the fight and to hear she'd lost not a single man came as a shock.

"Should have yer own looked at, sir," Nabb said, nodding to the sealed cut in her own suit.

Alexis probed it gently and found that it didn't hurt. "I think the suit's taken care of it, now I've stopped running about." She frowned, considering what would have to be done next. "Find Matheny and put him on the helm," she said. "Bend a course for L1, that should still be closest. We'll follow *Hermione* out ... hopefully she'll still be in sight."

"Aye, sir." Nabb looked doubtful, but he went off in search of Matheny.

Alexis scanned the cutter's deck. There was so much yet to be done. First get into *darkspace* and on their way back toward New London space. If *Hermione* was still in sight, then they'd have to hurry to catch up. Hopefully the ship would see their signals and wait for them — a nice little cutter as a prize might make Neals more willing than the ship's boat alone had. If the ship wasn't in sight, then they'd have to make their own way home, which meant plotting a course. Alexis shuddered. At least she'd have a solid starting position, but the thought of their lives and freedom hinging on her ability to navigate chilled her to the bone.

She'd need an inventory of supplies, Penduli was four weeks sail from here — not an insurmountable range for a cutter, but only if there was adequate food and water aboard. Supplies of spare sail and cordage she'd need to know as well, and the state of the guns. How much shot there was aboard and what its condition was. All of the thousand things necessary to running a ship.

She caught sight of Isom seated against a bulkhead, a bloody cutlass still clutched in his fists. The man had been aboard *Hermione* longer than Alexis, but was still rated Landsman. The only reason he was in her division, working the masts, was because he was young enough and somewhat agile — someone aboard *Hermione* was convinced he could be made a topman. But he seemed to have no head for space and constantly complained that he shouldn't be there, that he was a legal clark who'd been caught up in the Press by mistake when the war started. Given the state of his weapon, he might have at least made some good use of himself during the action. Alexis made her way over to him and crouched down.

"Are you hurt, Isom?" she asked. "Do you need the surgeon?" Not that they had a surgeon. A couple of the lads could do a bit more than apply the wound sealant that their suits sprayed out, but that was all.

"I ..." Isom started to speak, but then trailed off. His eyes were wide and red-rimmed. His hands were white-knuckled and shaking where he clutched the cutlass.

Alexis draped an arm over his shoulders. "What's wrong, Isom? What is it?"

"I ... I killed a man, miss," he said, voice quavering. Alexis tightened her hold on his shoulders, ignoring that he'd called her 'miss' instead of 'sir'. "I stuck this sword right in him ..."

She reached out and grasped the blade. "Let me take that, Isom," she said.

"Stuck it right in ... it was like ..." He closed his eyes and shivered. "It *popped* when it went into him."

Alexis tugged harder on the blade and managed to get it loose. She set it on the deck to her side and slid it away. Men were hurrying by, busy at the tasks to get the ship moving. One of them looked about to speak and Alexis shook her head sharply. Isom was not well-liked and she wanted no harsh words now.

"You did what you had to do, Isom," she said.

"I heard him scream."

Alexis wrapped her other arm around the man and he sank against her, head against her chest. She felt him shudder as he began to sob. The *popping* he'd felt would be the suit, she knew, and any screams were likely from his mates. With the compartment in vacuum he'd certainly heard no enemy scream unless he was helmet to helmet. It was likely he hadn't killed anyone at all, merely wounded them, and not gravely at that. But telling him that wouldn't be a kindness — he'd either not believe or it could make him hesitate in the next action. Better for him to think he'd killed once already, and that it was the right thing, so he'd be better prepared next time.

Nor could she really tell him it had been his duty — not when he'd been taken up by the Impressment Service. Not even the men who'd volunteered fought for that, really. Not when the guns were firing or the blades were out. No, they fought for themselves and their mates — to stay alive and so the others wouldn't think them shy.

"You did right, Isom," she said. "You fought beside your mates and we're all alive, yes? We're all safe and there's not a one of them can say you didn't stand and do your part." She felt him nod, then held him until she felt the sobs start to subside. "I have to see to the ship now, Isom. I'm going to have your mates find you a place to rest, do you understand?" He nodded.

Alexis caught the eye of a passing spacer. "Ficke, find a place for Isom out of the way and let him get some rest." She stood and grasped Ficke's arm. "Be easy with him," she whispered.

NINE

HERMIONE WASN'T visible when they transitioned to *darkspace*, but the little cutter — *Sittich,* Alexis found she was called — made good time. She was a joy to sail, well-kept and far more agile than a frigate or other square-rigged ship. Once she was sure they were out of Hanoverese space and safely within New London's borders, Alexis took to spending at least one watch each day experimenting with her. The fore-and-aft rig was so much simpler than *Hermione's* sail plan that Alexis almost felt she'd be able to sail the ship herself — certainly it was no hardship doing so with such a large crew aboard.

She stood at *Sittich's* bow, one arm upraised as she watched the sails. They were close-hauled on the port tack, the *darkspace* winds streaming over the port bow, filling the sails and making their azure glow spark and flash with white. She'd never seen a ship sail this close to the wind's eye before and she resisted the urge to order her just one more point closer — she thought she might be able to, if she rolled *Sittich* just a bit and took the winds against her sails at an angle, but then they might also end up in irons again. Head on into the wind, dead in space until they were able to thrash and flog the sails around to catch a bit and move again. No, the watch was almost over and she'd soon have to go back inside and stop her playing.

She flung her arm down and the waiting men went into action. Her order was relayed inside to the quarterdeck and the helmsman turned the ship. Men on the sails hauled on lines, far fewer than there were aboard *Hermione*, to bring the long boom that anchored the bottom of the sail across the deck.

Sittich's bow came up into the wind, slowing as the sails hung loose for a moment and the winds played along both sides, then the bow continued on, faster and more agilely than Alexis would have credited it if she hadn't seen it for herself. The sails shuddered, lifted, then filled with a snap Alexis swore she could hear through the vacuum, and *Sittich* seemed to leap forward again, now on the starboard tack.

Alexis cried out with glee, glad that her vacsuit's radio wouldn't transmit in *darkspace* and that none of the crew could hear her. A vacsuited figure came toward her, gliding over the hull as he pulled himself along the guidewires that ran the length of the ship. Alexis went aft to meet him and recognized Nabb as they came close enough to touch helmets and speak.

"Sail, sir," Nabb said. "Fine on the starboard bow, near dead ahead."

Alexis turned to look, even though she knew she'd likely see nothing at this distance, not without the optics that brought images inside the ship.

"Thank you, Nabb," she said. She sighed. The time she'd spent sailing *Sittich* back to New London had been so different, almost a joy, and now it was likely over. Whoever captained the ship ahead of her would likely put his own prize crew aboard and start her and her lads back to *Hermione*.

WHEN THEY WERE close enough to exchange signals, Alexis

found that the other ship was *H.M.S. Lively*, a 32-gun frigate commanded by a Captain Crandall. Alexis signaled that *Sittich* was a prize and *Lively* ordered her to heave-to. The larger ship came alongside after her crew unstepped the foremast so that her starboard side was clear of rigging and made fast.

Once the two ships were side by side and a boarding tube extended, Alexis crossed to the frigate. She faced forward as she exited the tube and saluted the ensign painted on the bulkhead there to represent the colors lit on the masts. A lieutenant stepped forward to greet her.

"Welcome aboard. Carew, is it?" he asked. Alexis nodded. "Waithe, Third Lieutenant. Captain Crandall's in his day cabin, just this way."

He gestured aft and Alexis followed him, pausing for the marine sentry outside the captain's cabin to announce them. She entered to find Crandall seated at his dining table which was clearly doubling as a large desk, given the number of displays showing on its surface.

"Have a seat, Carew," Crandall said. He was a large man, muscular not gone to fat, with light hair. "You have a written report, have you?"

"Yes, sir." Alexis raised her tablet and sent the report to his. She sat in the indicated chair, edging forward on the seat so as to keep her back straight. She was unsure of how her report of the action would be received.

"Wine? Something else?" Crandall offered.

"Thank you, sir. Tea, perhaps?" She wanted to keep her wits about her for this interview.

Crandall nodded to his steward, who set about pouring a cup of tea, then he lowered his eyes to his tablet and began reading. "Tell it to me, as well, Carew," he said, not looking up.

Alexis took a deep breath. Her report covered the time from *Hermione's* dropping her and her division in the ship's boat, but she started telling it from when *Hermione* had captured the merchant vessel that had sent them there, so that Crandall would have the whole of it. Crandall interrupted only once, when she described *Hermione's* last messages and transition to *darkspace*.

"Thought it was some kind of trap, he said?" Crandall asked.

"That is what Midshipman Ledyard relayed, sir."

Crandall grunted. "Well, must've seen something that set him thinking that." He lowered his eyes to his tablet again and gestured for Alexis to continue. She related the short action with the Hanoverese ship, glossing over, as she had in her report, the details of how she'd drawn him in to boarding range. The deception still left her a bit uncomfortable and she was unsure of how it would be received.

"And so we transitioned and made course for Penduli, sir," she finished.

"Penduli? You're four days *past* Penduli, Carew — missed it all entire!"

Alexis felt her face flush and looked down at the deck. "I ... navigation has not been my greatest talent, sir."

Crandall laughed. "I should say not, if you were trying for Penduli, no." He took a long drink. "But practice will improve that for you. Though I'd not recommend another attempt like this one until you've improved."

"No, sir."

"Oh, chin up, Carew. Navigating isn't the whole of it, lord knows. Ask Bligh!"

"Sir?"

Crandall raised his eyebrows. "Add some naval history to your studies, as well, Carew. Bligh. Salt-water, planet-bound sailor. Conned an open boat across seven thousand kilometers of ocean with no charts. Damned fine navigator." He grinned. "Not so fine a captain, if why he was in that boat to begin with's any sign."

"No, sir," Alexis agreed, feeling that was the safest course.

Crandall lowered his eyes to his tablet and frowned. "Still, Carew, you've not said, and there's no mention in your report, of why that Hanoverese ship tried to board before you'd surrendered. Just

'The Hanoverese attempted to board our boat and we took their ship.'" He raised his gaze to her again. "You didn't attack after striking, did you?"

"No, sir!" Alexis hastened to assure him. "I didn't strike our colors."

"Then why did he approach to board instead of standing off and firing into you until you struck?"

"Sir, I —" She looked down at the deck, flushing. "— convinced him that the men were in no condition to resist."

Crandall narrowed his eyes. "How, exactly?"

Alexis sighed and caught her lower lip between her teeth. "I told him that they were drunk." She clenched her eyes shut, dreading his reaction. "And that I'd locked myself in the cockpit with no idea how to fly the boat or work the console ... and that I was quite ... frightened at being abandoned by *Hermione*."

Crandall was silent for a moment, so long that Alexis became convinced he was furious, and then he laughed. And kept laughing, covering his mouth with one hand. Alexis opened her eyes, a bit relieved but still wary that it had been wrong thing to do.

"So ... it was not a dishonorable thing to do, sir?"

Crandall cleared his throat, still chuckling occasionally. "You neither struck your colors nor surrendered?"

"He asked me to surrender sir, but I didn't agree to."

"What did you say, exactly?"

"That there didn't appeared to be an alternative, sir."

Crandall laughed again, a hearty, honest laugh from deep in the belly.

"No, Carew," he said finally. "Not dishonorable. Not against the laws of war, at least." He leaned forward to rest his arms on his desk. "War's about deception, you see, Carew. Oh, there are rules — we respect surrender given or quarter asked for and such — but at its heart it's about making the other bloke think you're doing what you're not, so he never sees the knife coming for him." He shook his head. "No, you spoke to him in a naval uniform from a naval boat. If he chose to see —" His lips twitched. "— a little girl in pinafore lost on a street corner, well, more pity him, then."

Alexis flushed at the description. "Thank you, sir."

Crandall laughed again. "The beauty of it, Carew, is that you'll be able to use that bit again if you have need." He sat back. "After all, do you think the lad'll ever tell anyone how you snookered him?" He sobered. "Now, the question is what to do with you."

"Sir?"

"I'll have my bosun transfer some stores to your ship, of course."

Alexis inhaled sharply. She'd expected Crandall would send his own prize crew aboard, but it appeared she'd be allowed to stay in command a bit longer. Hearing even the little cutter referred to as *her* ship did something odd to her insides.

"And you'll follow us on to Penduli ... *back* to Penduli." He grinned. "I see that look on your face, Carew. Got a taste for command, did you?"

Alexis grinned back. "Yes, sir, I suppose I have."

"Good — enjoy it while you have the chance." He nodded. "But I'll examine your navigation plot myself when we arrive, so mark it well."

"Aye, sir."

Crandall frowned, then sighed. "I'm sorely tempted to steal you and your lads for *Lively*, I must admit." Alexis felt her eyes widen. Would he? Did they have a chance to get away from *Hermione*? But Crandall shook his head. "No, I've a full midshipmen's berth and a full crew, coming out of the Core. Wouldn't do to leave Captain Neals short an entire division — and such a capable one, at that. So, assuming *Hermione's* not in system when we arrive, you'll report with your men to the Port Admiral."

"Aye, sir."

ALEXIS STOOD in front of the wide desk in Penduli's Port Admiral's office. Admiral Piercy had not invited her to sit, nor had he offered her a drink. In fact, he seemed quite put out to be spending any of his time on her at all — a thing for which Alexis didn't really blame him. It was not, after all, common for an admiral to have junior midshipmen underfoot. *No, once you're an admiral you have lieutenants to do your bidding.*

The offices she'd passed to reach the admiral's were, in fact, full of lieutenants busily working. The only reason Piercy had asked to see her personally, she suspected, was for news of *Hermione. Why he couldn't wait to bring me in until he'd read my report, instead of leaving me to stand here ...*

"Hmph," Piercy grunted, putting his tablet aside. "Seems you did well enough, Carew, given the circumstances."

"Thank you, sir."

"Clever business drawing that Hannie lieutenant in. Quite."

"Thank you, sir." At Captain Crandall's suggestion, she'd added the details to her report, so as to make it clear she had not struck or surrendered before the action.

"So, now my only thing is what to do with you." He pursed his lips. "I'm loathe to deprive Captain Neals, but there are any number of ships in port that have a dire need for men and officers."

Alexis' spirits lifted. She'd been quite disappointed at the lost chance for her and her lads to join *Lively* and Captain Crandall, perhaps this was another. Any ship would be better than returning to *Hermione.*

"*Hermione's* due soon," Piercy went on, "if Neals keeps to his past patrols."

"If I may, sir," Alexis ventured, "I'd hate to be idle, on the chance *Hermione's* out longer than before. Or even just the men, so that they get into no mischief aboard the station?" Even if she couldn't find another ship herself, if she could get her lads away from Neals, it would be worth it.

Piercy was turning to another portion of his desk, as though already dismissing the matter and moving on.

"No," he said. "Neals is due soon. We'll give him a fortnight before I strip him of a full division." He frowned. "Take your men to the Assize Berth to wait — they'll be put up there and kept out of trouble."

Alexis caught her breath. The Assize Berth was where the men brought from the gaols were kept until assigned to a ship. The thought of her lads locked up with thieves and murderers was intolerable.

"The Assizes, sir? These are good lads, is there not somewhere —"

"I'm running a station, not an inn, Carew! The Assize Berth is where there's room for them. Take them there or put them up at your own expense, for all I care, but make sure they're all accounted for when *Hermione* puts in or I call for them. It's your responsibility."

"Aye, sir."

"Now about this little ship you brought in." His frown deepened. "You're certain *Hermione* had transitioned before you took her?"

"Yes, sir. By nearly an hour, sir."

"Hmph. Well, I'll have to put it to the Prize Court as yours, then. Neals won't be happy, I'm sure, but it's on his head."

"Sir?" she asked, unsure of what he meant.

"It'll be your claim, Mister Carew. You and your little band, as there were no other ships In Sight."

Alexis was stunned. On her previous cruise with *Merlin*, the pirate ship *Grappel* had been deemed her prize by a fluke of the Prize Court's misunderstanding, to have another prize submitted so was astounding.

"Quite," Piercy said. "Can see from the look on your face you hadn't expected that. Don't count it too quickly, though, there's a chance Captain Neals might appeal any award. He's that right, you know." He busied himself with his tablet. "See Dawbers outside, he'll complete the submission on that."

"Aye, sir. Thank you for your time, sir."

Alexis left his office and paused by the marine sentry just outside. "Dawbers?" she asked. "I assume he'll be a lieutenant?"

The marine nodded toward a nearby desk where a harried looking lieutenant was hunched over his desk.

"Thank you." She approached the desk and waited for a moment, but the lieutenant appeared not to notice her. Finally she cleared her throat gently. The lieutenant looked up.

"Yes?" His voice was resigned.

"Lieutenant Dawbers, sir? Carew, midshipman off of *Hermione*. Admiral Piercy said that you'd be the one to submit a prize on my behalf."

Dawbers drew a deep breath and let it out in a prolonged sigh, as though he were most put upon.

"Of course he did," he said. He slid his fingers over his console rapidly. "What is the ship name?"

"*Sittich*," Alexis told him. "Brought in this morning, in company with Captain Crandall and *Lively*."

"Here it is." Dawbers frowned. "Yourself and ... twenty-five men? No other claimants?"

"Admiral Piercy said it should be submitted so."

"Hmph," Dawbers snorted, sounding remarkably like his admiral. "Well, if he's said." His fingers flew over the console again. "Very well. A Hanoverese cutter, one hundred fifty tons burthen ... no cargo to speak of, I see." He looked up. "We'll submit it with a value of a thousand pounds for the agents. The Prize Court may raise that, of course, if they see fit." He frowned. "I'd advise you not to rely on getting all of your share, Mister Carew. If your captain should challenge the award ..."

"No, sir, I shan't."

"Good." He smiled suddenly. "Though if you were to sell your certificate to an agent, you'd come out well ahead, I think. Even at ten percent, you'd receive a tidy sum and the risk would be on the buyer. Be nice to see one of those sharps stick himself for a change!"

"Yes, sir, it would," she agreed, smiling herself.

The less reputable prize agents haunted the naval stations, looking for spacers and less well-off officers who hadn't the patience or means to wait for the Prize Court to make a final determination. They'd purchase the initial certificates, rights to what the award would eventually be, for a much reduced rate — sometimes even less than the ten percent Dawbers had mentioned — then collect the full amount when the Prize Court finally paid out.

Of course, if the Prize Court found that the ship was not lawfully a Prize or valued it lower than the initial estimate, the agent might receive significantly less or nothing at all. Generally, though, they paid so little that their profit was quite high.

"Well, here you are, then." He ran a finger over his console and Alexis' tablet *pinged*. "Yours and those for your men. You'll have to release those, in lieu of your captain being here."

"Yes, sir. And thank you."

Dawbers waved a hand in acknowledgment, already back at work on some other task.

Alexis left the offices and walked up the station corridor to where she'd left Nabb in charge of the men. They were clustered nearby, keeping out of the traffic moving up and down the corridor. She pulled out her tablet to review the certificates and froze. She'd known what the amounts would be, but seeing them was somehow different. *Sittich* was submitted to the prize court with her as the only officer. At six full eighths of the thousand pound value, the claim was for seven hundred fifty pounds. A sizable amount. Moreover, the two eighths that went to the crew, two hundred fifty pounds, amounted to ten pounds for each of the two dozen men of her division and Hearst, the pilot.

A year's pay for most of the spacers. Or a few days' drunkenness if they sold them to an agent — which they'd likely do. Her own certificate she'd simply deposit with her agent, or their branch on Penduli, a reputable firm recommended to her by Captain Grantham on *Merlin*. They'd *charge* her ten percent and handle all of the dealings with the Prize Court for her, simply adding any award to her holdings already in their accounts. Cupples, Beesley, and Stokes, though, were prize agents for officers — and officers with a certain amount of coin to put on account to start with — not for common spacers.

Alexis considered for a moment. She'd already decided that she'd find a place for the lads to wait out the next fortnight. The thought of sending them into the Assize Berths was more than she could bear. And she hated to see them cheated out of the prize money, but if she advised them to put their certificates aside and wait out the Prize Court's findings, they'd likely not listen. For a spacer, a pound in the hand while in port was worth far more than ten at some later day. And with no guarantee the award wouldn't be split with all of *Hermione's* crew in the end, if Neals challenged the award and won.

And it's sure and certain he'll challenge it when he hears. She had a sudden thought.

"Nabb," she said, feeling for how much coin she had with her and pulling out several shillings. "I've one last thing to do. Find the lads a pub and buy them a pint or two. No more than two, mind you, and watch them so no one runs off."

"Aye, sir."

"Watch Isom, especially. Now we're back on a station ... well, the temptation might be too great."

"I'll have Matheny sit with 'im, sir. Steady lad, he is."

"Thank you. I shouldn't be more than an hour or two."

"Aye, sir. Sir?"

"Yes?"

"I'll watch 'em, sir, but there's not a one who'll run." He looked down at the deck then back to her. "They'd be in a Hannie prison if it weren't fer you and know it. They'll not run on your watch."

"Well, without them I'd be in one myself, so we'll call it even all around, shall we?"

TEN

"Are you quite well, Mister Tapscott?"

Alexis watched the man with concern. Small, no more than a few centimeters taller than Alexis was, and nervous looking, he was walking close to her, his eyes darting quickly from place to place. More than his eyes, really, for he seemed to be unable to look somewhere without moving his entire head to point at it.

She could understand his nervousness. There were no pubs near the Port Admiral's offices that would welcome two dozen common spacers, nor that the spacers would choose to frequent, come to that. Nabb had led the men down two levels to an area where they'd be more comfortable. Though the corridor here had just as many lights as the others, it seemed dimmer and narrower. Or, perhaps, it was that the many tables and food carts the merchants had set up outside their shops, or someone else's shop, simply took up the space. Regardless, it was not a place that a representative of Cupples, Beesley, and Stokes, Registered Prize and Investment Agents, would normally frequent.

Tapscott licked his lips, head never stopping. "Quite all right,

Miss Carew! Very well, in fact. A part of the station I've never visited — fascinating! Simply fascinating."

Alexis smiled. *Well, he's not nervous, then.* "We're here, then," she said, stopping short of the pub's hatchway. "You're quite clear on the way of this, Mister Tapscott?"

"Absolutely, Miss Carew!" The man actually rubbed his hands together. "A spot of intrigue, yes?"

"But important, Mister Tapscott. Please do remember that."

Alexis thought she'd found a solution to the men's prize certificates, but it would take a bit of deception. She knew they'd not accept any funds from her — a pint of beer, perhaps, but nothing more. She'd likely even have to hide that she planned to pay for their berthing while on the station from her own funds, or they'd march themselves straight to the Assize Berth on their own. No, they were proud men and looked poorly on what they considered charity from anyone, even officers they liked.

The amounts of the prize awards, even at a bit over ten pounds each, were too small for most reputable agents to bother with. In fact, her own accounts, at well over a thousand pounds now, were smaller than what Cupples, Beesley, and Stokes would normally handle, and it was only Captain Grantham's referral that had gotten her an account. Luckily for her, their resident agent, Mister Tapscott, was enamored with the intrigue of her request and willing to go along with her.

"I will, Miss Carew. Have no fear."

"All right, then," she said, sliding the hatch open and entering.

The pub was small, barely large enough to hold the two dozen spacers of her division. Nabb had chosen it well, since it made keeping an eye on the men easier and the large crowd would keep the pub owner happy. Tapscott followed her in and Alexis made her way to the center of the room. The men had been loud when she entered, but they quieted quickly and looked at her.

"Had a good wet, lads?" she asked. When they'd settled down again, she pulled a free chair from underneath a table and stood on it so they could all see her. "I've news of the prize submission, so settle in and listen well." The room was suddenly dead quiet, with only the gentle clink of the pub tender washing glasses. "They've submitted *Sittich* at a thousand pounds value — moreover, they've said our boat was the only ship In Sight for the action. *Hermione* isn't in it." She waited while those who realized what that meant cheered. "Yes, the whole lot's to go to us in this room." More cheers and she held a hand up. "But—"

"*Quiet up, you lot!*" Nabb yelled.

"Thank you," she said, smiling at him. "*But*, and you know there's always a 'but' with the Prize Court, isn't there? Captain Neals could still challenge it for *Hermione* and all her crew."

"*Quiet!*" Nabb yelled again into the shouts.

"Nothing's set, lads," Alexis said. "But the certificates are out and yours are each quite a bit — ten pounds even." She waited a moment for the new cheers to be silenced. "So I've your certificates here and you can take them out to some sharp who'll give you, what, one or two of ten? Well, that seems a poor bargain when you mean to give some lubber a full eight pounds you risked your lives for, doesn't it?"

She gestured Tapscott forward. The little man looked around at the spacers and raised one hand to give a shaky wave. "This is Mister Tapscott of my own prize agents. A *proper* prize agent, one that officers, even my last captain, use, right? Tell them the offer, Mister Tapscott."

Tapscott cleared his throat, clearly uncomfortable being the center of so much attention. "Yes, so, the offer is that my firm will hold your certificates for the fee of ten percent—"

"What! We can get ten on the bloody corridor out there! Make it twenty!"

Tapscott looked around bewildered.

Nabb made his way through the tables and smacked the spacer on the back of the head. "Allmond, ya stupid git, it's him what gets the ten!"

"Who gets the rest then?" Allmond asked, rubbing his head.

"We do!" Nabb shook his head in disgust.

"But —" Allmond furrowed his brow, then his eyes opened wide. "That's nine tens, that is!"

"Ah, yes," Tapscott said. "So, a ten percent fee and we will hold the certificates until the Prize Court makes its final determination, but we will advance you two pounds now and indemnify you against any loss should the Prize Court's final award be less than that."

There was silence for a moment, then, "What's that mean, then?"

Isom stood up. "It means," he said, "that it's two pounds for each of us now, the rest, less his ten percent, when the Prize Court finally decides, and he's the only one gets buggered if they send it sour."

"Well that's all right then!"

"More'n all right! Let's hear it for Mister Tapscott, lads!"

Tapscott looked around, grinning and eyes wide at the sudden cheers.

Alexis smiled too as Tapscott pulled out his tablet for the men to sign over their certificates and receive their two pound advance in coin. Smiled, at least, until it was Isom's turn and she watched as he carefully read the contract then looked up at her in surprise. She shook her head, willing him to remain silent. *Of course it would be Isom, the legal clark, who'd be the only one of the crew to actually read the thing and see that it's my money for the advance and me taking the risk.* Ten pound accounts were far too small for Cupples, Beesley, and Stokes to bother with, but they'd manage just about any sort of arrangement for a fee.

Isom signed the contract, accepted his two pounds, and stepped aside for the next man. He paused by Alexis. "Thank you, sir."

Alexis squeezed his shoulder gently, then hopped back onto the chair. "All right, lads! One last round here, then it's off to find a berth for you. Nabb, do you have any thoughts on that?"

ALEXIS STOOD in the crowded civilian corridor, uncertain as to whether she really wanted to do this. The smaller corridor branching off this one was much as she remembered ... as much as she *could* remember it, given her state the last time she was here. Where the main corridor was clearly commercial, with well-lit storefronts and signs for each establishment, the side corridor was narrow, narrower than she remembered, with no signs, only numbers, above each hatchway. She clenched her hands tightly, running her thumb over the smooth glass of the bottle she held and wondered at her nervousness.

Her lads were all off carousing with their newfound coin and the inn Nabb had found for them was empty. Well, pub, really, for they'd discovered that none of the inns in the Naval section of the station would cater to common spacers, only to officers. Spacers were rarely granted more than a watch or two stationside and then expected back aboard their ship — if they were between ships the Navy housed them in the Assize Berths to keep them from running.

They'd had to settle for a pub that offered a few sleeping pods available for those who merely wanted a quick nap before resuming their carouse. Ten pods between them, so Alexis had assigned one each to herself, and the pilot, Hearst, then placed the lads onto three watches to split time in those remaining. But with so much coin in their pockets, none had felt the need to sleep or relax the first night, so the pub was empty and Alexis left at loose ends.

She'd realized suddenly, sitting by herself in the empty pub, just how alone she truly was. Not just on the station, where she knew no one but her lads from *Hermione* — and an officer certainly couldn't simply sit and talk to them, they wouldn't stand for it — but even aboard the ship itself.

The hatchway she was watching slid open and a woman in a merchant ship's uniform came out. She ducked her head and hurried to the main corridor, quickly easing herself into the flow of people. Alexis shook her head in wonder.

The lads make a visit to a bawdy house and it's a public event, with three cheers and slaps on the back, but I've yet to see a woman leave there with her head up. She hesitated, realized she was doing the same by hanging around uncertainly, and squared her shoulders.

Alexis strode across the corridor, down the narrower side corridor, and tapped her finger to the hatchway's call button. In a moment, the hatch slid open and Alexis recognized the woman who opened it from her previous visit.

"Navy?" the woman said, then her eyebrows went up and she stood aside. "Come in, dear, I remember you. Six ... eight weeks, has it been?"

Alexis entered, flushing a bit and clearing her throat at being remembered. She nodded, uncertain what to say, and realized that she didn't recall the woman's name from her first visit.

"And what can we do for you tonight, dear?"

"I ..." Alexis swallowed hard. "I was wondering if Mister Blackmon might be available?"

The woman smiled. "'Mister Blackmon', is it?" she asked, causing Alexis to flush more as she realized patrons of the establishment would almost certainly be on a first name basis with its inhabitants. The woman glanced at the screen of red and green circles. "As it happens, 'Mister Blackmon' is indeed available for you." She raised an eyebrow again. "Will it be all night in again, then?"

Alexis felt as though her face might burst into flames at any moment, but nodded. She fished in her pocket for the coins, not wanting the transaction to appear on her accounts, even though she was the only one who reviewed them. "One pound ..." She cleared her throat again on hearing an odd catch in her voice. "One pound seven, yes?"

The woman nodded and took the coins. "Room seven, dear."

Alexis climbed the stairs and paused outside the hatch to the room, then clutched her bottle tightly and rapped softly on it. She flushed again, remembering how she'd simply walked in the last time, thinking it would be an empty room. *What if he'd just been standing there in ...*

The hatch slid open wide and Alexis realized her nervousness had her gazing down at the deck, which was not such a demure thing to do when a man opens the hatch to his room wearing only a very short silk robe that barely covered his ... *Does he own any trousers at all, I wonder?*

She jerked her gaze upward to his face.

Cort Blackmon's face broke in a wide grin. "Alexis?"

She cleared her throat. "Yes, I ..."

"Come in, lass," he said, standing aside. "Come in." Alexis hurried inside and he slid the hatch shut behind her. "Ha'ye been well, lass?"

"I have, I suppose," Alexis said, then hurried on, wanting to make herself clear. "I thought we might ... talk again? That is to say, the last time ... you said it was not uncommon." She bit her lip. "To talk, that is."

"Aye, talkin's common enow," Cort said, his lips twitching. He reached out and took the bottle from her hand. He held it up and raised an eyebrow. "Bourbon? An' 'ere it was the Scotch whiskey y'were goin' on aboot so, last y'were here. Been a fair bit since I was home an' tasted it m'self." He took two glasses from a nearby table, gesturing to a chair next to it, and opened the bottle.

"Perhaps a bit too much, last I was here," Alexis said, accepting a glass and taking a small sip, barely wetting her lips.

"Y'were a bit jaiked up." He seated himself on the edge of the bed, glass in hand. "An' what's on yer mind tonight, lass?"

ALEXIS CAME AWAKE SLOWLY. She clenched her eyes shut and burrowed her face into the warm body next to her. Cort's arm tightened around her, pulling her close.

"D'ye sleep well, lass?"

However does he do that? Does he lay awake waiting for one to wake up?

"I did," she said, realizing it was true. She felt quite rested for the first time in quite a long while.

"Nae bad dreams?"

Alexis smiled. "None," she said. Whether from their talk or simply from the comfort of being with someone she could talk to, Horsfall hadn't come to her dreams that night. She hadn't even had the anxiety of dreading it before falling asleep.

She felt a wetness against her cheek and sat up abruptly, wiping at her face.

"Oh ..." She stared at the wet spot of drool staining the chest of Cort's silk robe and grimaced.

"Aye, lass, an' y'snore nae a little bit."

Alexis smoothed her jumpsuit, tugging things into place — anything, really, to avoid looking at him.

Cort laughed and reached out to take her hand and squeeze it. "Trust me, lass, a man'll put up w'both drool an' snorin' fer you."

Alexis felt her face grow hot, both from his touch and his words. She glanced up and met his eye, lip caught between her teeth. She had a feeling she might one day regret doing no more than talk with Cort Blackmon. *Especially if he's as skilled at ... other things as he is at listening.*

For he was remarkably good at listening, giving her his full attention and just letting her speak, without forever trying to interject solutions. Occasionally he'd prompted her with a comment or question, but for the most part had let her work her thoughts out on her own.

Though he had answered her questions readily enough regarding those matters she was curious about. Such as the workings of the houses and the ladies who worked the naval port. She had a better understanding now, she thought, of the men who'd send most of their pay home to wife and family then spend the rest on a portside bawd. *A bit of comfort's welcome, far from home.*

She swung her legs over the side of the bed and stood, frowning at how rumpled her jumpsuit was.

"I should be getting back to check on the lads," she said.

Cort nodded and stood, retrieving her beret from a corner of the compartment. Alexis paused in pulling on her boots, remembering the rather obscene rant she'd been on about Captain Neals when she'd thrown it there. He rounded the end of the bed to hand her the beret.

"Droolin' an' snorin' an' profane oaths," he said with a teasing grin. "Powerful lot o' bad habits fer sich a tiny package."

Alexis pulled her boot on and accepted the beret. She stood and grasped the mostly empty bottle of bourbon from the table. "You've left off the drinking," she said, answering his grin with one of her own.

"Drinks nae a bad habit, lass. The bloody Navy sails on it."

ALEXIS MADE her way back to the pub, uncomfortably aware of her appearance.

A midshipman roaming the corridors in the station's early morning with a rumpled jumpsuit and tousled hair all astray, for she'd lost the tie for her usual ponytail at some point, and a nearly empty bottle of whiskey clutched in her hand. *I'll be lucky if I'm not taken up by the Station Patrol before I get there.*

She managed to make it back, though the looks she received from other officers made her cringe, and almost sighed with relief as the pub's hatch slid closed behind her. Nabb and a half dozen or so of the crew were up and about their breakfast.

"Are y' all right, Mister Carew?" Nabb asked.

Alexis smiled at the concern in his voice. "Quite all right, Nabb," she assured him. "I've just had a fine evening out." She cleared her throat seeing a couple of the lads look from her to their breakfasts and back with raised eyebrows. "Everything all right with the lads?"

"No troubles, sir. All back by the start o' the Morning Watch an' time in the sleep pods is settled."

"Thank you, Nabb." She bit her lip at the implication. She herself was returning almost five bells into the Morning Watch, though as an officer she wasn't strictly required to be adhere to the schedule she set for the crew. Still, she wondered what the lads would think of it. She crossed to the bar and set the bottle of bourbon on it.

"Would you keep this someplace safe for me?" she asked the publican. At his nod, she turned back to Nabb and ran her hands over her hair, trying to get it into some sort of order. "I'll just ..." She headed for the hatch to the sleeping pods and heads. "I'll just freshen up a bit and we'll see what needs doing today."

"Aye sir."

Alexis slid the hatch to the pods and heads closed behind her, ignoring the comment she heard one of the spacers, Scholer, make.

"'at's a proper spacer, her."

ELEVEN

"Are you Carew?"

Alexis looked up from her tablet and the plate of breakfast, the pub they'd found for their berthing served a respectable plate of sausage and beans, to find a lieutenant beside her table. She'd been reviewing the ships in-system. There were but five days left on Admiral Piercy's promised fortnight and she was beginning to allow herself to hope that *Hermione* would not show. She hadn't said anything to the men about the chance of being sent to another ship, though, as she didn't want to get their hopes up.

"Yes, sir, I am," she said, standing. She caught sight of the Station Patrol insignia on the lieutenant's uniform and her shoulders slumped. "Drunk or fighting?" *And, please, let it be one of those and not the third over breakfast.*

In the nine days they'd been on station, not a one had gone past without the Station Patrol dragging some of her lads back to the pub. It was an expected thing for ships in port, but Alexis had never had to deal with the aftermath directly. She began to understand why some captains would keep the men aboard ship, or at least limit the time they had for liberty.

The most common reason was drunkenness — meaning so implausibly drunk that the spacer had actually stopped drinking, for no pub owner would think to call the Patrol on an active patron. A distant second was fighting — distant not because the lads got into few fights, but because fights were so common that the Patrol simply wasn't called unless the pub owner felt the property damage was excessive and couldn't be settled up privately. Those two were the most common reasons for the Patrol to ask for her, but she held a special dread for the third. Six times now a spacer had been brought back over a contract dispute with one of the station's ladies of negotiable virtue. 'Negotiable' being the sticking point, and Alexis found it rather uncomfortable to stand there with a Patrol lieutenant and no few marines while one of her lads explained exactly what he felt he'd negotiated and not received. The sheer variety was enlightening, though.

She'd even had to begin holding her own little Captain's Mast each day, assembling the men and assigning punishments to the three or four who'd been brought back by the Patrol in the previous twenty-four hours. Usually confinement to the pub for a day and an assignment to clean it spotless. The publican had looked askance the first time her spacers had grabbed buckets and headed for his kitchen, but now he seemed to eagerly await the results of each day's gathering. He'd be sad to see them go, she suspected, for her group had not only filled the ten sleeping pods the publican kept, but took many of their meals there as well.

She'd even been able to negotiate a reasonable price. Sixpence per man each day bought them the use of all ten sleeping pods, a breakfast of beans and sausage, a dinner of soup and bread, each with half a pint of beer, and the publican's wife had thrown in a laundry day each week.

And lucky I could draw them an extra uniform from the station's quartermaster, or it'd be a sight on laundry day.

"Neither, Mister Carew," the lieutenant said, unsmiling. "This one's tried to run."

Alexis' eyes widened in shock. "Where is he?"

"Outside," the lieutenant said, nodding toward the pub's hatchway.

Alexis hurried past him and into the corridor. Isom was there, arms held by two marines, head hanging and blood running down his chin.

"What happened to him?"

"Spouted some rot about the regulations and my boys shut him up."

Alexis clenched her teeth. If Isom had spouted anything in the regulations, he was most likely right and this lieutenant a fool, but there'd be little gained in arguing it.

"Would you bring him in, please," she said to the marines, "and set him down."

"I only brought him here to inform you before taking him to the brig," the lieutenant said. "I was expecting a captain when he said he was berthed here, not a midshipman."

Alexis tried to smile. "I understand, Lieutenant ...?"

"Garman."

"Thank you, sir," she said. "If we could only let him sit down while you and I sort this out, Lieutenant Garman? My ship hasn't returned yet and Captain Neals left me in charge of the men in his absence." *Which, strictly speaking, is the truth.*

Garman frowned but nodded to the marines. They entered the pub and let Isom slump in a chair. The half dozen or so men who were having their breakfast looked up, curious about what had happened, but Alexis waved them away and they sat back down, but not before throwing a few dark looks toward the marines.

"Now, Lieutenant Garman, sir, may I offer you and your men a drink?" She caught the eye of the publican who grabbed glasses and came over to them.

Garman grunted, as though surprised to be offered something by a midshipman. "A glass of port wouldn't go amiss, I suppose," he said. "Beer for my men."

Alexis nodded to the publican and waited until the three had been served. "May I ask what Isom did, sir?"

"Tried to leave the naval section of the station. Clearly planned to sign aboard some merchant and run."

"Not runnin'," Isom mumbled.

Alexis knelt in front of his chair and grasped his hands. She looked up into his battered face. "What were you after, Isom?"

"Tryin' t'see Mis'er Grandy," he mumbled, the words thick through his battered face. Alexis had no idea who Mister Grandy might be, but didn't see that it mattered to the problem at hand.

"He had no pass from an officer, Carew," Garman said. "He was trying to run."

"Don' need pass. No regulation."

"I'm confused, sir," Alexis said, turning to Garman. "*Is* there such a regulation?"

Garman frowned. "Well, it's usual for them to have a pass, certainly — something that states their business and such. Don't know that there's a specific regulation, come to think on it."

And you couldn't be bothered to think on it before beating the man bloody? "I see, sir." Now it was Alexis' turn to frown. "You see I have charge of these men until my ship returns, and Isom here wasn't at all late for watch or checking in — he's effectively on liberty."

"He had your permission to hare off like that, then?"

"Rather I haven't expressively forbidden it." She resumed her seat. "The men have some prize money and we're at loose ends until *Hermione*, our ship, returns. So long as they're back here when I ask them to be and get into no more than the usual and expected bit of trouble, they're free to do as they wish."

Garman grunted. "I think you allow them too much license, Carew."

"My captain may, as well, when he returns, Lieutenant Garman." She smiled and spread her hands wide. "But if there's no regulation violated and I don't consider him to have run ..."

"Hmph." Garman drained his glass and stood. "No sense dragging him to the brig if you intend to say he had your permission to go where he did, I suppose." He frowned. "I think you'll regret it, though." He nodded at Isom. "This one'll run. He's got the look about him."

"Thank you, Lieutenant Garman. I'll take that under considera- tion and review my dealings with the crew, for certain, sir." Garman nodded and gestured for the two marines to follow him out. Alexis waited until the hatch had closed, then muttered, "And you're welcome for the drink, you arrogant sot." She turned back to Isom, who was trying to rise. "No," she said, easing him back. "Sit still. Matheny! Broady! Come help Isom to the head and get him cleaned up."

Isom shook his head. "Have to see Grandy."

"We'll talk about that after you've cleaned up and had a bit of a lie down. I promise."

Isom nodded and the two other spacers draped an arm over his shoulders and helped him up. They went off into the back where the sleeping pods and head were while Alexis returned to her table. Her breakfast was cold and she hadn't the appetite for it, in any case.

When Isom returned he was cleaner, still battered but not as bloody. Alexis gestured for him to sit and she nodded to Nabb who was standing nearby. "A bit of grog, I think Nabb," she said. Isom sat hunched in the chair, head bowed and silent. Nabb brought a small mug of grog, watered rum and lime juice, to the table and set it before Isom.

"Thank you, sir." Isom at the same time Alexis said, "Thank you, Nabb."

Nabb stepped away and Alexis turned her attention to Isom. "Now, then, have a drink and tell me about it. What's so important that it was worth a beating, for I believe you when you say you weren't running."

Isom looked up at her and took a long drink. "I was a legal clark on Uffington."

"So you've said."

"Well, sir, there's a firm on Penduli, name of Grandy, Penthurst, and Dulle, sir. There was a property matter some time ago and I had an extended correspondence with Mister Grandy, you see."

Alexis frowned. "So this was all about seeing some friend?"

"No, sir! Mister Grandy, he's a full solicitor and I'm merely a clark ... was a clark. No, sir —" He lowered his gaze again. "— just thought that, perhaps, Mister Grandy might..."

Alexis suddenly understood. "You think this Mister Grandy might be able to get you out of the Navy?"

Isom nodded, turning red. "It's not that I think I'm better than the Service, sir ..."

Alexis stood. "Isom, I'm sure you're a fine legal clark, but if there were ever a man less suited to naval service than yourself, I should dearly wish not to make his acquaintance. Come on, man, don't dally," she said, gesturing for him to rise.

Isom looked at her in surprise.

"*Hermione* and Captain Grantham could return at any moment. If this Grandy's to have a chance, we'd best be about it."

Alexis led Isom to the nearest boat bay and booked them passage to the planet's surface. While they waited, her initial enthusiasm began to wane as she asked him more questions, but she'd already committed to taking the man to Grandy's offices.

"So there's been no response from him to your messages?" she asked.

"No, sir, I've tried to call when we're in port and sent him messages, but no response at all. I think ..." He trailed off and stared at the deck. "Perhaps because messages are from a common spacer and not a clark at a law firm, he may not recognize me?"

Alexis doubted that. She had a moment's thought that Isom's messages might be affected by whatever had kept her from receiving hers as well, but he'd received responses from others he'd written to. The next boat came and they boarded for the short flight to Penduli's surface.

They stepped off the boat onto a landing field covered in water from a persistent, light rain. Alexis looked around, wishing the day were clearer, for Penduli was a well-established planet with a population of over a hundred million. The main port itself had half a million permanent residents. She looked around in wonder, as some of the buildings lining the landing field were as much as ten stories tall — Dalthus rarely built above three, and that counting attic space.

She led Isom to the edge of the field where there were cars for hire, all ground vehicles, though the occasional air car darted through the space above them.

And not a horse in sight anywhere — what must the Core Worlds themselves be like?

They arrived at the address, a suite of offices on the fourth floor above a coffee house. A stunning young woman looked up from her console as they entered. She ran her eyes over the two of them, clearly taking in Alexis' rank and Isom's disheveled appearance. "May I help you in some way?" she asked.

Alexis took an instant dislike to the young woman. She'd seen that look on the faces of her peers on Dalthus, usually directed at some farmhand or shopkeeper. An instant appraisal, judgment, and dismissal as unworthy of further attention or any real courtesy. She forced her face into a smile.

"Yes, please. Mister Isom to see Mister Grandy, if it's convenient."

The woman pursed her lips into a delicate moue. "Oh," she said. "I'm afraid that would be impossible. Mister Grandy is quite busy today."

Alexis had a sudden understanding. Isom's description of his correspondence with Mister Grandy had given the impression of a warm, jovial man. Not the sort who would ignore messages from a colleague's former clark, even if the circumstances were somewhat unusual.

"I see," Alexis said. "And you are the keeper of Mister Grandy's schedule, I take it?"

The woman nodded, a self-satisfied smirk on her face. "If you'd like to leave a message, I'm sure we'll contact you when Mister Grandy has an opening."

Alexis nodded. "And you are the passer of Mister Grandy's messages, as well, I assume?"

Another nod.

"Well, then," Alexis said, settling herself into a nearby chair and gesturing for Isom to do so as well.

The woman looked confused for a moment. "What do you think you're doing?"

Alexis pulled out her tablet and settled back in the chair, giving every impression that she intended to be there for some time. "Waiting for Mister Grandy," she said.

"You can't do that!"

"Dear," Alexis said, "if you're capable of a thought that's at all beyond the ornamental, you'll see clearly that I'm already doing so."

"I shall call the authorities!"

Alexis looked up from her tablet and narrowed her eyes as though thinking hard, then nodded. "Yes, please do."

"I ... what?"

"I'm sure the arrival of the authorities will cause some sort of ruckus, at which Mister Grandy will appear and we can be about our business." She waved her hand dismissively and settled back into the chair. "Do as you think best, dear."

The woman clenched her jaw and turned back to her console. Isom made to speak, but Alexis held out a hand to restrain him. She checked her tablet for messages — she was receiving occasional messages from the Port Admiral's station, addressed to her at Penduli Station, but still nothing addressed to her on *Hermione*. She'd thought, at least, that their extended stay on the station would allow her messages to catch up with her. After a few minutes, she noticed the woman at the desk speaking lowly into her console. The woman nodded, but her lips were pursed, clearly unhappy with what she'd heard.

"Shouldn't be long now, Isom," Alexis whispered.

In fact, it was less than a minute before a man hurried out of the back offices. He was past middle-age and balding, with a thin mustache. His gaze passed over Alexis and the rest of the waiting area before fixing on Isom.

"Mister Isom?" he asked, his smile faltering a little. Alexis couldn't blame him for being unsure, as Isom was dressed as a common spacer and still sported the bruises and cuts from the beating he'd taken from the port marines.

"Mister Grandy!" Isom said, standing and holding out his hand. "Thank you so much for seeing me."

"Of course," Grandy said. "Of course! It's a pleasure to meet you finally. Your work on the Wickholm property was first rate — my client was exceptionally pleased with the result." He looked Isom up and down. "But what is this? You've given over the law for naval service?"

Isom flushed and looked at the floor. "That is the matter I wished to speak to you about, Mister Grandy," he said. "The joining was not by choice, you see."

Grandy's face fell. "Oh, dear," he said. "Caught up in the Press? Indeed?"

Isom nodded.

"I see. Well, come back to my office and tell me what's happened. We'll see what can be done." He turned to Alexis and held out his hand. "And you, Miss ..."

"Carew, sir," she said. "Midshipman aboard *Hermione*, the ship Isom is serving on."

"Would you come back with me, sir?" Isom asked. "In case Mister Grandy has questions about the ship or the Service?"

"Of course, Isom."

Alexis followed Grandy and Isom back to his office. Rather than sitting behind his desk, Grandy ushered them to a sitting area with four deep chairs around a low table. Grandy waited, making small talk about legal matters with Isom, until the woman had brought coffee for them all, served with cream, sugar, and a dark look for Alexis.

As soon as the coffee was served, Grandy became quite business-like. His tablet was suddenly in his hands and he was tapping away as he asked Isom to tell his tale, interspersed with questions about minute details. Alexis sat back and sipped her coffee. Isom's tale was common one for spacers since the start of the war and the reinstatement of the Impressment Service. Less so for a landsman who'd never been to space, but he'd been caught up in it nevertheless.

"Well, sir," he said, "I'd been out one night near the port, you see, and was making my way home. It was a bit late, but there were still plenty of people about —"

"Why were you near the port to begin with?" Grandy asked. "It hardly seems the place for you." He inclined his head to Alexis. "Meaning no offense, Miss Carew, but naval crews are somewhat rowdier company than one expects of a law clark."

"None taken, Mister Grandy," Alexis said smiling. "I'm sure 'rowdy' is quite the politest thing my lads have been called in port."

"Indeed," Grandy said and looked expectantly at Isom.

"I ... well ..." Isom flushed and Alexis had a sudden suspicion.

A legal clark with prospects, but no real standing as yet. His opportunities for meeting a woman would be limited, while the port would offer access at a cost affordable on a clark's wages. *Or a cost much greater, as it turned out for him.*

"There was a lady involved, Isom?" she asked gently.

Isom flushed more and nodded.

Grandy cleared his throat and waved a hand. "I see, well, the reason you were there will likely have no bearing on the case. Do continue, please, Mister Isom."

"I was making my way home," Isom repeated, "and suddenly there were men running down the street past me. Running hard and shouting from ahead, so ... well, I turned and ran with them." He looked from Alexis to Grandy, eyes wide. "I wasn't sure what they'd be running from, you see, and ... it's a hard area, as you said. The next

I knew, there were men ahead of us. They rushed into the crowd and started striking people with stunners. One of them struck me and I blacked out."

Isom was hunched over in his chair and Alexis saw that his eyes were wet and she reached out to lay an arm across his shoulders.

"When I woke I was in the hulks. Twenty of us jammed into a compartment, waiting for transfer to some ship. I tried to tell them I wasn't a spacer! Never been to space at all. I was a bloody clark, for pity's sake, never been outside the city, even!" He rubbed at his eyes. "They'd taken my tablet and they wouldn't call down to the city to check who I was at all. Said I was a liar and a spacer." He spat out a laugh. "Pointed to a tattoo on my arm as proof." He rolled up his left sleeve to show a tattoo on his inner arm, a fouled anchor many spacers got as their first tattoo. "I've never wanted a tattoo and it was still bleeding when they pointed to it. I suppose they had it done while I was unconscious to prove I was a spacer." He shrugged. "Then I was put aboard *Hermione* and sailed for the border."

Alexis felt her eyes burning. It was one thing to choose the naval life, another to be forced to it by circumstance as she had been, but something very different to have had your life stolen and be thrown into it against your will. She couldn't imagine how Isom must feel.

And to be put onto Hermione *to top it all?*

Grandy was silent for a time, brow furrowed. "Mister Prescott is aware of your situation?" he asked. Alexis assumed this was Isom's former employer.

"He is," Isom said. "First I had access to send a message, I informed him. He's said he'll look into it, but it's hard with me aboard ship so far away and not there to make the complaint myself. I thought, being here …"

"Yes," Grandy said, "but I have some experience with the naval courts. In some ways they are superior to the civilian courts, in others …" He shook his head. "No, the court on Uffington will say that you must be there to make a complaint, while the court here will say that they must have the impressment records from Uffington."

"We must send for those records, then," Alexis said.

Grandy nodded. "Which shall be done." He gave her a thin, rueful smile. "And when they arrive some months from now, where will your ship be?" Isom's shoulders slumped. "That is presuming, of course, that they send the correct records in response to the request. The Impressment Service there will not wish its actions known. Your Navy, Mister Carew, can be remarkably efficient in its inefficiencies."

Alexis wanted to defend the Service, thinking of Captain Grantham and *Merlin*, but the knowledge that captains like Neals also existed stopped her. She remembered Williard's words. *Two Navies*.

"All this is not to say that you must give up hope, my good man," Grandy said, reaching forward to pat Isom on the leg. "Between me here and Prescott on Uffington, we'll work it out. They'll have a much harder time failing to produce the proper records with him right there. Once he sends them to me, I'll be in a better position to file the case."

Isom looked up at him, eyes wide with hope. "So you'll take the case, sir?"

"Of course!" Grandy said, taking up his tablet again.

Isom's face fell and he looked suddenly worried. "I haven't much in the way of money, sir, a bit of savings, but —"

Grandy waved his hand. "No matter, Mister Isom. This will be a professional courtesy." He smiled. "I'm sure you'll have ample opportunity to repay the favor when you're back on Uffington ... with your own practice one day."

"Thank you, sir."

Grandy asked Isom a few more questions and then sat back. "Sadly, there's nothing more we can do until we have the records from Uffington. I assume I may contact you by sending the message care of ... *Hermione*, was it?"

"Yes, sir," Isom said.

"Well, then," Grandy said, standing. "We'll try to get this cleared up as soon as may be."

"Mister Grandy?" Alexis said. The man seemed to have a grasp of the law; and Isom, for all he was a sad sight as a spacer, seemed a knowledgeable clark. Dalthus had no real solicitors yet, the population was too small, and she hadn't had the thought to speak to one since joining the Navy. Perhaps he might have some insight into the issues of her inheritance.

"Yes, Miss Carew?"

"If you have a moment, there's a matter I might wish to consult with you regarding."

Grandy smiled and sat down again. "Two new clients at one go? A banner day."

It took a surprisingly short time for Alexis to lay out the situation she faced on Dalthus. Being her grandfather's only heir, but unable to inherit because of a law of male primogeniture. *For something so important, it should take longer to explain.*

Grandy frowned when she was done and she took this as a bad sign. He'd been smiling and reassuring throughout the talk of Isom's situation.

"Yes," he said finally. "We see things like this in the Fringe so often. It's a patently illegal law, you see, but there's no real system in place to deal with it. The colonies are generally allowed to do as they will, provided there's no real human rights violations. And even if there are, they're left alone if their emigration policy is liberal enough. A sort of 'if you don't like it, leave' policy." He sighed. "The problem for you is standing, you see."

"Standing?" she asked.

"Yes. You see, in order to bring a case before a magistrate, you must have standing. You must have been injured by the law in order to challenge it. Unfortunately, you have not been injured."

Alexis drew in a deep breath. "I have, sir, I assure you. Were it not for this law, I would be at home this minute, tending to my grandfather's lands."

Grandy nodded. "Yes, and there's the rub, you must understand.

Your *grandfather's* lands, still. As he's alive, the inheritance laws have not yet injured you, do you see?"

Alexis was shocked. "Do you mean to say that the courts will not hear my case because my grandfather is not dead?"

"Bluntly, yes." He nodded at her look of outrage. "I quite understand your feelings, Miss Carew. This would be one of those areas where your naval courts are superior to the civilian, in my opinion. The civilian court must follow the law — that's their oath, on all sides — while the naval court, the captains presiding, even the prosecutor, well their oath is 'to seek justice and the best interests of the Service'." He sighed. "Gives them greater latitude to seek a just resolution. Like your Articles of War, yes? Full of 'shall suffer death' for every offense, but then gives the captain the option of 'or such other punishment as shall be decided'." Alexis began to think that Grandy had a great deal more knowledge of the Navy than she'd originally suspected.

Grandy frowned. "I assume your family is not titled?"

"No, sir," she said. "Would that make a difference?"

"If you were titled, they would be family lands and must pass with the title."

Of course, the aristocracy would have an out for it. Above the law, even the bad ones.

"Let me do some further research," Grandy said. "Dalthus, was it?"

"Yes, sir. I have some funds with an agent, if you —"

Grandy waved his hand. "No, Miss Carew, I suspect that I should not have the opportunity to help my friend, Mister Isom, were it not for your kindness. A bit of research is the least I can do in thanks for that."

"Thank you, Mister Grandy," Alexis said. "I do appreciate it."

Her tablet began beeping insistently and Alexis pulled it out. Her face fell and she felt a chill run through her.

"Are you quite all right, Miss Carew?"

Alexis looked up at him, eyes wide and struggling to regain her composure. She hadn't realized just how much she'd been hoping, and the disappointment she felt on reading the message made her want to scream.

"*Hermione's* returned."

"DRUNKENNESS! BRAWLING! *DESERTION!*"

"Sir," Alexis said, back straight, eyes focused on the bulkhead of Captain Neals' day cabin. "There was no desertion, sir. All the lads are accounted for."

Neals slammed his tablet onto his desk. "I've the reports from Station Patrol right here, Carew! That they caught the man before he could succeed doesn't excuse it!"

"Sir, Isom wasn't deserting. He was free to do as he wished until reporting back — the lieutenant misunderstood something about a pass and —"

"Will you forever argue with me, Carew? Forever play the space-lawyer?" Neals stood, palms on his desk and looked down at his tablet. "I have never in my life seen —" He raised his eyes to look at her. "— such a list of offenses."

Alexis stared at him in shock. What Navy had the man been serving in all these years? While she'd been on station, she'd seen the Penduli Station Patrol take up virtually the entire crews of two other ships, rival captains in some matter, and ban the lot from landing for six months over brawling. Her lads had been piddling puppies in comparison. Why, her brawlers were welcomed back into pubs as soon as the damages were settled, and her drunks ... well, publicans had sent boys to wait outside the berth to make sure her lads found their way back the next night.

"This is what happens from putting a woman in the mix," Neals went on. He slammed his palm down on the desk. "No *discipline!*"

Alexis clenched her jaw and resumed staring at the bulkhead.

Neals came around the desk and stood near her. This close, she could feel him trembling with anger.

"I thought I was finally shut of you, Carew," he whispered. "Cost me a boat and some crewmen, but well worth it at twice the price. Yet now you're back."

Alexis swallowed hard to stifle a gasp. It sounded almost as though he'd left them behind deliberately and not just as an accident of his running, but not even Neals would do something like that, would he?

"I *will* be shut of you, Carew, do you understand? I'll have you out of my Navy, no matter the cost." His jaw worked, breath ragged, before he stepped back.

"Sir —"

"Shut up, Carew." Neals resumed his seat and picked up his tablet. "No discipline. That's what comes of trying to play at Captain Goodfellow with the men. They should have been in the Assize Berth where they belong, not ... coddled by a little girl." He sighed. "Well, I'll have them back under proper naval discipline." Neals narrowed his eyes and tapped the tablet. "You'll write them up for next Captain's Mast, Carew, every one of these offenses."

"Sir! I held Masts myself and issued punishments. They've already been —"

"Punishments?" Neals raised the tablet. "Yes, I read your report as well as the Station Patrol's, Carew." He snorted. "Cleaning? A bit of pay stoppage for the worst? Confined to the berth ... *in a pub?*"

Alexis cringed. Yes, confinement to a pub for drunkenness might seem odd, but the lads had taken the spirit of it. The offenders had kept to themselves at a corner table for the duration and not had a bit to drink past their daily issue. All of them had taken their punishments as willingly as they would have aboard ship. And she feared their reaction if they had to appear before another Captain's Mast for the same offenses — the men would accept punishment for an offense, even the lash, but they expected that to be the end of it. "Over, done with, and no more said about it," was their view — to be punished twice for the same offense wouldn't be tolerated lightly.

"As for yourself, Carew," Neals was saying, "I must say that I find myself disappointed beyond measure."

Well, of course, why would I expect any different?

"This coarse, money-grubbing scheme of yours to steal from your shipmates goes beyond even my lowest opinion of you."

Alexis blinked and her mouth dropped open in shock. *What on earth —*

"Trying to claim a prize for yourself alone? Cheat *Hermione's* crew of their just reward? Shame, Carew. You can be sure I'll be challenging this in the Prize Court ... on behalf of the crew."

Alexis steeled herself. Well, of course he'd try to get a piece of what her lads had accomplished in taking *Sittich*. She wouldn't begrudge at all sharing the award with *Hermione's* crew, but for Neals to accuse her of cheating and stealing from them ...

"Sir, it was submitted so at Admiral Piercy's order."

"Yes, I've seen the tale you spun the admiral about being 'abandoned', Carew. Not a word about your utter, contemptible failure to dock with *Hermione* as ordered? As ordered *more than once!* You can be assured that I've corrected Admiral Piercy's perception of the events ... despite your conniving efforts to beguile the poor man."

"Sir, I —"

"And that Crandall, too! Why the man had the *nerve* to contact me and *compliment* me on having such an officer as you!" Neals slammed his hand onto the desk again, his face growing red. "What kind of slattern are you to have so befuddled good officers?"

Alexis flinched and stared at the bulkhead. She felt her eyes burn and her muscles clench with the effort to fight back the urge to speak. She'd forgotten, at least for a time, how easily and quickly Neals' moods could swing. The time aboard Penduli Station, out from under Neals' thumb, had caused her to relax — perhaps not such a good thing now she was back aboard *Hermione*.

TWELVE

Alexis started for the base of the mast, easing herself along the hull in the gliding walk that always kept one magnetized boot in contact with the hull at all times, so she wouldn't drift free and have to pull herself back toward the ship by her safety line. The men of her division had just finished trimming the sails to Captain Neals' latest orders and were hurrying down.

The captain had again ordered that the last man down be flogged, a practice that made Alexis sick to her stomach. She understood the use of flogging for discipline — with months spent in space, well away from any planetside authority, the captain had to have some means of enforcing order. As one of the spacers on her first ship, *Merlin*, had explained it to her, even the men understood the need, and typically faced their punishment with an attitude of 'over, done with, and now forgotten' for both the flogging and the offense for which they'd earned it. They understood that there was no way for a captain to imprison or otherwise discipline a man while spending months in space, and so the corporal punishment allowed for an immediacy of consequences.

And then there are the Tartars. The captains who didn't just use the lash for serious offenses, but for every little thing, thinking it motivated the men to work harder or, as she suspected of Neals, because they enjoyed ordering it.

So stupid, she thought as she took her place at the base of the mast. She hated this task, as she'd have to identify the last man down herself and report him to Neals. Her stomach turned at the thought of being complicit in his barbarous cruelty, but she couldn't refuse a legal order.

It was the best of the topmen who bore the brunt of Neals' order, for they were the ones who went highest and farthest out on the yards to work the sail. Naturally it was they who were last down. *Flog your best and most skilled men — for no more reason than that they are the best. The man's a fool.*

High above her, the men had started down. Those nearest the mast on the yards clipping their safety lines to the guidewires and pulling themselves toward the hull. Those further out began jockeying for position, trying to reach the mast ahead of their fellows. The men were already dreading the next Captain's Mast, for Neals had announced that he'd be passing judgment on them for their offenses aboard Penduli Station. There was no little resentment about that, in addition to the dread, and not just from her own division — she'd heard the muttering and dark looks from the rest of the crew when Neals had announced his intentions.

One of the men on the topgallant yard, almost forty meters from the mast's base, unclipped his line and leapt off the yard for the mast. He caught hold of it in a narrow space between two shipmates, but it was as though his actions had spurred the others. A half dozen more spacers on the topgallants unclipped their lines and pushed off downward at an angle toward the mast. Bodies were suddenly flying across the intervening space, crashing into those already on the mast and knocking them loose to be pulled up short by their safety lines. But those who'd leapt had no lines attached and Alexis' blood chilled as she saw two, knocked off course by their fellows, miss the mast and sail past.

Several spacers already on the mast reached out to them or jumped from it themselves, relying on their own safety lines to keep them attached in an effort to reach their mates, but the two men were already too far away. The would-be rescuers were brought up short by their lines and could only watch helplessly as the two drifted away from the ship.

Alexis cried out and reached for the rescue gun at her belt. The officers each carried one for these circumstances, it used a charge of compressed gas to shoot a weighted bag attached to a line. She'd used hers once on *Merlin* when two men were cut loose from the masts during an action and she'd managed to save one of them.

Crying out again, this time in frustration, she saw that it wouldn't work. The men had already drifted out of the ship's field and entered the morass of *darkspace*. As their momentum slowed, the ship continued to sail away from them and she was too far down the bow of the ship, near the mast's base just above the sail locker. *Hermione* was too large for her shot to reach the men, so she began scrambling up the bow. If she could reach the top of the hull and a clearer shot, or even pull herself aft and catch up with them.

Her breath rasped, echoing in her helmet as she cleared the top curve of the hull. She transferred her safety line to one of the guidewires that ran the length of the ship and grasped it with both hands. Her lower mass meant she could accelerate faster than someone larger and if she could just get close enough to fire off the line. She glanced up and saw that she couldn't. The two men were already more than halfway down the hull and the squat bulk of the quarterdeck took up a full third of the upper hull. She'd have to maneuver around that to reach the stern and a clear shot, but the men were falling farther back faster than she'd be able to travel.

The bosun, on the other hand, had a clear shot. Alexis gripped the guidewire, fists tight as she watched him squat on the hull and aim his own rescue gun upward. There was a puff of escaping gas and the weighted bag flew toward the two men, *Hermione's* lights sparkling off the wire that trailed behind it.

The bag left the ship's field about ten meters up and started to slow and fall behind the ship as well. It arced slowly through the void toward the two figures, whose arms and legs were flailing in a vain effort to turn or propel themselves back to safety. The nearer man saw the bag crawling toward him and reached out his hand, straining to grasp it, but it slowed to a stop just out of his reach.

The men and the bag continued to fall behind, the rescue line playing out, and Alexis screamed in frustration at the horrifying tableau. The nearer man continued to reach and grasp, his hand opening and closing in a desperate effort to reach the bag that remained always just centimeters away.

The bosun dropped the now useless rescue gun and rushed for the hatch to the quarterdeck. Alexis yanked on the guidewire and pulled herself toward it too. If they could notify the captain in time to begin turning the ship, then the men could still be saved.

There was no battle in progress, no reason not to bring the ship about and sail back to retrieve the two spacers. If they saw the ship turn, then they'd have a chance to activate the chemical lights on their suits so that *Hermione* could find them, but they'd have to see the turn begin before they gave up hope of rescue, for many spacers would dump their air if a ship wasn't clearly returning for them, preferring to end things quickly rather than suffer through an extended period of time under the effects of *darkspace*.

Ahead of her, the bosun had entered the quarterdeck airlock. Alexis kept her speed up along the hull, barely slowing as she closed on the hatch herself and finally slammed bodily into the closed hatch.

She slid it open and then closed behind her, leaping across the small room for the valve that would fill the lock with air. She unsealed her helmet, grimacing as the difference in air pressure made her ears pop painfully. When the pressure in the lock had equalized with the quarterdeck she slid that hatch open and rushed in.

She froze as she saw the bosun facing Captain Neals. The bosun's face was set, the muscles in his jaw clenched and his eyes tight. Alexis saw his eyes narrow as he spoke, voice low and the only reason Alexis could hear his words was because the rest of the quarterdeck crew was deathly still and silent. The spacers at their stations stared fixedly at their consoles and even Lieutenant Dorsett and the marines stationed at the airlock and ladderway looked pointedly away from the two.

"Sir," the bosun said, "they're just behind us — it'd take no time at all."

Neals' nostrils flared and he clenched his own jaw. "Are you deaf, Mister Maslin? I believe I was clear." The bosun swallowed and started to speak, but Neals cut him off. "The answer is no."

Alexis couldn't believe what she was hearing, the captain couldn't be talking about stopping for the two men who'd gone overboard. He could not possibly be refusing to come about and pick them up. *Hermione* wasn't facing the enemy, she was on no urgent errand — coming about for the two who'd gone over would affect their speed less than the pointless sail evolutions he'd been putting Alexis' division through. Behind her, she was dimly aware of the lock cycling again and the hatch slid open.

"That is an order, Mister Maslin," Neals continued.

The bosun squared his shoulders and took a deep breath. "Aye, sir."

"*No!*"

All eyes on the quarterdeck turned to her. She knew it was a pointless, but couldn't stop herself. She couldn't let those men die without protesting the decision.

"You forget yourself, Carew," Neals said.

"Captain, please, you can't just leave them out there! It would take but a little time to come about!"

"This ship is on course and making good time. Come about and waste that for two lubbers who couldn't be bothered to clip on a line? I think not — worthless, the lot of them."

Alexis opened her mouth, but couldn't find the words to respond. She'd known Neals was cruel, heartless even, but to leave men to die like this? To call them worthless and lubbers, a deadly insult to experienced spacers, when they were, in truth, the most skilled sail handlers aboard? Her eyes burned as she tried to think of some argument, some words that would change the captain's mind.

Neals looked over her shoulder and his face grew angrier. "*What are you lot doing in my quarterdeck lock?*"

Alexis glanced behind her and saw that a half dozen spacers had crowded into the lock, their faces dark as they'd clearly heard what the captain had said about their mates. "No one sets foot on the quarterdeck without my leave — clear out!"

Despite the angry looks, discipline held and the spacers began affixing their helmets in preparation to return to the hull when a voice echoed from the airlock.

"*Bastard!*"

Everyone on the bridge froze. Neals' eyes widened and his face flushed red.

"Who said that?" He spun on the bosun. "Mister Maslin, take that man's name!"

The bosun swallowed heavily and took a step back. "Sir, I was looking away ... I didn't see who spoke."

"Damn you!" Neals' face grew redder. "Carew! Those men are of your division! Whose voice was that?"

Honestly Alexis had not been able to tell, with the voice's harshness and echoing from within the airlock combined with her own distraction at the captain's cruelty she hadn't recognized it. "Sir, I couldn't say ..."

"*What are you men still doing there?*" Neals yelled. "Clear the quarterdeck this instant! Marines!"

The marines reached for their sidearms, but the airlock hatch was already being closed by the men inside. Just before the hatch slammed shut, the voice sounded again.

"Bloody *bastard!*"

Neals stood still for a moment, staring at the hatch. His breath was ragged and Alexis could see the muscles of his jaw working. His lip curled up in a sneer.

"Carew," he said.

"Sir, I'm sorry," she said hurriedly. "The men are distraught, you understand ... their mates ..."

"Those men are of your division, Carew?"

"Yes, sir. I'm sorry, but I did not recognize the voice. I'll look into it, though, I swear —"

Neals raised a trembling hand to point at the airlock. "Get back out there, Carew, and bring them in through the proper lock, then assemble those men on the mess deck." He turned to the bosun. "Mister Maslin, pipe *All Hands* to the mess deck to witness punishment, then pass the word for Lieutenant Blowse — I want the marines turned out, every one, for I will surely hang the next man who speaks so to me."

ALEXIS LEFT the quarterdeck airlock and stepped out onto the hull, waving to get the attention of the men in her division even as *Hermione's* hull lights began flashing to call the full crew inside. She hurriedly made her way to the bow and gathered her men around her, ensuring that they entered the sail locker together and with no others.

She faced the inner hatch while the compartment filled with air, not wanting to turn around and see the others. Not wanting to see who was missing. Finally, the air stopped hissing in and she couldn't delay it any longer. She unsealed her helmet and lifted it over her head, turning to face the men.

"Matheny and Urton," she said dully, seeing who was missing.

"Yes, sir," Nabb said.

Alexis clenched her eyes shut, feeling them burn, but she didn't have time for tears. Matheny and Urton were gone, likely dead by now for they'd surely dumped their air when they saw that *Hermione* hadn't turned back for them. But the men in this room were still alive and she vowed to keep them so. She opened her eyes and met theirs in turn. Their gazes were hard and angry, red-rimmed and some with tears mixed into the sweat on their faces, but more angry now.

"The captain —" she began.

"That —"

"*Goodnowe!*" she barked harshly. "Not a word!" She took a deep breath and let it out, shuddering. "Not a single word from any of you, do you understand me? The captain, whatever else you may think of him, is the *captain* and he's promised to hang the next man who says a word against him."

"He can't —"

"Shut *up*, Goodnowe! Are you mad?" She looked around at the others desperately. "He will hang you, then put it in the log and go to his dinner with never a second thought." There was a pounding on the hatchway into the ship and she knew that she hadn't much time. "Please, lads, hold your tongues." She met each of their eyes in turn. "Matheny and Urton are gone, but I cannot bear to lose another of you this day."

"Aye, sir," Nabb said nodding and the others followed suit.

Alexis took another deep breath and slid the hatchway open then led the men up the companionway to the mess deck. The marines were already assembled, as well as most of the hands. She made her way aft to the wardroom hatch where the other officers waited. After a short wait while the rest of the hands made their way inside the ship and assembled, Captain Neals stepped forward. He surveyed the assembled men.

"Lieutenant Blowse," he said.

"Sir—"

"As I ordered, Lieutenant!"

"Arms!" Blowse ordered and the marines drew their sidearms. There was a collective intake of breath from the men, followed by muttering.

"*Silence!*" Neals yelled. "Lieutenant Blowse, the first man who moves from his place without orders is to be shot down, do you understand?"

"Sir—"

"Do you understand, Lieutenant?"

Blowse nodded to his marines who readied their weapons. "Aye, sir."

Neals took a deep breath. "Carew, bring your division forward — here in front."

Alexis stepped forward, wondering what Neals had in store. "Come on, lads, form up in front." The men of her division stepped forward, nervously eyeing the marines, and formed into lines in front of the officers. Neals stepped forward and jerked his head at her to stand back with the other officers.

"Two men short, this division is." Neals narrowed his eyes. "Two useless lubbers who couldn't be bothered to look to themselves Outside!"

Alexis concentrated on keeping her face impassive. She looked from man to man, meeting their eyes in turn. *Please, lads, hold your tongues. He'll do what he will, but, please, don't give him cause for more.*

"And someone in this division is an insubordinate cur!" Neals' face was turning red again. "Mister Maslin!"

"Aye, sir?"

"Every man in this division ... two dozen. Every man left, that is."

Alexis was stunned and she could tell by the silence on the deck that the others were as well. She looked around at the other officers and saw that their eyes were wide. Williard was pale and his mouth had fallen open. There were over two hundred men gathered on the deck and not a sound was heard for several seconds, then there a soft murmuring. Not from Alexis' division, she was relieved to see. All of them stood still, faces blank and jaws set. The murmuring grew louder and some of the gathered men shifted in their positions.

"*Silence!*" Neals bellowed. "I will have order on this ship! I will have discipline and attendance to my orders!"

The bosun cleared his throat and started to speak. "Sir, is this—"

"Be about it, Mister Maslin, you have your orders! And do not shirk, or I will see you at the gratings yourself, and your backbone bared this very day!"

"Aye, sir." The bosun jerked his head at one of his mates who rushed off to fetch the cat. He returned in a few minutes, all the while the assembled men stood still and silent, but Alexis watched their faces. *Hermione* had never been a happy ship and floggings were common. It was rare for a Captain's Mast to go by without at least one spacer finding himself bound to the gratings for some offense, but this ... a full division flogged at once? Twenty-two men?

The bosun took the red baize bag he stored the cat in from his mate and reached inside. He withdrew the cat o' nine tails, made from length of ship's cable. The cable was unwound to free its three cords, each made from three strands of braided line. Almost a meter long, its nine strands were knotted to add weight and stiffen the blows. Half its length was left solid, the better for handling. The boson grasped the handle and shook his arm loosely.

He eyed the assembled men and then looked to Captain Neals who gestured for him to get on with it. He drew a deep breath nodded to his mates. "Seize one of them up, lads."

The bosun's mates looked uncertain and Nabb stepped toward them, fists clenched.

"Nabb," the bosun warned.

"Ease off, Maslin," Nabb said. He met Alexis' eye and nodded curtly. "Someone's got to go first and show 'em how it's done. Form a line, lads," he called over his shoulder as he angrily stripped open his jumpsuit and shrugged out of it. "Captain's pleasure to see it in job lots today, so best be about it."

"Three dozen for that one, Mister Maslin," Neals said.

Nabb snorted and stepped over to a grating two of the bosun's mates had rigged to stand upright against a nearby column. He raised his hands to the corners and they bound him there with a thick cord.

The bosun looked down at the deck, shook his head once, and then lashed out with the cat. The strands struck Nabb's back with a sharp *crack* and drew lines of crimson across his flesh. The second blow followed closely on the first, the bosun not wanting to delay.

Alexis felt herself trembling. She'd stood through floggings before, far more often than she liked since coming aboard *Hermione,* but this was quite different. The crowd was strangely silent and she flinched as the *crack* of the next blow echoed through the quiet space. Usually there were shouts and calls from the assembled men — catcalls if they felt the offender deserved the punishment or, more common aboard this ship, shouts of encouragement if not. This time, though, there was no sound other than the cat landing across Nabb's back. The crew stood silent, faces set and staring, not at Nabb nor even the bosun, but at Captain Neals and the assembled officers.

When the last blow was dealt, the bosun's mates released Nabb's arms and he sank to his knees, blood flowing down his back and soaking his jumpsuit. The ship's surgeon started forward, but Neals held up a hand.

"No, Mister Rochford, I don't think so. He and his mates can care for one another when this is done, leave him there."

Rochford looked as though he might object, but then lowered his eyes and resumed his place.

Alexis grasped her hands, trying to stop their shaking.

I should have let them run when we were on Penduli. Should've walked every last one of them onto a merchantman myself and seen them well away.

The silence continued as the next man was bound in place and Alexis watched, horrified, as his back too was laid bloody by the bosun's cat. At some point, she felt wetness on her cheeks and realized that she was crying, tears flowing down her face as a third man took his place at the grating.

Blood was beginning to pool on the whiteness of the deck where the men who'd already been flogged knelt and the bosun was forced to run the strands of the cat between his fingers, stripping the blood from the strands for they'd become soaked with it and begun sticking together and landing as a solid clump. When the third man was cut down and allowed to collapse next to Nabb, the bosun tossed the cat angrily aside and jerked his head at one of his mates.

"Get another," he said quietly. "Bring them all." He looked to those waiting their turn. "And get to making more."

The wait was agonizing, though only a few minutes before the mate returned with three red bags and then rushed off again. Isom was bound up next and he was visibly terrified. He struggled with the bosun's mates and had to be dragged to the grating, thrashing and throwing his head from side to side. His struggles were so great that the bosun had to use his belt knife to bare the man's back, slicing his uniform open down its length. Isom's screams, shrill and panicked, when the first blow landed seemed to break the spell of silence and the murmurs of the crew could be heard between blows.

Alexis' vision blurred and she swayed on her feet as one after another the men of her division, the men she was most responsible for, went under the lash. She heard a soft noise to her left and looked over to see Lieutenant Williard swaying on his feet, pale and with one hand to his mouth. Ledyard caught her gaze and one corner of his mouth raised in a smirk. Through it all, Neals stood immobile, watching every blow.

THIRTEEN

When it was over and Captain Neals dismissed the hands, Alexis barely made it into the companionway before she ran. She leapt down the steep ladder, hardly letting her feet touch the narrow steps, past the gundeck, past the orlop deck and deep into the ship's hold. She slammed the hatchway open and then closed behind her and ran forward through the narrow aisles between the ship's stores. She didn't stop until she was far forward — as far from the quarterdeck and Neals as she could possibly get.

She'd wanted to rush to her men when it was over and see to their care, but they'd want their mates around them now, not an officer. Any officer.

"You *bastard!*" she cried, slamming her fist into the side of a container. "Vile, *bloody*, bastard!"

Over and over again she slammed her hands into the container until, finally exhausted, she sank to her knees. She wrapped her arms around her legs and buried her face in her crossed arms. The thought that she should have done something kept entering her mind, but what? And what good would it have done? If she'd said or done anything that stirred the men, then surely someone would have hung.

She'd seen the desire to do so in Neals' face, he'd simply been waiting for an excuse. She certainly couldn't have stopped him herself, the marines would have simply dragged her off to quarters or the brig.

Nothing had ever made her feel this helpless before, not even the inheritance laws on Dalthus that would keep her from her family's lands. At least those she could speak out against and try to change — here she had no power at all.

She sat for a long time, trying not to think about what she'd just witnessed — trying to think about nothing, really — when she heard footsteps approaching. Blinking and sniffing, she realized that she shouldn't be seen like this — the men should not see an officer behaving so and she certainly didn't want any of the other officers to see her.

Perhaps being found by Lieutenant Williard would not be so bad, he might have some advice or insight, though it would most likely be to simply ignore it all in the hopes for future advancement, but none of the others. She scrambled quickly to her side and eased her way into a narrow opening between two containers, vat nutrients to one side and thermoplastic precursor to the other, she saw. The shadows deepened the farther she went back and she crouched down, hoping that no one would notice her.

"This'll do, then."

"Can't be far enough away from that lot to suit me."

"And that's what I wanted to talk to ye about — gettin' far away."

"Ah, bollocks, Carville. More of that? I've told you before, running's a bad bet — and Neals'll give you no chance, besides."

Alexis recognized their voices now, Hacker and Carville, two men in Ledyard's division. She edged farther back into the recess, wanting even less to be seen now that she'd heard the men speak of running, deserting the ship at some opportunity.

Likely it was just talk, but no good could come of them knowing she'd heard. If she did nothing it would seem like she condoned it and if she reported them they'd likely face the lash themselves. After what she'd just witnessed, she'd have no hand in sending someone else to that fate. In fact, though she knew it was her duty to put an end to such talk or report it, she couldn't help but empathize with the two men. *Hermione* being what it was, life on the run as a deserter might seem preferable to many.

"Not runnin', no ... takin'."

"Taking what?"

"The ship, boyo, what'd y'think?"

Alexis' breath caught in her throat. The two weren't discussing desertion, they were talking mutiny. She froze and ducked her head. It was a much more serious matter now if the two men discovered her and knew she'd heard them. Desertion was serious, but mutiny, even the plotting of it with no action, which was how Neals would view even the barest mention, meant death.

"You're daft," Hacker said, whispering now. "I'd not say that on any ship ... on this one, bugger me if I'll listen to another word!"

"Have ye not had a enough, then? Two deaders fer no cause, an' the whole lot flogged fer afters!"

"Keep your bloody voice down, Carville! What if someone hears you?"

"Like Ledyard, the pissy, pox-ridden bastard? Did ye see the look he had? He's a taste fer seein' the lash, he does — you *know* he's put men up fer Captain's Mast just t'see it happen!"

"Carville—"

"Look," Carville said, his voice lower. "We could do it, we could. Most o'the crew'd stand aside an' see which way things blew. No more'n twenty men movin' at the right time and the ship's ours."

"To do what with? Can you navigate enough to get anywhere? Didn't think so. You haven't thought this through."

"Need one o' the officers, then. Carew might — she's no great love of the captain, neither, her. Williard'd want t'save his own skin any way he could. One o' t'other snotties, once we'd scared 'em proper."

"And do what with the rest of them? Have you even thought about after?"

"Too bloody right I've thought about after! Bloody *dreamed* about it! Neals gets his and that little shit, Ledyard, too!"

"Shh! Damn you, Carville, you'll get us both hung!"

"It's comin' 'ave no doubt. Weren't the onliest ones headin' off fer a private talk, us. Never seen a ship this bad — it's comin'."

There was a long pause.

"You may be right—"

"You mark me, Morrey Hacker, it's comin'."

The two men were silent for a time and Alexis began to wonder if they'd left without her hearing their footsteps. Then Hacker spoke again and his words sent a chill through her.

"If it's coming, Carville, I'll not want to just be towed along in it."

The two men walked off, still murmuring to each other. Alexis waited in the shadows until she was certain they were gone and then emerged. She straightened her uniform and bit her lip, wondering just how many other secret meetings were taking place deep in the ship's hold. And what was she to do now?

She couldn't imagine telling Captain Neals — his reaction would be something she'd not wish on any of the men. The First Lieutenant, Dorsett, was who she should tell, according to all propriety. It was his responsibility to see the captain's orders carried out and to manage the crew, but Dorsett was a non-entity aboard the ship, so overshadowed by Neals that he rarely left his cabin when not on watch. Ostensibly Williard was in charge of the midshipmen and was who Alexis should go to for advice, but she'd thought more about what he'd said over dinner on the station. She didn't feel that he would know how to handle what she'd heard. There were, in fact, no officers aboard *Hermione* that she felt enough respect for to confide in.

Maslin, she thought. The bosun stood in an odd place aboard ship, neither an officer nor fully one of the crew. The men might hate him for his role in enforcing discipline, but they respected him too. *Yes, I'll speak to Maslin.*

"LADS, there's something I'd like to say before we head out."

The chatter in the sail locker quieted, though it hadn't been that great to begin with. Alexis had spoken to Mister Rochford about the men in her division, but to no avail — he'd already suggested to the captain that they be excused from duty while the wounds from their floggings healed, but Neals had rejected the idea out of hand. By the time Alexis had approached Rochford after supper, he was quite put out about it, but there was nothing he could do.

And so, the very day after being flogged, all twenty-two men left in her division were crowded into the sail locker, shifting uncomfortably as the heavy vacsuits settled against their backs, preparing for a watch Outside working the sails. Alexis was grateful for a chance to go out on the hull herself, for it would give her an opportunity to speak to the bosun in private, but she did wish that her men could be spared the work until they healed.

"I know yesterday was hard, lads." She hesitated, not sure of how far to go or what to say, then pushed on. "It was horrible, and I wish I could have done something—"

"Never blamin' you, Mister Carew, it's that bastard Nea—"

"That's what I mean to speak about, Nabb. You must all watch your tongues and not give him any excuse. I've … I've heard some things that others aboard are saying." She looked around the compartment, meeting their eyes in turn and noting which faces had gone still and guarded. "If there's talk aboard this ship, dangerous talk, then I should be very put out if any of you were to be involved."

"Only so much a man can take, sir," Nabb said, staring down at the deck.

Alexis nodded. "I think a man might take quite a lot more than he expects, if he'll only look ahead to where another course might land him." She shifted her vacsuit's helmet in her hands in preparation for donning it. "Just think of the consequences before acting, lads, and don't disappoint me, will you?"

She settled her helmet over her head to a chorus of "Aye, sir."

They'll trade a pound's worth of prize certificates for a three-penny upright and I ask them to think through the consequences?

Once they'd all donned their helmets, Alexis dumped the air from the sail locker and they filed out onto the hull. The men who'd had the sail watch before them waited impatiently to reenter the ship. Alexis walked to the base of the mast and looked around. Being Outside normally calmed her, the roiling, black shapes of *darkspace* in the distance and the cerulean glow of the charged sails were something she eagerly awaited the chance to return to, but not today.

She caught sight of the bosun's distinctly colored vacsuit and swallowed hard. She did not relish the thought of this conversation — surely no good would come of telling anyone of what she'd overheard, but she couldn't think of any good that would come of *not* doing so either.

Consequences, indeed.

She made her way to the bosun's side and gestured that she'd like to speak with him. He leaned toward her and touched his helmet to hers.

"Yes, Mister Carew?" he asked, voice echoing in her helmet.

Alexis opened her mouth, but found that she simply didn't have the words. She'd tossed and turned most of the night wondering what to say to him, how to describe what she'd heard. Should she just come right out and say, "Hacker and Carville and some others I don't know are plotting mutiny?" Or, perhaps, try to hide their identities, but would Maslin believe that at all? And what about the hypocrisy of why she, herself, had been in the hold, what if he asked about that?

Why, yes, Mister Maslin, I was down there cursing the captain's soul to Hell itself and quite wishing the vat of nutrients I was pounding my fists on was, indeed, his vile, toadish face ... but, please, do focus on two men I overheard.

"Mister Carew?"

Perhaps they were only venting their spleens, as I was. But, no, the closed faces of the men back in the sail locker told her that things had gotten further than two mates talking. She could, possibly, try to talk to the other hands — start with Hacker and Carville, then move on to others, and appeal to them take no rash action.

"Mister Carew?"

"I'm sorry, Mister Maslin, my thoughts flew away with me for a moment." No, the bosun was the only choice. "There's talk I think you should be aware of, Mister Maslin. Amongst the men. No names, but I —"

Alexis grunted as she was suddenly shoved forward, stumbling and almost losing contact with the hull. She spun around and saw Ledyard standing near the bosun, his vacsuit recognizable by the midshipman's stripes and the fact that it was only a little larger than her own and his arms still outstretched from shoving her. He gestured abruptly to her and she touched her helmet to his.

"Damn you, Ledyard!" she said. "I'm senior to you and I've had enough of your games! This isn't the time for them."

"Captain Neals sent me for you, as you seem not to be watching the lights. His compliments and he'll see you on the quarterdeck instanter."

Her irritation at Ledyard's disrespect vanished, replaced by worry. If she'd missed a signal to report, Neals would be furious, but what on earth could he want when they'd only just come out onto the hull?

She followed Ledyard back to the airlock and through onto the quarterdeck.

"Carew," Neals said as soon as she entered, "your division is suited and on the hull?"

"They are, sir."

"Very good." He looked down at his tablet, tapped it a few times, and then looked back to her. "I should like them to unstep the mainmast, Carew. Please report back to me the moment this is done."

Alexis blinked, uncertain she'd heard correctly. The masts were normally unstepped, folded down to lie flush against the hull, only when the ship was in normal space — and even then only when they'd be using the conventional drive. The fore- or mizzen-mast might be unstepped in *darkspace* to clear a way for another ship to come alongside, but rarely the main. Unstepping the mainmast while still in *darkspace* and relying only on the fore- and mizzen-masts would cut their speed by almost half.

"Unstep the mainmast and report back instanter, sir," she repeated to ensure she'd heard correctly. "Aye, sir." She went back out onto the hull, still wondering at the purpose, but relayed the order to her men.

They set about the complex task, first furling the mesh sails and taking them down to be stored in the sail locker, then lowering the long, bulky yards for storage as well. Though there was no gravity, the sails and yards still had mass and controlling them, each tens of meters long, was grueling. Following the yards, the men had to release and coil the rigging, both standing and running — hundreds of meters of cable that secured and braced the mast and yards to the hull and each other. And finally the mast itself, where they had to unlock and lower each of the telescoping segments carefully into the one below it and, at last, unlock the base of the mast to let it hinge back onto the hull and lock into place.

All told, it took the twenty-two men of her division over an hour to complete the process. Alexis watched them through every step, lending a hand where she could and ensuring that no step was overlooked. She could see the men were moving slower and more carefully than they normally would, their backs painful from the flogging the day before.

When the last clamp was in place around the now folded mast, she returned to the quarterdeck.

"The mainmast is unstepped, sir," she reported.

Neals consulted his tablet. "Your men are slow, Carew. Unhappily so." He frowned. "Please step the mainmast and set all plain sail. Report back here when it's done."

"Aye, sir." She left the quarterdeck and went out onto the hull once more, relaying the order to her men. She could see their shoulders slump even through the bulky vacsuits as they, too, came to understand the reason for Neals' orders.

The flogging wasn't enough for the bastard, was it? She clenched her jaw, furious. *No, he'd make them work the day after, reopening the cuts from the lash let their sweat from the effort add to the sting.*

Alexis watched as the bulky mast was raised again and extended, the rigging made fast and the yards hoisted up, before the sails were brought out. All plain sail, he'd ordered — main, top, topgallant, and royal sails sent up the mast, made fast to their yards and let go. Even the sight of the sails glowing with azure light and sparks of white as they were charged and filled with the *darkspace* winds to pull the ship along couldn't alleviate her anger.

"Mainmast stepped and all plain sail, sir," she announced, restraining the urge to slide the airlock hatch closed with as much force as she could muster.

"Far too slow, Carew," Neals said, not bothering to look up from his tablet. "Again, if you please."

FOURTEEN

Alexis closed her eyes and slumped under the stream of hot water. She'd be using most of her water allotment for this shower, but felt the need to wash away the last several hours. Neals had kept her division working throughout their watch and on into the next, never letting up — the only respites they'd had were brief trips into the sail locker to charge the air and water in their suits and then return to the masts.

As soon as she'd realized the captain's purpose, Alexis had joined in the work, lending a hand wherever she could to lessen the load on the men of her division. Always rushing from the mast to the quarter-deck hatch when they were nearly done, so that she could report to Neals as quickly as possible. She truly had no idea whether they were completing the tasks faster or slower each time, for Neals never said — he responded to each of her reports with a grunt and, "Again and faster, if you please."

When he finally ordered them back inside after stepping the mast for the last time and furling the topgallant and royal, the men collapsed onto the benches in the sail locker. Alexis slumped against the wall next to the inner hatch, for, by tradition, officers stood in the locker while the men sat, in recognition of their hard work. She didn't even have the strength to feel moved when Nabb elbowed his neighbor to slide down the bench and motioned for her to join them. She simply sat gratefully and pondered that the men she commanded were so much more her familiars than the officers who were her peers.

"Two lads left behind to die soes we'd not lose time — and what was all this about, then?"

"Enough, Nabb," Alexis said quietly.

"Can't take no more," Isom moaned, doubled over to rest his head on his knees. "I'm just a bloody clark!"

"No clark you! Yer in the Navy now!"

"Neals' Navy! Which're a damn sight harder than t'other one!"

Alexis stood and resumed her place by the inner hatch. Her legs were a bit weak, but she felt it best to be clear she was speaking as an officer.

"Look, you lot, I know a good whinge is a spacer's natural right—" She glanced at the pressure gauges. Once all of the suits were recharged with air and ready for an emergency, they'd be going back into the ship, which gave her little time. "— and you've far more cause than most or ever, but watch your tongues. Give no one cause to call you out for it."

"Sorry, sir," Nabb said. "And you lot mark her, too. Best t'be still on this boat."

The sharp trilling of a bosun's whistle sounded from the speakers in the head and broke her out of her reverie.

All hands? she wondered as she shut off the water and hurriedly grabbed a towel. She quickly rung most of the water from her hair and tried to dry it as much as she could in the few moments she could spare, then threw on a new uniform and grabbed up the pile of her vacsuit and the sweat-soaked uniform she'd worn Outside. What could Neals possibly want now?

She dumped her vacsuit and uniform in a corner of her berth and tied her wet hair back in a ponytail before hurrying to the companionway and up to the mess deck where the men were assembling. She'd come up forward and the space in front of her was blocked by the broad backs of the assembled men.

"Make a lane!" she yelled.

The crew moved to either side, clearing a space for her to hurry down the length of the deck to where the officers were grouped aft. She was beginning to count herself lucky that Neals hadn't arrived yet when he stepped through the aft hatch and glared at her.

"Good of you to join us, Carew," he said as she took her place in line with the other midshipmen.

Neals was in a vacsuit and carrying his helmet, which surprised her because he very rarely left the interior of the ship, relying on the officers and bosun to see to things on the hull.

"I'm sorry, sir," she said, taking her place.

Neals handed his suit helmet to Lieutenant Dorsett. "As you're here, call your division forward."

Alexis swallowed heavily, dreading what he might have in store for them now, and stepped forward. "Port watch, main topmen, up front with you!"

"I've just been out to inspect the state of my rigging, Mister Carew, and what do you suppose it is I've found?"

"I could not say, sir."

"I found the port-four gasket on the topgallant left untied, Mister Carew! That is what I have found!"

Alexis clenched her jaw. She wanted to scream at him. *Work them for nigh seven hours and then go looking for aught to complain of? A single bloody gasket left undone?*

"Who was responsible for that gasket, Carew? Name the man for me, please."

Alexis froze. *He's looking to flog one of them again — he'll not be satisfied until a man dies there before him.*

"The name, Carew!"

She glanced toward the men and caught his eye. Isom, the little legal clark, caught up by the Press and who should be spending his days reading judges' decisions instead of hauling on lines in the depths of *darkspace*. He knew it, as well, she saw in his face. He paled and might have fallen if the men to either side hadn't grabbed his arms and steadied him. *No, I'll not give you another of my lads.*

"The responsibility is mine, sir," she said.

Neals' eyes narrowed.

"They were in my charge. I knew they were tired," she continued, "and I should have checked the work, sir. The fault lies with me. I am sorry." *Confine me to my berth, stop my pay ... dismiss me from the Service, if you like, you bastard, but I'll not play this game for you.*

Neals blinked as though confused by what she'd said. "Sorry?"

"I apologize, sir, for my inattention."

The captain was silent for a long moment, then, "Beg."

Alexis wasn't sure she'd heard him correctly. "Sir?"

"Beg, Carew. You wish to apologize, to be forgiven your lapse? Then beg for it."

Her world seemed to have narrowed to her and the captain. She was dimly aware of the assembled crew and a low muttering. She sighed — it was a small price to pay, she supposed, but still it galled her. She might be new to the Navy, but she did know that officers should not be treated so.

"Sir, I ... I apologize for my lapse and beg you to forgive it."

Neals narrowed his eyes and she saw his lips twitch. "From your knees, Carew."

She heard a gasp and Lieutenant Williard stepped toward the captain, saying something about officers and honor but she couldn't seem to focus on anything but Neals.

"She has no honor, lieutenant! She's a jumped-up little bint who's no place here!"

"No," Alexis said softly.

Neals spun back to her. "What did you say?"

"No, sir, I will not kneel. I admit my fault in not noticing the gasket. I will even beg your forgiveness for it." She shook her head. "I will kneel to my Queen, sir, and to no other."

"Are you refusing to obey my orders?"

"I believe no Queen's Officer would obey such an order, sir." She knew it would be too much, going too far, but the words came from her mouth as though of their own accord. "And no honorable man would give it."

There was silence for a moment. Neals' face grew very still and then he smiled.

"Mister Youngs!"

"Aye, sir?" the purser called.

"You have the ship's muster book?"

"Aye, sir." He pulled his tablet from pocket and looked to the captain expectantly.

Alexis close her eyes, almost feeling relief. The tension ebbed out of her. *And here it comes, dismissed.* She'd be put ashore at the next port and have to make her own way home to Dalthus. Her grandfather would be quite disappointed in her ... or perhaps not, after he'd heard the details. She felt a twinge of guilt at abandoning her men, but they might get on better without her. If she were not there as a focus for Neals' ire ... he'd still be a brutal, cruel bastard, but her lads might catch less of it.

"Carew is disrated. Mark it accordingly."

Alexis' eyes sprang open and her blood ran cold.

"Sir!" Williard called out and shouts sounded from the assembled men.

"Arms!" Lieutenant Blowse shouted and his marines drew their sidearms. The men stilled, but there was a low current of muttering.

Alexis was dimly aware of what was occurring around her, but she focused on the captain's words. *Disrated? Could he really?*

Disrating was something she'd heard of happening to the petty officers — the bosun, the warrants, and master's mates who came up from the ranks of spacers. To be disrated was to be demoted back to the crew, it was not something that happened to officers who held a commission. Midshipmen, however, lived in an odd, middle-ground — being officers-in-training and not holding commissions from Admiralty. They were, in fact, on par with the master's mates in some respects.

He can, she thought. *And I've turned sixteen, so there's not even that to keep me off the crew.*

She'd expected to be dismissed and have to leave the Navy. She had not expected to be sent into the crew as a common spacer. She had no real objection to it — she'd originally tried to join as a common spacer before Captain Grantham of *Merlin* had brought her aboard as midshipman — but not on this ship.

Not on Hermione.

Neals was speaking again and she stared at him in shock, the words not truly registering.

"And as you've been good enough to admit the untied gasket was your fault ..." He smiled. "Mister Maslin, rig a grating and send for your cat, if you please."

ALEXIS WAS MOVING as though in a dream.

She was peripherally aware of the sounds and movement around her — more shouts from the assembled men, Neals' voice and that of Lieutenant Blowse barking out commands, Williard saying something to the captain and being shouted down, and, lastly, the bosun's mates upending a grating and affixing it to a column — but she seemed unable to move or speak. Which was quite odd, because she *was* moving. Stepping away from the other officers — *not 'other' now, I suppose* — and towards the men. She heard a voice which sounded quite like her own, which was even odder, as she was certain she was entirely unable to speak.

"*Nabb!* Broady! Scholer! Back to your places the lot of you and mind your tongues! Don't you dare disappoint me, lads, or I'll know the reason why!"

Is this really happening? How on earth had things gone so wrong so quickly? Though she probably should have expected this or something like it. Neals had made it clear from the moment she'd come aboard that he hated her and thought she had no place on a Queen's Ship.

Her vision seemed to have narrowed to the rigged grating and it was drawing closer, though she had no conscious awareness of walking toward it. The thought entered her head that she would not be dragged to her place screaming as Isom had been. She thought of Nabb, stepping forward first to "show the lads how it's done," his disdain for the man who'd ordered it clear in his every movement. And of Robert Alan — the first man she'd ever seen flogged aboard *Merlin* — who, for whatever else he might have been, had stepped forward and grasped the grating with an almost casual indifference.

I must do no less.

She looked down and found her hands already at the collar of her jumpsuit, but trembling and shaking so that she was unable to make them grasp the fastenings. She heard the bosun speak and realized that he was right beside her.

"Leave that, Mister Carew," he said, his voice soft and not unkind. "We'll cut the back and ... and leave you what decency there is aboard this ..."

"Thank you, Mister Maslin." Her voice, at least, sounded steady to her, though she wasn't at all certain where the words were coming from. "I do find myself altogether unable."

She tried to raise her hands to the grating's corners, but found her arms were too weak. Two bosun's mates took her wrists gently and raised them. She almost laughed when the straps they'd attached to each corner wouldn't reach and they had to reattach them lower on the grating.

"Thank you," she heard herself whisper, absurdly, and one of them looked at her in surprise, then quickly away unable to meet her eyes. "It's not your fault, Lain — nor yours, Hayer. Do as you're ordered."

She felt someone close behind her and she flinched as cold metal touched her neck just under her collar. It ran down her spine, sending a shiver through her and she heard the hiss of tearing cloth. She heard Neals was saying something and then the bosun, but she didn't understand them. All of her attention seemed focused on the white thermoplastic of the grating directly in front of her.

Then came the whistle of something moving fast through the air and a loud *crack*. An endless moment, in which she thought to herself, *This must be another nightmare. It can't truly be happening.* And lines of fire flashed across her bare back.

FIFTEEN

ALEXIS WOKE LYING on her stomach, an odd position for her to be sleeping in. She pulled her arms under herself and started to rise, but gasped and fell back to the surface of the cot as pain tore through her back. Though the room was dark, she could tell from the slightly antiseptic smell that she was in the sick berth on the orlop deck.

"Mister Rochford?" The memory of what had happened and why she was here came to her, and she wondered if it was even appropriate for her to call for him directly, seeing as how she was no longer a midshipman. "Mister Rochford, sir?"

She twisted, slowly and carefully, and eased her legs off the cot to sit up, feeling the skin on her back pull and then gasping as something separated. The captain must not have allowed them to seal the wounds. They'd hurt more that way and for longer, serving as a reminder. *And scar.* She'd seen enough of that in her short time in the Navy. Well-treated, the marks of the lash would leave thin, white lines that would fade in time. Left alone to be pulled open again every time she moved wrong, the scars would form wide and knotted. Either way, she'd bear a remembrance of Captain Neals for the rest of her days.

Moving more slowly and carefully, she sat up and looked around in the dark, puzzled. The lights were off completely, something that she'd never seen in the sick berth. They'd be dimmed so the men could sleep, but there was always some light for the berth attendants to move about.

"Mister Rochford, sir!" she called out more loudly.

"*Shh!*" There was a clatter in the darkness. "Damn your eyes, be quiet! They'll hear you!"

She sensed someone moving toward her in the darkness. "Mister Rochford?"

"It is," he whispered. "Lie back down and be still, now, but especially be quiet!"

"What's happening? Why are you hiding here in the dark?"

"The men are about and there've been gunshots. They've someone just outside the door. Quiet now, or he'll hear!"

They've done it. She closed her eyes and her heart fell. For the men who'd mutinied, and even for some of those who hadn't, there'd be no turning back. Admiralty would sentence them to death and hunt them the rest of their days.

"If there's a man outside the hatch, Mister Rochford, do you think they don't know you're in here? Help me stand, please."

"It's best you stay here, I think. Wait until it settles down and see what happens."

Alexis eased off the bed, ignoring the pain from her back and shuffled through the dark toward where she thought the hatch must be. She wished she had a uniform to put on, but was uncertain which she should wear — that of a midshipman or a common spacer. *Anything but this, I suspect.* She had on only a sick berth gown, open at the back, and regulation underpants. As she shuffled through the dark sick berth, she felt the underpants sticking to her body where her blood had dried after the flogging. *I must be a sight.*

"Will you turn a bloody light on, Mister Rochford? There's little point in hiding, I think." The ship's surgeon didn't answer, so Alexis continued on her way. She felt along the wall until she reached the hatchway and slid it open.

She squinted against the light outside and recognized the spacer standing by the hatchway. The man straightened from where he was leaning against the bulkhead and Alexis saw that he was holding a pistol. *They've done it. They've really gone and done it.*

"Lufkin."

"Mister Carew, sir, I'll have to ask that you stay in the sick berth, sir."

Alexis considered how to proceed. A mutiny could go one of many different ways. She wondered how many of the officers and crew were dead already. "Is the ship taken, then, Lufkin?"

The spacer looked down at the deck, then back at her. "It's done, sir. They're all up on the mess deck considering things right now."

"And how many are dead already?"

Lufkin looked down again and said nothing. Alexis took a step around him and headed for the companionway.

"Mister Carew, sir! I'm to keep you here!"

"Follow and help me or shoot me in the back, one, Lufkin," she said, not looking back, "but I'm going up to speak to the lads."

"Mister Carew, sir, at least dress a bit!" Lufkin said, rushing after her.

She started climbing the steep ladderway to the gundeck and then up to the mess deck. A few steps up and she gasped as she felt a new tear in her back and a warm trickle flowed down her skin.

"You're bleeding, sir, please come back down and let the surgeon fix it up!"

"Just keep them off me, Lufkin, and let me have my say. Then I'll do as you ask. Fair enough?"

She could hear them now, a muted roar of shouting from the deck above. She reached the hatch and rested her hand on it and took a deep, steadying breath. She slid the hatchway open and the roar of shouting men flowed over her. Men were crowded onto the mess deck, many pushing and shoving. She could only see a few feet in, as her view was blocked by the backs of those standing closest to the hatch.

"Let me through, lads!" she called, but they didn't move. There were more shouts and a gunshot rang out, followed by a cry of pain. Alexis raised her arms and struck the two nearest men hard on their backs. *Make a lane! Lively now!*" The men spun around angrily, arms raised to strike, but froze when they saw her. "Did you hear me, lads? *Make a lane!*"

The two men stepped aside and she strode out into the mess deck, but didn't get far — the deck was crowded and chaotic and her first steps brought her to face two more backs. Without her having to ask, the two men who'd first gotten out of her way tapped the next two on the shoulder. They turned around and after a moment's stare at her, quieted and moved out of her way. She stepped forward and the process repeated, until, by the time she was halfway down the length of the deck, all of the men were silent and had turned to watch her.

She knew she must look a fright. Her hair, which she'd never properly dried, was out of its customary ponytail and it had dried in an unkempt rat's nest. She was barefoot and barelegged below the sick berth gown that reached past her knees. That gown gaped open in the back and the air was cool on her bare skin and the marks from the bosun's cat. More than one of the stripes from that cat had reopened and several trickles of blood ran down her back. The sting from those marks made her wince with each step, but she clenched her jaw and kept going.

A lane had opened up to the other end of the deck and she could see what had been the focus of the men's attention. Captain Neals, dressed in his nightshirt and surely dragged from his bed, was kneeling on the deck, his hands bound behind him. Next to him were several of the officers, in uniform or not depending on whether they'd been on watch, also kneeling and bound. She saw that Lieutenant Dorsett was missing, and Lieutenant Roope, as was Midshipman Brattle.

As she drew closer, she saw the first bodies. Three, scarlet-clad, piled by the far bulkhead. She swallowed hard and forced her eyes away. She'd known the marines would be the hardest hit by this — the men would have to take those on guard and stop the others from rallying to defend the officers. Some of those she'd sparred with every day and who'd become the closest thing to friends she had aboard *Hermione* would be lying dead on the deck, killed by spacers she'd worked with and cared for just as much.

She forced that thought down, as well — this wasn't the time for the right and wrong of what the men felt they'd been forced to and there'd be time enough for the dead later, now was for the living and to see that they stayed that way.

Morrey Hacker, pistol in hand, was standing amongst the kneeling officers on the raised platform from which Captain Neals typically addressed the crew. He glared at her as she approached and then behind her.

"I told you to keep her in the sick berth, Lufkin!"

"And what was I to do when she wouldn't, then?"

Hacker waved his free hand in frustration. "Put her back through the bloody hatch, man! She's not but half your size, for pity's sake!"

"I see you weren't just towed along in it after all, Morrey Hacker," Alexis said.

He returned his gaze to her and narrowed his eyes at her words. "We've no quarrel with you, Mister Carew, you're not like these others." He waved his hand at the kneeling officers. "Best you stay in the sick berth until it's all over."

"Until what's all over, Hacker? It appears it is. What's left to be done, then?"

"Back to the sick berth, Mister Carew — this is none of yours here!"

"I think I'd like to address the crew, Hacker." She stopped just short of the platform at the very edge of the crowd.

"We've taken the ship! We'll hear no more from officers!"

"But I'm not an officer, am I, Hacker?" She took a step forward.

She could see some confusion in Hacker's eyes. He hadn't wanted to be involved in mutiny, but if it was coming he'd wanted to lead it. And now she could tell he wasn't entirely sure where to take it. "If I'm disrated and one of the crew, then I've as much right to be here as any man aboard, haven't I, Hacker?" He started to speak, but Alexis cut him off, seeing an opportunity. She hopped up onto the platform, feeling yet another line on her back split open and fresh blood flow. "And if I am an officer, then I should be with the others, yes? Kneeling there. Are you captain now, Hacker, and we should kneel for you? Do you want me kneeling, just like Neals did?"

Hacker looked around and realized what it must look like, him standing alone on the platform with the officers kneeling. "No, damn you! That's not what I meant! You're twisting —"

"Let her speak!" Someone in the crowd yelled, followed by others.

"Her back's bloodied as ours, she's the right!"

Hacker shrugged and Alexis turned to the assembled crew. Her eye was drawn to the port side where a small group of men, perhaps no more than sixty, huddled looking on. Those would be the ones who'd not participated in the mutiny. Most of those who held a warrant position to the ship where there — the carpenter, the gunner, the purser, and their mates. Those men held too much position to risk it in mutiny. She didn't see the bosun and wondered if Mister Maslin was now one of the dead, but she did see most of the men of her division in the group. She didn't take the time to mark them all, but she was relieved they hadn't participated.

But the rest of the crew clearly had and she was surprised that it had been so many. She would have expected, as she'd overheard in the hold, that it would be a much smaller group.

She took a deep breath.

"So what should I speak to, lads? You've taken the ship and there's no going back from that," she called out. She tried to meet each man's eyes in turn, noting who looked away and who glared back at her. She waved a hand at the kneeling officers. "Is it this lot you're deciding on?"

She could tell from their silence that this was it. With the actual fight for the ship over, there'd be some who'd be eager to take their revenge on the officers and others who'd have had enough of the violence. Could she appeal to the latter and how? She scanned their faces again. The hard cases, the ones from the gaols, would be no help — they'd not care, might even relish the killing. And they'd, none of them, want to hear about the right or wrong of it. She wasn't sure of that herself. For Neals, at least, she could see the justice in it for the men to have their revenge.

But that would be all it was, revenge. Not killing in the heat of a fight, but cold with the victim unarmed and defenseless. And she knew from her dreams that it was a thing that haunted you, even when it was needful as it had been with Horsfall. She'd not want Captain Neals haunting any of her lads' dreams. But that wasn't a thing they'd want to hear, either. They'd not welcome the suggestion that they'd one day regret the act — it would seem cowardly to men like this. No, the reason would have to be something else.

"You can't kill them," Alexis said simply. "Not now they're taken."

"After all they've done it's only just!"

"Even little Ledyard, there?" she asked pointing.

"He's the worst of the lot!"

"And look at what example he had!" she cried pointing at Captain Neals. "Will you kill a child for doing as he's taught is right?"

"Neals then!"

"Not even him!" she yelled back. "Look, lads, you've taken the ship and you'll be known for that now, but don't make it worse with more killing."

"Hang for the ship or hang for the ship and killin' them! It's all the same!" one of the men called out.

Alexis hopped down from the platform and rushed forward to confront him, the other men standing quickly out of her way.

"It's not all the same, Waller Campton! Not one bit! It's one thing to kill a man in heat, but to do it cold, as this would be? That'll be looked on differently and you well know it!" She turned slowly looking at the men around her, singling out those she knew sent part of their pay home. "You all have families. Wives, children, fathers, mothers ... what you've done will affect them, too. Annis, what will your mum think when she hears?"

"You leave me mum out o' this!"

"Well, and it's you who brought her into it, didn't you! When the word reaches her, what will she think of you? What will her neighbors think of her?" She tried to remember what she knew of the men around her, who had a wife and children and which sent money home to an elderly parent each month, singling them out one by one.

"'There goes old Mrs. Whitehurst, there, aye — you know her boy, Halden, was part of that business on *Hermione*, poor lad to be serving under that bastard of a captain, just couldn't take it no more.'" She turned to another. "'Poor Mrs. Ficke, her man Dunleigh had no choice but to run, the way he were treated.'

"But kill them in cold blood, lads, and you know it'll be different. It'll be the busy neighbors whispering and the cuts from the shopkeepers and the parson's ladies talking. 'Oh, Mrs. Hatchell, her boy went bad, you know. Fair bathed in blood on that ship.'"

She froze as she turned, seeing Nabb in the circle around her. *Oh, Nabb, not you.* She felt her chest clench at the thought of what would be in store for him now. He'd have to run far, for any of the mutineers caught would surely hang. There'd be no more of his pay sent home to wife and children, and surely there'd never be enough coin for them to join him wherever he made his way.

"'Look at Mrs. Nabb, there,'" she continued, hardening her gaze, "'walking bold as brass with her little ones, and the oldest just the age of the boy her Wallis strangled with his own hands on that *Hermione*.' Is that what you want for them, lads? Is it?"

"Why're ye trying to save 'em, Mister Carew? They treated ye bad as us, the lot of 'em."

Alexis stepped up to Nabb and raised her hands to cup his face tenderly.

"Damn you, Wallis Nabb, are you so blind? It's not them I'm trying to save."

SIXTEEN

"WAIT. Commodore Balestra, she will come soon," the Hanoverese lieutenant said as he slid shut the hatch. The two armed guards stayed behind, one to either side of the hatchway.

Alexis shuffled nervously into line with the other officers from *Hermione*, not at all certain she should be there with them. Though the crew had kept her with the officers since the mutiny, Neals had not spoken to her — not a word, and the other officers had followed his lead. So not only was she at loose ends as to her status amongst *Hermione's* crew, she was even more confused about her status with the Hanoverese.

After her appeal to the crew aboard *Hermione* had been successful in quelling their desire for revenge, the officers had been locked in Neals' cabin for the duration. Alexis had gone with them and so knew little more than they did about the decisions the crew made, but she did feel their decisions made a certain sense. Left with control of a warship, they had few choices of where to go — two, really. Or only one, if one considered that the ship was in a border area between only two nations and staying in New London space would see them taken up and hanged for mutiny.

Instead, they'd sailed for the nearest Hanoverese port.

In the end, they hadn't needed Alexis or any of the officers to navigate the ship. It had only taken a very bright helmsman who had his eye on one day becoming a sailing master, and, so, had listened intently to the navigation lessons the midshipmen were given while he was at the helm. After successfully proving himself by sailing to the nearest uninhabited star system, he'd plotted *Hermione's* course toward the border.

What the Hanoverese had thought of a New London frigate sailing into their system with her colors doused and signaling surrender without a single shot being fired, Alexis couldn't imagine. She did know that many amongst the crew, even amongst the mutineers, were unhappy with the decision — it was one thing to rebel against Neals, it was quite another to turn the ship over to the enemy in time of war.

Alexis didn't approve, but she also couldn't see an alternative that would leave the men alive and free, for the butcher's bill from the mutiny was already greater than she could bear. Fully half her beloved marines and their officers, down to the last sergeant, were dead, along with two dozen of the crew. None of her own lads were dead, thankfully, but she'd lost Nabb forever, no matter what the Hanoverese had in store.

At least for her, Rochford had been allowed — ordered by the crew, really — to treat the wounds from her flogging. The pain was mostly gone now, though her back still felt tight and odd, something the men told her she'd get used to in time.

The Hanoverese lieutenant slid the hatch open and gestured for them to enter. Alexis was at the end of the line, behind even Ledyard. The Hanoverese had insisted on keeping her with the officers so far, despite Neals' attempts to tell them she belonged with the crew.

As she entered the commodore's day cabin, Alexis felt her mouth open in shock and quickly closed it. It wasn't the commodore's rank, nor even the uniform, which was rather more ornate than Alexis felt strictly necessary — no, it was the fact that Commodore Balestra was the first other female naval officer Alexis had ever seen. Tall and blonde, with sharp, striking features, and a uniform covered in gold braid, medals, and a gaudy sash.

The woman sat down at her desk and began reviewing her tablet without a glance at those assembled before her. After a moment, Neals' face began to redden and he cleared his throat. Balestra held up one hand, index finger extended in a "wait a moment" gesture, never looking up from her tablet. Alexis saw Neals' face redden further and she suppressed a smile of satisfaction. *I shouldn't like her — she's the enemy, after all — but it's worth a bit to see the captain put in his place.*

Finally, Balestra took a deep breath and looked up.

"*Capitaine* Neals, I have reviewed the situation and I am prepared to dispose of you."

Neals' eyes widened, as did those of *Hermione's* other officers. The Hanoverese lieutenant cleared his throat.

The commodore leaned back. "*Que?*"

The lieutenant whispered in her ear and Balestra frowned.

"*Merde. Non.* I make the ... disposition? Of your status, yes?" she said. Seeing them relax, she continued, "The *mutins*, the ones who take the ship, they are free to go where they will." Neals opened his mouth to speak, but Balestra held up her finger again. "*Non*, this is decided. I have no love of *mutins*, but we are at war with you. It is decided. They will go free. The others, the crew who stay with you, and yourselves, you are now prisoners of *le Hanovre*. Do you understand?"

Neals clenched his jaw tightly and his nostrils flared. "Yes."

Balestra's eyes narrowed and she raised a hand to her shoulder. She tapped two fingers sharply on her rank epaulet. "Do you understand, *Capitaine* Neals?"

Neals flushed again. "Yes, *sir*."

Balestra frowned and turned to the lieutenant. "'*Monsieur*', Delaine?" The lieutenant whispered to her again. "*Porcs sexistes*," she muttered and shook her head. Alexis watched this with gleeful fascination. Neals was clearly in a position he hated and she was relishing his discomfort.

"Your crew, of course, will be under guard, but you, the officers, may give your parole, yes?"

Neals nodded. "You should know, Commodore Balestra, that Carew there is no longer an officer."

Balestra turned to look at Alexis. Alexis met her eyes for a moment, but wasn't at all sure how she felt that the foreign commodore had known exactly who she was when Neals named her.

"*Oui,*" Balestra said, "I have seen your log." She smiled thinly as Neals blanched white. Bad enough he'd lost his ship, Alexis knew, but he'd not had an opportunity to purge the logs or other systems. In addition to *Hermione,* the Hanoverese had received all of her logs and signals, as well. Until Admiralty was notified and able to change them, the enemy would be able to read all of New London's private signals. "And seen your … Delaine, the word, *un enfant pétulant agissant en colère?*"

The lieutenant looked at Neals with a slight smile. "Tantrum," he said distinctly.

Neals' face turned scarlet. "How I run my ship, Commodore Balestra, is none of your concern, I think."

Alexis might have been mistaken, but she was quite sure she saw the lieutenant wink at her as the commodore replied.

"But, *Capitaine* Neals, you have no ship." She paused, allowing that to sink in. "So, the parole, yes? *Capitaine* Neals?"

"Yes, of course, my officers and I give our parole."

"*Non, Capitaine* Neals, the parole is a personal decision. An agreement of honor — each must make his own, *oui?*"

Neals looked aggravated and as though he simply wanted to get out of the cabin and on with whatever was next. "Very well. *I* give my parole. All proper now, commodore?"

"*Oui.* And you, Lieutenant Williard?"

"Yes, sir."

And on down the line with each officer agreeing in turn and

Alexis wondering just what it was they were agreeing to. She understood that parole had something to do with an agreement between a prisoner and captor, but not the details and she didn't want to agree blindly, even if it did appear to be a formality.

"*Aspirant* Carew?"

Alexis blinked, both from confusion at what to answer and as it had been some time since she'd been addressed as anything other than "mister". And how was she to address the commodore? She seemed to grow irritated as each officer addressed her as "sir", but what was appropriate to the Hanoverese? And would doing so irritate Captain Neals even more ... which, having thought about it, might not be a bad thing. *What more can he do to me now we're prisoners?*

"I'm sorry, Commodore Balestra, I don't understand this 'parole'."

"Oh, just agree, Carew!" Neals said. "Do let us get on with this!"

Alexis started to answer, but was cut off by Balestra, who stood and slammed her palms down on the desk.

"*Ta gueule, capitaine!*" Neals blinked and looked shocked. "Her *décision!* Her *accord!* Her *honneur! Mon dieu, vous cul arrogants* ... Delaine! Show these others away, I will explain to *Aspirant* Carew the parole." She waited until the lieutenant had led *Hermione's* other officers away and then muttered under her breath, "*Connard.*"

She took a deep breath and looked Alexis in the eye. "*Pardonner, mademoiselle.* I have not the patience with these men." Another deep breath and she smiled. "So, the parole, yes? It is an agreement between us. You, all of you, will go to the town of Courboin — a small town, but it has ... the comfort, yes? With the parole, you will have the freedom of the town. You may shop in the market. You may walk in the hills. You will have a room in a house with the other officers. Very nice, yes?" She frowned. "Perhaps you will have a room in a house without the other officers. No matter. Without the parole you will stay in the prison. Not so very nice. No market, no hills, always under guard, yes? For this we ask very little — you do not fight us, you do not plan the escape, you do as we ask of you. It is a small thing."

"So it means I just ... give up?" Alexis didn't understand how to reconcile this, and how quickly the other officers had agreed to it, with the exhortations of the Naval Gazette — to fight on, to never give up. Neither, though, could she reconcile the Gazette's description of the Hanoverese as the vicious instigators of the war with this woman and her lieutenant.

Balestra frowned. "*Aspirant* Carew, you are the prisoner now. The parole is ... the word, courtesy, yes? You do not fight with us and we do not guard you. Until comes the release or *le échange,* the trading of officers, or—" She smiled. "— *la délivrance,* some great rescue, yes?"

"And the men, Commodore Balestra? Do they also give parole?"

"*Non. Le ordinaire?* Only officers. The crew, they go to the prison ... or what we may make a prison here."

"I'm sorry, Commodore Balestra." Alexis wasn't sure of the reason, but it simply didn't feel right. Perhaps it was the speed with which Neals and the other officers had accepted the offer — she had little respect for them or what they thought was the right course of action. Perhaps it was the feeling that whatever effort went into guarding her would mean that much less effort available to fight New London — not so much that she cared about the course of a war she didn't truly understand, but what if those who could have been guarding her were then free to attack others? Better, she thought, for them to be guarding her than shooting at Captain Grantham or Philip or even Roland. And, more so, it would feel like she was abandoning her lads, if they went off to prison while she remained free. "I'm afraid I cannot agree to this parole."

Balestra regarded her for a moment, then pursed her lips. "So. Very well then."

"I'm sorry, I just —"

"*Non, non.* It is for you to know your heart, your *honneur.* If you cannot, then you cannot." She looked toward the door and Alexis realized that the lieutenant had returned while they were speaking. "Ah, Delaine, *bien. Aspirant* Carew will not take the parole. See her to her place, will you? And to that other thing we discussed?"

"*Oui*, yes. *Mademoiselle* Carew? This way?"

Alexis was unsure of the courtesy due a foreign commodore, so she nodded to Balestra and followed the lieutenant through the hatchway. Once they were outside the commodore's cabin, he led her through the ship and to the forward companionway before speaking.

"Your Captain Neals, I do not think he approves of my commodore, *Mademoiselle* Carew."

"Captain Neals does not approve of women in the Service. It is entirely possible that he does not approve of women in the more general sense, come to think of it."

"Ah. This foolishness you have in your colonies still. I know it is not from your capital, for I have visited New London myself."

"I never have, only a few worlds on the Fringe and now the border."

"We here are not so foolish as to believe these things. Not so foolish as to believe that men and women are the same, you understand, but neither so foolish as to think they are so very different." He shrugged, an eloquent gesture that seemed to communicate a great deal. "A man may do a thing, a woman may do a thing ... so long as the thing is done well, who is to be concerned that it was a man or a woman who did the thing?"

"I have cause to wish that belief were more widespread, Lieutenant Delaine."

"*Non, Mademoiselle* Carew ... but I am remiss." He stopped and faced her. "Lieutenant Delaine Thiebaud, at your service." He held out his hand and she gave him hers, stifling her surprise when he raised it to his lips. "*Enchanté, Mademoiselle* Carew."

"Very well, Lieutenant Thiebaud, then," Alexis said, retrieving her hand. The lieutenant's behavior was, she thought, a bit exaggerated ... and not at all appropriate for an escort to prison. "You are to take me to a cell, now, I believe? Or perhaps you have decided to escort me to a ball instead?"

"Pardon me, *mademoiselle?*" he asked, looking downcast. "It is my nature. I am French, after all."

Alexis followed him as he resumed his way down the companion-way. "French? Not Hanoverese?"

"*Oui*, but ..." He pulled out his tablet and held it where she could see as well. He brought up a star chart and did something that colored two areas of space, one quite a bit larger than the other. "Here we have your New London and Hanover, yes?"

He drew his finger along the tablet where the two areas met and it turned red. "And here we fight." He highlighted another section of space that bordered both of the first two. "This, then, *La Grande République de France Parmi les Etoiles* ... The Grand Republic of France Among the Stars." He took a deep breath and shook his head. "Yes, I know, but ... we are French. Still, these —" He indicated a cluster of systems hanging down from that French Republic and between New London and Hanover. "— all the way to Giron, here, where we are, were once French, *le Baie March*, and are now of *le Hanovre*."

Alexis frowned. "If they conquered you, why are you fighting for them?"

He shrugged as though to dismiss the thought. "Oh, this was long ago. We are of *le Hanovre* since my father, my grandfather, his grandfather." He shrugged. "But, too, we are *Français*. Others go to the stars and are of New London or *Hanovre* or Ho-hsi. For us, no matter the star that is in our sky, we are of *la belle France*."

"And what of who claims to own that star?"

Theiebaud's face tightened a bit. "We are loyal to *le Hanovre*, of course, *mademoiselle*."

They walked along in silence for a while, then he stopped in the hold near the lower airlock.

"Before we go to the planet's surface," he said, "these men have asked to speak to you before they go and my commodore has agreed." He opened the hatchway and gestured for her to proceed him.

Alexis entered a large space in the hold. A group of about thirty men were gathered at the far side all with heavy bags beside them. They looked up as she entered.

"The other *mutins* have gone on, but these, they insisted to see you."

"Please stop calling them that," Alexis said quietly as she crossed the compartment. There was only Nabb from her division, as none of the others had joined in taking the ship. She recognized men from all over the ship, though, some she only knew a little and didn't understand why they would have waited to see her. She stopped short of them and waited, unsure of what to say, but the men quickly formed a line and approached her.

"Jus' wanted ter tell yer it weren't about you, Mister Carew," the first one said. "The ship an' all, I mean. You was always fair."

He lowered his eyes and Alexis nodded, unsure of what to say other than, "Thank you."

He nodded to her, nodded to Theiebaud, then shouldered his bag and walked off to the open hatchway. The next man took his place.

"Wisht I were in yer division, sir. Been a better sail if I were."

The line moved on with each man having his say and quickly leaving. Alexis found her chest tightening further as each man spoke and could hardly stand it when only Nabb was left.

"Oh, Nabb," she said sadly.

"Sorry, Mister Carew. I disappointed you."

"Why? Whyever didn't you just stay out of it?" She took his hands in hers. "Your family ... you can't ever go home again."

Nabb looked away. "Some of the lads, the younger ones, were hot to join in. Worried about after and where it'd leave 'em if they didn't, you see? Others were after seein' as no one went fer you in it." He shrugged. "You'd said you didn't want us in it, soes I told 'em I'd go an' they hang back. Call 'em in, like, if it were needful." He shrugged. "Only ways I could think to keep 'em out."

Alexis stared at him in shock as understanding dawned. She wrapped her arms around him and buried her face in his chest. "You protected my lads," she whispered.

Nabb patted her back awkwardly. "Weren't but what were

needed, sir." Alexis stepped back from him and he shouldered his bag. "Best be going."

"Wait!" Alexis grabbed his arm to stop him. "Your family!"

"Can't go back to —"

"If they must, if things get too hard for them —" She considered. Yes, her grandfather would understand. She'd write to him and if the holding hadn't a need for hands, a little of her prize money could be used. "Dalthus. Carew Holding. If they can make their way there, even as indentures—" She held up her hand to stop Nabb's objection. "Even as indentures, Nabb. My grandfather will make it right for them."

Nabb nodded. "Aye, sir." He walked on.

"Nabb!" she called out as he reached the hatchway. "Tell the others," she continued when he turned. "For their families. Carew Holding on Dalthus, if they've need."

"Aye, sir."

Thiebaud waited until he had left. "I do not understand why you do this for the *mutins,* they have—"

"Stop calling them that!" Alexis rounded on him. "You weren't there! You don't understand what they went through on that ship!" She shoved him away from her, at a loss for how to explain the months she'd spent aboard *Hermione.* "You do not know."

Theiebaud looked from her to the empty hatchway then back. "You love them very much."

"No, it's not that ... well, I care about them, certainly —"

"*Non,* you love them and they love you. One does not argue with the French about this matter, it is a thing we know." His brow furrowed as he looked toward the hatchway. "*Très fidèle. Pardon.* I was mistaken. I should wish for such a crew, I think." He looked back at Alexis. "Or such a captain as you."

Alexis frowned. "I am not a captain, Lieutenant Thiebaud. Only a midshipman ... if even that."

"There are captains of ships, *mademoiselle,*" he said, nodding, "but also captains of men."

SEVENTEEN

"DINNER, SIR?"

Alexis rolled over on her cot and opened her eyes. The light was muted by blankets draped over upended spare cots to form a sort of room for her. The Hanoverese "prison" was actually a converted warehouse in the town of Courboin. The small town of Courboin ... barely more than a rural village, really, and the warehouse was the only one in the town.

The men had been herded into the warehouse with a stack of cots and blankets, their bags and chests dumped through the doors, and left to make the best of the empty space. Hanoverese marines — or French, as Alexis had noted they all spoke that language and not the German of Hanover — guarded them. The guards were stationed at the doors and some walked a catwalk midway up the high walls of the warehouse, but, other than being watched, the New Londoners had been left to their own devices.

"And is it a good, thick chop today, Isom?" Alexis asked.

"Ah ... rice and them beans, sir," Isom said.

Alexis rolled on to her back and stared up at the warehouse ceiling far above. "Of course." There was ample food sent up from the town, but only that. It'd been rice and beans since they'd arrived, and little in the way of seasoning for flavor. Certainly none of the beef the men expected and were used to, not even beef from the vat. And, worse from the men's perspective, no wine, beer, or spirits. If that wasn't corrected soon, the Hanoverese would face their own mutiny, for the spacers cared not at all how fresh the water was if they were being denied their daily tot.

"I find myself not at all hungry, Isom." She rolled back onto her side to face away from the blanket "doorway" where Isom stood.

"You should eat, sir ... been three days since you ate more than a bit."

Alexis frowned. Had it been so long since she'd eaten? It didn't seem so ... and she wasn't hungry. She was just so very tired. She closed her eyes.

ALEXIS JERKED AWAKE. There was shouting and banging from the main room outside her blanketed partition. She sat up partway, then fell back to the cot. Her limbs felt leaden and her head hurt — or, rather, it both felt as though it were wrapped in cotton and pained her at the same time. A dull ache at the back and a pressure around the sides and front that made her want to lay back down and close her eyes.

"Mister Carew, sir," Isom said, coming in. "Askren and Durand are fighting, sir, you've got to come."

She started up again and then fell back with a sigh. "I'm not one of the officers any longer, am I, Isom? There's little I can do."

"I ..."

"We're not aboard ship, Isom, nor even a station. It's prison." Alexis rolled on to her side and clapped a pillow over her head. "The guards will handle it, I'm sure."

"MADEMOISELLE?"

"She just lays there anymore, Lieutenant Thiebaud, sir. Eats a bit now and then, but ..."

Alexis sighed and rolled over. She wanted nothing more than to be left alone and sleep a bit longer. Sleep seemed to dull, at least for a time, the sharp ache of uselessness she felt.

Thiebaud and Isom were beside her, looking down with concern on their faces. She closed her eyes again, wishing that they'd be gone when she opened them, would leave her be. Couldn't they see that there was no point? She'd be stuck here for the duration of the war — her and the lads. And there was nothing more to be done. This was their lives now.

"Leave me be, please," she whispered. Stuck here, couldn't help the lads a bit and couldn't do a thing about her grandfather's lands. *Not even a message from them.* Useless ... just useless.

"Do you see, sir?" Isom asked.

"*Mademoiselle* Carew?" Thiebaud asked. He sat on the edge of the cot and rested a palm on her forehead.

"I'm not *sick*, lieutenant," she said, rolling away from him and closing her eyes again. "I'm simply tired."

"Do you see, sir," Isom repeated. He lowered his voice. "She's not even —" He whispered. "She's not bathed in some time, sir. Not like her at all."

Alexis wanted to scream at them to leave, but couldn't find the energy. Of course she hadn't bathed — the warehouse had no bath or shower, and only a pair of heads. Their condition, with seventy men in residence, was entirely unpleasant. It was all she could do to make her way there for necessary business, the thought of trying to bathe there was more than she could bear. *And what would the point of it be, anyway?*

"Will you please take some food, *mademoiselle?*" Thiebaud asked.

"I'm quite capable of telling when I'm hungry. Enough, please, the both of you," Alexis said, eyes still closed.

"Something from the market, perhaps, *mademoiselle?*" Thiebaud persisted. "There is a shop with the *chocolat, oui?*"

That stirred her a bit, but probably not as Thiebaud intended. Alexis rolled to face them and raised herself on one arm. Even that little movement seemed to be too much, but the flash of anger she felt at his suggestion spurred her.

"Chocolate, lieutenant? You'll offer me this while my lads eat your beans morning, noon, and night?" The brief flash of anger faded, replaced by weariness. She collapsed on the cot, burying her face in the pillow. "Will you please just leave me be?"

THE SHADOWS WERE BACK. *Black, swirling masses that spun around and around her before coalescing into shapes. The figures formed and moved toward her — pointing, accusing. More of them than ever before — how could she possibly have failed so many?*

Alexis tried to scream, but no sound emerged. She tried to turn and run, but her legs felt rooted in place.

The figures grew closer, far closer than they ever had before and Alexis felt her heart hammering in fear. She knew this was a dream and tried desperately to wake herself, but failed. What would happen if they reached her? This darkness, so like darkspace *yet so different, terrified her.*

Closer. Shadowy, outstretched hands reached for her. She thought to sway her body from them, even if her feet were rooted to the ground, but they were all around her. Surrounding her and moving ever closer.

ALEXIS WOKE WITH A GASP, heart hammering and breath ragged. Her undershirt was drenched in sweat and every movement brought a chill from the damp fabric. She lay for a moment, trying to control her breathing.

Need for the head drove Alexis from her cot. She pulled the

fabric partition that made up her doorway to one side and stepped out. The men were lying about, some pacing aimlessly, others gathered in small groups. She made her way to the head, acknowledging the nods of those nearby. Those in line moved out of her way and she thanked them, though why she should be in any hurry to enter the little compartment was beyond her.

Seventy men and two toilets is not a pleasant spectacle. The condition of the head had gotten worse and worse as time went on, until Alexis dreaded having to use it. She considered cleaning it herself, but hadn't the energy. She washed her hands in a sink not much cleaner than the rest and looked at herself in the grime-covered mirror. She had dark circles under her eyes and her hair hung dank and limp.

When was the last time I brushed it, let alone washed? Of course the thought of bathing in this room was somewhat terrifying to begin with. And the effort it would take.

Her mouth, though, felt fuzzy and it might be time to brush her teeth. Despite the terror of the dream, fatigue dragged at her. Later, perhaps, after she'd eaten. She'd surely feel hungry enough to eat a bit later — just a brief nap first, perhaps an hour or two.

She stepped out and nodded thanks to the men again, then made her way back to her cot. Across the warehouse, there was shouting and a two groups started shoving each other. Alexis looked around, expecting the bosun or one of his mates to break it up, but of course Maslin was dead along with one of his mates back on *Hermione* and a second mate had been one of the mutineers. There was only Lain left with them of the bosun's mates, and he likely had no authority here in the prison. Her throat constricted and her eyes burned. She picked up her pace, despite how very tired she was. Once back in her cot she could sleep and not think so much about things. The dream surely wouldn't come again so soon, would it?

"I heard you were about, Mister Carew. I've a bit of soap and a fresh uniform, if you like?"

Alexis turned and found Isom waiting beside her, one of her uniforms held out.

"No, Isom, I don't believe that's necessary. I'll just lie down for a bit." Her attention turned back to the scuffle, which had broken up, but she could see that one of the men was sporting a bloody nose.

"I've been talking with the lads, sir. This lot aren't meant to be idle. Hard to go from working all day to loose ends, it is."

"I suppose, yes."

"Captain should see to that."

"I suppose so, yes, Isom." She started walking again, but his words nagged at her. It wasn't like Isom to mention the captain, not at all. "Wait, what do you mean?"

"The idleness, sir, it's not good for the men. They're used to being set their tasks — left on their own like this, it's like a too long holiday. The captain should see to that. And to the other things."

"What do you mean? What other things?"

"What needs doing. Those heads for one, they're a right mess. But more than that, we've need of a few more of them. He should tell the Hanoverese what we need."

"The captain's given his parole, Isom, he's off in town with the others."

"Well, yes, but it's still his responsibility."

Alexis turned to him. "What makes you think this?"

"Spoke to the others, sir. Some were taken in the last war and know the way of it. Captain's supposed to check in on us, see we're keeping up as we should, and have what we need."

"He's not been here even once, has he?" She looked around the large space, noting the disarray and clumps of men idling about. Plates of half-eaten food and dirty clothing strewn everywhere. Even the marines' area was a cluttered mess.

What must they be thinking? He wasn't much of a captain to begin with, but now even he's abandoned them. A horrible thought occurred to her. "And if the captain's not part of those captured, who's to do it then?"

"Most senior officer, I suppose, as with anything."

Damn me. Alexis closed her eyes. None of them, not Neals nor even Williard, nor any of them had bothered to come and check on the men. *And I abandoned them, too, sulking in my cot — too sorry for myself to care for them.*

"I'm sorry, Isom."

"Sir?"

Who to start with? Her eyes fell on the marines. They'd lost their lieutenant, and both sergeants, along with so much of their company in the mutiny. She'd never known them to leave a thing out of place, but their cots were now covered with discarded uniform bits and twisted blankets, and not a one of them was properly in uniform.

Alexis strode over to them, Isom following her. "Sir?" he asked again.

"A moment, Isom, I need to—" Her eye fell on Moberly, one of the corporals she'd sparred with regularly. She knew the others respected him. She stopped near him.

"Help you, Mister Carew?" he asked, looking up from his cot.

Alexis was suddenly at a loss for what to say. Should she talk to him about what to do to correct things? *No, most of them have spent their lives aboard ship — it's what they know, all they know. They need a ship's way of doing things.* She clenched her jaw. *Not Neals' ship, though, a proper ship.*

"Is that how you address an officer, Moberly?"

"Sir?"

"*Moberly!* Why are you on your arse when you're speaking to me?" Alexis paused while he jumped to his feet. She ran her eyes over him, seeing him flush as he realized what a state he was in. "Is that proper kit for a marine, Moberly?"

"No, sir!"

"Is this how marines keep a berth, Moberly?"

He looked around desperately. "No, sir!"

"I'm naming you sergeant, Moberly!"

"Sir? Can you do that, sir?"

"*Do you see anyone here who'll stop me, Moberly?*"

"No, sir!"

"Then you're a sergeant until I say differently. You'll be paid a sergeant if it has to come out of my own pocket. And you'll behave a proper sergeant or I'll bloody well know the reason why! Do you understand me, Moberly?"

"Yes, sir! Aye, sir!"

"I'll inspect this berth in one hour's time, sergeant! Do not disappoint me."

"Aye, sir! No, sir!"

Alexis turned to the other side of the warehouse and found the rest of the crew still and staring at her. She ran her gaze over their faces until she saw the man she wanted.

"*Lain!*"

"Sir?"

"You're bosun now, Lain! Pick two mates and do I need to tell you what I want in an hour's time?"

"No, sir! Aye, sir!"

Alexis watched the sudden flurry of activity with satisfaction. "That's what Lieutenant Thiebaud was here for, wasn't it, Isom? None of the other officers would speak to him about the men, so he came to me?"

"I expect so, sir."

Damn me for a self-indulgent fool. "All right, then." She walked over to one of the guards. "I'd like to speak to Lieutenant Thiebaud when he's time for it, if you please."

"*Que?*"

"Oh, don't you '*que*' me. There's not a one of you doesn't understand every word we say, I can see it in your eyes. Now my compliments to Lieutenant Thiebaud and I'd be pleased to speak to him at his convenience."

The guard looked at her, swallowed once, and then nodded.

Alexis looked around, pleased to see that there wasn't a man in sight who wasn't involved in some task. Even the line for the head had disappeared.

"How much of that soap did you say you had, Isom?"

"YOU WISHED to speak to me, *Mademoiselle* Carew?"

Alexis nodded and gestured for Thiebaud to sit, she'd had a pair of chairs added to the space partitioned off for her in preparation for this meeting.

"Thank you for coming, lieutenant. Yes, there are some things I'd like to speak to you about." She settled herself in the other chair. "First, I think, is this *'mademoiselle'* business. I do not believe, Lieutenant Thiebaud, that you refer to fellow officers in your own service in such a way." She hurried on as she saw him start to speak. "I do not mean that I think you intend any disrespect with it. I truly don't. But I do believe that it ... is a different sort of respect, and not at all what you would show to a midshipman in your own service. Am I mistaken?"

Thiebaud hung his head. "*Non*, you are not mistaken. I have spoken to you not as the fellow officer, but as the beautiful woman." He looked at her without raising his head. "You must forgive me, it is my nature ... I am French."

Alexis had to bite the inside of her lip to keep from smiling, even as she felt her face flush. The man was entirely irrepressible, it seemed.

"Tell me, lieutenant, this 'I am French' — does it work well on the girls in Hanoverese ports?"

Thiebaud raised his head, grinning broadly. "*Très bien, Aspirant* Carew. Very well."

Alexis laughed despite herself. Irrepressible, entirely too handsome, and the devil himself was in that smile. "You are a bad man, lieutenant."

Thiebaud shrugged. "I—"

"You are French. Yes, I begin to understand, I think."

"It is good for you to laugh, *Aspirant* Carew. The day is brightened."

Alexis felt herself blush again and took a deep breath. At least she'd won the first round and he'd stopped the '*mademoiselle*' business. *Aspirant* was likely French for her rank. She sat up and squared her shoulders. "To business, I think, lieutenant?"

"*Bien sûr*, of course. What do you wish to speak of?"

"Toilets."

Thiebaud blinked. "*Les toilettes?*"

"There are two." She saw his shocked look. "For seventy men. And myself." She lifted a bucket from behind her chair and placed it between them. "There are no showers. I bathed in that today." She slid the bucket toward him and raised her eyebrows. "This is acceptable to the French?"

"*Non*," he stammered. "No, not even to *le Hanovre*."

"Did no one review these facilities before you put my crew here, lieutenant?"

"We asked the town for a place —"

"And received an empty warehouse with no facilities. This must be corrected."

"It will take some time to find another place, I think."

"No," Alexis said. "My men have already suffered here. There's room enough for more heads, bring in workers and have them built."

"*Non*, this is not possible. So many are at the war, there are none to spare for this."

"Then bring in the tools and supplies," Alexis said. "My men are idle and it would do them well to have some honest work."

Thiebaud looked shocked. "Give to prisoners the tools?" He shook his head. "*Non*, this is not done."

"Well one or the other must be done, lieutenant. I want ten '*toillettes*' out there within the fortnight and a dozen or more showers."

"*Aspirant* Carew," Thiebaud said stiffly. "You forget yourself.

You are *aspirant* and I am *lieutenant* — it is not for you to give to me the orders."

"I apologize, lieutenant. But I *am,* as I'm sure you've found, the highest ranked New London officer here who gives a bloody fig about those lads." She sighed. No, there were likely all sorts of rules the Hanoverese had about such things. Thiebaud would have to *want* to help her, and that wouldn't come as an enemy officer. *Well ... winnings are only worth it if you spend them on something useful, I suppose.* "If my asking you as a fellow officer will not move you, then I am afraid you leave me no other choice but one."

"And what is this?" Thiebaud asked.

"I will ask you as a beautiful woman," Alexis said, grinning broadly. "You are French, are you not?"

Thiebaud regarded her for a moment. "You have just this moment demanded I address you as *aspirant,* not as the beautiful woman. And now you seek to use it for what you want?"

Alexis nodded. "Yes. Though it would have been far simpler if you'd just agreed to what I asked in the first place."

The corners of Thiebaud's mouth twitched then he nodded. "This thing, I cannot agree to, but my commodore, perhaps." He stood. "Come, we will ask."

"Now?"

"*Deux toilettes?* This very minute, I think."

He led Alexis past the guards and out of the warehouse. It was her first view of the town, though a brief one as they immediately boarded Thiebaud's boat. Like most ship's boats, it had no windows in the passenger compartment, but Alexis was able to see a bit of the town as they walked to it.

The town of Courboin was larger than the village she'd grown up near on Dalthus, but smaller than the main port town there of Port Arthur. Based on what she saw of it, she estimated there were, perhaps, a thousand people living in the town itself. Set in a long, narrow valley, she could see fields stretching away in all directions, smaller near the town, for the workers, and much larger farther away where the more mechanized farms for export were. *Much like Dalthus.* She could look down the road from the warehouse toward the main street and see the town square no more than a kilometer away.

"*Hermione's* other officers are there?" she asked.

"*Oui,*" Thiebaud said. "They share a house there, near the square."

So close and couldn't be bothered.

They boarded the ship's boat and Alexis settled into her seat.

"Lieutenant?" she asked.

"*Non.*" Thiebaud sat next to her and adjusted his seat straps. He looked at her sternly. "You have decided to work your — the word, wiles, yes — upon me, *mademoiselle.* You cannot do this and still I am *Lieutenant* Thiebaud to you and you are *Aspirant* Carew to me. We must now be Delaine and *Alexis, oui?*"

Alexis narrowed her eyes. It was a bit surprising that he knew her given name. It was in her records, of course, but would he have remembered it from weeks before when she was first captured? Or had he looked it up more recently? And did she really care? It had been quite some time, since she'd left *Merlin,* in fact, since she'd been on a first name basis with anyone. Certainly she'd never met anyone who spent nearly as much effort trying to charm her, obvious and flamboyant as his efforts were. It was, in fact, a relief after the stiff formality and thinly veiled hostility of *Hermione's* gunroom. Her earlier resolve that he respect her rank wavered. *Is it so very wrong to want a friend?*

"Very well ... Delaine." She restrained a smile and waved a finger at him. "But do not make presumptions or it will be right back to *lieutenant* and *aspirant* for you, understand?"

"I shall be always on the best behavior, *Alexis.*"

He very definitely — *and deliberately, I'm sure* — put more of his accent into her name than was absolutely necessary, something she found, to her surprise, that she rather liked. *It is* not *so very wrong to want a friend.* Or just someone that she could talk to. She realized suddenly that Delaine, a foreign officer — an *enemy* officer — was the first person she'd felt comfortable talking to in ... *How long? More than six months aboard* Hermione *and another month here. Nigh half a year with no one to speak to but those other midshipmen and not even a message from someone else.* How she longed for news from home. *No one save a paid evening with Cort Blackmon?*

"Your face is clouded, *ma petite.*"

"It has been a trying time. And odd that capture and imprisonment have been the least of it." She forced a smile. "What was that you called me?"

Thiebaud shrugged. "It is a way of naming someone. It is no matter." He gestured forward. "We will arrive at my commodore's ship soon."

Alexis studied him, but he looked steadily forward, betraying nothing. *Which for someone so expressive, betrays quite a lot, doesn't it. I shall have to find out what this* ma petite *actually means ... and all his other French bits.* What she'd just thought struck her and she felt her face grow warm.

"Are you well, *Alexis?* Your face has colored."

She studied the seatback in front of her, face as expressionless as she could manage. "It is no matter."

They sat in silence for a while until the boat docked with Commodore Balestra's flagship. Alexis realized that she had been so concerned with other things that she had paid no attention to the ship when last she was aboard.

"Delaine, what is the ship? I should have asked before."

Delaine smiled. "She is *Forte*, fifty guns, for your Navy they would be of twenty-four and eight pounds."

Alexis followed him down the companionway and then aft to the commodore's cabin. She noted the guns, larger and more numerous than those on Hermione. *Half again as many, I'd not want to meet this ship in combat.*

She also noted the looks from the crew, mostly suspicious or angry. She didn't blame them, she was the enemy, after all, but listening to their muttered comments led her to notice something else. The crew, all of them that she heard, seemed to be speaking French — or, at least, as near to French as she could recognize — and not the German of Hanover.

"Delaine, the crew — are you *all* French?"

"*Oui*, we are the ... the word, force for local defense, you understand?" He glanced at her, sliding a hatch open. "All are from these worlds nearby, *le Baie March*."

Alexis nodded. She began to suspect, despite Delaine's claim that these systems were taken from that French Republic in his "grandfather's grandfather's time," that the folk here did not yet think of themselves as Hanoverese. *I wonder what difference that makes in the war with New London.*

The marine guarding the door announced them, looking odd to Alexis in a blue uniform instead of the scarlet she was used to New London's marines wearing. Delaine motioned her to wait and stepped inside, closing the hatch behind him. Alexis waited patiently until Delaine reopened the hatch and waved her inside.

"So, *Aspirant* Carew" Commodore Balestra said when she entered. "You wish tools for your men, so that they may improve the prison?"

"Yes," Alexis said. "And some other things, commodore."

Balestra frowned. "Other things?" She raised an eyebrow at Delaine, who shrugged and shook his head.

"Yes, if you please. Since I'm here, you understand, and so as to not have to bother you again." Alexis had thought about this on the trip up. Isom had been a font of information he'd garnered from former prisoners and his own reading of the regulations, if she were going to ask, she should ask for everything she could think of that would make the men's lives in captivity easier. "I understand that the other officers may draw on their pay to support themselves in the town — that the pay will not arrive until you have informed New London of *Hermione's* capture, but that they may borrow against its arrival?"

Balestra nodded.

"I should like to do the same in order to purchase supplies for the men's mess. The food you supply is quite good, please don't mistake me, but they could do with a bit of meat now and again, I think." *What was the term the guards used?* "We are '*bifteck*', after all." The term had not been used in a pleasant way when she'd heard it, no more than the spacers who referred to their captors as 'frogs'. She tried to gauge Balestra's reaction to this, but the commodore's face was impassive. "And they should have some opportunity to get out and about instead of being cooped up forever inside."

"This is all?"

"Perhaps they could be allowed to send messages home. To their families?"

Balestra regarded her steadily and Alexis fought to keep her own face impassive.

"When last you are here, I ask you for your parole. I say to you, you may shop in the market, you may walk in the hills. Very nice, yes?"

Alexis nodded. Her stomach fell at the thought that her decision to refuse parole might now jeopardize her crew.

"Now you ask of me to shop in the market and walk in the hills. Is this all to change this decision?"

"I ..." Alexis wasn't sure how to respond or what Balestra wanted to hear. If she gave her parole now, it might seem that her requests were merely for herself, not for her crew — and truthfully she still felt parole was not the right decision. "If you prefer, commodore, I will not profit by this. Someone else may shop, I only ask for access to my pay so that supplies may be bought. I will eat only the food you provide. I will remain in the prison, I only ask that my men be allowed some small amount of time outdoors. I do not ask these things for myself, only that I do not wish to see the men remain in these conditions."

Balestra half rose, her voice angry. "Do you say I mistreat these men?"

"No, I—"

Delaine coughed loudly and ran a hand over his mouth. *"Deux toillettes."*

Balestra glared at him, but sank back into her chair. "I was not informed of this."

"That is what I meant, commodore," Alexis said, "not that you mistreat them, but that those who should have informed you of ... oversights did not do so."

"Non, I have heard nothing from your *capitaine* or *lieutenants* of this. Nothing from them but asks for more of their pay. *Les putes* of Courboin grow rich from them." Balestra took a deep breath. "I will not ask for the parole *entièrement* — by force, it has no *honneur.* But you must give the parole in these things you ask. The treatment of your men is a matter of *honneur, oui?"* She frowned. "The soldiers, I know for them it is not so, but we in navies may still hold to older ways, you understand?"

Alexis thought she did, but Balestra continued.

"Messages, I may not allow. Until New London is aware of your ship's loss, we will not tell them. You will have the tools, but you must give your word, as *le officier* — the tools are for the building, no escape and no harm to the people, you understand?" Alexis nodded. "You will have your pay and may go to the market, but you will return, yes? Your word on this?" Alexis nodded again. "You and your men may go and ... frolic in the sun as you wish. Of the men, one in three, only for two hours a time, *oui?* At the end, all return to *la prison.* Do you agree? Your word?"

Alexis nodded again. "Yes, my word on it, commodore. Thank you!"

EIGHTEEN

THE NEXT MORNING, Alexis wakened to shouts and the slamming *crack* of steel on concrete. She threw on her uniform and rushed from her blanket-walled cubicle to find a dozen men swinging picks into the warehouse's concrete floor near the head. The rest of the men were crowded around, laughing and yelling encouragement.

"Put yer back into it, mate!"

"Put yer wife's backside into it and make a real swing!"

Alexis made her way to the back of the crowd. "Make a lane!" she shouted, jabbing the two nearest men in the back. They stepped aside, grinning, and she walked through to the front. Delaine was there and made his way to her side.

"The tools must be returned to the truck outside each day, *mon mignon*, and will be counted by the guards, you understand?"

Alexis nodded, a little surprised that the tools and supplies had arrived the very day after she'd spoken to Commodore Balestra. "You wasted no time. Thank you."

Delaine grinned. "I am not so foolish as to waste time in pleasing you, *Alexis*. And now I shall escort you to the market, yes?"

Alexis was a bit shocked. She'd expected an escort, but hadn't thought it would be Delaine. The ease with which he'd gained a meeting with Commodore Balestra made her suspect that he was not simply any lieutenant, but was, perhaps, the commodore's Flag Lieutenant, an officer designated as her personal assistant. Though he might also have simply been given responsibility for the New London prisoners, and that would explain his presence. Regardless of the reason, she was pleased to see him.

She followed him out of the warehouse and saw Lain and a number of her crew unloading a truck full of supplies under the eyes of the French guards. Bags of concrete, piping, and plumbing fixtures. She smiled. Clearly the men had things in hand, they could keep a ship repaired and running after all, and she could tend to the market. They'd be glad of some real meat for once.

"We will walk, yes?" Delaine said, nodding down the road to the town some kilometer away. "It is a pleasant day."

"It is," she agreed. The air was cool, Courboin was well into autumn and harvest time, but the sky was clear and the sun warm. The sight of the town reminded her of Dalthus — it was a bit the size of Port Arthur, seeming to be struggling with the transition from agriculture to commerce. Large enough to need a warehouse the size of the one she and the men were housed in, but not so large that it had lost the feel of a farming village.

The walk was quite nice and Alexis found herself enjoying herself a great deal. It had been ages since she'd seen the sky for any length of time. The lighting aboard ships and stations never wavered, except inside the cabins. There was no night and day, only the schedule of the watches. She'd once complained that she couldn't tell night from day aboard ship and been told, "Day is when the captain's awake."

She took a deep breath of the air and felt a pang of longing for home. The scents were subtly different, but much closer to Dalthus than the dry, stale air aboard ship.

Delaine led her to the center of town where an outdoor market thrived throughout the town square.

"That is where the other officers from your ship reside, *Alexis*," he said, pointing to a nearby building. It was a tall building for the town, three stories with a vacant storefront on the ground floor and a residence, intended for the shop owner, behind and above. It was certainly a step up in accommodations from a converted warehouse, and Alexis felt her anger at Captain Neals and the others grow again. She fought it down, determined not to think about it. If she'd given her parole as well, she'd be more comfortable, but she never would have known that the men were being so neglected, nor that she could do anything about it.

They entered the market area and Alexis began shopping in earnest. The first stop was a butcher's stall, where she asked to have an entire side of beef delivered immediately. She had confidence that the cook would find the fairest way to divide it between the men. Though what he'd do when faced with beef that looked like a cow instead of a pudding, she didn't know. *The shock may do him in, poor man.*

She assured Delaine that she had more funds than just a midshipman's pay to draw upon, as all of the costs would be fronted to the merchants by the Hanoverese Navy until New London was notified of their capture and her accounts became available to her. The full side of beef was an extravagance, a treat from her, given the time the men had done without. For future deliveries she arranged for only less expensive cuts, as well as pork and chicken to provide some variety. Those the men would likely not thank her for, thinking beef, even from the vat, was their due, but she wanted to hold the ongoing costs down as best she could, not knowing how long the war would last. There'd certainly be no more prize money flowing into her accounts while she was a prisoner.

She also arranged for fruits and vegetables to be delivered regularly and bought a bag of apples to take with her, opening it and biting into one before she'd even left the vendor's stall. The sweet tang filled her mouth and she sighed with delight. Real Fall apples, fresh from the trees and not boxed for cold storage for weeks on end.

"You have been long aboard ship, *Alexis*?" Delaine asked.

She swallowed hurriedly and held the bag out to him in offering. He selected one and bit into it, nodding his thanks.

"Ships and stations," she said. "Very little time on planets since I joined, and less even since I went aboard *Hermione*." She looked around the market, realizing that she had placed orders for everything she thought she and the crew might need. Disappointment set in that she'd have to return to the warehouse so soon, but she didn't want to take advantage of Delaine's good will. "I suppose that's everything. We can go back now, I'm sure you have other duties you should be attending to."

Delaine smiled. "Ah, but I wish to see the rest of the market myself," he said, "and I am told there is a pastry at the cafe there which I should not miss, so you must accompany me until I have the time to return you, yes?"

THE DAYS TURNED into a comfortable pattern. Lain had the men hard at work on building the new heads. They broke up the concrete floor to expose the piping for the current heads, then Delaine arrived with new pipes and fixtures for them to install. Walls went up with surprising speed, and Alexis had the men divided into three watches, each of which she escorted outside for two hours' time during the day. They even organized a bit of sport, and she thought she might ask if she could be allowed to bring all the men outside at once for one day each week and have a sort of competition between the watches.

Every third or fourth day, Delaine would escort Alexis down to the town market. There was little for her to do there, frankly, as the deliveries she'd arranged arrived on schedule each week with no issue, but Delaine insisted it was best for her to confirm them periodically with the shopkeepers, something she suspected was not entirely true. She appreciated their days together, but felt a bit guilty that she was taking him away from his other duties to escort her.

"I appreciate the time with you, Delaine, I truly do, but I wonder at it. It seems to me I shouldn't have this much freedom without giving my parole."

They were walking back from the market, taking a roundabout route along the edge of town. The houses were far apart here, separated by expansive fields and gardens. They'd lingered long in the market and at the cafes and the sun was low, sending long shadows over the path.

"Ah, *ma fifille*, but that is exactly why, you see." Ever since their first trip to the market, he'd begun referring to her in different ways that she suspected were quite French and quite not the way to refer to an officer, but she didn't object.

I played that card, won, and then spent the winnings on toilets.

The fact was, she didn't object because the attention was flattering. On Dalthus, her interactions had always been colored with her grandfather's position. Boys from the village were quite proper and respectful, at least once she'd reached a certain age and throwing each other into mud puddles was no longer appropriate. Her suitors, from the class of landholders like her grandfather, and their attentions held the unspoken knowledge that her grandfather's lands were far more interesting than she herself was.

With Delaine, it was different. She had no position or lands here, in fact, she was simply an enemy prisoner. It was probably not appropriate or officer-like for him to pay her such attention or for her to accept it, but she found herself not caring. It was the first time someone was so clearly interested in her for herself alone, and the knowledge filled an emptiness she hadn't realized existed.

"The others," Delaine continued, "they have given parole, so we cannot question them. You, though, I may ply you with my charms and soon you will give to us all the secrets of New London. Do you see?"

Alexis felt a moment's alarm that he might be serious, but saw his eyes and his lips twitched, and relaxed with a smile. He was simply being outrageous — which was either very Delaine or simply very French. She had yet to discover where the one truly ended and the other began. She laughed. "I'm a midshipman but two years in. I doubt I have any secrets for you."

Delaine's face was very serious, but she could see his eyes dancing. "But how am I to know this until I have plied you? And then —" He shrugged, a gesture that seemed to have a language all its own for him. "— secrets, no secrets ... still I am the winner, *mais oui?*"

"Hmm," Alexis said, fixing a stern look on her face. "I think you will find, sir, that I am not so easily plied."

Delaine reached out and took her hand as they walked. Alexis almost stumbled as her fingers warmed within his. The sensation seemed to flow up her arm into the rest of her. She shivered, though not from the chilling air.

Oh, dear, perhaps I am ...

Delaine stopped walking and turned her to face him, taking her other hand in his. Warmth flowed through her from his touch and she found herself trembling. Delaine moved closer to her, not touching, but she could feel the heat of his body. Her vision narrowed until all she could see was his face, leaning closer to hers and then her eyes closed.

Why did I close my eyes? His lips touched hers and she gasped. *It seems I am disturbingly pliable after all ... what an odd thing to discover.*

Delaine's lips left hers and she opened her eyes to find his face still close to hers. She blinked rapidly, trying to clear her thoughts. She felt the circumstances called for her to say something, but she wasn't at all sure what might be appropriate.

"That was ... quite pleasant," she whispered.

Delaine's brow furrowed. "*Plaisant?*"

Alexis cleared her throat. "Yes, well you may be French, but I am of New London and we are not ... unduly expressive."

He grinned and leaned toward her again. "'Pleasant' is all I am due?"

Her eyes closed again.

How very odd ... it's like a reflex, I'm simply not in control of ...

Delaine's lips touched hers again. This time she felt a warm, soft, wetness and her lips parted with his, again without any conscious thought. What thoughts she did have blurred and she lost track of time. His lips left hers again and she opened her eyes, breathing deeply.

"Very nice?" she ventured.

Delaine's arms went around her, one hand behind her back and the other cupping the back of her head. He pulled her to him force-fully and she found it was time for her eyes to close again.

I believe I've found something one does not tease the French about ...

Reality narrowed to where Delaine was touching her. Which was quite a lot of places, really, as her knees buckled and she found herself remaining upright only with his support.

No ... no, teasing the French about this is actually quite produc-tive, I think ...

Her eyes opened again and she stared at Delaine's face inches from hers. She swallowed hard and braced herself.

"Adequate."

"YES, ISOM?"

"The men're finished with the head, sir. They'd like to show it to you."

Alexis laughed. She could understand them being proud and satisfied that they'd done good work, but being asked to tour a head was certainly new. "I've seen most of it every day, Isom. Used a bit, in fact. But, yes, I'll come see it finished."

She crossed the warehouse floor to the area they'd walled off to create the new head. It seemed as though all of the men who'd worked on it were gathered there, grinning widely.

Can't imagine them being so pleased with a toilet.

The crowd made a lane for her to the new head's doorway and she entered. It was much as she'd last seen it the day before, though they'd cleaned up all the signs of construction. The tile and pipework fairly gleamed, in fact. At the end, they'd somehow gotten far more material from the Hanoverese than they'd asked for. Down one lane from the doorway were a full two dozen toilets and down the other stood the same number of sinks and shower stalls. Each with far more privacy than the men were used to aboard ship. At the end of the showers, a group of two dozen men stood, grinning even wider than those outside.

Nicer than they had aboard ship, come to that — but what are they so pleased about?

"All right, lads," Alexis said, smiling. "What's the joke, then?"

The men parted and what yesterday had been a bare wall at the end of the lane now had a new doorway.

"Open 'er up, Mister Carew, and 'ave a look!"

Alexis walked to the door, still smiling but eyeing them warily. They were up to something, and a spacers' joke could be quite crude. They'd not normally play jokes on an officer, but the close quarters and laxer discipline of the prison might have made them forget that.

She pulled the new door open, stepped through, and froze, mouth agape.

Somehow, without her noticing, they'd enclosed one end of the newly built head and installed a single toilet and sink. They'd even acquired some thick rugs to lay on the tile floor. And, most amazing, there at the far wall.

"A bath," she breathed, hardly believing it. "A proper bath."

She spun around to thank them, but found that someone had quietly closed the door behind her.

"I'll not be disturbed for an hour, Isom!" she yelled, wiping her eyes.

"WHAT IS IT, DELAINE?" His face was quite serious and she felt her stomach drop. Whatever the news was, it could not be good.

"I am sorry this did not come to you sooner," he said, "but it has only just been told to my commodore." He pulled out his tablet. "On your ship, the *Hermione*, yes? Our men did the investigation. In the *système de communication*, for the messages? They found ... the word ... a thing through which things pass? But only some of the things?"

"A filter?"

"*Oui*, I think it is this word. A filter of the messages." He held his tablet out to her. "My commodore, she says this was an evil thing."

Alexis took the tablet and her heart fell.

"No," she whispered.

It was a list of messages. All addressed to her, with timestamps ranging from the day she'd boarded *Hermione* to when they were last on Penduli Station. Messages from her grandfather, from Philip, even from Roland, Captain Grantham, and others. All marked as *received*, so that they'd be removed from the messaging systems and she'd not get them from other sources, not even when on a station. "No," she breathed, seeing that her own messages were there as well. Dozens of them — every message she had sent while on *Hermione*.

"None of them were sent?" she asked.

"*Non. Alexis*, I am sorry."

She scrolled quickly to the last message from her grandfather. He started, as he always did, by letting her know that everyone was well, so there was that, she supposed. But then she could fairly hear his worry that he hadn't heard from her in so long. *And longer now — it's been nearly a year since I boarded* Hermione. She clenched her eyes shut tight. *He must be frantic.*

It was the last message from Philip, though, that broke her heart.

ALEXIS,

NOT AT ALL sure what I did wrong — thought we were mates and all. I know my messages have made it to Penduli and Hermione's *been through there three or more times — gotten receipts that you've received them, even — but I've heard nothing from you. I guess you don't want to hear from me, so I'll not bother you more. I'm truly sorry — whatever it was. You can hit me, if that'll fix it?*

PHILIP

"DELAINE, you must let me send a message. Just one, please?"

"*Alexis,* I cannot. Until my Navy is certain that your ship's loss is known."

The tears finally overwhelmed her. "Please, Delaine ... my family, my friends, my ... please?"

He shook his head slowly.

Alexis sank onto the cot and covered her face with her hands. Delaine sat beside her and gently placed an arm around her shoulders. She leaned into him, burying her face in his chest and sobbing. "Please?"

"I cannot, *Alexis,*" he said, voice rough. "The very moment we have word that your Navy is aware, I will come to you. I swear this to you, my *honneur* upon it."

She sat up, sniffing and wiping at her eyes. "I should like to speak to Commodore Balestra."

"My commodore has foreseen this request, *Alexis.*" He shook his head again.

Alexis closed her eyes and swallowed hard. If she couldn't fix one thing, then she'd deal with another. "Who?" She opened her eyes, breathing deeply. "Who did this, Delaine?"

"*Alexis—*"

"There's no filter that didn't have the name of who set it up, Delaine. Tell me."

"It is best, perhaps, if you did not —"

"And there's no commissioned officer would waste his time on this. Only one of the midshipmen would be this petty and cruel. I'll have the name from you."

Delaine sighed. "*Oui.* This I can do for you, but—" He looked at her for a moment, then sighed again and shrugged. "You will do what you will do. *Aspirant* Timpson."

Timpson. Her berthmate. Probably the midshipman she should have been closest to, if *Hermione* had been a proper ship with decent officers. She clenched her teeth and stood. She was dimly aware of Delaine following her. She saw the guard at the door hold up a hand as she approached, but behind her Delaine called out and he stepped aside, eyes wide as she drew near.

She burst through the door and across the lot to the road down to the town. Delaine had arrived by ship's boat, as usual, but there'd be no where to land it in the town, so she'd have to walk the kilometer. Timpson would be near the town square, probably in a pub or whatever they called it here.

Delaine said something to her, but she ignored him and started walking. If anything her rage grew during the walk. How could they? For so long? She could see it as a joke for a time, perhaps through the first return to Penduli Station, then allow all the messages through and have a laugh about it. Would they have ever ended it?

As they got further into town the traffic on the road increased and Alexis moved to the side of the road, then on to the sidewalks when they began. With only a short distance left before the town square she stopped and turned to Delaine.

"Where do they drink? I'm certain you know."

"The cafe, across the square by the market. This is where they spend their days."

"Thank you." She started walking again.

"Only, please, do not kill the boy, *mon loup*," Delaine said. "There would be many questions for such a thing."

Alexis wasn't sure what she intended, only that she knew she had to confront Timpson. She strode across the square and through the market to the cafe. The sight of *Hermione's* midshipmen there enraged her further.

The four of them were sharing a table littered with bottles and plates. All but Ledyard had a girl seated in his lap and they appeared quite friendly. *So, this is what they do all day instead of taking care of the men?* Alexis' frustration with the conditions the crew had been living in before she'd spoken to Commodore Balestra flared again and added to her rage. She stopped short of their table and stared at them. It took a moment for them to notice her.

"Carew?" Bushby asked. "Didn't expect to ever see you again."

Canion laughed. "Did you finally give parole and come to join us?"

"Ledyard's lap is free, if you have," Timpson said. "You're just his size."

Ledyard flushed, but laughed along with the others.

As Alexis struggled to find the words to express what she was feeling, Delaine stepped past her and held a hand out to the girl in Timpson's lap. "*Mademoiselle, s'il vous plaît, vous voulez aucune partie de ce.*"

The girl looked puzzled, but she stood and Delaine drew her aside. Timpson glared at him.

"My messages," Alexis finally managed to say, staring at Timpson.

"What?"

"My messages. All of them? How could you?"

Timpson looked confused, then he threw his head back and laughed. "I'd forgotten about that! What? Did the Frogs tell you, I suppose?"

Alexis stepped closer to him.

"Have you still been writing to them, Carew? It'll make a nice bit of reading for them, if they ever go through. Especially that Philip fellow."

Ledyard piped up, making his shrill voice even higher. "'Oh, Philip, I miss you so much. You are my only friend and the boys here are ever so mean to me.'"

The four laughed again.

Alexis struck out, her open palm connected with Timpson's cheek in a resounding *crack* that echoed through the cafe. Timpson's head rocked to the side and the laughter stopped.

"Damn you!" he yelled. "You can't—"

Crack.

"You are filth," she said coldly into the silent cafe. Everything the four had done overcoming her. Her isolation, their snide remarks, stealing her stores, their cruelty to the men, it all overwhelmed her. "Thieves and bullies, the lot of you!"

Timpson stood and glared at her. "Damn you, Carew! If you were a man—"

Alexis shoved him in the chest with both hands. "What would you do? Call me out?" She shoved him again and he staggered back, toppling his chair. "Do it!"

"Can't and you well know it!"

"Why? Because we're officers?" Rage filled her and, though she hadn't known what she wanted when she started into town, she was certain now that she wanted to kill Timpson. She wanted him to challenge her, despite the Navy's ban on dueling, and she wanted to see him fall.

Not for what he'd done to her, that had been cruel, but at least she'd known she wasn't receiving her messages. No, what burned in her was the knowledge of her grandfather's worry and what Philip and the others must have thought. *Still thought*. Receiving no answer at all, though they'd known she must have received theirs.

"Look around you, Timpson," she said. "We're not aboard ship — we're captured. Do you think the Hanoverse will care? Us dueling would be great sport for them!" She shoved him again. If he wouldn't call her out, then at least he could fight back. "Fight me, damn your eyes!"

"The Navy—"

"Will give not a fig that one less midshipman comes back after the war!"

She stepped back from him and looked around the cafe. The town residents had all stood and moved away from the table of midshipmen, staring on in fascination. All but the girls who'd been sitting with them. The two with Bushby and Canion were still on their laps, frozen and staring at Alexis along with everyone else. Delaine was whispering into the third girl's ear and she was staring at Timpson, her eyes narrowed and her mouth set in a firm line.

Alexis looked back to Timpson. "I name you a thief and a coward, Penn Timpson. What will you do about it?" She waited as Timpson straightened his jacket and looked away from her, jaw clenched but saying nothing. "I thought as much." She spat at his feet, turned, and left the cafe.

She was a hundred meters from the cafe when Delaine caught up with her. She gripped her hands together to stop them shaking, shocked at how viscerally disappointed she was that Timpson had not, in fact, called her out.

The rage she'd been feeling in the cafe was very like what she'd felt when she'd shot Horsfall. Then, and after, she'd told herself that it was necessary, that it was the only way to ensure the cooperation of the other pirates. Now, though, she had to admit that a part of her had looked at the harm he'd done to her crew and was glad for the excuse to kill him. The same part that had just tried to goad Timpson into challenging her. She clutched her suddenly roiling stomach and stretched her hand out to the wall of a nearby shop to steady herself. *What am I? To do these things?*

"*Alexis,*" Delaine said, grasping her arm. "Are you unwell?"

"I'm sorry —"

"*Non,* do not." He turned her to look back at the cafe. "But look, there."

Hermione's midshipmen were in a heated conversation with the three girls. As Alexis watched the three girls spun and strode from the cafe, heads up and hair flipping behind them. Canion called something after them, but the girl Delaine had spoken to threw her hand up in a universal gesture of contempt.

"What did you say to her?" Alexis asked.

"I gave her no words but your own — and my oath that they were true." Delaine smiled. "These *aspirants,* they will be quite lonely in Courboin now, I think."

Alexis smiled. That was probably a much more fitting punishment for them than what she'd attempted. What would she have done if Timpson had challenged her?

"You frightened me, *Alexis.*"

Alexis' heart froze. Had Delaine seen that darkness rising up in her and been put off? Would she lose him too?

"If he had challenged you ... I could not bear to see you harmed."

Alexis laughed, the sound a little shrill to her ears. Was that what he was frightened of? She'd trained with the marines aboard *Merlin* and *Hermione* for almost a year. Though she was nowhere near as skilled as they, the other midshipman barely bothered themselves to practice the minimum required.

"No fear there, Delaine," she said. "If ever I step onto the field with the likes of Penn Timpson, it won't be me left lying on the grass."

He took her hand and placed it on his arm to escort her back to the prison. "There is steel in you, *ma chatte.*"

There's something in me ... I only wish I knew what.

ALEXIS CLOSED her eyes and settled back against Delaine. They were sitting beneath a tree on a hillside some distance outside of town. In the far distance, she could hear the massive harvesters working the export fields. Nearer, the voices of those from the farms and town working their own fields by hand. The sun was very warm, but the shade of the tree and the occasional breeze made a pleasant contrast, and that breeze brought the scent of cut grain along with the workers' voices. For a moment, she could almost believe that she was home on Dalthus, the sounds and smells of harvest time were so familiar.

She reached for the remainders of the picnic lunch Delaine had brought for them and found the grapes, taking one and holding it over her shoulder for him. The feel of his lips on her fingertips made her shiver and flush. She giggled suddenly and covered her mouth with her hand.

"What amuses you so, *mon lapin?*"

She smiled and put her head back to rest against his chest. "Only that this is not at all what I should have imagined a foreign prison to be like."

She'd expected him to laugh, but felt him tense instead and she opened her eyes. The sky was blue and half full of soft, white clouds. The fields were full and prosperous. It was an idyllic sight and a perfect day, but she was suddenly worried. "What is it, Delaine?"

"I had thought to speak of it much later, but ..." He took a deep breath. "I would ask that you make the parole to my commodore, *Alexis.*"

Alexis felt a chill run through her. If Delaine was calling her by name instead of his duck or his hen or — *What was that last one? His rabbit?* No, if her name was all he could come up with then it was a serious thing indeed. "Why? After all this time?"

"I will be leaving soon. My commodore, she has received orders to meet a fleet of *le Hanovre.*"

Alexis' heart fell. She'd known it would happen someday. He had a ship and the ship would have to sail somewhere at some time. She'd miss him terribly, though. She raised her hand to his cheek. "I'll be all right with the lads, Delaine. Better there than in town with the others, I suspect."

"*Non*, you do not understand. This fleet will come and *le Hanovre* will ... the officers with the parole, *Alexis*, they will be allowed to stay, but your men will go. It has happened before elsewhere. Not always, but ... I would not take this chance with you."

She sat up and turned to face him. "Go? Where will they be taken?"

"Deeper into *Hanovre*. The war is hard and there are few to do the work. I have heard it is ... difficult in these places."

A chill went through her. "You mean some kind of work camp? They can't do that!" It was expressly against the laws of war to force captured spacers to work for the enemy.

"*Le Hanovre*, I do not think they care."

"You have to stop them!"

"*Alexis,* I will not be here. My commodore will not be here. We are to sail — all of our ships, all of our men — to meet this fleet and *le Hanovre amiral,* the admiral. Where he will send us, I do not know." He lowered one hand to the grass and caressed it, seemingly unaware of the gesture. "*Le Hanovre*, with the war, I think they no longer trust us beneath stars that were once *Français*."

"Sail to meet them? All of you?" she asked, not understanding. "Even the guards?"

Delaine nodded. "I do not think this admiral knows of your men yet, or he would not have ordered it so." He shrugged. "But the orders are clear and my commodore, she must obey. All ships of the fleet, all men of the fleet, will sail and meet this admiral. Men from the town will guard you from tonight, until the admiral arrives."

"Tonight?"

"*Oui*." He looked down. "I am sorry. The orders, they only came this morning. As it is, I take time from my own ship, my *Bélier*, to see you once more."

Alexis raised her hands to her mouth, trying to take in these changes. He was leaving so soon and what would this new admiral really do with her and her lads?

"You see, *Alexis*, yes? You must give the parole now, before —"

She pressed her fingers to his lips, silencing him. "No, Delaine. *Non*." She smiled. "You must go with your ship and I must stay with my lads. We can do no other." She leaned forward to kiss him, sorrow at being parted from him warring with excitement at an idea that was just forming.

NINETEEN

"Remember what I told you," Alexis whispered to Lain and Moberly.

"Aye, sir," Moberly said. "We'll take care."

"See that you do. They're simply men from the town, set to a task they never asked for. I don't want them injured if it can be avoided."

"My lads will see to it, sir," he said. "Take 'em down gentle like."

"And you've told them the words I gave you?"

"Aye, sir," Moberly said, nodding. "Hands up and throw down yer gun, all Frenchified. Couple of the lads had trouble wrapping their tongues around it, but the meaning'll come through, I think."

Alexis nodded, though not very confident. *My mangled guesses at the words and their thick tongues, we'll be lucky to get by without asking the guards to the summer dance.* "Good then. Go see to it. We'll give it an hour past dark and then move. Lain, do you have the man I asked for?"

"I do, sir. Collison's the man you want. Pinched fer stealing aircars on Etal and says he can pilot anything and steal most."

"Good," Alexis said.

She stood and pulled the blanket of her little compartment aside for them to leave. She laid back down on her cot to wait, wondering if this was the right thing to do. If Delaine hadn't told her the men would be transferred, she likely wouldn't even attempt it. Escape depended on too many variables. She had confidence that her men would be able to overpower the guards, but she also had to be right that the antigrav hauler she'd seen in the fields would return early in the morning, before dawn. That was the norm on Dalthus, but she was making a huge gamble that it would be the same on Giron.

Delaine had to be telling the truth that the entire fleet had sailed to meet this new admiral. A single warship in orbit would put paid to any chance they had. At the same time, there had to be at least one merchantman in-system, and at least one of its boats landed at the port. It would be rather embarrassing to break out of prison, steal a hauler, and rush over two thousand kilometers to the port ... only to be left standing on an empty landing field when the Hanoverese fleet arrived.

Alexis closed her eyes, hoping to nap, but she still had a decision to make about the night's plans. What to do about the officers in town? Entering the town to retrieve them would increase the risk to the entire group. And did she really want to? Williard, perhaps, was worth saving, but there was no doubt New London and the Fleet would be far better off to never see the likes of Neals again.

Part of her longed to leave the midshipmen behind, but that was a vengeful, spiteful part of her. In the end, she couldn't predict the Hanoverese reaction when they arrived and found she and the crew had escaped — would they honor the officers' paroles, or would they punish them? That was what decided her — no matter her feelings about Neals, she couldn't take the risk they'd suffer for her actions and decisions.

She managed to sleep fitfully, but wasn't at all rested when a spacer lightly shook her shoulder and whispered, "It's time, sir." In the dark and with his voice so low, Alexis couldn't tell who it was. She rolled off the cot and put her boots on, having slept in her uniform.

"Sergeant Moberly said as you're to wait here 'til it's over, sir, if it's all right with you. Be more'n enough confusion out there in a bit."

"Yes, Scholer," she said, recognizing him now. "At least until it starts."

"That's not what Sergeant Moberly said —"

Somewhere in the darkness there was a muffled *clang* followed by a shout and then more shouting. Alexis ripped the curtain aside and strode out onto the warehouse floor. The lights came on, blindingly bright after the darkness, and Alexis could see that the struggle, at least inside, was over already. Each of the guards, even the ones walking the upper catwalk, was down on the floor, three or four marines and spacers surrounding them.

Within a few minutes, Moberly came in from outside, leading a file of marines, spacers, and chastened-looking French guards. "Lock 'em in the office, lads," he said, "and make sure they've no weapons or coms on them." He crossed to Alexis. "All taken, sir," he said, "and naught more than a bump or bruise to show for it."

Alexis reached out and grasped his forearm. "Thank you, Moberly," she said. "I'm afraid I have something more to ask of you, though."

"Sir?"

"While Lain's off to retrieve the hauler, I need a small group to come with me to bring back Captain Neals and the others."

Moberly paused. "Is that wise, sir?"

Alexis saw the same look of doubt on Scholer's face, as well as those of the spacer's nearby. She could understand, even felt the same way herself. Entering the town to retrieve Neals and the others was an additional risk — both from being discovered in the town and from the officers themselves. There was no way of predicting how Neals would react. "Wise or not, it is what we will do, sergeant. I'll have no one from *Hermione* left behind. No one."

"Aye, sir." His brow furrowed. "Four marines, do you think? So's not to be too many tramping through the town?"

Alexis nodded. "That will do nicely." She saw Lain approaching with another spacer.

J A SUTHERLAND

"Collison's ready to go, sir," he said.

"Are you certain you can start a Hanoverese hauler, Collison?" Alexis asked. "And fly it?"

Collison grinned. "Never seen nothing I couldn't steal and fly, sir." His grin grew wider. "It's keeping it too long that got me pinched."

"Well, that won't be an issue this time," she assured him. "Once we're at the port we'll leave the hauler behind and there'll be something new for you to steal for us."

Collison laughed. "Always suspected the Navy was a good fit for me."

"It's quite possible it won't be locked at all," she said, "if they treat it as we did on Dalthus. There's little point in stealing something everyone on the planet can recognize."

Collison looked vaguely offended at the prospect of someone not locking their vehicle.

Alexis clasped him on the shoulder. "We're all counting on you, Collison. Get that hauler back here instanter."

"Aye, sir."

She watched Collison walk away with Lain to join the spacers and marines who were going after the hauler. "You picked steady men to go with them?"

"Aye sir," Moberly said. "And Lain chose a man or two who knows his way about sneaking in the dark."

Alexis nodded. The Navy's penchant for sweeping the gaols for crew was coming in disturbingly handy. "I'll want only marines with us when we go to town, Moberly," she said. "I think it best the captain not see any of the spacers until absolutely necessary."

"And them not see him, sir? The lads'll not be happy to see him and the others."

"He's still the captain, Moberly." She saw that he looked uncertain. "What is it?"

Moberly hesitated as though deciding whether to speak. "Only

220

that, well, is he, sir? Still the captain, I mean … with him giving parole and all?"

Now it was Alexis' turn to hesitate. She hadn't considered that. Parole was an agreement not to escape, after all — *could* Captain Neals and the others accompany them or would it violate their parole? Would the trip into town and its danger of discovery be for nothing? And what would the captain's reaction be if he must stay while she left?

"Let me and the captain worry about that, sergeant," she said.

ALEXIS LED Moberly and four other marines out of the warehouse. The night was cool and quiet, with only the occasional buzz of an insect to break the silence. The guards from town had arrived in an old, decrepit ground-truck with an open bed, rather than the ship's boat the fleet guards had used. *And wouldn't it make things easier to have that for our use?* But, of course, if the fleet was still guarding them they'd have no opportunity to escape.

"Can any of your men drive this, Moberly?"

"I can, sir," one of them spoke up.

"Well, get to it, Simcoe," Alexis said. She took a seat in the driver's compartment with Simcoe while Moberly and the others clambered into the back. They'd taken the time to arm themselves with the stunrods and pistols of their former guards, but Alexis dearly hoped they'd not have the need to use them. *In and out, then back here with the officers to meet the hauler. After that …*

Well, after that she had only the vaguest of plans. Cram the men into the hauler and make for the nearest port. Hope that a ship's boat from some merchant was on the landing field and could be taken. Hope further that they could take the merchant ship itself and that Delaine had told her the truth about all of the local fleet's ships having left the system to meet the Hanoverese.

The quiet whine of the truck's motor and the soft sound of its tires against the road barely disturbed the night as Simcoe pulled away from the warehouse and headed toward town. In a surprisingly short time they pulled to a stop in front of the building that housed *Hermione's* officers. It had been a vacant shop and residence when they'd arrived and had been rented to house the officers much as the warehouse had been converted into a prison for the men.

"We should go to the back, sir," Moberly advised. "If there're servants they'll be housed back there and might think it's a tradesman come early, or a servant from another house."

Alexis nodded. "Lead the way, sergeant," she said. "This is your bailiwick."

The six of them made their way to the alleyway behind the building and Moberly knocked sharply on the rear door. When there was no response for several minutes, he knocked again, then a third time. Finally they saw a light in the window and heard a shuffling behind the door before a voice called out.

"*Que?*"

Moberly opened his mouth and looked at Alexis, eyes wide and panicked. Alexis met his gaze, heart beating wildly. *No, we didn't consider that bit, did we?* She stepped beside Moberly and leaned close to the door, wracking her brain for what French she'd picked up from Delaine and the guards. *And hope it's more than 'my little hen'.*

"*Pardonnez-moi, madame. Je suis tombé ...*" *I've fallen and ... oh, hell, what's the word for leg?* "*... ma cuisse est blessé.*" She blushed and bit her lip. *Have to go with 'thigh' and not just leg ... and you'd think with all the body parts Delaine murmured in my ear ...* No, Delaine's murmurings were quite a bit more ... specific. Alexis flushed, knowing it wasn't the time for such thoughts.

"*Oh cher!*"

Alexis heaved a sigh of relief as she heard the rattle of the lock and stepped back from the door. "Don't harm her," she whispered to Moberly.

He nodded and as the door started to open pushed forward, shouldering the door open and grasping the old woman behind it. He spun her around and clasped a hand over her mouth before she had time to more than gasp in surprise. The four other marines hurried past him, Alexis following behind.

"*Calmer. Non blessé. Calme. Nous serons partis,*" she whispered to the old woman, trying to calm her and assure her that they'd be gone soon and not harm her. The woman's eyes were wide and darting around the room and she was breathing harshly behind Moberly's hand. Alexis was certain she was butchering the words, but her meaning seemed to be getting through. "*Calmer. Sil vous plaît? Nous voulons ...*" *Well, no, I don't actually want them, I suppose.* "*Les* New London *hommes.*"

The woman stopped struggling and stared hard at Alexis. She made muffled noises behind Moberly's hand, trying to speak. "*Calme, oui?*" Alexis whispered and the woman nodded. Alexis nodded to Moberly and he took his hand away from her mouth.

"*Vous venez pour les hommes?*" she whispered.

"*Oui,*" Alexis said, nodding. "We've come for the men, the New London men, *oui.*"

The woman jerked her head to the side, spitting on the floor. "*Vous êtes les mutins? Bon! Prendre les! Les tuer, les brûler avec le feu, bon débarras!*"

Moberly's eyes widened in surprise at her tone and his grip must have slackened, for the woman shrugged out of his grasp and leaned back against the tall kitchen counter. She crossed her arms and raised her chin. "*Bâtards! Imbécile!*"

Alexis raised an eyebrow. She'd caught only a little of that. *Something about killing them and ... fire? I see Hermione's officers have endeared themselves as always.* She laid a hand on the woman's arm. "*Bientôt,*" she said. *They'll be gone soon.*

The marines were returning to the kitchen, having searched the ground floor, but she wanted to ensure it was only the officers above stairs. "*Domestique?*"

The woman snorted, nostrils flaring wide. "*Un!*" She grabbed her breast and waved a hand at the door. "*Pfft! Et deux!*" She grabbed her bottom and flung a hand at the door. *"Pfft! Et trois! Pfft! Pfft!"*

Alexis nodded, motioning for her to be quiet. She didn't fully understand what the woman was saying, but took it to mean that there were no other servants in the house.

"Well," Alexis said. "Now all we have to do is decide who'll wake Captain Neals."

IN THE END, she sent a marine to wake Lieutenant Williard, who woke the midshipmen and Mister Rochfort, and then sent Ledyard to wake the captain. He agreed with Alexis that the captain would not react well to being awakened by her or one of the marines, not after the mutiny and given his dislike of her personally. Ledyard soon returned with Captain Neals, who'd taken the time to dress himself in his full uniform before deigning to come downstairs, Wrigley and Patridge, his personal servant and his clerk, trailing behind.

Reina, the housekeeper, had introduced herself while they waited and busied herself with putting out plates of bread, cheese, and pastry for the marines. She even brewed coffee and spoke pleasantly to them as she poured. She understood some English, but spoke mostly French and Alexis was just as glad the marines spoke none of it as she overheard the woman pleasantly whisper, *"Tuer le petit bâtard premier."*

'Kill the little bastard first'? Good lord, what's gone on in this house these last few months? She was almost afraid of what might happen if the woman realized they weren't here to harm *Hermione's* officers as she seemed to think. And what were they to do with her when they left? She'd have to discuss it with Moberly and find some way to restrain her until they were well away.

"What nonsense are you about now, Carew?" Neals demanded as he entered the kitchen. His gaze slid to Reina. "Coffee, you stupid, Frog bitch, and be quick about it!"

224

"Captain Neals," Alexis said. "I've found out that a Hanoverese fleet is coming. All the ships that were here have sailed to meet them and we've a chance to escape, sir."

Neals looked at her for a moment, then shook his head. "A Hanoverese fleet? There's already a Hanoverese fleet here, Carew. Many ships and a commodore, do you recall? That's a fleet, girl." He sighed heavily. "You've interrupted my sleep for this nonsense?" At the counter, Ledyard and Timpson smirked at her.

"Captain," Williard said. "Mister Carew's explained it to me while you were dressing, sir. Commodore Balestra's fleet isn't properly Hanoverese. It's more of a ... a local defense force, do you see? And the people of these systems, herself included, it seems, think of themselves more as French."

"That much was obvious from the first, Mister Williard," Neals said, "since the entire town speaks nothing but Frog."

"Yes, sir," Williard said, "but Commodore Balestra's been called to meet a fleet from Hanover proper, do you see? *All* of her ships, sir, and *all* of her men."

Neals narrowed his eyes and looked at Alexis. "Well, why didn't you say so, Carew? All their warships are gone? You're certain of this?"

Alexis fought down the urge to snap at him that she had, indeed, said so. Her time away from Neals, it seemed, had gotten her used to being in command of her men and not at all prepared for Neals' abuse again. "Such is the information I have, sir," she said, trying to keep her voice calm and respectful. "Bosun Lain has taken a few hands and some of Sergeant Moberly's marines to take a hauler from a nearby farm. It's my hope that —"

Neals' face had grown pinched and red as she spoke. "*Bosun Lain, Carew?*"

Oh ... bugger it, I'm done for now. She hadn't even thought of his reaction to the promotions she'd made, not in the middle of trying to escape.

"Lain is a bosun's mate, Carew, and a poor one at that!" He

turned his attention to Moberly. "And what's this 'sergeant' nonsense, corporal? Kill off your superiors and make a jump for yourself, is that it?"

"No, sir," Moberly said, clearly shaken at Neals' words.

Alexis stepped forward. "Sir, the men were idle and needed direction, sir." She thought frantically of how to phrase it. "I did the best I could as the only officer present, sir. I'm sure you'll wish to review everything yourself, sir, as captain, but —" She glanced at Williard, hoping he'd step in.

"Yes, sir," Williard added. "I'm sure you'll wish to review everything Carew's done in your absence ... and correct what messes she's made, sir, but with the time we have ..." He shrugged. "The very little time we have, sir?"

Neals clenched his jaw. "Yes, I suppose." He glared at Alexis. "I'll expect a most thorough report of all your actions, Carew, once we're aboard a ship and away from this bloody system. Now how many men do I have and what is our situation."

Alexis started to answer, but Williard cut her off.

"Sir," he said, his voice sounding unsure. He was reviewing his tablet. While Alexis' had been taken from her, the paroled officers had retained theirs. They'd have no access to the Hanoverese networks, but could use them to authorize purchases and for any information stored on them. "Sir, there is a ... difficulty."

"What?" Neals snapped.

"Sir, I've been reviewing the regulations and, well, we, all of us except Mister Carew ... well, we gave our parole, sir."

"What of it, Mister Williard? Speak up, damn you, it was just a moment ago you spoke of limited time!"

Williard's eyes remained on his tablet as he slid a finger over the screen. He swallowed heavily, as though not wanting to speak. "It's only, sir, that our parole was to neither escape nor take up arms against Hanover for the duration of the war."

"What are you saying, lieutenant?"

"Well, sir —" He cleared his throat. "— I'm reviewing the regulations as they pertain to parole, and ... well, we gave our word not to escape ..."

"That agreement surely doesn't hold when the entire fleet of guards has flown off and left the system to us," Neals said.

"I believe it does," Williard said. "We agreed, sir, upon our honor, not to escape."

Neals smiled. "But once we have," he said, "what will the Hanoverese do about it, eh?"

Williard looked shocked — even the midshipmen looked askance at Neals. A gentleman's word, a naval officer's word, was supposed to be inviolate. Their honor had been pledged to the parole they'd agreed to.

"It's not just our honor, sir," Williard said. "If we break our parole ... well, why would the Hanoverese trust the word of the next set of officers they capture? And what of the Queen, sir? As officers we represent Her Honor as well, do we not?"

"Damn you, Williard!" Neals almost shouted. "Are you telling me I should stay on this bloody rock because of some words I said to that jumped up whore Balestra?"

Williard took a step back from Neals. He looked around the room at the others. "Sir ..." He trailed off and swallowed heavily. "Sir, as an officer and ... and in my person as Lord Ashcroft, sir, I may not break my parole." He paled but met Neals' eye. "And I must advise you the same, sir." He glanced down at his tablet again and hurried on. "But there may be a way ..."

"Speak up!"

"Sir, we may not, none of us who gave our parole, escape. Not with our honor intact. But ..." He looked at Alexis and then back at Neals, as though dreading his next words.

"Spit it out, man!"

"Sir, we may not escape, but we may be *rescued*."

"CAPTAIN NEAL'S MAD, SIR."

Alexis nearly cried out with relief when Moberly squeezed in beside her and closed the door to the ground-truck's driving compartment. With Simcoe set to drive them all back to the warehouse, she'd been afraid that Neals would insist on riding up front, but Moberly had announced that he'd need to supervise Simcoe — with the two of them, there was just enough room for Alexis in the middle. Neals and the other officers had been relegated to the truck's open bed with the marines.

"Moberly ..." Alexis warned.

"Barkin' mad, sir," Moberly said. "I expect we'll see him running wild and howling at the sky come the next full-moon night."

Alexis struggled to maintain her composure. The stress of the day, the night, and, not less, the last quarter hour of listening to Captain Neals rant and harangue Lieutenant Williard over the thought of being 'rescued' by her — all of it had come together to put her on the very edge. The image of Neals baying at the moon was almost enough to put her over into hysterical laughter.

"That's enough of that, Moberly," she said instead. "He's still the captain."

"Not as Lieutenant Williard tells it, sir, least not as I heard him."

No, Williard had been quite clear on the point, standing up to Neals no matter how angry the captain had become. None of the officers could participate in the escape, they could only follow. They could not be armed, could not fight, could give no orders, could not even offer advice — not without breaking their parole. The entire responsibility for getting them back to New London space would fall upon Alexis and the crew.

In a way she was grateful to Williard, for she had little confidence that Neals could manage it if he were in command. At the same time, she held no illusions about Williard's motives. The man wanted to get home, and with his honor intact — he cared not one whit about Alexis or the men. In fact, the insistence that they "be rescued" protected not only the officers' honor, but their very lives.

If the group was recaptured, Alexis and the men could be executed as escaped prisoners while Neals, Williard, and the midshipmen would at least have the argument to make that they were still on parole and only being "rescued".

Alexis' own status as an unparoled prisoner complicated things even more. If a New London force had stormed the system and released them, they'd have been free to arm themselves and fight from that moment. But Williard's reading of the regulations and the wording of their parole was that Alexis didn't qualify — only making contact with a *free* New London force would free them from the terms of their parole.

For Neals the prospect of having to stand aside and follow Alexis' direction until they reached a New London system or made contact with the Fleet ... well, Alexis had feared the captain would fall to the ground in an apoplectic fit before he'd finished venting his spleen on Williard. *And so much the easier for all of us if he only had.*

If anything, Neals had been even angrier upon being informed that he would have to leave most of his personal effects and cabin furnishings behind. They'd been brought down from *Hermione* for him, along with the other officers' chests and belongings, but there was no way it would all fit in the ground-truck — and no way Alexis would take the risk of bringing the hauler into town. Instead all of the officers had been limited to what they could stuff in makeshift bags and carry along with them.

"Get us back, Simcoe," she said.

"Aye sir."

She settled back for the ride, only now that her own part in retrieving the officers was done she began to worry about the men who'd gone off after the hauler. They should have arrived at the fields where she thought the hauler would return by now. Their return trip, if they were successful, would be much quicker. Quicker even than her little group in the ground-truck. If they hadn't been successful then ... well, that didn't bear thinking on. For her and the men there was no turning back now. They had no choice but to succeed.

She breathed a heavy sigh of relief as she saw a hauler's lights ahead of them, landing at the warehouse. Simcoe picked up the pace and sent the ground-truck speeding forward without having to be told. Neals would probably have something to say about the jostling as the truck careened up to the warehouse and rocked to stop, but Alexis was too relieved to care.

The men left in the warehouse had heard the hauler or one of the lookouts had informed them, and they poured out, lining up to board. Alexis crowded past Moberly and rushed to the hauler, finding Lain as he clambered out of the hauler's massive, box-shaped cargo compartment.

"Trouble?" she asked.

"Not a bit, sir," he said. "Found it just like you said at the edge of that field. Looked like some men were up and at breakfast nearer the farmstead, but no guard a'tall. Might as not even know we took her yet."

"Moberly!" Alexis called over her shoulder. "You and Lain see to loading the men!" She turned to face the growing crowd. "It'll be crowded, mind you, lads! So watch your tempers!"

"Aye sir!" came the chorused reply.

Alexis hurried to the hauler's cab. It would be crowded, indeed, with more than seventy men and their bags crammed into the hauler's cargo compartment. Moreover, it would be uncomfortable, with no seating — and no pressurization or heat for the long flight to the nearest port almost two thousand kilometers away. Even at the hauler's top speed the trip would be hours long with little room to sit down.

"I hear it all went smoothly, Collison," she said, climbing into the hauler's cab.

"Weren't even locked, sir" Collison said, lip curled in disgust.

"I'm sorry, Collison. The very next time we're captured, I'll try to ensure it's a properly distrustful planet, shall I?" She settled herself behind him. "Where do we stand, then?"

"Disabled the transponders right off, sir," he said. "Such as they was. This system don't have enough satellites fer proper navigatin', ferget about trackin'." He gestured at the sparse console. "By guess and by eye ter get us anywheres, but there's a decent map." He tapped one of the panels that showed a map. "I've an idea of the proper course for the port, sir."

"Anything on the radio?"

"Nothing, sir, but it's nearing dawn. I'd 'spect they'll find this thing's missing soon."

"All right, Collison," she said. She opened the cab's door to hop out and check on the loading. "Good work."

"Thank you, sir."

Alexis made her way to the rear of the hauler, trying to think of what might happen next. What would happen on Dalthus if a hauler went missing? First whichever holder had hired its use would try to raise it on the radio ... no the hauler's pilot, there at the holding, would try to raise it. He'd want to know what fool was off joyriding in it and he wouldn't want to alert the dispatcher that he'd gone and lost one of the most valuable things on the planet.

Then there'd be the sheepish call to the dispatch office. More calls to locate the other pilots. Had someone made a mistake and taken the vehicle on another run? It could be an hour or more, she hoped, from the time they discovered it missing to when they suspected foul play. Longer, perhaps, if the original pilot received a response to his initial queries — something garbled, with a great deal of static, but just enough to make him think there had been a misunderstanding or emergency? It was certainly worth a try.

TWENTY

"I MAKE IT ONE BOAT, SIR."

Alexis reached forward and turned off the hauler's radio. They were in sight of the port's landing field and the hauler's original pilot and dispatcher had grown angry and suspicious with her anyway. She'd managed to put them off a bit, at least until the prison guards' replacements had arrived to find their fellows locked up. Once that news had filtered from place to place over the radio, it had been pretty clear who had taken their hauler. Now she could only hope that whatever response was organized took enough time for her and the crew to reach the port and take a boat. The only boat, she saw as the port's landing field came into view. She'd hoped for more than one boat to be on the field, which would mean more than one ship in orbit — more than one chance for it to be a ship large enough for her crew and not some pinnace or cutter that would hold less than half of them. *One's better than none, though.*

"I'd hoped there might be more than one, Collison," she said, "but we'll make do, yes?"

"Aye sir," he answered. "Makin' do's done us well so far, it has."

Alexis took a deep breath. "Let's be about it, then," she said.

Collison nodded and hunched over the hauler's controls. He seemed to have the hauler aimed directly for the ship's boat and as they got closer and lower with the hauler still at high speed, they overflew the boat with barely a meter's space to spare and dropped to the field immediately past it. If the hauler hadn't had its own gravity generator and inertial compensator, the men in the cargo compartment would have been flung about like rag dolls. As it was, Collison slammed those compensators off as soon as the hauler had stopped moving and that was the signal for the men in back to a.

They threw open the doors of the cargo compartment and fell on the few merchant spacers around the boat. It was over before Alexis and Collison were even able to exit the cab and rush to the rear of the hauler. Shocked by the hauler's abrupt arrival and the rush of men, the boat's small crew was overwhelmed. Lain and Moberly wasted no time in identifying the boat's pilot and dragging him to Alexis.

"What ship?" Alexis demanded.

"*Que?*"

Oh, I'm bloody tired of hearing that, I am. "*Navire! Ce navire?*" Her crew was busy crowding aboard the boat.

"*Trau Wunsch.*"

"How big? *La taille?*" In the corner of her vision she could see Neals and the other officers standing to the side while the crew streamed aboard. *Are they really?* Would Neals really stand on precedent and insist on boarding last even given the circumstances?

The pilot was pale and shaking. "*Barque, une cent de tonnes.*"

Alexis almost shouted with delight. It would be large enough ... just. The ride up in the boat would be standing room, with most of the crew stuffed into the boat's hold or stacked like cordwood, but a ship that size would be enough for them. It would be tight, and they'd have to sleep in shifts with many berthing in the hold, but it would be enough — there'd be enough air and water to sustain them the week or two it would take to reach New London space, and food might grow short, but they could do it.

"*En haut! Immédiatement!*" She gestured for the pilot to enter the boat.

"*Que?*"

"On the boat and take us up!" Alexis yelled, pointing at the ramp. "*Vous prenez l'avion!*"

The man blanched and Lain gave him a shove toward the ramp. "Up you go, lad, a'fore the cap'n feeds ya yer own liver!"

Alexis followed them, calling out, "Get aboard, lads, and hurry!" she called out.

She rushed up the ramp and into the cockpit, seating herself beside the pilot. She wracked her brain for the French to make him understand.

"*Vous nous prendre pour le navire. Aucun avertissement.* We take your ship and you have the boat and your life, yes? *No warnings!*" She drew a finger across her throat to underscore the threat. "*Comprenez vous?*"

"*Oui!*" the pilot nodded, head bobbing rapidly.

Lain and Moberly crowded into the cockpit behind them.

"Lads're aboard, sir," Lain said. "Captain Neals is on the ramp."

THE TAKING of *Trau Wunsch* went quickly. The boat's pilot made some excuse for returning to the ship so quickly. Alexis didn't know exactly what, because the pilot was speaking German, *Trau Wunsch* being from Hanover proper and not one of the formerly French worlds. She was confident, though, that Moberly's hulking presence next to him kept the pilot honest.

They likely could have taken the ship simply by announcing their intentions on the way up to orbit, though, as *Trau Wunsch* had only three men aboard as an orbit watch. The rest were on leave or about business in the port. Once the boat made fast and the hatch opened, there was no resistance as Alexis' crew stormed aboard and took control.

"All hands to the sails, Mister Lain! At least those we've vacsuits for and'll fit."

"Aye sir!"

Alexis ran her fingers over the barque's navigation plot, confirming, for the third time since entering the quarterdeck, that the ship's systems were unlocked. *Unlocked ... but in bloody German, which'll be a challenge in itself.*

"Sergeant Moberly, are our reluctant benefactors well away?"

"Aye sir! Into the boat and the cockpit locked against them. Shoved away and drifting. They'll not bother us 'til a boat from one o' them other ships comes for them."

"Thank you, Moberly." She rested her palms on the plot. "Take the signals console, Simcoe, as best you can. Get us underway, Ficke." She tapped the plot. "This moon here is closest — we'll transition at L1. No more than half power to the conventional drive, mind you, Ficke ... lord help us if they're in the same state as the rest of this tub. Mister Lain, I'll want the masts raised and all plain sail ready to charge the moment we transition."

"Aye sir!" the men chorused.

The ship's quarterdeck was a bustle of activity. The mess deck was even worse, with all her crew crowded in and trying to sort out who would best fit the bare two dozen vacsuits aboard. Most merchant ships carried the minimum of crew, and this one was no different. That was lucky for them in taking her, for half the crew had been planetside and there'd been only three of those left awake when their stolen boat arrived and made fast. *Awake and eating bloody breakfast on my quarterdeck!* Alexis shoved a dropped plate and its contents aside with her boot. Eating on the quarterdeck, indeed. *Their orbit watch was as slovenly as the rest.*

Trau Wunsch was not well-kept. The decks and bulkheads were filthy, her mess deck was cluttered and strewn with the crews' possessions, and the air had an odor to it. Not just the staleness and undertone of old sweat that a normal ship had, but a sour, gagging reek, as though some long forgotten cargo were rotting in the hold.

"Sergeant Moberly!" Alexis went on, returning to the long list of tasks that would see them underway.

"Sir?"

"Two marines to the hold, if you please, and they're to see no one goes down there on a lark." She had faith in most of the lads, they were still in far too much danger to take things less than seriously, but one or two might take the chance for a bit of exploring. She'd need her lads whole and sensible, not raiding whatever wine or spirits were stored aboard.

On the monitors, Giron fell away and behind them as Ficke applied power and pointed the ship toward the nearest moon and its Lagrange point. *Did I just feel the ship move?*

"Mister Lain!"

"Aye sir?"

"Two lads to engineering, lively now, and they're to see to the compensators. They'll not be able to read the consoles until we've changed them to proper English, mind you, so pick those who'll know what to look for in the readouts."

"Aye sir."

"And two more to the hold, while you're about it, please. Steady lads, and I'll have an accounting of our stores." They'd need to know how they were set for food and water. With so many more men aboard than the ship normally held, they could be on short rations for this trip. She looked around the quarterdeck, trying to think of what else needed doing before they transitioned, and after. The myriad little things it took to keep a ship running and safe. Her foot slid out from under her as she turned and she barely caught herself on the edge of the plot. Her face twisted with disgust at the smear of egg yolk across the deck and on her boot. "And an idler with a bucket, Mister Lain — handsomely, but I'll have this mess cleaned off my quarterdeck!"

"Aye sir!"

Alexis heard a muttered oath and looked up from the plot in

shock. She scanned the quarterdeck for who might have made the outburst. *Oh dear ...*

Captain Neals, along with the other officers, stood to the side. Crowded into the corner, really, as the quarterdeck itself was far smaller than a Navy ship's. He was scowling at her, face red. Alexis had all but forgotten him — having him locked away in the hauler's cargo compartment, in the passenger compartment of the boat on their way up, and, certainly, at the rear of the short, anti-climactic boarding action to take *Trau Wunsch* had been a great relief. She hadn't even noticed that he and the others had made their way onto the quarterdeck, so focused was she on getting underway. *Her* quarterdeck, as she'd just named it, clearly to Neals' greater displeasure.

"Ah, captain?" She caught her lip between her teeth. "Since you cannot ..." She shot Williard a pleading look, but found no help there. "Would you, perhaps, like to retire to the master's cabin? Mister Lain! A detail to the master's cabin to make it habitable for Captain Neals, if you please!" *Oh, bugger it, I did it again ... could I've made it clearer I only want him gone? And then give more orders while he's here?*

Neals' face grew redder, but he said nothing. Simply nodded curtly and stalked to the quarterdeck hatch, followed by the others.

Alexis turned back to her plot before the hatch had closed. The other ships around Giron were staying steady in their orbits. She breathed a silent sigh of relief at that, if any of them had chosen to come after *Trau Wunsch*, they'd be hard pressed to resist.

"Simcoe," she said, turning to the signals console. "My compliments to the gunner, please, and I'd admire a report on the state of our armaments."

"SAIL! Starboard beam, down thirty! Close aboard!"

Alexis rushed from the navigation plot to the tactical station, a jolt of fear running through her. They were still well within Hanoverese space and unless Hache hadn't been paying attention, close aboard meant it had to be a warship lying with sails dark and unpowered.

"I was watchin', sir," Hache said. "Just appeared like, right where she is."

A picket, then. With the border and space so vast Alexis had hoped the odds would be on their side and they'd be able to avoid any Hanoverese ships and make it to New London space without incident. Apparently they wouldn't have that luck.

"Signal, sir!" Moreton called from the signals console. "She's flying Hanoverese colors ... *Heave to for inspection.*"

Trau Wunsch was flying Hanoverese colors as well. Alexis had hoped that would get them past any cursory look by an enemy ship, but that wouldn't fool them once they boarded.

"Small, sir," Hache said. "Pinnace, no more than six guns."

Alexis caught her lip between her teeth. Six would be more than enough, given the state of *Trau Wunsch*. The merchantman was large and had ports for eight guns, but only four aboard — tiny two-pounders, no better than flashlights. Of those, one's barrels were so scarred and pitted from previous use that the gunner had declared it unusable. Another he allowed they could try in dire straits, but reckoned it more of a danger to their own ship.

The guns weren't the only thing the merchant captain had skimped on. They'd found that *Trau Wunsch* had barely three dozen cartridges for the guns aboard and those were so ill-kept that the gunner had immediately had them all torn down and reassembled. Their contacts would need replacing and their capacitors checked for wear. A capacitor failure on the gundeck would be catastrophic. They had, perhaps, a dozen rounds they could rely upon and a dozen more that might or might not fire.

Alexis wanted to scream in frustration. They were so close, she suspected, to the border that the next ship they encountered after this would likely be from New London. Instead she forced her voice to stay calm and level, hearing her first captain's words in her head.

Decorum, Mister Carew. You must keep a steady hand to steady the men.

"Beat to quarters, Mister Lain," she said, a bit surprised at how calm she sounded. "But keep the guns inboard. Half those with vacsuits to the sail locker and half to the guns, please." She waited while the bosun rushed forward to the ship's mess deck where the guns and the bulk of the men were.

Vacsuits were another thing they lacked. The merchantman normally had a crew of twenty-six, including the captain and mates, far fewer than the number of *Hermiones* now crammed aboard. She'd told the bosun to assign those suits to the sail and gun crews as best he could. Some of the men would be in suits that were ill-fitting and all of them have complaints about the plumbing. Alexis would have no suit at all — there'd be none small enough for her, and as for that plumbing, well, *Trau Wunsch* had an all-male crew.

When the mess deck was cleared for action and the air evacuated, those without suits would have to cram onto the quarterdeck or into the holds as best they could. The thought of going into action in this fragile hulled scow with most of her crew unsuited filled Alexis with dread.

"Keep the Hanoverese colors flying, Moreton," she said, "but be ready to replace them with our own." Flying false colors was a legitimate ruse of war, but the first shot had to be fired under their true colors.

Alexis looked at the navigation plot for a moment and shook her head. There was no chance of outrunning the Hanoverese pinnace. Even though *Trau Wunsch* had three large masts to the much smaller pinnace's one, the maintenance on her particle projector had been neglected and none of the sails could be fully charged.

I do believe I've stolen the worst-kept ship in the entire universe.

"Signal *Will Comply*, Moreton," she said. "They'll expect us to take a moment to send men out to work the sails."

The bosun returned, followed by ten of the men all in vacsuits. Shortly after they'd made their way into the sail locker, Captain

Neals and the rest of *Hermione's* officers entered the quarterdeck. Alexis had given them the master's quarters, crowded though it was. It gave them some privacy and kept them out of the way of the rest of the crew. Alexis herself had been standing watch-and-watch, bedding down for a few hours' sleep in a corner.

"What are you about, Carew?" Neals demanded. "Why was quarters sounded?"

"Sir, there's a Hanoverese pinnace after us," she said. "If you could please —"

Neals rested his hands on the edge of the navigation plot and leaned over, eyes narrowing. "You let him get this close? You incompetent ..."

Alexis clenched her jaw.

"Sir," Williard said. "We may really not participate in the action, we—"

"Oh, bugger the parole, Williard," Neals snapped. "I'll not put my life in this ... girl's hands." Neals continued to study the plot and shook his head. "Look at what she's gotten us into. We can't outrun him and there's certainly no way we can fight with this tub she dragged us onto. Our only hope is to strike."

Alexis stared at him for a moment, then her stomach clenched with rage. He thought he'd just walk in and take over? Strike without a single shot being fired and send her lads back? Back to whatever work camp the Hanoverese had in mind for them if they were lucky, or to be executed for escaping at the worst?

Alexis leaned close to Moreton and whispered. "My compliments to Sergeant Moberly, Moreton, and he's to come to the quarterdeck with three marines. Armed." *Or as much as they can be with what we have aboard.*

She squared her shoulders and stepped to the plot opposite Neals. No, she wouldn't allow it. These lads were her crew now, not his. This ship was hers. She taken it with her crew and this was her quarterdeck. If there was one thing she'd learned of the Navy, it was that a captain was sole master of her ship. No one except the ship's captain, not even an admiral, gave orders to a ship's crew. Moberly and three marines had just entered from the companionway.

"Captain Neals," she said, forcing her voice to remain calm and low. "I'm afraid I must ask you to leave my quarterdeck."

There was silence for a long moment. Neals slowly raised his eyes from the plot to meet hers. His face red with fury. "*Your* quarterdeck?"

"You are on parole, Captain Neals, you have no authority to give orders. *I* took this ship. It is mine and this crew is mine. I'll not allow you to send them back to the Hanoverese just because you have no stomach for a fight."

Williard stepped over to Neals and whispered in his ear.

"Moreton," Alexis said, not caring what Williard was saying. "Send the lads out of the locker to the sails."

"Aye, Captain."

Alexis felt the corner of her lip twitch and her heart swelled. The master of a ship was addressed as captain, regardless of her actual rank. Moreton had just clearly stated where he stood. She resisted the urge to walk over and hug him.

"Allmond, tell me the moment that pinnace comes within range of our guns."

"Aye, Captain."

Neals was staring at her, face now white and eyes wide. Alexis could almost sympathize — to him, it must seem almost as though he was facing a second mutiny.

Alexis caught Moberly's eye and he nodded slightly. Alexis squared her shoulders, the marines would follow Moberly.

"Sergeant," she said, "Captain Neals and the other officers from *Hermione* are distraught. Please see them safely to their quarters and that they remain safe there throughout the action."

"Aye, Captain." Moberly stepped over to Neals. Williard faded back to stand with the midshipmen.

Neals glared at her. "I'll see you hang for this, Carew."

"As you wish, Captain Neals, but I'll see my lads safely home first."

"ON MY WORD, gentlemen, and not before." Alexis alternated her gaze between the navigation plot and the image of the approaching pinnace. *Trau Wunsch* sat dead in space, her sails doused, but only lightly furled. It would be but a moment's work for the spacers, still on the masts and fumbling as though they were an incompetent merchant crew, to let them fall again. The pinnace closed, taking in her own sails to heave to close to *Trau Wunsch*. The timing would be critical.

"Guns," she said. She forced herself to count silently to herself. On the mess deck, the gun crews would be ripping the covers from the gunports. Once those were off, they'd lose communication to the guns except by runner, for this ship carried no gallenium nets to block the radiation of *darkspace*.

"Colors!" she cried. "And sails, now!"

Moreton, on the signals console, stabbed a finger on his console and announced, "Flying the ensign, sir!" just as the first shots flashed out from *Trau Wunsch's* guns. The sails dropped and charged, filling with a faint, azure glow instead of the bright color shot through with white sparks and lightning that Alexis longed for. *What a piece of shite!* The sails billowed and filled and *Trau Wunsch* began to plod forward, not the rapid leap Alexis had experienced on other ships.

The pinnace fired back, *Trau Wunsch's* first shots seeming to have done no damage. Her sails dropped as well and flashed azure in the console's image. *Trau Wunsch* shook and Alexis bit her lip. *Lord, is the hull so frail we can feel a pinnace's shot strike?*

Alexis watched the plot carefully. This action would be a brutal exchange of shot. She couldn't escape and the pinnace wouldn't let her, so it would come down to who could pummel the other more thoroughly. The Hanoverese had more and heavier guns, but Alexis had faith in her crew being the faster to reload and fire. Faith that was well justified as the next shots were fired. A trio of light, ineffectual bolts that splashed against the pinnace's hull with no discernible damage. It was a full forty-five seconds more before the pinnace reloaded and fired again. The ship shook again, the energy of the lasers vaporizing the hull's thermoplastic.

Damn! "Target their gunports! We have to reduce their rate of fire." She watched a runner in a vacsuit hurry off to relay her orders.

Trau Wunsch fired again, but only two bolts this time and the ship shuddered more than before. *What? They didn't fire.*

The runner returned. "Targeting gunports, sir, but the number two gun's tubes have blown!"

Alexis clenched her eyes shut. The gunner had warned her, but she'd hoped they'd last longer. She felt a moment's fear for the crews on the guns. When the tubes blew, overloaded and worn out from focusing the energy of the lasers, the shot would splinter and fire off within the hull. There was no telling how many had been wounded or killed. The pinnace fired again and *Trau Wunsch* shook, the energy of the thermoplastic hull vaporizing transmitted along her length.

She briefly considered attempting to board the other ship. There were enough men with vacsuits to outnumber the other crew, but not substantially so. The extra fifty or more men on *Trau Wunsch* were useless unless they could be brought to the fight, and all the Hanoverese would have to do was depressurize a compartment to kill them all.

Damn me, but we could outrun them if we only had a decent projector. But even with its single mast, the pinnace would be able to keep up with them. *A single mast.* Alexis had a sudden thought. *Trau Wunsch's* guns weren't heavy enough or many enough to damage a mast in time. They might cut some rigging, but that was all and could be quickly repaired. But without that single mast, the pinnace would have no chance of catching them.

"Everyone in from the sails! All brace for collision!" she shouted, rushing to the helm and hoping the messages could be relayed in time. She waited, anxious, while the order was relayed. *Trau Wunsch* shuddered again as the pinnace fired. She watched the other ship's position carefully, judging the angles. Another exchange of fire and quarterdeck lights flickered. Somewhere the ship had been holed and some wiring cut. She couldn't wait any longer. *Please let them be down from the masts.*

"Drop the keelboard! Hard a'starboard, up twenty!"

"Keelboard, aye, sir!" From the bottom of the ship the narrow, telescoping keelboard would be extending. Twenty meters out from the ship, well outside the ship's field, and containing no gallenium itself, the keelboard would drag and cut against the morass of *darkspace.* Slowing *Trau Wunsch,* but allowing her to turn more sharply and sail at an angle to the winds. The helmsman turned the wheel hard to starboard, toward the Hanoverese pinnace and angling to pass above it. The other ship reacted, but not in time.

Trau Wunsch slid into its path. The foremast struck first, angled down and to starboard off *Trau Wunsch's* bow. Its tip struck just behind the pinnace's bow, yards and rigging entangled. Both ships shuddered and shook, the force of the impact transmitted through their hulls. *Trau Wunsch* kept moving, what she lacked in speed she made up in sheer mass, mass that wouldn't be stopped by a much smaller ship.

The keelboard struck, crumpling, but also slicing into the pinnace's hull. Vapor rushed out, forming light colored streams in the ships' lights. Alexis blinked at the image, it was so odd to see white clouds form in *darkspace* where the sky was full of blackness.

Trau Wunsch groaned and shook. The images on the console started to roll as she was pulled to the side by contact with the other ship.

"Hard roll a'port!" Alexis yelled. She didn't want to be pulled into the other ship and become entangled. She needed to crush through it, past it, and be free beyond. *Trau Wunsch* rolled to port, swinging the mizzen mast hard against the pinnace's bow. Alexis

245

winced as she saw the bow crumple, she'd likely just killed anyone in the other ship's sail locker. "Everyone up from the guns! Out to the sails and cut us free — save the mainmast, but cut everything else loose!"

Trau Wunsch ground on through the other ship. Men streamed through the sail locker onto the hull, some even crawled out through the gunports on the mess deck. Rigging was cut, masts and yards cut away without regard to saving any of the materials. The pinnace's lights flickered once, twice, and then went out completely. Then, when *Trau Wunsch* was loose and again underway, the bosun entered the quarterdeck.

"Mizzen and foremasts are but stumps, sir. The main's intact but the rigging's a scandalous mess. Quarter of the keelboard's gone and another quarter crumpled so's it won't retract." He paused. "Four men dead below when we were holed. Three on the guns when the tubes burst."

Alexis closed her eyes. She desperately wanted to ask who was dead, who she'd failed to get home safely, but there'd be time enough for that later. Now she had to see to the living.

"Thank you, Mister Lain," she said. "See to the rigging as best you can and cut away the damaged portion of the keelboard. We'll make do with half so as not to have it always dragging. Lord knows we'll move slowly enough with but a single mast."

"Aye, sir."

"And see about transferring some vacsuits to the marines, please. We'll see about taking on any survivors from the pinnace as soon as it may be done."

Alexis waited on the quarterdeck while the men worked, knowing that, even if she had a vacsuit, her place wasn't out among them. Moberly came to ask if he should let Neals and the other officers out of the master's quarters yet, but Alexis shook her head. "No. I do not believe I wish to see Captain Neals at this time. Possibly for the rest of this trip. Have some food and wine brought to them, but keep a guard on the door."

"Aye, Captain," Moberly said.

Lain reported that they'd rerigged the mainmast to account for the others being missing and it would likely hold at speed. Vacsuits were transferred to the marines and Alexis carefully took *Trau Wunsch* toward the pinnace, heaving-to beside the other ship. The marines made a boarding and came back to report that all aboard were dead.

Swallowing hard to hold down her distaste at the act, Alexis ordered all of the supplies transferred from the other ship. It would make *Trau Wunsch* even more crowded, but there was no telling how long their journey would be. She even ordered the bodies stripped of vacsuits if the suits might still be usable.

ALEXIS STUDIED THE NAVIGATION PLOT. By all measures, they should be well inside New London space and within days of reaching Penduli. She'd considered going elsewhere, there were closer New London systems, but she knew Penduli and it seemed like home to her. It was also more developed and had an orbital station. Along with that went the assurance that there would be a senior officer there, someone senior to Captain Neals.

Neals had hardly left the master's cabin since the action with the Hanoverese pinnace, but when he had it had not been pleasant. He wanted command back and Alexis' refusal infuriated him, but he had no support from Williard and certainly none from the crew. Alexis feared what he would do if they sailed into a system and he could announce his parole was over and take command.

More, she feared what the crew might do in reaction to that. They'd managed to avoid participating in one mutiny and were on their way home. She didn't want them to face that decision a second time.

"Sail! Off the starboard beam, down fifteen. Might be a sloop or brig, sir. Two masts, ship-rigged."

"Thank you, Scholer." Alexis examined the navigation plot. If her calculations were correct, even reasonably so, they were certainly no more than a few days from Penduli, well inside New London space. The winds seemed to indicate that she'd done a better job this time, as they were running straight along her course. Without a storm to disrupt them, *darkspace* winds tended to run directly towards the nearest star system, so there was something there, at least. The new ship was almost directly off their starboard side and a few degrees below their line of sail.

She smiled, allowing herself a moment to feel relief. Even if she'd gotten the navigation wrong, the new ship would be able to tell her where they were. "Send the men out to the sails, Mister Lain. Bring us eighty degrees starboard and down ten."

"Aye, sir."

Alexis rested her hip against the navigation plot and closed her eyes. On closing courses, they'd have, perhaps, a half an hour before they could read the other ships signals and find out how close to Penduli they were. She stretched her shoulders, feeling them loosen. Now that they were so close to being home, she was able to relax a little.

The half hour passed quickly and when she judged they were close enough to begin exchanging signals, or at least identify each other, she crossed to the signals station. "All right, Silk," she said to the spacer there. "Raise our colors, New London over Hanover." She smiled at him. "Don't get the order wrong or we'll find a very different welcome."

He smiled back. "Aye, sir." And a moment later, "Colors are lit, sir. New London over Hanover."

"Very good, Silk." She crossed back to the navigation plot to wait on the other ship to identify itself. "As soon as they respond, please do think of a polite way to ask them where in hell we are, won't you?"

Silk laughed. "Aye, sir, that I'll —"

Alexis turned as he fell silent and felt a sharp jab of fear at the look on his face. "Out with it, Silk! Report!" she said, crossing to his station.

"Sail's raised colors, sir." He turned to her, eyes wide. "Hanover."

Alexis looked at his screen and saw the other ship's masts and yards steadily lit with the blue and gold of Hanover. Not alternating with New London's red and white, to indicate a prize, as her own were.

"Come about, Mister Lain!" she yelled. "One eighty to port and lively now!"

"Aye, sir!" Lain replied, rushing to the sail locker.

Damn you, Delaine! It was him, she knew. How she knew, she couldn't say, but she was certain of it. What other Hanoverese ship would be this deep in New London space all but waiting for her? She clenched her fists and watched the plot as *Trau Wunsch* turned away from the other ship. First to run with the wind, then further to take it on her port beam, running directly away from the other ship. That would slow his closing, but not stop it. *He's the legs on us for any point of sail, damn it!* Trau Wunsch wasn't designed for speed, she was too bulky and lumbered along like a fat sow at the best of times. Damaged as she was, they'd been making barely two or three knots.

Alexis stared at the plot, willing some solution to come to her, but there was none. No matter where she turned, the other ship would be the faster and would surely close with them. She'd turn and fight, but that would be useless as well — with but two guns left and only a few charges.

And those so old I doubt their capacitors would hold a charge. She cursed her ship's former masters, who'd left it so defenseless. *Would I fire into him if I could?*

Alexis drew a deep breath. *Can't escape and can't fight.*

"Come back ninety to starboard, Mister Lain. We'll run for Penduli, or whatever system lies before us, and hope for rescue before we're caught."

"Aye, sir."

"Full sail, Mister Lain. Stunsails and stays if there are any in the locker. I know the mizzen and foremasts are but stubs, but rig something." She clenched her teeth. "Send the lads aft and have them fart off the bloody stern if you think it'll gain us anything."

Lain looked at her in surprise. "I ... aye, sir."

ALEXIS KEPT watch over the navigation plot while the minutes passed. Jaw tight, arms crossed, she stared at the plot with narrowed eyes. She resisted the urge to have the log thrown again to determine their speed, checking the time instead and seeing that it was but five minutes since the last throw. It would give her no good information for the chase, in any case. It was simply something to do other than stare at the plot and watch the slow, inexorable creep of the other ship growing closer. The fat oval of its estimated weapons range, shorter fore and aft where it likely had smaller guns and wider to the sides, was far too close for her comfort. *It won't be long before he could turn and strike with his broadside.* The turn would slow him, but he'd soon make up the lost distance. *Will you fire, Delaine?*

"Signal, sir," Silk said. "*Heave To* then ... not a proper signal, sir, it's all spelled out, but just some gibberish ... *m-a-b-i-c-h-e-t-t-e* ..."

Alexis laughed in spite of the tension she felt. She'd known before, but this left no doubt that it was Delaine behind her. "*Ma bichette*," she said.

"That mean what it sounds like, Mister Carew?" Lain asked, his face growing dark and angry.

"'My little doe', Mister Lain." She sighed and her smile fell. "He is French, after all."

Lain flushed. "Well ... that's all right, then ... I suppose."

Alexis looked around the quarterdeck, fixing each man in her mind. She closed her eyes for a long moment, then opened them. For a moment, she considered putting on a vacsuit and going out on the hull. If she were to leap off the stern, Delaine would surely see and stop for her before she was affected too much by being adrift in *dark-*

space. The delay might allow *Trau Wunsch* and her lads to be well away.

No, there's no telling what Neals will do if I'm not aboard.

"Mister Lain?"

"Sir?"

"Take the best gun we have — one that's not likely to destroy our own ship if it's fired, that is — take it to the stern gallery along with the gunner and whatever shot you can find. I find this pursuit troublesome and should like it slowed. A few bolts into his sails, perhaps, once in range?"

Lain nodded. "Aye, sir. I'll see it done."

"Lain," Alexis said. "Be sure it's into his sails, I don't ..."

Lain nodded again. "Aye, sir. I understand."

Alexis returned her gaze to the plot, jumping in surprise when she noticed Lain at her side again. She hadn't thought so much time had passed.

"All set, sir," he said. "Coad and Lufkin are on the gun. They'll aim fer his sails when you order it."

"Thank you, Mister Lain."

"Sail!"

Alexis rushed to the tactical console. "Where away, Scholer?" she asked, staring at the image.

"Fine on the port bow, down twenty, sir. Large sail." He ran his fingers over the image, tracing three blobs of light. "I make it a frigate, sir."

Alexis almost cried out with relief. "Port ten, down fifteen, Mister Lain."

"Aye, sir."

The frigate surely belonged to her own Navy, there couldn't possibly be two Hanoverese ships this deep in New London space, and it would see *Trau Wunsch* soon if it hadn't already. All she had to do was keep sailing closer and the pursuing ship would find itself well outmatched. *Delaine's ship.*

"Make a signal to the frigate, Silk," she said. "*Enemy In Sight* and keep it flying."

"They won't be able to read it for a bit, Mister Carew, should I wait so the Hannie don't see —"

"Fly it now," Alexis said quietly. She closed her eyes. *I do not bluff, Delaine.*

"Aye, sir."

She waited, trying not to count the minutes.

"The Hannie's come about, sir. She's running."

Alexis released a breath she hadn't been aware she was holding and opened her eyes. Had she done the right thing? No matter, it was done. If there were consequences she'd accept them.

"Take down *Enemy In Sight*, Silk. It'll do that frigate no good now." She saw Lain staring at her. "There are many duties, Mister Lain. The path between them is not always clear, it seems."

Lain nodded. "You're sure it were 'doe' he called you and not t'other?"

Alexis smiled. "Quite sure."

"Glad he'll get away, then. Good man, that Frenchie lieutenant."

"Yes." She watched the line of the other ship's retreat on the plot for a moment. "Silk, make *Request Assistance,* if you please, and prepare the signals to explain our state to that frigate." She grimaced. "And I suppose I should send someone to inform Captain Neals that he is rescued."

GIVEN *TRAU WUNSCH'S* CONDITION, the approaching frigate, *H.M.S. Vestal,* ordered her to heave-to and leave it to the frigate to maneuver into range for docking. The larger ship unstepped her foremast and settled along *Trau Wunsch's* port side before extending a boarding tube.

Alexis made her way to the crowded mess deck and port airlock. Neals and the other officers were there waiting as well, but none of them acknowledged her presence. "Captain Neals ..." she began, but stopped. What could she say, really? He'd hated her before and their flight from Giron would certainly not have improved his opinion of her. Come to that, she despised him as well — perhaps the best that could be hoped for was that they'd all be sent off to different ships now and never meet again.

The lock cycled and the hatch slid open to reveal a party of marines, spacers, and a lieutenant from *Vestal*. He took a step forward then actually rocked back on his heels, a grimace of disgust on his face.

Yes, I suppose we are a bit ripe. Though large for cargo, *Trau Wunsch* had been designed for a much smaller crew. Alexis and the others were used to it by now, but it must come as a shock to someone boarding for the first time.

Alexis stepped forward with a smile. "Welcome aboard, lieutenant. I must say we're quite glad to see you."

"Enough, Carew!" Neals stepped forward as well. "Is this enough to satisfy your 'honor', Lieutenant Williard?"

"Yes, sir, I think we may safely say our parole is at an end."

"Good enough," Neals said. "Come aboard, lieutenant."

"Lieutenant Lakes, sir," the officer from *Vestal* said, breathing through his mouth as he entered the ship. His men entered as well, struggling to find space on the crowded deck.

Neals stepped past him and stood in the lock's hatch, turning to face the mess deck. Lakes turned to face him, clearly puzzled. "Captain?"

Neals locked eyes with Alexis and she slumped. *No ... it's not over, is it?*

"Arrest them, Lieutenant Lakes," Neals said.

"Sir?"

"Every man-jack of them, this instant." Neals raised a hand to point at Alexis. "But especially that one." He smiled. "The charge is mutiny."

TWENTY-ONE

"BE SEATED and come to order! Captains Crandall, Hazlewood, and Barks presiding in the Court Martial of Ordinary Spacer Alexis Arleen Carew! Charged in violation of the Articles of War!"

Alexis seated herself and looked around the compartment that would serve as courtroom for her trial. The three Post Captains who would be acting as judges sat against the far wall, resplendent and severe in their full dress uniforms. She knew Captain Crandall from her brief meeting aboard his ship, but nothing about the others, save what her defense counsel, Lieutenant Humphry, had told her, and that next to nothing. She knew little more about Humphry himself, as she'd only seen the man three times in the week she'd been back aboard Penduli Station.

In fact, she'd spent more time with Lyulph Grandy than she had with the lieutenant appointed to represent her. Grandy, who couldn't even be in the courtroom, as space was reserved solely to naval officers, had promised to visit her during recesses, if he was allowed.

She glanced at Humphry, seated next to her at the defense table, but the man stared straight ahead, not meeting her eyes. She looked next to her right, where the prosecutor sat. Lieutenant Lonsdale appeared ready to proceed, shoulders squared and tablet in hand. Behind him *Hermione's* officers sat in the first row of the gallery, Captain Neals closest to her. None of them spared her a single glance.

She clenched her fists on the table in front of her and bowed her head. They'd not even maintained her rank as midshipman, instead accepting Neals' insistence that he had ordered her disrated.

And not even rated Able, but only Ordinary, as though I had no skills at all. I'm surprised he didn't insist on Landsman.

It surprised her that she could be stung by such a thing when she was about to be tried for offenses, the least of which could result in a death sentence. But she was proud of what she'd done, what she'd learned of the ships in such a short time. To have it all ignored and mean nothing was somehow worse than the charges themselves.

"Thank you," Captain Crandall, the Court's head, said. "Read the charges, if you please."

"The accused shall rise!"

Alexis stood and stared levelly at the bulkhead behind the three captains.

"Alexis Arleen Carew, charged in violation of the Articles of War, the specification as follows:

"Article the Third, if any officer, spacer, soldier, or other person of the fleet, shall give, hold, or entertain intelligence to or with any enemy or rebel, without leave from the Queen's Majesty, or the Lord High Admiral, or the commissioners for executing the office of Lord High Admiral, commander in chief, or his commanding officer, every such person so offending, and being thereof convicted by the sentence of a court martial, shall be punished with death!

"Article the Eighteenth, if any person in or belonging to the fleet shall make or endeavor to make any mutinous assembly upon any pretense whatsoever, every person offending herein, and being convicted thereof by the sentence of the court martial, shall suffer death: and if any person in or belonging to the fleet shall utter any words of sedition or mutiny, he shall suffer death, or such other punishment as a court martial shall deem him to deserve: and if any officer, spacer, or soldier on or belonging to the fleet, shall behave himself with contempt to his superior officer, being in the execution of his office, he shall be punished according to the nature of his offense by the judgment of a court martial!

"Article the Nineteenth, if any person in the fleet shall conceal any traitorous or mutinous practice or design, being convicted thereof by the sentence of a court martial, he shall suffer death, or any other punishment as a court martial shall think fit; and if any person, in or belonging to the fleet, shall conceal any traitorous or mutinous words spoken by any, to the prejudice of Her Majesty or government, or any words, practice, or design, tending to the hindrance of the service, and shall not forthwith reveal the same to the commanding officer, or being present at any mutiny or sedition, shall not use his utmost endeavors to suppress the same, he shall be punished as a court martial shall think he deserves!

"Article the Twenty-first, If any officer, spacer, soldier or other person in the fleet, shall strike any of his superior officers, or draw, or offer to draw, or lift up any weapon against him, being in the execution of his office, on any pretense whatsoever, every such person being convicted of any such offense, by the sentence of a court martial, shall suffer death; and if any officer, spacer, soldier or other person in the fleet, shall presume to quarrel with any of his superior officers, being in the execution of his office, or shall disobey any lawful command of any of his superior officers; every such person being convicted of any such offense, by the sentence of a court martial, shall suffer death, or such other punishment, as shall, according to the nature and degree of his offense, be inflicted upon him by the sentence of a court martial!

"Alexis Arleen Carew, you are so charged! Be seated and the prosecution shall present evidence!"

Alexis sat as Lonsdale rose at the other table. *They can only hang me once, I suppose.*

"The prosecution now calls to the stand Captain Tylere Neals,"

Lonsdale said. He waited while Neals made his way to the chair set aside for witnesses and swore to tell the truth. "Captain Neals, would you be so kind as to relate to the Court the events leading up to the mutiny on *H.M.S. Hermione?* Strictly as they pertain to the accused, if you please."

"Of course," Neals said. He settled himself comfortably in the witness chair and nodded to the three captains who sat as judges.

"Easy, Carew," Lieutenant Humphry whispered to her. He nodded to her hands, which were clenched and white knuckled on the defense table. "Confidence and restraint will serve you best."

Alexis forced her hands to relax and looked straight ahead, struggling to remain impassive. There was now no man she hated nearly so much as she despised Captain Neals — and now she'd have to sit silently and listen to him spew his lies and accusations.

Neals cleared his throat. "The crew of *Hermione* was always a surly, undisciplined lot, you understand. I did my best to bring them into line after taking command, but there was an undercurrent. A bad element amongst the crew ... too much new blood from the gaols and assizes at the start of the war, I think. My officers and I were making some progress." He nodded toward *Hermione's* surviving lieutenant and midshipmen who were seated in the gallery. "Kept the men busy and out of mischief. But when Carew came aboard, I noticed a decided change."

"And what change was that, captain?"

"Well, it's never a good idea to put a woman aboard a warship in the first place, is it? Takes the men's minds off their work. And Carew, well, she seemed unnaturally close to the men from the start. Especially those in her division."

"Captain, are you suggesting—"

"I have no proof of anything, of course. If I had, I would've put her off the ship at once." He straightened. "But in retrospect, there were signs. She always was touching them, you see. A hand on their arm or a pat on the back. Encouraging those thoughts, I think. And she went quite easy on them — rarely enforced discipline or drove the men to excel. Quite lax. Garnering their favor, if you see it."

"And the mutiny, captain?"

"Yes, of course. The day before, you see, we'd had two men overboard and lost. Men of Carew's division, I point out. They were lax with their lines coming down the mast — likely due to Carew's allowing such dangerous behavior — and by the time it was reported to the quarterdeck they were so far behind that it was pointless to try and recover them. Again, I fault Carew for the delay as well. She slipped onto the quarterdeck and stood there with her mouth gaping like some fresh-caught fish before she reported the men had gone over."

Neals poured himself a glass of water from a pitcher nearby and took a long drink.

"Well, the men were understandably distraught — all of them, but especially those of her division — but Carew didn't take them in hand. She let them fester and fret about it until they spoke out in such a way that I simply couldn't ignore. Crowded almost onto the quarterdeck itself and were close to mutiny right then and there, in my opinion. Since Carew was clearly incapable of controlling her men, I took a direct hand and settled things down. Had to flog the worst offenders — no choice — but the rest settled down right enough.

"The next day I did what I should have done earlier, I admit. I took a direct hand in that division, as Carew simply wasn't up to it. Worked them hard and gave them no chance to dwell on things. There was a great deal of improvement, I might add. Cut a full three minutes from their time to step the mainmast and rig all plain sail just in that one day's work. Shows how lax Carew was with them, that they'd been lazing about all that time under her.

"Well, even with the improvement, they were still a lax lot and I found some minor issue — an unfastened gasket — in my inspection of their work. Asked Carew for the man's name so that I could give him a talking to — set his mind right about his work, you understand

— and Carew ... well, she outright refused to give me the name. Defied my order in front of the entire crew."

Neals looked down at the floor for a moment and then at the judges. "Gentlemen, I wish that I could communicate to you the depths of my disappointment in myself. I'm sure you agree that it is a captain's responsibility to mold and teach his young officers. My own captains, when I was a midshipman, were instrumental in forging my ability to command and my career itself. Vice-Admiral Beesley, for instance, and Admirals Waithe and Hearst. Even old Lord Daigrepont, though he left the service to join the House of Lords before rising to flag rank himself. Good men all, and instrumental, critical I tell you, in making me the man I am today. I remember serving with them all fondly and am grateful to call them friends to this day." He sighed. "I had hoped, gentleman, to do justice to the good they did me by doing the same for my young officers.

"But with Carew ... I failed. And for her to disobey, to refuse a direct order ... gentlemen, such a thing cannot be let stand. It cannot be tolerated or all discipline will break down. I had no choice. And so, with great regret, I ordered her disrated. I should have dismissed her from the service entirely," he continued quickly, "but think of my position. We were on patrol, with limited provisions. Should I have kept her aboard and set men to guard her? No, I thought, perhaps, that some little time before the mast might make an improvement in her. And, if it did not, better to have her working and contributing to the ship, than taking up time and resources during a war."

He turned his gaze on Alexis and her hands clenched again. She met his eyes and it was all she could do not to speak out or, worse, rush forward and strike him for the lying bastard he was.

"Still she defied me, gentlemen," Neals continued. "I felt I had no choice, you understand. It was a difficult decision, but I ordered her flogged."

"Order!" one of the captains called as the watching crowd became louder.

"As I would have any *man* amongst the crew who so defied a

direct order!" Neals raised his voice to be heard. "Yes, gentlemen," he continued when order had been restored. He met the eyes of the judges and then looked out in the crowded courtroom gallery. "Yes, I can well understand your shock. I would be shocked too, if I had not directly experienced the arrogance and defiance of that girl. Had I but known what Carew's next actions would be, I can assure you I would have ordered far more than a mere flogging!"

"And what actions were those, captain?" Lieutenant Lonsdale asked.

"Carew, in conjunction with the men of her division, conspired to incite the crew to mutiny that very night!" Neals paused and took a long drink. "Your pardon for my outburst, gentlemen, the events of that night are quite distressing still."

"I understand, Captain Neals," Lonsdale said. "Do you require a brief recess, perhaps?"

Neals drew a deep breath. "No. No, 'twere best done quickly, yes?" He smiled at the judges. "That evening I had dinner with my senior officers and retired early. It was late, perhaps six or seven bells of the Middle Watch, when I was awakened by a gunshot. I rose and went to my arms cupboard, but it was too late. Some eight or a dozen men overpowered the marine sentry and stormed into my cabin." He took another drink. "They roughly bound me and dragged me out onto the mess deck, where I found several of my officers in similar condition.

"The crew was quite excited and loud, but then ... then she—" He pointed steadily at Alexis. "—came up the companionway and they quieted. In an instant two hundred and more men went silent. It was uncanny, the power she had over them somehow, and I cannot understand how I did not see her machinations before this. She came up to us ... they had us kneeling, you must understand, like supplicants ... and then she began talking to the crew about whether they would kill us all!"

"Order!" Crandall yelled.

"Said they'd bathe in our blood!" Neals yelled to be heard over the shouts of the crowd.

"*Order!*" Crandall was standing now, but the crowd's outrage was too great for them to obey.

"Taunted young Ledyard there that he'd be strangled!" Neals shouted, pointing Ledyard out for them.

"Order, damn you all, or I'll have this room cleared!" Captain Crandall shouted. He waited while the watchers took their seats and quieted.

Lonsdale consulted his tablet for a moment.

"Captain Neals, please do continue. The events that followed this?"

"Yes, well, cooler heads than Carew's prevailed, as you can see from our presence here." He smiled at the brief laughter from the crowd. "We, my officers and I, were confined to my quarters and under guard. Carew herself entertained to remain in that compartment, as well. I presume to keep watch over us. During this time we had no real knowledge of what was happening to the ship, though I did note many of the mutineers seemed to consult with Carew. Given her presence amongst us, of course, we were unable to even discuss retaking the ship. Though had I known their plans for it, I would have acted regardless."

"And what were those plans, Captain Neals?"

"After some days of sailing, we found ourselves in the hands of the Hanoverese. Not through capture, mind you, but due to the mutineers sailing *Hermione,* bold as brass, straight into an enemy system and handing her over!"

The shouts from the gallery behind her were the loudest yet and as the presiding captains again shouted for order and decorum. Something struck the back of Alexis' head and she turned. It was the first time she'd really looked at the crowded gallery behind her and she gasped in shock. The watching officers were on their feet, shouting and glaring at her. A dress beret lay on the floor behind her chair and as she looked back up, two more flew from the crowd to strike her in the face.

"*Order!*" Crandall stood and glared at the crowd. "I will tolerate no further outbursts, no matter the provocation, or this courtroom will be cleared! Decorum, gentlemen, no matter the provocation! Continue, please, Captain Neals."

Neals cleared his throat. "Well, sirs, it was at this point that I began to suspect that these events were not just happenstance. After being removed from *Hermione*, we were taken to meet with a Hanoverese commodore and at the end of this meeting, Carew remained behind and met with the foreign officer in private. Now I ask you, gentlemen, what commodore would have the time to meet privately with a very junior midshipman? Not even a midshipman, really, for she'd been disrated at this time. And not just once, for I became aware of many meetings between this commodore and Carew during our captivity. More, in fact, than I myself, the senior officer of the prisoners, was granted."

"What is it you suspected, captain?"

"I came to believe, and still believe to this day, that Carew was in league with the Hanoverese from the start, that she colluded with them to foment dissatisfaction amongst *Hermione's* crew, and that the loss of my ship was not a spontaneous act of mutiny, but the deliberate, planned actions of a foreign agent!"

TWENTY-TWO

"He can just do that?" Alexis demanded. She threw herself onto the cot in her small cell and glared at Lieutenant Humphry. After the reaction to Captain Neals' testimony, Captain Crandall had ordered a recess for the day and sent Alexis back to her cell. "Just spout lies and those ... *vile* insinuations of his? And there's naught you can do to stop him?"

"I will have an opportunity to question Captain Neals, certainly, when it comes time to present your defense. Should I find it advisable to do so." Humphry had stopped near the door to the cell where he could see the marine sentry stationed outside. "But, as I've warned you, the court will give great credence to the testimony of a full Post Captain. Without something to refute him —"

"He's a bloody liar!"

"Ah, well, I'll go with that tomorrow, shall I? 'Captain Neals, isn't it true that you are a bloody liar?' 'No.' 'There you have it, gentlemen of the Court, Carew is free to go and let's all be off to an early pint, yes?'"

"He—"

"As may be, Carew, but can you prove it? It's your word against his and he has the greater status. Did you not hear the gentlemen he named as friends? Lords and admirals. "

"You said the statements from the men support me!"

"They do." Humphry nodded. "But, again, the words of a captain carry more weight. Captain Neals and the other officers will face their own courts martial for the loss of *Hermione*, but that will come after yours. And yours is pivotal to their own. If you're convicted of mutiny and sedition, Captain Neals will likely be acquitted of *Hermione's* loss."

"More than seventy spacers and marines came out with us, lieutenant. How can one man's words carry more weight than all of them?"

"All of those men will be facing their own courts martial for mutiny, Carew. Captain Neals' contention is that they were all, every one of them, involved in the mutiny and came back with you to work further mischief within the Service. The statements of the other officers support Captain Neals' version of events ... at best, and it is a poor best, is that of Lieutenant Williard who insists on saying —" He consulted his tablet. "— 'I do not recall this, but, perhaps, Captain Neals' recollection is the sharper.'" He shrugged. "I do wish you would take my advice, it is the only way you might save yourself."

"I will not." She picked up the pillow from the cot and hugged it tightly to her chest. "You're supposed to be defending me! How can you even suggest such a thing?"

"This is not a civilian court, Carew, with a bought and paid for defense such as your Mister Grandy. My oath, as with all the officers of the court, is to seek justice and the best interests of Her Majesty's Navy. As I see it, this can best be served by hoping for some mercy from the court and being done with it." There was a knock at the hatchway and he looked out. "Ah, speak of the devil, indeed. Your Mister Grandy is here." He laid a hand on the latch to slide the hatch open, but paused. "Explain to the court that you are were simply an impressionable young woman, caught up in events that you did not fully comprehend the consequences of — this, I believe, is your only chance to avoid the noose."

"You want me to admit to everything that bastard's accused me of and then beg them not to kill me because I'm just a silly little girl! I'll not do it." She threw the pillow across the room. "And if I did, you'd then have me turn on the men and say they were guilty as well? What of them, then?"

"They'll likely hang in any case, Carew. Testify against them, before they do so against you. The Navy must show swift action and put this mess behind us!"

"They did *nothing*, damn you! You have the men's statements. 'To a man,' you said — to a man they've said the same as me!"

There was another knock at the door. "A moment!" Humphry yelled. "Yes, Carew, 'to a man'. Each was offered leniency to testify against you and rejected it. Over seventy of them? That in itself's suspicious enough. It makes Captain Neals' contention that you exerted some ... unnatural hold over the crew all the more believable."

"Good *lord!* What is wrong with you people? I feel like I'm through the bloody looking glass!"

"In my experience, Carew, to find no man in such a group who will act to save himself? Very odd indeed."

"It must be quite sad for you, Lieutenant Humphry."

"Sad?"

"To be in a Service that speaks so much of loyalty, and yet cannot recognize the same within its very midst." She closed her eyes. "Do, please, leave, lieutenant. I have no more stomach for your counsel today."

Humphry slid the hatch open and left without another word.

Grandy entered, paused, and slid the hatch shut with a nod to the marine outside then a raised eyebrow for Alexis. His short mustache twitched as he made a place to sit on the edge of the cot. He couldn't represent either Alexis or Isom in the court martial, as he wasn't in the Navy, but he'd been offering what advice he could.

"I take it things did not go well?"

"One could say that, Mister Grandy." She stood to retrieve her pillow, then returned to the cot. She put her back to the compartment's corner and drew her legs up, cradling the pillow between her legs and chest. "I do believe they're going to hang me."

Grandy sighed and crossed one leg over the other. "So it seems. You and more than a few of the crew, as well."

Alexis choked on a laugh that turned into a sob. "You do not comfort me, sir."

"Not my place to comfort you, girl. Just to give you my legal opinion." He shook his head. "From what I was told of Neals' testimony ..." He shook his head again. "You need one of the officers to turn and denounce Neals. That's the only thing the captains will listen to. Some proof, other than a common spacer's word." He paused. "Look, then, is there any of them that might come around and change their story? If there is, I'll try to speak to him before he's called to testify tomorrow and see what I can do — it's certain-sure that Humphry won't bother."

Alexis snorted. "He seems worse than useless. I don't at all understand how he intends to defend me."

"He doesn't," Grandy said, then continued at her shocked look. "The man's more concerned for his own position, I wager. He'll lose no prestige or patronage if you hang, but will if he's seen to attack a Post Captain with Neals' sort of friends."

Alexis was silent for a moment. "Then why ..." She sighed. "Why would they assign him to defend me?"

Grandy shrugged. "His name was next on the list for defense, I'd suppose. But you can't rely on him, clearly, and dwelling on the why will do you no good either. Is there any of the officers who might be convinced to go against Neals? Even one of the midshipmen, though they're not commissioned — a friend, perhaps?"

Alexis laughed. "No, most certainly not one of the midshipmen." She considered the question for a time. "Lieutenant Williard, perhaps."

"Lord Atworth?"

She nodded, a little surprised that Grandy knew of Williard's title. "He's no fan of Neals. Not like the others."

"I'll speak to him, then. Perhaps I can convince him to break ranks with the others."

"Will they let you in to see him?"

"In?" Grandy frowned. "Likely just ask to speak to him at the club over dinner."

"The club? *Dorchester's?*" Alexis felt her breath catch. "Do you mean to say he's *out?*" If Neals and the others were to face their own courts martial, how could Williard be out and about? She saw the look on Grandy's face and knew the truth. "Well, then, they all are, aren't they? Of course. I don't know why I expected differently ... Neals, Williard, all the way down to that little shite Ledyard, yes? Walking around free while the lads and I are locked up. Through the looking glass, indeed." She laughed. "Do make room, Mister Grandy. There'll be a damned great rabbit joining us any moment. Fur like snow, he'll have."

"DID MISTER GRANDY speak to you about Lieutenant Williard, Lieutenant Humphry?" Alexis whispered. They were back in court for a new day of testimony. The captains had not yet arrived, but the gallery was full, including Neals and the rest of *Hermione's* officers and she didn't want them to overhear.

"Lieutenant Williard? Why would Grandy speak to me about him? Why, for that matter, should I speak to Grandy at all?" Humphry snorted. "You would do well to ignore your Grandy, Carew, and listen to me instead. He is not Navy."

Alexis started to answer, but the bailiff entered and called the court to order. She stood with the others as the captains entered and took their seats, then sat herself. She turned to tell Humphry that Grandy had been going to speak to Williard about his testimony, but there was no time.

"You may proceed, Lieutenant Lonsdale," Crandall said.

"Thank you, sir. Lieutenant Adam Williard, Lord Atworth, if you please."

Alexis tried to catch Williard's eye as he took the stand and swore the oath, but his gaze never wavered from the rear of the compartment. He didn't look to the captains standing judge, nor even at Lonsdale when the questioning began.

"Lieutenant Williard, you were, until the death of Lieutenant Dorsett during the mutiny, Second Lieutenant aboard *Hermione*?"

Williard paused for a moment before answering. "I was."

"And you were Second Lieutenant aboard *Hermione* at the time Captain Neals took command of the vessel, is this correct?"

Again the pause. "Yes, that is correct."

"So," Lonsdale said. "It would be a fair statement that you witnessed the entirety of Captain Neals' tenure aboard the ship, as well as that of Carew?"

This time, Williard's pause was longer. "I was aboard and Second Lieutenant during that time, yes."

"And as Second Lieutenant, it was your responsibility to oversee the midshipmen, correct?"

Williard's brow furrowed. "It is generally the responsibility of all the officers and senior warrants to oversee the midshipmen, as to their training and education."

Lonsdale frowned. "But as Second Lieutenant, it fell to you to oversee the midshipmen's berth. You would have spent the most time with them?"

"I kept details neither of my own time spent with the midshipmen nor that spent by the other officers, so could not truthfully say who spent the most."

Alexis lowered her head and closed her eyes. Williard was clearly determined to put as little meaning into his testimony as possible. While he might not condemn her, it was certain he had no plans to contradict Neals either. Lonsdale was plainly frustrated with him, and even the three captains were regarding him with furrowed brows, but she didn't see how that would help her. He'd been her last, only, chance. Perhaps if Humphry were to press him, but when she turned to her counsel to suggest it, she saw that Humphry wasn't even listening to the testimony, he was engrossed with his tablet and barely paying attention.

Lonsdale soon allowed Williard to step down, seeming to have elicited nothing from him but that he had, indeed, been aboard some ship which may have been called *Hermione*. Williard stalked out of the compartment without looking at anyone, his eyes steadfastly forward.

"Midshipman Coleman Bushby, please," Lonsdale called when Williard had stepped down.

And that's it for me, there's not a one of the midshipmen who'll say aught in my favor.

"Mister Bushby," Lonsdale asked, "are you familiar with Carew, there?"

"I should say so!" Bushby said. He caught Alexis' eye and grinned broadly. "She tried to poison me!"

Lonsdale's eyebrows rose, as did those of the three captains. "Poison you, sir?"

"Indeed. Didn't know it was her, at first, but there were tainted stores brought aboard. Burned my gut something fierce. Canion, there, got the worst of it — almost died, he did. Had to be dragged to the surgeon barely able to breathe!"

"I see," Lonsdale said. "And you're certain it was Carew that was responsible?"

"In cahoots with the gunroom steward, yes," Bushby said. "He's one of the crew came back with her to cause more trouble. He had access to all our stores and she was quite ... close to him."

"So you concur with Captain Neals' belief, sir, that the mutiny along with these poisonings were deliberate acts on Carew's part?"

"No doubt in my mind. First she weakened us, you see — the officers — then she and the crew were better able to take over. She was never a real part of the berth with us — not a proper officer at all —

but it was only once we were captured that I realized what she'd been up to. When she and her Hannie friends beat Timpson."

"Beat him, you say?" Lonsdale asked. "Along with the Hanoverese?"

"She did the beating, mind you. Had her Hannie partner stand by so the rest of us couldn't stop her and there was nothing Timpson could do but take it. Would've been shot by the Hannie if we'd done aught to stop her."

"And did Carew, at any point—"

A klaxon began sounding from the compartment's speakers, harsh and grating.

"That's the invasion alarm," Crandall said, standing. "Marines! Get the prisoner back to her cell — the court's in recess!"

ALEXIS REMAINED ALONE in her cell for two days after the alarm, with no visitors and no word of what was happening. After the initial alarm, there had been no others, so perhaps it wasn't an invasion, but she had no way of knowing. A marine guard slid the hatch open three times a day to deposit of plate of food — a spacer's portion of vat-grown beef and plain ship's biscuit, a tot of watered rum, and no more. She ate what she was given, mindlessly, barely noticing how bad it was.

Lieutenant Humphry did not visit her to discuss the case, nor did Mister Grandy. She suspected that Grandy had, at least, tried to do so. Why he would be turned away now, and why Humphry would not bother to come at all, she didn't know.

It was almost a relief when the hatch slid open on the third day and a marine informed her that the court was prepared to resume her trial. She straightened her jumpsuit as best she could, fingers lingering for a moment at the collar where her rank tabs had once been, and followed the marine to the courtroom.

"ARE YOU PREPARED TO RESUME, Lieutenant Lonsdale," Crandall asked.

"I am, sir," Lonsdale said, standing. He picked up his tablet and came out from behind his table. Alexis looked to Humphry, hoping for some sign of encouragement, or even acknowledgment that he was paying attention. "If it please you, sirs, I should like to resume the prosecution's case with evidence, rather than testimony."

"Sirs!" Humphry said, rising, the first reaction Alexis had seen from him in the entire trial. "I renew my objection to this ... this evidence! Its providence is suspect, to say the least!"

Renews? Alexis looked at him in shock. He'd barely spoken the entire trial, much less objected to anything that Lonsdale or the witnesses had said. Something must have happened while she was in her cell.

"Your objection has been heard, Mister Humphry," Crandall said. "It is denied. Mister Lonsdale, you may proceed."

"Sirs, for the presentation of this evidence, I should like Captain Neals returned to the stand for corroboration." Neals rose in the gallery, a puzzled look on his face, but made his way to the witness stand. "I remind you, Captain Neals, that you remain bound by your earlier oath."

"I understand, lieutenant."

"Very well, Lieutenant Lonsdale," Crandall said, "for the record, please tell the Court the nature of your evidence."

"Thank you, sir," Lonsdale said. "The prosecution shall now enter into evidence the ship's log of *H.M.S. Hermione.*"

TWENTY-THREE

IF ANYTHING, the outcry from the gallery at Lonsdale's announcement was louder and more prolonged than at any point in the trial. All of the watchers knew that *Hermione's* log had been lost, turned over to the Hanoverese by the mutineers, along with the ship itself. Alexis looked to Humphry, but he stared straight ahead, face fixed and unhappy.

"Wherever did he get the ship's log?" Alexis whispered to Humphry.

"It doesn't matter," Humphry whispered back. "I tried to keep it out, but failed." He shook his head. "Only Lonsdale's actually seen it, but you can't even clamor for mercy now, Carew, they'll see everything you did shortly."

What did I do? Alexis wanted to scream it. What on earth would *Hermione's* log show she'd done that was so horrible? She thought back over the months aboard ship.

"Captain Neals," Lonsdale said, "I wish you to cast your memory back to April third, some three days after Midshipman Carew came aboard *Hermione.*"

Alexis looked up, startled. It was the first time since she'd returned to New London and Neals had demanded her arrest that anyone had referred to her as a midshipman. She could tell from the look on Neals' face that he'd taken note of it as well and didn't like it.

Neals nodded, and Lonsdale continued. "I will now show a portion of your ship's log from Captain's Mast on that date." He ran a finger over his tablet and a screen to the side of the courtroom illuminated with a view of *Hermione's* mess deck. Alexis gave a startled gasp and covered her mouth with her hand. She hadn't expected to react so, but the image, with the faces of so many men she'd never see again, shocked her. The scene played out and she averted her eyes, remembering the day and her first taste of life aboard *Hermione* under the hand of Captain Neals. The grating was rigged and the cat brought out, she remembered. A harsh sentence for a stupid, meaningless offense.

"Would you tell us the man's name, Captain Neals," Lonsdale was asking, "and the offense for which he was flogged on this date?"

Alexis clenched her ears shut against the sharp *crack* of the bosun's cat coming from the room's speakers.

"I do not recall exactly, lieutenant," Neals said. "I am certain it was recorded in the log."

Alexis bit her lip. *Batterton, topman on the mizzen. Made the mistake of whistling in the hold where Neals could hear him.*

"I see, Captain Neals, no matter," Lonsdale said.

No, no matter, you bastards all. Alexis wanted to scream at the court. *Just a man beaten bloody for* whistling, *damn you all.*

"And this scene, captain?" Lonsdale asked. "Some four days later, April seventh? The name and offense, if you recall?"

"I do not. I'm sorry, lieutenant."

Alexis opened her eyes and looked at the screen. *Sartin. Twelve lashes. Last down from the mast.*

"I see, captain," Lonsdale said. "And this? April twentieth?"

The scene changed again. The same location, *Hermione's* mess deck. The same participants, the crew crowded around the rigged grating while the officers stood by. Alexis stared at her own image, wanting desperately to leap back in time and shake herself out of the stunned inaction she remembered feeling. *Stop it! Do something! Standage, his bloody bunk wasn't closed up early enough, and this was reason to beat him?*

"I fail to see the point of this, lieutenant," Neals said.

"I must say," Captain Barks said from the bench. "I fail to see the point as well."

"If you'll indulge me, sirs," Lonsdale said. "I believe my point will become clear with just a bit of leeway."

"Carry on, Mister Lonsdale," Crandall said, "but please, do get to this point you speak of."

"Thank you … Captain Neals?" There was silence broken only by the *crack* of the cat from the compartment's speakers. "Captain?"

"Was there a question, lieutenant?" Neals asked.

"The man's name and offense, sir."

"I've told you, *lieutenant*," Neals said, clearly irritated. "I do not recall every instance of punishment. The details are in the log!"

"Thank you, Captain Neals," Lonsdale said. "I beg you to bear with me."

Alexis buried her face in her hands, not wanting to face any more of it. She heard the change from the speakers as the scene changed.

"And this, captain? Some seven days later on April twenty-seventh?"

"Leachman, topman, last down from the mast." Alexis looked up into the silence that followed, unaware for a moment that she'd spoken aloud.

She looked at Neals first, seeing his dismissive, angry face. Then at Lonsdale who stared back at her impassive and then at the three captains who were staring at her in shock that she'd spoken. She shrugged off Humprhy's hand as he grasped her shoulder to quiet her. She looked at Lonsdale again. He was looking back at her, almost expectantly, and the man's calm infuriated her. How dare he? How dare he drag these up again to somehow discredit her, when it was Neals who'd ordered it. Rage built in her, both at Lonsdale and at herself, for standing by and letting it happen to begin with.

"You want their names?" she asked. "Next will be Isom. A bloody legal clark with no business aboard ship, but he got a round dozen for stepping back into Timpson's path." She started to rise, but Humphry's hand on her shoulder pulled her back down. It bothered her how easy it was to remember them, each of the floggings she'd witnessed. She'd thought that they would all run together in her memory, one long endless horror, but found that she remembered them all, every one.

"After him was Standage — two dozen for ... for no better reason than that Neals' pet bastard Ledyard wanted to see a man's back bloody. Langwell, twelve for shirking, though he'd wrenched his shoulder the previous day and been to the surgeon. Twyford, three dozen for swearing at a bosun's mate, and Lain would've seen to it with a cuff and a strong word if left to handle it himself." She shook off Humphry's hand and stood.

The captains were staring at her in shock, but Alexis didn't care about them. She turned her gaze to Neals, wanting him to acknowledge her words. Infuriated that he wouldn't even name the men who'd served aboard *Hermione*.

"Then Worrick, a dozen for being last down from the yards, your favorite sport, you bastard!" She longed to throw herself over the table and strike Neals, all of her rage and frustration welling up inside her. She pointed at the screen. "You can't be bothered to look at the log and put a name to their faces?" Her anger at Neals overwhelmed her. "They were yours! You were supposed to take care of them!"

Her vision blurred. She'd never understand why Neals had been allowed to command a ship, command men who were willing to fight and die for their kingdom, yet asked so very little in return.

"You are unworthy to command such men ... I should have let them kill you."

Now the captains reacted, Crandall calling for her to resume her seat, but she ignored him and the sounds erupting from the gallery behind her.

"Should've left you behind on Giron!" She did start forward then, but strong hands on her shoulders shoved her back into her seat. She hadn't even been aware of the two marines who'd approached her. "*God forgive me for not killing you myself!*"

"*Order! Damn your eyes, order! Or I'll have the lot of you in chains!*" Crandall shouted.

The marines pressed her firmly into her chair and Humphry leaned close to her ear. "Shut up, Carew! You do yourself no credit!"

The courtroom quieted again. Through it all, Neals sat, face impassive and calm. Alexis found Lonsdale staring at her, an odd look on his face. The three captains huddled together for a moment, whispering.

"Mister Lonsdale," Captain Barks said after some time, "I believe we understand the difficult conditions Captain Neals faced with an unruly and near mutinous crew." Alexis almost spoke again, but the warning pressure of Humphry's hand on her shoulder kept her silent. "Is this really necessary?"

"I simply wish the court to fully understand conditions aboard *Hermione* — to put Midshipman Carew's actions into context." He consulted his tablet. "For the record, sirs, Mister Carew accurately described the floggings I've yet to show you."

"Is there much more of this?" Barks asked. "Do you intend to show every flogging aboard that ship?"

"I do, sir."

"Well, how much more, Lonsdale, as I, for one, have had enough of watching this."

"Until the events starting the day before the mutiny? Thirty-six, sir."

The courtroom was silent.

"Thirty ... six." Crandall glanced at Neals briefly. Neals calmly poured himself more water and took a drink. "Well, Captain Neals had been in command near a year. That is not so terribly out of reasonableness for a ship with an unruly crew."

"You misunderstand me, sir," Lonsdale said. "Thirty-six is the number of floggings ordered only during Carew's time aboard *Hermione*. Some —" He consulted his tablet. "— one hundred seventy-four days."

Captain Hazlewood narrowed his eyes. "What were the total floggings for Captain Neals' time in command, lieutenant?"

"Eighty-five, sir," Lonsdale said immediately. "And three men dead of it. That was the count immediately before the events that ended in mutiny."

There was silence for a moment, then Crandall spoke. "I believe we do not need to see each and every one, Lieutenant Lonsdale. Nor," he said, with a look first at Neals then Alexis, "do we require their names and offenses recited here in court."

Lonsdale nodded. "Of course, sir." He consulted his tablet. "By that do you mean to say that you do not wish to see the additional twenty-two floggings carried out the day before the mutiny?"

Silence followed Lonsdale's question, save for a single outburst from the gallery, "Sweet Jesus."

"No," Crandall said, face white. "No, I do not believe we need to view that."

Captain Barks stared at Lonsdale for a long moment, eyes narrowed. "I begin to question your purpose in this, lieutenant."

"My purpose, sir?"

"Yes, your purpose!" Barks nodded toward Alexis. "I think you forget, sir, who it is your task to convict! Captain Neals is not on trial here!"

Lonsdale squared his shoulders and raised his chin. "My task, sir, is to fulfill my oath to the Court. Justice and the best interests of the Service, sir. The same as your own, if I may remind you."

"You may not, Mister Lonsdale!" Barks yelled, his face red. "You impertinent —"

Crandall held up a hand, cutting Barks off. "Tempers are high, gentlemen, I understand. But I'll have none of this bickering." He took a deep breath and looked around the courtroom. "Mister Lonsdale, what do you intend to present next?"

Lonsdale consulted his tablet. "Mister Carew's actions which precipitated her disrating, sir. If it please the Court."

"I very much doubt that this Court shall be pleased by anything remaining in this case, Mister Lonsdale," Crandall said, "but you may continue."

"Thank you, sir."

Alexis slumped into her chair. At least she wouldn't have to watch her lads being flogged again. That was something she could be thankful for. She looked down, not wanting to watch her disgrace and what would likely convict her. She'd disobeyed Neals' order, after all. There was no denying it and the entire court would soon see for themselves.

She listened as the events played out. The courtroom was curiously silent, as though no one present could bear to miss a word. She heard Neals' demand for the name of the man who'd left the gasket undone and her own refusal to give it. Heard herself saying that the fault was hers and apologizing, then begging his forgiveness when he demanded it. The court and gallery remained silent until Neals' voice came from the speakers.

"*From your knees, Carew.*"

Alexis pressed her eyes tightly shut. *How different would things be if I'd just complied?* Perhaps she'd have had time to speak to the bosun before the mutiny. He might have been able to head it off with a well-placed word. There'd have been no deaths that night and Nabb ... She felt a tear leak from her eyes and run down her cheek. Nabb and the others wouldn't be on the run with a death sentence hanging over them, should they ever return to New London space.

She heard her own voice, surprisingly strong and clear. Odd, since she remembered being horribly angry at Neals' attempt to flog one of her lads again.

"*I will kneel to my Queen, sir, and to no other.*"

"Bloody right!" a voice called out from behind her and others chorused agreement.

They quieted again, though, as Neals ordered her disrating and flogging. On the screen she knew the grating was being rigged and the bosun's mate sent for the cat.

She heard her own voice again, shockingly calm and clear given that she remembered being terrified and shaking.

"*Nabb! Broady! Scholer! Back to your places the lot of you and mind your tongues! Don't you dare disappoint me, lads, or I'll know the reason why!*"

I guess I did say that ... I thought I'd imagined it. Alexis felt her hands begin to shake and clasped them tightly on the tabletop in front of her. She wanted it to stop, but, no, *this* flogging it seemed they still wanted to see. Blindly brush away the ones before, but not this one. She knew what they were seeing. Her halting steps toward the grating, her inability to shrug out of her jumpsuit and take her lashes as the men did, her shaking hands having to be dragged up by the bosun's mates. She felt her face grow hot with shame. *I'm sorry, lads, I wasn't as strong as you.*

"Enough, Mister Lonsdale." Alexis looked up to see Crandall speaking. He glanced toward her, his face pale. "Enough."

He gestured for Barks and Hazlewood to come closer and the three captains whispered together for almost a full minute before Crandall stood.

"We've let this go on far too long," he said. He gestured to the marine sergeant near the rear doors. "Sergeant, I want the name of everyone in the gallery. Gentlemen —" He had to raise his voice over the mutters this order ensued. "Gentlemen! This case is sealed! You will not repeat what you've heard here today on pain of court martial. We will review the rest of *Hermione's* log in private. Take Mister Carew back to her cell. Mister Humphry, Mister Lonsdale, you two remain, but everyone else is to be removed this instant!"

ALEXIS WAS TAKEN BACK to her cell and left alone again. She laid down on the bunk and stared at the bulkhead, unsure of what had happened. It seemed she was forever being dumped back into her cell and no one would tell her what was going on. Right now the three captains were reviewing *Hermione's* log, they'd said, but why wasn't she there? Would she even be given an opportunity to defend herself? And where had they gotten the log to begin with?

She closed her eyes and must have slept, for she was suddenly being shaken awake by a marine.

"They're asking for you back in the courtroom, sir," he said.

Alexis swung her legs over the side of the bunk and rubbed her eyes. "How long?" she asked.

"Four hours, sir." The marine stepped back and offered her a hand to help her up. Alexis looked at him in shock, both from the offer of assistance and being addressed as 'sir'. "Wouldn't've knelt, myself, sir. Told that bastard straight, you did."

"Thank you." She took his hand and stood, reading the nametag on his uniform. "Thank you, Enright."

Enright nodded toward the small head built into a corner of the cell. "Do you need a moment to freshen up, sir?"

Alexis shook her head. Her hair was a mess, she was sure, and her face felt puffy with sleep, but whatever was coming when she returned to the courtroom would likely be the end of this nightmare. She wanted it over, not delayed.

Enright led her back to the courtroom. It was quite different from the other times she'd entered. The gallery was empty and virtually all of the court personnel were absent as well. The three captains, Humphry, and Lonsdale were there. A single lieutenant sat to the side tapping away at his tablet and two marines stood at each of the doorways. Other than these, the room was empty. Alexis took her seat at the table with Humphry and Crandall spoke immediately.

"Thank you for joining us, Mister Carew," he said. "Mister Humphry, Mister Lonsdale, you may leave. Your service is concluded and this Court thanks you."

Alexis blinked in shock, looking around as Humphry rose and left without a glance or word to her. Lonsdale grasped her shoulder as he passed, but said nothing either. She was left facing the three captains alone. Only Barks showed any emotion, his face red and his jaw clenched tightly. Every so often he looked at her and his nostrils flared. When the door was closed behind Humphry and Lonsdale, the three captains stared at her for a moment. Alexis swallowed and met their eyes in turn.

"We, the three of us, have reviewed *Hermione's* log with Mister Humphry and Mister Lonsdale," Crandall said finally. "We believe, at this time, that we have sufficient information to render a decision in this case, do you understand?"

Alexis stared at him in shock. Humphry, worthless as he was, wasn't here and she'd not been allowed to speak a word in her own defense, but they'd made a decision? She considered objecting, but what good would it do? Lonsdale had, at least, seemed to have expressed some sympathy for what was to come. Her shoulders sagged and she looked down at the table. "I believe I do, sir."

"There are contingencies to this decision, Mister Carew," Crandall said. "Contingencies you will be expected to abide by, so listen carefully, if you please."

Alexis looked up, suddenly hopeful. *I can't very well have to abide by anything if I'm hung, now can I?* Possibly she'd survive this mess — dismissal from the service wouldn't be the worst outcome.

"The Court will shortly announce its decision to the public," Crandall was saying. "Our finding is that you are blameless as to all counts."

Alexis felt herself pale in shock, a chill running through her. *Blameless?* From Crandall's talk about contingencies, she'd expected to be found guilty of something and receive a sentence less than hanging. Possibly, if she were lucky, to be acquitted of some of the charges. But blameless? That went beyond acquittal. It was a statement from the Court that the charges should never have been brought, that they were baseless and unfounded. It was a very public rebuke of Captain Neals.

"The decision is public," Crandall continued sternly. "The proceedings are not. These proceedings, all testimony, and, most particularly, the log of *H.M.S. Hermione* are to be sealed. You are not to speak of these things to anyone at any time in the future, do you understand?"

Alexis felt her jaw tremble and her eyes burned. *Speak about it? I don't want to ever bloody think about Hermione again!* She swallowed and cleared her throat. "I understand, sir."

"You will be discharged from this courtroom and go immediately to a new ship —" Crandall took a deep breath. "A happier ship than *Hermione,* I should hope, but far from Penduli."

They want nothing said about it. They want to hide what Neals did as much as they can. With the threat of hanging no longer over her, it was like a veil had been lifted from her thoughts. She was thinking more clearly than she had in days. *Whoever it was who said the threat of hanging clarifies the mind was quite mistaken.*

"Sirs ... where did the log come from?" she asked. *The invasion alarm ... it must have been Delaine.*

"Mind your place!" Barks said. "And do as you're told if you know what's good for you!"

Crandall waved a hand at him. "I was going to inquire if she had any questions, regardless. She's a right to know some things."

Barks sat back, jaw clenched and red-faced.

"A Hanoverese brig," Crandall said. "Sailed in bold as brass with a flag of truce flying."

"Thank you, sir," Alexis said, suppressing a smile. She could almost picture Delaine handing over the log with a grin and some outrageous comment. She lowered her gaze. "And is Captain Neals' case decided as well, sir?"

Crandall paused for a moment. "Captain Neals and his officers, yourself included, will be acquitted of the loss of *Hermione.* The ship is found to have been lost due to mutiny, through no fault by any of her officers."

Alexis closed her eyes and took a deep breath. She might be doing herself in, but she couldn't remain silent. She'd done too much of that aboard *Hermione*.

"He can't be allowed to command a ship again, sirs, please! You don't know what it was like!"

"You forget yourself!" Barks yelled.

Hazlewood held up a hand. "It is likely, Mister Carew," he said, "that Captain Neals has been ... much affected by his ordeal in captivity. I believe he will find the need to rest and ... recover himself."

"Should he return to service," Crandall said, "it will certainly be some shore position and not a spacegoing command. He will remain upon the Captain's List, of course, and one day may be promoted to admiral." Crandall spared a glance for Barks. "Of the Yellow."

Alexis wanted to protest, to insist that something more must be done, but she could see it would be pointless. They clearly wanted nothing more said about the events aboard *Hermione*, and doing any more to Neals would require some public reason. But if he was kept ashore he'd not have the power over the men he possessed in space. There'd be a Port Admiral looking over his shoulder all his days and there to review every bit of discipline. Being an admiral of the Yellow Squadron one day would be no honor for him — the Yellow Squadron had no ships. It was a resting place, a dumping ground for those too politically powerful or embarrassing to dismiss, but too incompetent or dangerous to allow in a command.

Hazlewood nodded to her. "The best interests of Her Majesty's Service." He shrugged. "If you take our meaning."

"I understand, sir." She did. She longed to see Neals punished, but clearly there were naval politics to consider. She bit her lip. "And the men, sir?"

Crandall sighed. "Those who ran, obviously, will be convicted of mutiny, there's no doubt about their guilt. Most of those who came back with you will be acquitted. We'll have to review their cases still."

Alexis felt the shock go through her. She'd expected that those who'd run would be convicted in absentia, there was no getting around that. But they still intended to try the men who'd come back with her? And possibly convict them?

Of course, they need to hang someone. Saying they'll hang those who've already escaped them isn't enough — they need bodies on the gallows today.

She closed her eyes, silently praying for strength. *Why? Why must it be so hard?*

"No," she said, standing. She met each of the captains' eyes in turn, seeing the shocked looks on their faces. "I cannot accept your conditions, sirs."

"Are you mad, Carew?" Barks asked.

I get asked that so very often ... perhaps I should consider the possibility. "There's not a one of my lads more guilty than I, sirs," she said. "You can't hang them." She smiled, realizing that she had card left to play. *Thank you, Delaine, for my life and those of my lads.* "And you'll realize that yourselves, if you'll give it a moment's thought, sirs."

"What are you saying, Carew?" Barks asked.

"You want this kept quiet, sir," Alexis said. "Even I can see that. You want nothing said about the log and what happened aboard *Hermione*, but you can't have that if you harm my lads."

Barks' face reddened and he half stood, but Crandall was looking at her with an odd half-smile and Hazlewood was staring at her intently, though not unkindly.

"Don't bargain with us, Carew!" Barks yelled. "We can just as easily hang the lot of you and keep the whole mess quiet!"

"No, sir, you can't." Alexis squared her shoulders and met his gaze evenly. "You forget where you received the log from in the first place, I think. My guess is that Hanoverese brig is still in port, yes? And I'm sure you must suspect they've kept a copy or two."

Barks' face was scarlet now and his eyes wide. "That's treason, Carew. You'd ask them to release the log if you don't get your way?"

Alexis steeled herself, trying not to show how afraid she was. If this didn't work, then they likely *would* hang her along with the men, but she had to try.

"Never, sir. But inaction is not treason. And if a single one of my lads is harmed, I'll not ask the Hanoverese *not* to release it."

Captain Hazlewood cleared his throat. He leaned forward, regarding her with narrowed eyes. "Why are you doing this, Carew? You were free and clear a moment ago."

Alexis looked at him for a moment. How could he even ask? Why was it even a question for him? She felt like the vision of the Navy she'd had aboard *Merlin* was just that, a vision that existed nowhere else. Perhaps it would be best if she went back to Dalthus, if the home she'd thought she'd found here truly didn't exist.

Then she realized that it did exist. She'd seen it even aboard *Hermione* — in Boxer offering her his own bit for a meal, in Nabb's sacrifice to keep the rest of her division out of the mutiny, even in the simple gesture the crew had made in building her a proper bath. They returned the love and loyalty she felt for them, and that was what she'd seen in Captain Grantham and his officers.

Two Navies. Williard had been right about that, though not about what should be done about it. Captain Grantham's Navy was fighting two wars — one with Hanover and one with the likes of Neals within its very midst. She could no more abandon him and those like him to fight alone than she could have left her lads back on Giron.

"They stood with me, sir," she said. "Aboard ship, in prison, during the escape ... even through this trial — to a man, they stood." She shook her head slowly, bewildered that it even had to be said. "I ... would you truly have me do less?"

Hazlewood nodded and turned his head to look at Barks. "I'm with Crandall about the men, Captain Barks. I see no need to drag it out."

Barks stared at him open mouthed for a moment. "You'll take her word for their innocence?"

"Yes," Hazlewood said simply. "Yes, I will."

"And it solves our problem, Barks," Crandall said. "You know the Hanoverese would love nothing more than to embarrass us with that bloody log. What do you think that young lieutenant will say if *you* ask him to keep it quiet?"

"You think her asking will make a difference?"

Crandall shrugged. "I think it is the only possibility," he said then looked at Alexis. "And I think I should not like to bet against this officer, if she says that she will do a thing."

Hazlewood stared at Barks until he nodded, then turned back to Alexis. "None of the crew ..." His lips twitched. "None of your lads will hang, Mister Carew. They'll be split off to other ships, mind you — we can't have them together after this — but they'll not be harmed. Will that satisfy you?"

"Yes, sir." Alexis sank back into her seat, eyes closed. She'd not see them again, but that was the way of the Navy in any case, constantly changing ships. They'd be safe from this, at least. "Thank you."

"I'm with Crandall on the other thing, as well, Barks," Hazlewood said, "so let's be about it."

Barks clenched his jaw. "I'll give no leeway on this," he said stiffly.

"I rather suspect she'll need none," Hazlewood said.

Alexis looked from one to the other, confused.

"May we begin it, then?" Crandall asked.

Hazlewood nodded to the lieutenant. Alexis had completely forgotten his presence, concentrating on the three captains. The lieutenant walked over to where she was seated and laid a short coil of thin ship's line on the table in front of her.

If they want me to hang myself, I'll need more rope than that.

Crandall smiled at her. "Will you tie for me a sheepshank, Mister Carew?"

Alexis looked from the coil of line to the captains. She frowned, not understanding why they asked this, but picked up the line and quickly tied it into the requested knot.

"Thank you, Mister Carew."

The lieutenant placed three long rods on the table, then returned to stand behind the captains.

Hazlewood gestured to the rods. "Your mainyard has split at the crosstrees, Mister Carew, please splice it."

Alexis stared from the rods to the captains and back again. "Sir, I don't understand ..."

"Your mainyard, Mister Carew! Splice it. Lively now!"

Alexis jumped, and scooped up the rods after quickly straightening the knotted line. The rods were far smaller than a mast's yard, of course, and the line too thick by far for the scale, but she managed to make the turns of rope required and shortly had the three pieces bound in some semblance of a spliced yard, using one of the pieces to brace the other two. It was a common enough repair when a new yard couldn't be fashioned and brought outboard. As she gently placed the bound rods on the table, her heart beat faster and she realized, or at least suspected, what was happening.

"You can't," she whispered.

One corner of Hazlewood's mouth rose and Captain Barks raised his eyebrows.

"We are three Post Captains at a quite remote station and in time of war, Mister Carew," Hazlewood said. "You will find, in fact, that there is remarkably little we cannot do."

"You are on the quarterdeck of a sloop, Mister Carew," Crandall said, "much like your previous ship, *Merlin,* if you will. You are close-hauled on the starboard tack, with *darkspace* shoals to leeward and a ten knot wind. A kilometer off, the shoals extend into your path. What will you do?"

"I've not three years," Alexis whispered, dazed. They really did intend to examine her for lieutenant, not minutes after she sat trial for mutiny. *A looking glass, indeed.* But a promotion to lieutenant required three full years in service as a midshipman. "Not even two."

"A bloody war," Crandall said. "It's what hungry young midshipmen and lieutenants crave, Mister Carew, and cast toasts to around the gunroom table. Men die and their juniors are promoted to replace them. Peacetime rules do not apply."

"And you've had, by my count, command of a full three ships, Mister Carew. Not just idle prizes, but under trying circumstance," Hazlewood said. His face grew grim. "This war has been bloodier than most, and I'll not waste another day of you as a midshipman, Carew. As Lieutenant Lonsdale pointed out to us — our duty is justice and the best interests of Her Majesty's Service." He smiled. "It's rare enough we can satisfy both with one act, so I'll not waste that chance either."

"Your ship, Carew!" Barks yelled. "The shoals are now eight hundred meters off and you draw nearer!"

"Wear ship," Alexis said, leaning forward in her chair. She saw a look of surprise cross Crandall's face. "My *Merlin* could wear in half that distance, Captain Crandall, without the risks of tacking into irons." She squared her shoulders and gazed back at them calmly. "And my lads would have no trouble doing so, or I'll know the reason why."

"Not another wasted day, Carew," Hazlewood said, smiling broadly.

TWENTY-FOUR

ALEXIS SLUMPED against the bulkhead as the courtroom's hatch slid closed behind her. The corridor had been cleared of people, save for a single marine outside the hatch, and hatches at either end of the corridor had been closed as well. Captain Crandall had told her she'd be escorted well-away from the courtroom in order to avoid crowds and questions before the court announced its verdict.

She realized her hands were shaking and she was soaked with sweat. The examination had in some ways been more grueling and stressful than the trial itself. The knot tying and questions of fact, naming sails and such, had not been bad at all, but the situations ... suddenly appearing enemy ships, fires in the galley just as one went into action, dismasted by squalls, shot that holed the quarterdeck, dismasted by enemy fire, failure of the fusion plant during action, and to leeward nothing but bloody shoals. *Good lord, they're fairly wed to leeward shoals and made a mistress of dismasting.* She took a deep breath and closed her eyes.

I shall message Stanford Roland immediately and apologize for ever making fun of his fear of this.

No, she reconsidered. *No*, Roland would not take the news kindly — he'd stood for lieutenant too many times before passing. While she ... Alexis opened her eyes and raised the paper she held in her hand. *Real* paper, all archaic in proper, *traditional*, Navy-fashion, festooned with red wax seals and an actual ribbon to tie it closed. *Signed with their names, even, and not a proper thumbprint.* But signed, indeed, by all three captains and naming her, Alexis Arleen Carew, as a fully commissioned lieutenant in Her Majesty's Royal Navy.

Commissioned and promoted, she thought with glee, grinning widely. Not just a passed midshipman, stuck in that role until a lieutenant's position opened, but fully promoted and ordered to report aboard ship as such. Her grin fell a bit. A ship she was to meet almost six week's travel from Penduli — still on the border, still part of the war with Hanover, but far, far away from Penduli and the events on *Hermione*.

The captains of the court martial were clearly trying to keep these events quiet. They'd said as much to her, ordered even, as part of the decision they'd announce would be that the entire proceedings, even those that had been held in open court, were to be sealed and never spoken of. Not even the spectators who'd been present would be allowed to speak of it. And part of her wondered if she really deserved the document she held or if it was simply a sop ... payment to keep her quiet. She *thought* she'd done well in the examination, but ...

"Rough examination, sir?" the marine asked.

Alexis looked at him and felt her face grow hot as she realized she'd been leaning against the bulkhead for quite a long time.

"Are any of them not?" she asked, feeling her grin return.

That got her a smile in return. "Seen a passel of midshipman who'd agree with that," he said. His face sobered. "Begging your pardon, sir," he added quietly, "but I'm right glad the truth come out for you in there."

Alexis nodded. "Thank you." She shouldn't be surprised he knew the details, they were likely already known by all the hands aboard station. Captains and admirals could order what they wished, but the rumor and details would make the rounds below decks before the orders had left their lips. She clutched her commission papers tightly, suddenly realizing what else they meant.

The commission was issued by Admiralty, but it bore the name of the Queen. While a midshipman served at the whim of her captain, liable for dismissal or disrating at his word, the same could not be done to a lieutenant. There were other, subtler, ways a captain could use to destroy a lieutenant's career, but outright dismissal wasn't possible — he'd have to ask for a full court martial and explain his reasons.

No, if they'd merely wished to buy her silence, there were other, far easier, things they could have offered. The commission bound her more tightly to the Navy. It was more than acceptance, it meant that those captains, even Captain Barks, *wanted* her in their Navy. Alexis felt her chest tighten and clenched her jaw tightly.

Damn me, my first act as lieutenant will not *be to start bawling in the station corridor.*

The sound of one of the hatches blocking the corridor sliding open made her look to the side.

"*Delaine!*"

Alexis dashed down the corridor and flung herself at him. She wrapped her arms around him and buried her face in his chest, never minding that now her first act as a lieutenant was to hug an enemy officer in the station corridor. She'd thought she'd never see him again.

She heard the hatch close again and someone cleared his throat uncomfortably.

"Thank you," she murmured, releasing him and stepping back. She raised a hand to wipe her eyes and realized that she'd managed both with one go. The throat clearer had been Lieutenant Lonsdale, accompanied by Mister Grandy.

"Ah, *Alexis*," Delaine said, his grin as wide as ever. "For *mon cœur* to leave so abruptly, what could I do but follow, *oui?*"

"I think *le Hanovre* had more to do with that than your heart," she said.

"*Le Hanovre* were most ... the word, put out when they found you gone, *oui*. They tell my commodore, she is to send all her ships to find you." He grinned wider. "Those ships, they sail along the border ... but I know where you will go. You are predictable, *mon chérie*."

Lonsdale cleared his throat again. "I'm afraid Lieutenant Thiebaud must leave as quickly as possible," he said. "The captains feel soonest out of sight is soonest out of mind, you understand."

Alexis nodded. "Delaine, I have to ask you to do something ..." She trailed off, suddenly uncertain. *Could* Delaine ensure *Hermione's* log wasn't released? Was it even fair to ask him?

"*Lieutenant* Lonsdale has explained to me, *Alexis*," Delaine said, "but I wished to see that you were safe before agreeing." He turned his gaze to Lonsdale. "You should know, *lieutenant*, that this log was mistakenly *moved* from my commodore's ship to mine, not copied. And I must order some maintenance performed on *Bélier's* systems during my journey home, to ... the word, clean up, *oui*? Files no longer of need? This is sufficient for you?"

"It is," Lonsdale said, looking relieved. "Thank you, sir."

Delaine nodded.

"Delaine ... will this ..." Alexis caught her lip between her teeth. "Coming here, the log ... will it cause you trouble with the Hanoverese? Or for Commodore Balestra?" They were likely in enough trouble from her escape, she didn't want to cause them more — though what she could do about it, she didn't know.

Delaine pursed his lips and shook his head. "*Non*." He shrugged. "I could not stop your escape, and this will not please them. But for myself and Commodore Balestra, we will tell *le Hanovre* that we have still taken from New London a frigate captain, *oui*? The Captain Neals, he will not sail against *le Hanovre* again." He reached out and cupped her cheek, sending a shiver through her. "And my commodore and I, we shall pray for this war to be over before they find what we have given in his place."

He took his hand away and smiled. "But I am told you are now *lieutenant*, as well, *oui?*"

"*Oui!*" she cried out happily, holding up her commission papers, a bit rumpled and all but forgotten in her excitement at seeing him.

Delaine pulled a small box from his pocket. He glanced at Lonsdale. "It is tradition for New London, too, I think, for the new officer to have ... the word, *insigne*, the mark of rank, yes? From a friend?"

"It is," Lonsdale said, eyes narrowing, "but with the war ..."

Delaine shook his head. "*Non*," he said, opening the box. "These are not *le Hanovre*."

The rank tabs in the box were similar to New London's, but more ornate. And clearly old, archaic even. Worn, but well cared for, and clearly French — instead of the fouled anchor that New London used, these were crossed with the *fleur de lis*.

"These are from the *grand-père* of my *grand-père*, from *le Grande République*. To him even from his *grand-père*, I think."

"Delaine, I couldn't ..."

"*Non*." He closed the box and pressed it into her hand. "*Grand-père* fought *le Hanovre* for *le République*. His *grand-père* fought *le Hanovre*. Now you fight *le Hanovre*. They would wish it, I think, and be proud."

Alexis nodded, throat tight.

Lonsdale cleared his own throat once more and Alexis knew there'd be no more delay. She reached up and wrapped her hands around Delaine's neck, pulling him down to her. She pressed her lips to his and kissed him, as thoroughly and enthusiastically as she could. She heard a great deal more throat clearing, from Lonsdale and perhaps with Grandy joining in as well, but there was only them and the marine to witness her behavior and she might never see Delaine again.

When she finally pulled back, she was pleased to see Delaine's eyes were wide and a little unfocused. He opened his mouth to speak, but no sound emerged, then again.

"*Adéquat, ma caille*," he said finally, lips twitching. Alexis fought the urge to kiss him again, but she'd clearly scandalized Lonsdale and Grandy quite enough for the day. Those two were staring at her with wide eyes. "When this war is over, *Alexis*, you will come to visit me?"

"I will." She could see in his eyes that he understood all of the caveats a naval officer would have as well as her. *If I'm able, if the Service grants me leave, if we're both alive at the end of this.*

Delaine nodded to Lonsdale who gestured for him to follow and led the way down the corridor, leaving Grandy behind with Alexis. Grandy was, thankfully, silent as Alexis watched the two walk away. That section of corridor had been cleared as well, another marine stationed at the far hatchway.

"*Delaine!*" she called out as the pair reached it. He turned and looked back. "If you had caught me ... would you have fired?"

Delaine shrugged and she could see his mouth twitch again. "There are duties and duties, *mon chou*," he called back. "I pray we never need find out, *oui?*"

Alexis nodded, but her heart grew cold as she realized that she would have. To keep her lads safe, to get them home, she would have fired into his ship and not let up. She would have hated herself, and she thought a part of her would have died as she gave the order, but she would have done it. *Dear lord, what does that make me?*

Her mind translated what he'd just called her and her brow furrowed. *Really?*

"Cabbage?" She spread her hands. "The best you can do at a time like this is 'my little cabbage'?"

Delaine shrugged as the hatch slid shut between them.

EPILOGUE

"Alexis!"

She turned at the familiar voice, unsure of what she'd heard. She'd spent the last six weeks as second, last, and largely extraneous, lieutenant on a packet ship making its way quickly but erratically Fringeward from Penduli. Her orders were to remain aboard until she arrived here at Lyetham and then transfer to *H.M.S. Shrewsbury,* a seventy-four gun Third Rate for her actual position. Isom stopped beside her, sliding the antigrav sled he pulled with their baggage to a stop.

Strictly speaking, lieutenants were not allowed personal servants who followed them from ship to ship — that was a luxury reserved to commanders and captains — but Isom had somehow managed to attach himself to her. She suspected he'd received some advice from Mister Grandy about how to make use of the peculiarities of the Navy's personnel department, but chose not to inquire too closely.

He'd simply followed her aboard the packet and taken up duties as her hammockman and servant aboard, in addition to whatever shipboard duties he was assigned. When they'd arrived in Lyetham, he'd been waiting with her baggage packed and the lieutenant in charge of the packet had said not a word as Isom had followed her onto the station. For her part, Alexis was happy to have a familiar face going with her aboard a new ship.

She scanned the crowded corridor of Lyetham Station and saw who'd shouted rushing toward her.

"Philip!" she cried with delight.

He hurried up to her and stopped short, standing to attention and tugging his uniform jacket into some semblance of order, the untamable lock of black hair falling down his forehead, a scar he'd received from a cracked helmet in action ran from under that lock of hair and down his cheek. He squared his shoulders.

"Midshipman Easely reporting, sir!" he said, saluting smartly.

Alexis' heart fell. She'd known promotion and rank meant a great deal to some people, but she hadn't thought how her promotion might impact her own relationships. Then she saw the gleam in his eye and the corners of his mouth twitch.

"You tosser!" she cried, throwing her arms around him and pressing her cheek against his chest, not caring about the stares such a display between two officers might garner from passersby. "Don't you ever play at that nonsense!"

He's grown. Philip had been only a few centimeters taller than she on *Merlin*, but now she realized his chin cleared the top of her head with ease. His chest and shoulders were broader, too, no longer the lanky boy he'd been aboard *Merlin*. She stepped back and watched the red blush flow up his face to settle in his ears. *That's not changed, at least.* "How are you here?"

Philip grinned. "I'm aboard *Ruby*, now. We were deployed here a fortnight ago," he said. "I guess my message couldn't catch up with a fast packet."

Alexis wrapped her arms around him again, his words reminding her of the hurt his messages had contained when her communications had been filtered aboard *Hermione*. At least that was resolved, though she'd still be waiting weeks for more word from home — messages would have to reach Penduli and then be rerouted to her aboard her new ship.

"I'm so sorry about that, Philip."

"Oh, hell," Philip said. "That's not what I meant, Alexis." He grasped her arms firmly and pushed her away so he could look her in the eyes. "I know that wasn't your fault and I'm sorry I ever thought it was. I should've known there must be something amiss with your messages and that you'd never just ignore me." He lowered his eyes. "It's just ... " Alexis grinned as he flushed again, perhaps realizing where his new height and lowered head had placed his gaze. "Well, you're still the best mate I've found aboard ship," he said, blushing again. "I thought ... well, it doesn't matter now, does it?" He lowered his hands. "All's right with us, yes?"

Alexis smiled. She wrapped one arm around Philip's and they continued down the corridor.

"Yes."

"Good, then. And pity save your old shipmates if they ever step into a berth with me."

Alexis nodded. She had a moment's thought to tell Philip not to do a thing, if ever he had the chance, but Timpson and the rest had hurt Philip as well as her. It was his right to dish out retribution if he was given the opportunity. *And I'll relish the hearing of it.*

"Isom," she said. "This is my dearest friend Philip Easley, he and I were berthmates aboard *Merlin* when I first joined the Navy. Philip, Isom was with me aboard *Hermione*. And after."

Philip nodded to him while Isom ducked his head.

"How long are you in Lyetham?" she asked. "I've a full day before *Shrewsbury's* in port and I have to report aboard."

"I've all-night-in," he said, "but *Ruby* sails early tomorrow." He grinned. "You owe me a supper ashore, if I remember right."

"I do and more," she agreed. "And a fine supper. I've a lieutenant's pay now and a bit more prize money."

Quite a lot of prize money, in fact, for the Prize Court on Penduli had finally ruled on both *Hermione's* prizes and her *Sittich*. She suspected Captains Crandall and Hazlewood might have had a say in *Sittitch*, for the Prize Court had upheld it as her prize and not Neals'. *Trau Wunsch* had not even been submitted to the Prize Court, instead the ship had been condemned and sent to the breakers. Alexis shuddered at the memory of the surveyor's report on the ship's condition. *We were in more danger from that ship than ever from the Hanoverese.*

"I saw that Roland made lieutenant — and you were mentioned in dispatches, more than once."

Philip nodded. "That was a rough action," he said. "Roland showed himself well, and in sailing the prize back. He deserved the commission." He shot her an amused look. "Still a prat, though."

"Really?"

Philip's grin faltered. "More than ever, really." His brow furrowed. "I do think there's something ... I don't know. The more he succeeds, the more of an arse he seems. Haven't heard from him since he left *Merlin*, though."

Alexis frowned. She'd hoped Roland might have come around since he'd finally made lieutenant. She quickly shook the feeling aside, though. She'd have, at most, an evening to spend with Philip and didn't want to waste time on worries that were far away.

The thought of far-away worries brought Delaine to mind, though. She spared a moment's time to wish him well and safe. She began to understand why spacers seemed so much stronger about their relationships and passions. Two mates could meet after being months or even years apart on different ships, but they'd drink and carouse together as though they'd been together all along. The same men who'd spend half their pay on a doxie in port, sent the other half home to a wife they spoke of with words that brought tears to Alexis' eyes. *And speak with pride of a child born while they've been a year or more in space, they do.*

She and Philip were friends, there may have been a moment or two of more aboard *Merlin*, but nothing could have come of it, serving aboard the same ship; so those feelings, if they existed, had to be put aside. She'd had a few weeks with Delaine and then returned to New London. She might never see him again, couldn't even send him a message, at least for the duration of the war. *I'll not know if he's alive or dead until the war's over, even.*

Now she'd have a few hours' time with Philip, simply by the vagaries of chance that they were on the same station at the same time, then they'd both be off on different ships, with no telling when they'd meet again. *With so little time to exercise them, no wonder the men's passions run so strong.* One had to fit a lifetime's affection into a few hours' time — before you were torn apart again.

She realized Philip had been speaking, but her thoughts had been far away. "I'm sorry, what?"

"I was only saying that I've heard there's a pub two levels up that has a better than usual ordinary. My lieutenant recommended it highly."

"That sounds quite nice."

"This way, then," he said.

He laid his hand over hers where it rested on his arm and pulled her into a gentle turn, causing her to smile.

They made their way to the station's lifts, Isom trailing them with her baggage, and up two levels, then down the corridor to a pub called The Eagle's Beak, a grand name for a tiny place, whose storefront was crammed between a gin-stall and an establishment with suspiciously dark windows and furtive clientele.

"It doesn't look like much, I know," Philip said as they entered, "but Lieutenant Vallance says it's the best he's had."

Alexis sniffed tentatively as they entered, then inhaled deeply. The air inside was redolent with rich spices and cooking meats. "Heavens! If that's their ordinary I smell, I can well believe it!"

Philip grinned. "I'm glad you think so," he said. "I was hoping you'd like it."

"Isom," Alexis said. "Take a table over there with the baggage, will you? Have supper and a pint or two?"

"Thank you, sir." The pub was only a little more than a third full, so he was able to quickly find a table along the wall where the baggage would be out of the way. Philip led Alexis to another table and they sat.

"I'm glad I found you, Alexis," Philip said once they'd placed their orders for two meals and wine. "When I saw your packet was due here, I was afraid I'd have to sail before she arrived." He grinned. "Been checking the arrival boards every day."

Alexis grinned back. *He was waiting for me? Checking every day?* "I'm glad, as well."

"Yes, well." He glanced away and red crept up his face. "You see, I wanted to —"

"Mister Easely! I thought I'd find you here."

Alexis turned to the pub's entrance and saw a young lieutenant had entered and was heading for their table. The man stopped short and nodded to Alexis, taking in the rank insignia on her collar. "Lieutenant," he said, nodding.

Alexis nodded to him in return. "Lieutenant," she said.

"This is Lieutenant Vallance, Alexis," Philip said. "From *Ruby*. Sir, this is Lieutenant Carew — she and I were berthmates on *Merlin*."

Vallance nodded to her again. "Easley's said good things about you, Carew. I'm happy to make your acquaintance at last."

"Thank you, Lieutenant Vallance," she said.

"If you'll excuse me for interrupting," Vallance went on. "I have a bit of a mess aboard *Ruby* and need to ask Mister Easley a few questions. If you'll be so good as to excuse us for a moment, I'll have him back to you instanter."

"Of course."

Vallance pulled out his tablet and gestured for Philip to follow him. Alexis turned around to watch them leave, then turned back to her table.

She jumped and nearly screamed when she discovered someone was sitting in the seat Philip had just left.

"Lieutenant Carew?" the man said.

Alexis tried to catch her breath from the start. She looked quickly around the pub and found that Isom was watching her carefully, eyes wide as another stranger was seated at his table as well.

"Your man is safe, lieutenant," the stranger said. "As are you." He held out a hand. "Malcom Eades, Foreign Office."

Alexis took his hand reluctantly. "What is the meaning of this, sir?"

"There are some matters I wish to speak to you about and prefer to do so in private." He gestured to a narrow set of stairs along the pub's wall. "I've engaged a private room upstairs, if you'd be so kind."

Alexis' mind raced. Anyone could sit down at a table and claim to be from the Foreign Office, or any Office he pleased, really, but why should he? Why with her? What could the man, legitimate or not, possibly want?

She made a wait gesture to Isom, afraid he might do something, and looked at Eades carefully. He wasn't in uniform, but the Foreign Office had no uniform. In fact, his clothing was, if anything, so nondescript and general that no one could possibly remark upon it. Even his features were bland and unremarkable, with nothing at all that stood out.

"My companion will return soon, sir," Alexis said. "I cannot imagine what you might wish to speak to me about."

"Lieutenant Vallance will keep Mister Easley busy for as long I require, Lieutenant Carew," Eades said at the same time Alexis' tablet *pinged* for her attention. Shocked that Eades knew both Vallance and Philip, she pulled out her tablet and saw a message.

MISTER EADES of the Foreign Office will be contacting you this evening. Please follow his instructions.

ALEXIS BLINKED. It was signed *Captain Euell* of *Shrewsbury,* her next ship, but *Shrewsbury* was not in port. She checked the message headers to see if it had been sent some time ago and only just arrived on some other ship, but her tablet clearly informed her that the message had originated from *Shrewsbury* directly to the station and had been sent that very minute. She used her tablet to quickly check the system's arrivals, in case *Shrewsbury* had just transitioned, but it had not. *Shrewsbury* was, in fact, in *darkspace*, still en route to Lyetham and had been unable to send messages at all for over a week's time since leaving her last port of call. She looked at Eades in shock. How had he done that? He'd have to have the ability not only to send messages via the Navy's secure communications, but also to send them with perfectly formed message headers that would be accepted as from ships and officers that couldn't possibly have sent them.

Eades smiled slightly and gestured toward the stairs.

Alexis motioned for Isom to stay where he was and rose. Eades did as well and Alexis preceded him up the stairs to the pub's second floor where he nodded to a hatchway off the corridor. She entered and found a round table with seating for eight, but there was only one man in the room, seated at the opposite side of the table, facing the hatchway. In a bit of a daze, Alexis moved to the side and sat down.

"Will you have something to drink before we begin, Lieutenant Carew?" Eades asked.

"No, thank you, sir. I'll wait until I return to my companion."

"This may take some time, lieutenant."

Alexis looked from Eades to the other man and back. "You have me at a disadvantage, sirs."

"Ah, yes," Eades said. "The introductions, forgive me." He gestured to the other man. "Lieutenant Carew, may I present Vachel Courtemanche, representative to Her Majesty's Court from *La Grande République de France Parmi les Etoiles*. The Grand Republic of France Among the Stars."

Alexis' eyes widened and she found it suddenly hard to breathe. The Foreign Office and a French diplomat dragging her to a private room? She licked her suddenly dry lips.

"Bourbon," she said.

Eades looked at her oddly.

"To drink," she said. "Bourbon, if you please."

She settled back into her chair, stomach fluttering at the thought of what this meeting might mean. Eades' face had turned smug, as though he'd just won at something and her temper flared.

"No," she said, "make that Scotch." She narrowed her eyes. "And if they have none, ask them to send for a bottle. I'm sure there's a branch of Dorchester's aboard station that will have something suitable."

A NOTE FROM THE AUTHOR

Thank you for reading *Mutineer*. I hope you enjoyed it as much as I enjoyed writing it.

If you did and would like to further support the series, please consider leaving a review on the purchase site or a review/rating on Goodreads. Reviews are the lifeblood of independent authors.

As a reader, I've always been a fan of both science fiction and historical fiction from the Age of Sail. It's been a wonderful treat for me to bring those two loves together in the Alexis Carew series.

In the historical realm, the events that took place on HMS *Hermione* in September 1797 are always mentioned, but never depicted. It was the bloodiest mutiny in Royal Navy history, so an author would have a bit of trouble inserting his character into it. Most of the officers were killed and most of the crew was sentenced to death and relentlessly hunted down by the Royal Navy.

To some it might appear that Captain Neals' cruelty is exaggerated in *Mutineer*, but the historical Captain Pigot of *Hermione* was no less cruel.

In his previous command he had 85 men, fully half the crew, flogged over nine months and two men died of their injuries. He would order the last man down from the yards flogged, and this resulted in three men falling from the masts to their deaths in their attempts to avoid the punishment. And when the men complained after this, he had the entire division flogged ... and then flogged again the next morning.

It was this, along with his treatment of Midshipman David Casey that spurred the mutiny.

Casey was confronted by Pigot over an untied gasket on the main top and, after apologizing for the oversight, was ordered to beg forgiveness from his knees. Casey refused this humiliating order and Pigot ordered him disrated and flogged.

It's always bewildered me that Bligh – who by all accounts lost his ship because he *wasn't* harsh enough with the crew – is the one reviled by common usage while Pigot is all but forgotten.

I can only hope I've shown the crew of *Hermione* a bit of justice and honor in this story.

J.A. Sutherland
Orlando, FL, February 1, 2015

ALSO BY J.A. SUTHERLAND

To be notified when new releases are available, follow J.A. Sutherland on Facebook (https://www.facebook.com/alexiscarewbooks), Twitter (https://twitter.com/JASutherlandBks), or subscribe to the author's newsletter (http://www.alexiscarew.com/list).

Into the Dark

(Alexis Carew #1)

Mutineer

(Alexis Carew #2)

The Little Ships

(Alexis Carew #3)

HMS Nightingale

(Alexis Carew #4)

ABOUT THE AUTHOR

J.A. Sutherland spends his time sailing the Bahamas on a 43' 1925 John G. Alden sailboat called Little Bit ...

Yeah ... no. In his dreams.

Reality is a townhouse in Orlando with a 90 pound huskie-wolf mix who won't let him take naps.

When not reading or writing, he spends his time on roadtrips around the Southeast US searching for good barbeque.

Mailing List: http://www.alexiscarew.com/list

To contact the author:
www.alexiscarew.com
sutherland@alexiscarew.com

DARKSPACE

Darkspace

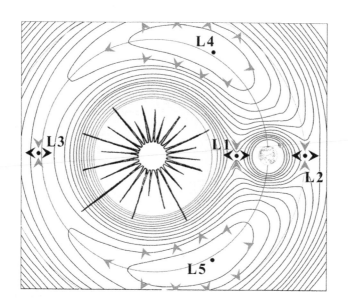

The perplexing problem dated back centuries, to when mankind was still planet-bound on Earth. Scientists, theorizing about the origin of the universe, recognized that the universe was expanding, but made the proposal that the force that had started that expansion would eventually dissipate, causing the universe to then begin contracting again. When they measured this, however, they discovered something very odd — not only was the expansion of the universe not slowing, but it was actually increasing.

This meant that something, something unseen, was continuing to apply energy to the universe's expansion. More energy than could be accounted for by what their instruments could detect. At the same time, they noticed that there seemed to be more gravitational force than could be accounted for by the observable masses of stars, planets, and other objects.

There seemed to be quite a bit of the universe that simply couldn't be seen. Over ninety percent of the energy and matter that had to make up the universe, in fact.

They called these dark energy and dark matter, for want of a better term.

Then, as humanity began serious utilization of near-Earth space, they made another discovery.

Lagrangian points were well-known in orbital mechanics. With any two bodies where one is orbiting around the other, such as a planet and a moon, there are five points in space where the gravitational effects of the two bodies provide precisely the centripetal force required to keep an object, if not stationary, then relatively so.

Humanity first used these points to build a space station at L_1, the Lagrangian point situated midway between Earth and the Moon, thus providing a convenient stopover for further exploration of the Moon. This was quickly followed by a station at L_2, the point on the far side of the moon, roughly the same distance from it as L_1. Both of these stations began reporting odd radiation signatures. Radiation that had no discernible source, but seemed to spring into existence from within the Lagrangian points themselves.

Further research into this odd radiation began taking place at the L4 and L5 points, which led and trailed the Moon in its orbit by about sixty degrees. More commonly referred to as Trojan Points, L4 and L5 are much larger in area than L1 and L2 and, it was discovered, the unknown radiation was much more intense.

More experimentation, including several probes that simply disappeared when their hulls were charged with certain high-energy particles, eventually led to one of those probes reappearing — and the discovery of darkspace, along with the missing ninety-five percent of the universe.

Dark energy that moved through it like winds. Usually blowing directly toward a star system from all directions, pushing those systems farther and farther apart, but sometimes coming in storms that could drive a ship far off course. Dark matter that permeated the space, slowing anything, even light, outside of a ship's hull and field.

Made in the USA
Coppell, TX
19 October 2021

64310774R00184